The Squatter's Dream

The Squatter's Dream

Dream

Rolf Boldrewood

MINT EDITIONS

The Squatter's Dream was first published in 1875.

This edition published by Mint Editions 2021.

ISBN 9781513291031 | E-ISBN 9781513293882

Published by Mint Editions®

MINT
EDITIONS
minteditionbooks.com

Publishing Director: Jennifer Newens
Design & Production: Rachel Lopez Metzger
Project Manager: Micaela Clark
Typesetting: Westchester Publishing Services

Contents

I

"Here in the sultriest season let him rest.
Fresh is the green beneath those aged trees;
Here winds of gentlest wing will fan his breast,
From heaven itself he may inhale the breeze."

—Byron

Jack Redgrave was a jolly, well-to-do young squatter, who, in the year 185—, had a very fair cattle station in one of the Australian colonies, upon which he lived in much comfort and reasonable possession of the minor luxuries of life. He had, in bush parlance, "taken it up" himself, when hardly more than a lad, had faced bad seasons, blacks, bush-fires, bushrangers, and bankers (these last he always said terrified him far more than the others), and had finally settled down into a somewhat too easy possession of a couple of thousand good cattle, a well-bred, rather fortunate stud, and a roomy, cool cottage with a broad verandah all covered with creepers.

The climate in which his abode was situated was temperate, from latitude and proximity to the coast. It was cold in the winter, but many a ton of she-oak and box had burned away in the great stone chimney, before which Jack used to toast himself in the cold nights, after a long day's riding after cattle. He had plenty of books, for he did not altogether neglect what he called his mind, and he had time to read them, as of course he was not always out on the run, or away mustering, or doing a small—sometimes very small—bit of business at the country town, just forty miles off, or drafting or branding his cattle. He would work away manfully at all these avocations for a time, and then, the cattle being branded up, the business in the country town settled, the musters completed, and the stockmen gone home, he used to settle down for a week or two at home, and take it easy. Then he read whole forenoons, rather indiscriminately perhaps, but still to the general advantage of his intelligence. History, novels, voyages and travels, classics, science, natural history, political economy, languages—they all had their turn. He had an uncommonly good memory, so that no really well-educated prig could be certain that he would be found ignorant upon any given subject then before the company, as he was found to possess a fund of information when hard pressed.

He was a great gardener, and had the best fruit trees and some of the best flowers in that part of the country. At all odd times, that is, early in the morning before it was time to dress for breakfast, in afternoons when he had been out all day, and generally when he had nothing particular to do, he was accustomed to dig patiently, and to plant and prune, and drain and trench, in this garden of his. He was a strong fellow, who had always lived a steady kind of life, so that he had a constitution utterly unimpaired, and spirits to match. These last were so good that he generally rose in the morning with the kind of feeling which every boy experiences during the holidays—that the day was not long enough for all the enjoyable occupations which were before him, and that it was incumbent on him to rise up and enter into possession of these delights with as little loss of time as might be.

For there were so many pleasant things daily occurring, and, wonderful to relate, they were real, absolute duties. There were those cattle to be drafted that had been brought from the Lost Waterhole, most of which he had not seen for six months. There were those nice steers to ride through, now so grown and fattened—indeed almost ready for market. There were ever so many pretty little calves, white and roan and red, which he had never seen at all, following their mothers, and which were of course to be branded. It was not an unpleasant office placing the brand carefully upon their tender skins, an office he seldom delegated—seeing the J R indelibly imprinted thereon, with the consciousness that each animal so treated might be considered to be a five-pound note added to his property and possessions.

There was the wild-fowl shooting in the lagoons and marshes which lay amid his territory; the kangaroo hunting with favourite greyhounds; the jolly musters at his neighbours' stations—all cattle-men like himself; and the occasional races, picnics, balls, and parties at the country town, where resided many families, including divers young ladies, whose fresh charms often caused Jack's heart to bound like a cricket-ball. He was in great force at the annual race meetings. Then all the good fellows—and there were many squatters in those days that deserved the appellation—who lived within a hundred miles would come down to Hampden, the country town referred to; and great would be the joy and jollity of that week. Everybody, in a general way, bred, trained, and rode his own horses; and as everybody, in a general way, was young and active, the arrangement was productive of excellent racing and unlimited fun.

Then the race ball, at which everybody made it a point of honour to dance all night. Then the smaller dances, picnics, and riding parties—for nearly all the Hampden young ladies could ride well. While the "schooling" indulged in by Jack and his contemporaries, under the stimulus of ladies' eyes, over the stiff fences which surrounded Hampden, was "delightfully dangerous," as one of the girls observed, regretting that such amusements were to her prohibited. At the end of the week everybody went peaceably home again, fortified against such dullness as occasionally invades that freest of all free lives, that pleasantest of all pleasant professions—the calling of a squatter.

Several times in each year, generally in the winter time, our hero would hold a great general gathering at Marshmead, and would "muster for fat cattle," as the important operation was termed. Then all the neighbours within fifty miles would come over, or send their stockmen, as the case might be, and there would be great fun for a few days—galloping about and around, and "cutting out," in the camp everyday; feasting, and smoking, and singing, and story-telling, both in the cottage and the huts, with a modest allowance of drinking (in the district around Hampden there was very little of that), by night. After a few days of this kind of work, Jack would go forth proudly on the war-path with his stockman, Geordie Stirling, and a black boy, and in front of them a good draft of unusually well-bred fat cattle, in full route for the metropolis—a not very lengthened drive—during which no possible care by day or by night was omitted by Jack or his subordinates—indeed, they seldom slept, except by snatches, for the last ten days of the journey, never put the cattle in the yard for any consideration whatever, but saw them safely landed at their market, and ready for the flattering description with which they were always submitted to the bidding of the butchers.

This truly important operation concluded, Geordie and the boy were generally sent back the next day, and Jack proceeded to enjoy himself for a fortnight, as became a dweller in the wilderness who had conducted his enterprise to that point of success which comprehends the cheque in your pocket. How he used to enjoy those lovely genuine holidays, after his hard work! for the work, while it lasted, *was* pretty hard. And, though Jack with his back to the fire in the club smoking-room, laying down the law about the "Orders in Council" or the prospects of the next

Assembly Ball, did not give one the idea of a life of severe self-denial, yet neither does a sailor on shore. And as Jack Tar, rolling down the street, "with courses free," is still the same man who, a month since, was holding on to a spar (and life) at midnight, reefing the ice-hard sail, with death and darkness around for many a league; so our Jack, leading his horse across a cold plain, and tramping up to his ankles in frosted mud, the long night through, immediately behind his half-seen drove, was the same man, only in the stage of toil and endurance, preceding and giving keener zest to that of enjoyment. Our young squatter was a very sociable fellow, and had plenty of friends. He wished ill to no man, and would rather do a kindness to anyone than not. He liked all kinds of people for all kinds of opposite qualities. He liked the "fast" men, because they were often clever and generally had good manners. There was no danger of his following their lead, because he was unusually steady; and besides, if he had any obstinacy it was in the direction of choosing his own path. He liked the *savants*, and the musical celebrities, and the "good" people, because he sympathized with all their different aims or attainments. He liked the old ladies because of their experience and improving talk; and he liked, or rather loved, all the young ladies, tall or short, dark or fair, slow, serious, languishing, literary—there was something very nice about all of them. In fact, Jack Redgrave liked everybody, and everybody liked him. He had that degree of amiability which proceeds from a rooted dislike to steady thinking, combined with strong sympathies. He hated being bored in anyway himself, and tried to protect others from what annoyed him so especially. No wonder that he was popular.

After two or three weeks of town life, into which he managed to compress as many dinners, dances, talks, flirtations, rides, drives, new books, and new friends, as would have lasted any moderate man a year, he would virtuously resolve to go home to Marshmead. After beginning to sternly resolve and prepare on Monday morning, he generally went on resolving and preparing till Saturday, at some hour of which fatal day he would depart, telling himself that he had had enough town for six months.

In a few days he would be back at Marshmead. Then a new period of enjoyment commenced, as he woke in the pure fresh bush air—his window I need not state was always open at night—and heard the fluty carols of the black and white birds which "proclaim the dawn," and the lowing of the dairy herd being fetched up by Geordie, who was a preternaturally early riser.

ROLF BOLDREWOOD

A stage or two on the town side of his station lived Bertram Tunstall, a great friend of his, whose homestead he always made the day before reaching home. They were great cronies.

Tunstall was an extremely well-educated man, and had a far better head than Jack, whom he would occasionally lecture for want of method, punctuality, and general heedlessness of the morrow. Jack had more life and energy than his friend, to whom, however, he generally deferred in important matters. They had a sincere liking and respect for one another, and never had any shadow of coldness fallen upon their friendship. When either man went to town it would have been accounted most unfriendly if he had not within the week, or on his way home, visited the other, and given him the benefit of his new ideas and experiences.

Jack accordingly rode up to the "Lightwoods" half an hour before sunset, and seeing his friend sitting in the verandah reading, raised a wild shout and galloped up to the garden gate.

"Well, Bertie, old boy, how serene and peaceful we look. No wonder those ruffianly agricultural agitators think we squatters never do any work, and ought to have our runs taken away and given to the poor. Why, all looks as quiet as if everything was done and thought about till next Christmas, and as if you had been reading steadily in that chair since I saw you last."

"Even a demagogue, Jack, would hesitate to believe that because a man read occasionally he didn't work at all. I wish *they* would read more, by the way; then they wouldn't be so illogical. But I really haven't much to do just now, except in the garden. I'm a store-cattle man, you know, and my lot being well broken in—"

"You've only to sit in the verandah and read till they get fat. That's the worst of our life. There isn't enough for a man of energy to do—and upon my word, old fellow, I'm getting tired of it."

"Tired of what?" asked his friend, rather wonderingly; "tired of your life, or tired of your bread and butter, because the butter is too abundant? Oh, I see, we are just returned from town, where we met a young lady who—"

"Not at all; not that I didn't meet a very nice girl—"

"You always do. If you went to Patagonia, you'd say, ''Pon my word I met a very nice girl there, considering—her hair wasn't very greasy, she had good eyes and teeth, and her skin—her skins, I mean—had not such a bad odour when you got used to it.' You're such a very tolerant fellow."

"You be hanged; but this Ellen Middleton really *was* a nice girl, capital figure, nice face, good expression you know, and reads—so few girls read at all nowadays."

"I believe they read just as much as or more than ever; only when a fellow takes a girl for good and all, to last him for forty or fifty years, if he live so long, she'd need to be a *very* nice girl indeed, as you say."

"Don't talk in that utilitarian way; one would think you had no heart; but it does seem an awful risk, doesn't it? Suppose one got taken in, as you do sometimes about horses 'incurably lame,' or 'no heart,' like that brute Bolivar I gave such a price for. What a splendid thing it would be if one were only a Turk, and could marry every year and believe one was acting most religiously and devoutly."

"Come, Jack, who is talking unprofitably now? Something's gone wrong with you evidently. Here comes dinner."

After dinner the friends sat and smoked in the broad verandah, and looked out over the undulating grassy downs, timbered like a park, and at the blue starry night.

"I really was in earnest," said Jack, "when I talked about being tired of the sort of life you and I, and all the fellows in this district, are leading just now."

"Were you though?" asked his friend; "what's amiss with it?"

"Well, we are wasting our time, I consider, with these small cattle stations. No one has room for more than two or three thousand head of cattle. And what are they?"

"Only a pleasant livelihood," answered his friend, "including books, quiet, fresh air, exercise, variety, a dignified occupation, and perfect independence, plus one or two thousand a year income. It's not much, I grant you; but I'm a moderate man, and I feel almost contented."

"What's a couple of thousand a year in a country like this?" broke in Jack, impetuously, "while those sheep-holding fellows in Riverina are making their five or ten upon country only half or a quarter stocked. They have only to breed up, and there they are, with fifty or a hundred thousand sheep. Sheep, with the run given in, will always be worth a pound ahead, whatever way the country goes."

"I'm not so sure of that," said Tunstall; "though I have never been across the Murray, and don't intend to go, as far as I know. As for sheep, I hate them, and I hate shepherds, lazy crawling wretches! they and the sheep are just fit to torment one another. Besides, how do you know these great profits *are* made? You're not much of an accountant, Jack, excuse me."

"I didn't think you were so prejudiced," quoth Jack, with dignity. "I can cipher fast enough when it's worth while. Besides, better heads than mine are in the spec. You know Foreland, Marsalay, the Milmans, and Hugh Brass, all longheaded men! They are buying up unstocked country or cattle runs, and putting on ewes by the ten thousand."

"Better heads than yours may lie as low, my dear Jack; though I don't mean to say you have a bad head by any means. And as to the account-keeping you can do that very reasonably, like most other things—*when you try*, when you try, old man. But you don't often try, you careless, easygoing beggar that you are, except when you are excited—as you are now—by something in the way of natural history—a mare's nest, so to speak."

"This mare's nest will have golden eggs in it then. Theodorus Sharpe told me that he made as much in one year from the station he bought out there as he had done in half-a-dozen while he was wasting his life (that was his expression) down here."

"Has the benevolent Theodorus any unstocked back country to dispose of?" asked Tunstall, quietly.

"Well, he has one place to sell—a regular bargain," said Jack, rather hesitatingly, "but we didn't make any special agreement about it. I am to go out and see the country for myself."

"And suppose you do like it, and believe a good deal more of what Theodorus Sharpe tells you than I should like to do, what then?"

"Why then I shall sell Marshmead, buy a large block of country, and put on breeding sheep."

"I suppose it wouldn't be considered perfectly Eastern hospitality to call a man a perfect fool in one's own house. But, Jack, if you do this thing I shall *think* so. You may quarrel with me if you like."

"I should never quarrel with you, dear old boy, whatever you said or thought. Be sure of that," said Jack, feelingly. "We have been too long friends and brothers for that. But I reserve *my* right to think you an unambitious, unprogressive what's-your-name. You will be eaten out by cockatoos in another five years, when I am selling out and starting for my European tour."

"I will take the chance of that," said Tunstall; "but, joking apart, I would do anything to persuade you not to go. Besides, you have a duty to perform to this district, where you have lived so long, and, on the whole, done so well. I thought you were rather strong on the point, though I confess I am not, of duty to one's country socially, politically, and what not."

"Well, I grant you I had notions of that kind once," admitted Jack, "but then you see all these small towns have become so confoundedly democratic lately, that I think we squatters owe them nothing, and must look after our own interests."

"Which means making as much money as ever we can, and by whatever means. Jack! Jack! the demon of vulgar ambition, mere material advancement, has seized upon you, and I can see it is of no use talking. My good old warm-hearted Jack has vanished, and in his place I see a mere money-making speculator, gambling with land and stock instead of cards and dice. If you make the money you dream of, it will do you no good, and if not—"

"Well, if not? Suppose I don't win?"

"Then you will lose your life, or all that makes life worth having. I have never seen a ruined man who had not lost much beside his years and his money. I can't say another word. Goodnight!"

Next morning the subject was not resumed. The friends wrung each other's hands silently at parting, and Jack rode home to Marshmead.

When he got to the outer gate of the paddock he opened it meditatively, and as he swung it to without dismounting his heart smote him for the deed he was about to commit, as a species of treason against all his foregone life and associations.

II

"Who calleth thee, heart? World's strife,
With a golden heft to his knife."

—E.B. BROWNING

The sun was setting over the broad, open creek flat, which was dotted with groups of cattle, the prevailing white and roan colouring of which testified to their short-horn extraction. It was the autumnal season, but the early rains, which never failed in *that* favoured district, had promoted the growth of a thick and green if rather short sward, grateful to the eye after the somewhat hot day. A couple of favourite mares and half-a dozen blood yearlings came galloping up, neighing, and causing Hassan, his favourite old hack, to put up his head and sidle about. Everything looked prosperous and peaceful, and, withal, wore that indescribable air of half solitude which characterizes the Australian bush.

Jack's heart swelled as he saw the place which he had first chosen out of the waste, which he had made and built up, stick by stick, hut by hut, into its present comfortable completeness, and he said to himself—"I have half a mind to stick to old Hampden after all!" Here was the place where, a mere boy, he had ridden a tired horse one night, neither of them having eaten since early morn, into the thick of a camp of hostile blacks! How he had called upon the old horse with sudden spur, and how gallantly the good nag, so dead beat but a moment before, had answered, and carried him safely away from the half-childish, half-ferocious beings who would have knocked him on the head with as little remorse then as an opossum! Yonder was where the old sod but stood, put up by him and the faithful Geordie, and in which he had considered himself luxuriously lodged, as a contrast to living under a dray.

Over there was where he had sowed his first vegetable seeds, cutting down and carrying the saplings with which it was fenced. It was, certainly, so small that the blacks believed he had buried someone there, whom he had done to death secretly, and would never be convinced to the contrary, disbelieving both his vows and his vegetables. There was the stockyard which he and Geordie had put up, carrying much of the material on their shoulders, when the bullocks, as was their custom, "quite frequent," were lost for a week.

He gazed at the old slab hut, the first real expensive regular station-building which the property had boasted. How proud he had been of it too! Slabs averaging over a foot wide! Upper and lower wall-plates all complete. Loop holes, necessities of the period, on either side of the chimney. Never was there such a hut. It was the first one he had helped to build, and it was shrined as a palace in his imagination for years after.

And now that the rude old days were gone, and the pretty cottage stood, amid the fruitful orchard and trim flower-beds, that the brown face of Harry the groom appears, from a well-ordered stable, with half-a-dozen colts and hacks duly done by at rack and manger, that the stackyard showed imposingly with its trimly-thatched ricks, and that the table was already laid by Mrs. Stirling, the housekeeper, in the cool dining-room, and "decored with napery" very creditable to a bachelor establishment;—was he to leave all this realized order, this capitalized comfort, and go forth into the arid wilderness of the interior, suffering the passed-away privations of the "bark hut and tin pot era"—all for the sake of—what? Making more money! He felt ashamed of himself, as Geordie came forward with a smile of welcome upon his rugged face, and said—

"Well, master, I was afraid you was never coming back. Here's that fellow Fakewell been and mustered on the sly again, and it's the greatest mercy as I heard only the day before."

"You were there, I'll be bound, Geordie."

"Ye'll ken that, sir, though I had to ride half the night. It was well worth a ride, though. I got ten good calves and a gra-and two-year-old, unbranded heifer, old Poll's, you'll mind her, that got away at weaning."

"I don't remember—but how did you persuade Fakewell to take your word? I should have thought he'd have forged half-a-dozen mothers for a beast of that age."

"Well, we had a sair barney, well nigh a fight, you might be sure. At last I said, 'I'll leave it to the black boy to say whose calf she is, and if he says the wrong cow you shall have her.'

"'But how am I to know,' says he, 'that you haven't told him what to say?'

"'You saw him come up. Hoo could I know she was here?'

"'Well, that's true,' says he. 'Well, now you tell me the old cow's name as you say she belongs to, so as he can't hear, and then I'll ask him the question.'

"'All right,' I said, 'you hear the paction (to all the stockmen, and they gathered round); Mr. Fakewell says he'll give me that heifer, the red beast with the white tail, if Sandfly there can tell the auld coo's name right. You see the callant didna come with me; he just brought up the fresh horses.'

"'All right,' they said.

"So Fakewell says—'Now, Sandfly, who does that heifer belong to?'

"The small black imp looks serious at her for a minute, and then his face broke out into a grin all over. 'That one belong to Mr. Redgrave— why that old 'cranky Poll's' calf, we lose him out of weaner mob last year.'

"All right, that's so," says Fakewell, uncommon sulky, while all the men just roared; 'but don't you brand yer calves when you wean 'em?'

"'That one get through gate, and Mr. Redgrave says no use turn back all the mob, then tree fall down on fence and let out her and two more. But that young cranky Poll safe enough, I take Bible oath.'

"'You'll do; take your heifer,' says he; 'I'll be even with someone for this.'"

"I dare say he didn't get the best of you, Master Geordie," said Jack, kindly; "he'd be a sharp fellow if he did. You were going to muster the 'Lost Waterhole Camp' soon, weren't you?"

"There's a mob there that wants bringing in and regulating down there just uncommon bad. I was biding a bit, till you came home."

"Well, Geordie, you can call me at daylight tomorrow. I'll have an early breakfast and go out with you. You know I haven't been getting up quite so early lately."

"You can just wake as early as anyone, when you like, sir; but I'll call you. What horse shall I tell Harry?"

"Well, I'll take 'the Don,' I think. No, tell him to get 'Mustang,' he's the best cutting-out horse."

"No man ever had a better servant," thought Jack as he sat down in half an hour to his well-appointed table and well-served, well-cooked repast.

Geordie Stirling was as shrewd, staunch a Borderer as ever was reared in that somewhat bleak locality, a worthy descendant of the men who gathered fast with spear and brand, when the bale-fires gave notice that the moss-troopers were among their herds. He was sober, economical, and self-denying. He and his good wife had retained the stern doctrines in which their youth had been reared, but little acted upon by the circumstances and customs of colonial life.

Jack applied himself to his dinner with reasonable earnestness, having had a longish ride, and being one of those persons whose natural appetite is rarely interfered with by circumstances. He could always eat, drink, and sleep with a zest which present joy or sorrow to come had no power to disturb. He therefore appreciated the roast fowl and other home-grown delicacies which Mrs. Stirling placed before him, and settled down to a good comfortable read afterwards, leaving the momentous question of migration temporarily in abeyance. After all this was over, however, he returned to the consideration of the subject. He went over Fred Tunstall's arguments, which he thought were well enough in their way, but savoured of a nature unprogressive and too easily contented. "It's all very well to be contented," he said to himself; "and we are very fairly placed now, but a man must look ahead. Suppose these runs are cut up and sold by a democratic ministry, or allowed to be taken up, before survey, by cockatoos, where shall we be in ten years? Almost cockatoos ourselves, with run for four or five hundred head of cattle; a lot of fellows pestering our lives out; and a couple of thousand acres of purchased land. There's no living to be made out of *that*. Not what I call a living; unless one were to milk his own cows, and so on. I hardly think I should do that. No! I'll go in for something that will be growing and increasing year by year, not the other way. This district is getting worn out. The land is too good. The runs are too small and too close to one another, and will be smaller yet. No! my idea of a run is twenty miles frontage to a river—the Oxley or the Lachlan, with thirty miles back; then with twenty thousand ewes, or even ten to start with, you may expect something like an increase, and lots of ground to put them on. Then sell out and have a little Continental travel; come back, marry, and settle down. By Jove! here goes—Victory or Westminster Abbey!"

Inspired by these glorious visions, and conceiving quite a contempt for poor little Marshmead, with only 2,000 cattle and a hundred horses upon its 20,000 acres, Jack took out his writing materials and scribbled off the following advertisement:—

"Messrs. Drawe and Backwell have much pleasure in announcing the sale by auction, at an early period, of which due notice will be given, of the station known as Marshmead, in the Hampden district, with two thousand unusually well-bred cattle of the J R brand. The run, in point of quality, is one of the best, in a celebrated fattening district. The cattle are highly bred, carefully culled, and have always brought first-class prices at the metropolitan sale-yards. The improvements are extensive, modern, and complete. The only reason for selling this valuable property is that the proprietor contemplates leaving the colony."

ROLF BOLDREWOOD

"There," said Jack, laying down his pen, "that's quite enough—puffing won't sell a place, and everybody's heard of Marshmead, and of the J R cattle, most likely. If they haven't, they can ask. There's no great difficulty in selling a first-class run. And now I'll seal it up ready for the post, and turn in."

Next morning, considerably to Geordie's disappointment, Jack declined to go out to the "Lost Waterhole Camp," telling him rather shortly (to conceal his real feelings) that he thought of selling the place, and that it would be time to muster when they were delivering.

"Going to sell the run!" gasped Geordie, perfectly aghast. "Why, master, what ever put such a thing into your head? Where will ye find a bonnier place than this? and there's no such a herd of cattle in all the country round. Sell Marshmead! Why, you must have picked up that when in town."

"Never mind where I picked it up," said Jack, rather crossly; "I have thought the matter over well, you may believe, and as I have made up my mind there is no use in talking about it. You don't suppose Hampden is all Australia?"

"No, but it's one of the best bits upon the whole surface of it—and that I'll live and die on," said Geordie. "Look at the soil and the climate. Didn't I go across the Murray to meet they store cattle, and wasna it nearly the death of me? Six weeks' hard sun, and never a drop of rain. And blight, and flies, and bush mosquiteys; why, I'd rather live here on a pound a week than have a good station there. Think o' the garden, too."

"Well, Geordie," said Jack, "all that's very well, but look at the size of the runs! Why, I saw 1,000 head of fat cattle coming past one station I stayed at, in one mob, splendid cattle too; bigger and better than any of our little drafts we think such a lot of. Besides, I don't mind heat, you know, and I'm bent on being a large stockholder, or none at all."

"Weel, weel!" said Geordie, "you will never be convinced. I know you'll just have your own way, but take care ye dinna gang the road to lose all the bonny place ye have worked hard for. The Lord keep ye from making haste to be rich."

"I know, I know," said Jack, testily; "but the Bible says nothing about changing your district. Abraham did that, you know, and evidently was getting crowded up where he was."

"Master John, you're not jestin' about God's Word! ye would never do the like o' that, I know, but Elsie and I will pray ye'll be properly directed—and Elspeth Stirling will be a sorrowful woman I know to stay behind, as she must, when all's sold and ye go away to that desolate, waesome hot desert, where there's neither Sabbaths, nor Christian men, nor the Word once in a year."

The fateful advertisement duly appeared, and divers "intending purchasers," introduced by Messrs. Drawe and Backwell, arrived at Marshmead, where they were met with that tempered civility which such visitors generally receive.

The usual objections were made. The run was not large enough; the boundaries were inconvenient or not properly defined; the stock were not as good as had been represented; the improvements were not sufficiently extensive. This statement was made by a young and aristocratic investor, who was about to be married. He was very critical about the height of the cottage walls, and the size of the sitting-room. The buildings were too numerous and expensive, and would take more money than they were worth to keep in repair. This was the report and opinion of an elderly purchaser (Scotch), who did not see the necessity of anything bigger than a two-roomed slab hut. Such an edifice had been quite enough for him (he was pleased to remark) to make twenty thousand pounds in, on the Lower Murray, and to drink many a gallon of whisky in. As such results and recreations comprised, in his estimation, "the whole duty of man," he considered Jack's neat outbuildings, and even the garden—*horresco referens!*—to be totally superfluous and unprofitable. He expressed his intention, if he were to do such an unlikely thing as to buy the wee bit kail-yard o' a place, to pull two-thirds of the huts down.

All these criticisms, mingled with sordid chaffering, were extremely distasteful to Jack's taste, and his temper suffered to such an extent that he had thought of writing to the agents to give no further orders for inspection. However, shortly after the departure of the objectionable old savage, as he profanely termed the veteran pastoralist, he received a telegram to say that the sale was concluded. Mr. Donald M'Donald, late of Binjee-Mungee, had paid half cash, and the rest at short-dated bills, and would send his nephew, Mr. Angus M'Tavish, to take delivery in a few days.

Long before these irrevocable matters had come to pass, our hero had bitterly repented of his determination. Those of his neighbours who were not on such terms of intimacy as to expostulate roundly, like Tunstall, could not conceal their distrust or disapproval of his course. Some were sincerely sorry to lose him as a neighbour, and this expression of feeling touched him more deeply than the opposition of the others.

Mr. M'Tavish arrived, and, after delivery of his credentials, the last solemnities of mustering and delivery were duly concluded.

The "nephew of his uncle" was an inexperienced but deeply suspicious youth, who declined to take the most obvious things for granted, and consistently disbelieved every word that was said to him. Geordie Stirling with difficulty refrained from laying hands upon him; and Jack was so disgusted with his "manners and customs" that, on the evening when the delivery was concluded, he declined to spend another night at old Marshmead, but betook himself, with his two favourite hacks, specially reserved at time of sale, to the nearest inn, from which he made the best of his way to the metropolis.

The disruption of old ties and habitudes was much more painful than he had anticipated. His two faithful retainers located themselves upon an adjoining farm, which their savings had enabled them to purchase. To this they removed their stock, which was choice though not numerous. Geordie, after his first warning, said no more, knowing by experience that his master, when he had set his mind upon a thing, was more obstinate than many a man of sterner mould. Too sincere to acquiesce, his rugged, weather-beaten lineaments retained their look of solemn disapproval, mingled at times with a curiously pathetic gaze, to the last.

With his wife Elspeth, a woman of much originality and force of character, combined with deep religious feeling of the old-fashioned Puritan type, the case was different.

She had a strong and sincere affection for John Redgrave, whom she had known from his early boyhood, and in many ways had she demonstrated this. She had unobtrusively and efficiently ministered to his comfort for years. She had not scrupled to take him to task in a homely and earnest way for minor faults and backslidings, all of which rebukes and remonstrances he had taken in good part, as springing from an over-zealous but conscientious desire for his welfare. His friends smiled at the good old woman's warnings and testifyings, occasionally delivered, when performing her household duties, in the presence of any company then and there assembled, by whom she was not in the slightest degree abashed, or to be turned from any righteous purpose.

"Eh, Maister John, ye'll no be wantin' to ride anither of thae weary steeplechasers?" she had been pleased to inquire upon a certain occasion; "ye'll just be fa'in doon and hurtin' yersel', or lamin' and woundin' the puir beastie that's been granted to man for a' useful purposes!"

She had been in the habit of "being faithful to him," as she termed divers very plain spoken and home-thrusting exhortations in respect to his general habits and walk in life, whenever she had reason to think such allocution to be necessary. She had taken him to task repeatedly for unprofitable reading upon, and lax observance of, the Sabbath; for a too devoted adherence to racing, and the unpardonable sin of betting; for too protracted absences in the metropolis, and consequent neglect of his interests at Marshmead; and, generally, for any departure from the strict line of Christian life and manners which she rigidly observed herself, and compelled Geordie to practice. Though sometimes testy at such infringements upon the liberty of the subject, Jack had sufficient sense and good feeling to recognize the true and deep anxiety for his welfare from which this excess of carefulness sprang. In every other respect old Elsie's rule was without flaw or blemish. For all the years of their stay at Marshmead, no bachelor in all the West had enjoyed such perfect immunity from the troubles and minor miseries to which Australian employers are subjected. Spotless cleanliness, perfect comfort, and proverbial cookery, had been the unbroken experience of the Marshmead household. It was a place at which all guests, brought there for pleasure or duty, hastened to arrive, and lingered with flattering unwillingness to leave.

And now this pleasant home was to be broken up, the peaceful repose and organized comfort to be abandoned, and the farewell words to be said to the faithful retainer.

Jack felt parting with the old woman more than he cared to own; he felt almost ashamed and slightly irritated at the depth of his emotion. "Confound it," he said to himself, "it's very hard that one can't sell one's run and move off to a thinly-stocked country without feeling as if one had committed a species of wrong and treachery, and having to make as many affecting farewells as I have no doubt my governor did when he left England for the *terra incognita* Australia."

"Well, Elsie," he said, with an attempt at ease and jocularity he was far from feeling, "I must say goodbye. I hope you and Geordie will be snug and comfortable at your farm. I'll write to you when I'm settled in Riverina; and, if I do as well as someothers, I shall make a pot of money, and be off to the old country in a few years."

He put out his hand, but the old woman heeded it not, but gazed in his face with a wistful, pleading look, and the tears filled her eyes, not often seen in melting mood, as she said—

"Oh, Maister John, oh, my bairn, that I should live to see you ride away from the bonny home where ye've lived so long, and been aye respeckit and useful in your generation. Do ye think ye have the Lord's blessing for giving up the lot where He has placed ye and blessed ye, for to gang amang strangers and scorners—all for the desire of gain? I misdoot the flitting, and the craving for the riches that perish in the using, sairly—sairly. Dinna forget your Bible; and pray, oh, pray to Him, my bairn, that ye may be direckit in the right way. I canna speak mair for greetin' and mistrustin' that my auld een have looked their last on your bonny face. May the Lord have ye in His keeping."

Her tears flowed unrestrainedly, as she clasped his hand in both of hers, and then turned away in silence.

"Geordie," said our hero, strongly inclined to follow suit, "you mustn't let Elsie fret like this, you know. I am not going away forever. You'll see me back most likely in the summer, for a little change and a mouthful of sea air. I shall find you taking all the prizes at the Hampden show with that bull calf of old Cherry's."

"It's little pleesure we'll have in him, or the rest of the stock, for a while," answered Geordie. "The place will no be natural like, wantin' ye. The Lord's will be done," added he, reverently. "We're a' in His keepin'. I'd come with ye, for as far and as hot as yon sa-andy desert o' a place is, if it werena for the wife. God bless ye, Maister John!"

III

"So forward to fresh fields and pastures new."

—MILTON

Jack's spirits had recovered their usual high average when he found himself once more at the club in a very free and unfettered condition, and clothed with the prestige of a man who had sold his station well, and was likely to rise in (pastoral) life.

He was bold, energetic, moderately experienced, and had all that sanguine trust in the splendid probabilities of life common to those youthful knights who have come scatheless through the tourney, and have never, as yet, been

> *"Dragged from amid the horses' feet,*
> *With dinted shield and helmet beat."*

He derived a little amusement (for he possessed a keen faculty of observation, though, as with other gifts, he did not always make the best use of that endowment) from the evident brevet rank which was accorded to him by the moneyed and other magnates. His advice was asked as to stock investments. He was consulted upon social and political questions. Invitations, of which he had always received a fair allowance, came in showers. Report magnified considerably the price he had received for Marshmead. Many chaperons and haughty matrons of the most exacting class bid eagerly for his society. In short, Jack Redgrave had become the fashion, and for a time revelled in all the privileged luxury of that somewhat intoxicating position. Notwithstanding a fine natural tendency *desipere in loco*, our hero was much too shrewd and practical a personage not to be fully aware that this kind of thing could not last. He had a far higher ambition than would have permitted him to subside into a club swell, or a social butterfly, permanently. He had, besides, that craving for bodily exercise, even labour, common to men of vigorous organization, which, however lulled and deadened for a time, could not be controlled for any protracted period.

He had, therefore, kept up a reasonably diligent search among the station agents and others for any likely investment which might form the nucleus of the large establishment, capable of indefinite expansion, of which he had vowed to become the proprietor.

Such a one, at length (for, as usual when a man has his pockets full of money, and is hungering and thirsting to buy, one would think that there was not a purchaseable run on the whole continent of Australia), was "submitted to his notice" by a leading agent; the proprietor, like himself in the advertisement of Marshmead, was "about to leave the colony," so that all doubt of purely philanthropical intention in selling this "potentiality of fabulous wealth" was set at rest. Jack took the mail that night, with the offer in his pocket, and in a few days found himself deposited at "a lodge in the wilderness" of Riverina, face to face with the magnificent enterprize.

Gondaree had been a cattle-station from the ancient days, when old Morgan had taken it up with five hundred head of cattle and two or three convict servants, in the interests and by the order of the well-known Captain Kidd, of Double Bay. A couple of huts had been built, with stock-yard and gallows. The usual acclimatization and pioneer civilization had followed. One of the stockmen had been speared: a score or two of the blacks, to speak well within bounds, had been shot. By intervals of labour, sometimes toilsome and incessant, oftener monotonous and mechanical, the sole recreation being a mad debauch on the part of master and man, the place slowly but surely and profitably progressed—progressed with the tenacious persistence and sullen obstinacy of the race, which, notwithstanding toils, dangers, broils, bloodshed, and reckless revelries, rarely abandons the object originally specified. Pioneer or privateer, merchant or missionary, the root qualities of the great colonizing breed are identical. They perish in the breach, they drink and gamble, but they rarely raise the siege. The standard *is* planted, though by reckless or unworthy hands; still goes on the grand march of civilization, with splendour of peace and pomp of war. With the fair fanes and foul alleys of cities—with peaceful village and waving cornfield—so has it ever been; so till the dawn of a purer day, a higher faith, must it ever be, the ceaseless "martyrdom of man."

> *"And the individual withers,*
> *And the race is more and more."*

Gondaree had advanced. The drafts of fat cattle had improved in number and quality—at first, in the old, old days, when supply bore hard upon demand, selling for little more than provided an adequate quantity of flour, tea, sugar, and tobacco for the year's consumption. But the herd had spread by degrees over the wide plains of "the back," as well as over the broad river flats and green reed-beds of "the frontage," and began to be numbered by thousands rather than by the original hundreds.

Changes slowly took place. Old Morgan had retired to a small station of his own with a herd of cattle and horses doubtfully accumulated, as was the fashion of the day, by permission of his master, who had never once visited Gondaree.

The old stockmen were dead, or gone none knew whither; but another overseer, of comparatively modern notions, occupied his place, and while enduring the monotonous, unrelieved existence, cursed the unprogressive policy which debarred him from the sole bush recreation—in that desert region—of planning and putting up "improvements."

About the period of which we speak, it had occurred to the trustees of the late Captain Kidd that, as cattle-stations had risen much in value in that part of the country, from the rage which then obtained to dispose of those despised animals and replace them with sheep, it was an appropriate time to sell. The station had paid fairly for years past. Not a penny had been spent upon its development in anyway; and now, "as those Victorian fellows and others, who ought to know better, were going wild about salt-bush cattle-stations to put sheep on—why, this was clearly the time to put Gondaree in the market."

As Jack drove up in the unpretending vehicle which bore Her Majesty's mails and adventurous travellers to the scarce-known township of "far Bochara," the day was near its close. The homestead was scarcely calculated to prepossess people. They had passed the river a couple of miles back, and now halted at a sandy hillock, beneath which lay a sullen lagoon. There were two ruinous slab huts, with bark roofs, at no great distance from each other. There was a stock-yard immediately at the back of the huts, where piles of bones, with the skulls and horns of long-slain beasts, told the tale of the earliest occupation of the place.

There was no garden, no horse-paddock, nothing of any kind, sort, or description but the two huts, which might have originally cost ten pounds each. Jack, taking his valise and rug, walked towards the largest hut, from which a brown-faced young fellow, in a Crimean shirt and moleskin trousers, had emerged.

"You are Mr.—Mr.—Redgrave," said he, consulting a well-thumbed letter which he took out of his pocket. "I have orders to show you the place and the cattle. Won't you come in?"

Jack stepped over two or three impediments which barred the path, and narrowly escaped breaking his shins over a bullock's head, which a grand-looking kangaroo dog was gnawing. He glanced at the door, which was let into the wall-plate of the hut above and below, after the oldest known form of hinge, and sat down somewhat ruefully upon a wooden stool.

"You're from town, I suppose?" said the young man, mechanically filling his pipe, and looking with calm interest at Jack's general get-up.

"Yes," answered Jack, "I am. You are aware that I have come to look at the run. When can we make a beginning?"

"Tomorrow morning," was the answer. "I'll send for the horses at daylight."

"How do you get on without a horse-paddock?" asked Jack, balancing himself upon the insecure stool, and looking enviously at his companion, who was seated upon the only bed in the apartment. "Don't you sometimes lose time at musters?"

"Time ain't of much account on the Warroo," answered the overseer, spitting carelessly upon the earthen floor. "We have a cursed sight more of it than we know what to do with. And Captain Kidd didn't believe in improvements. Many a time I've written and written for this and that, but the answer was that old Morgan did very well without them for so many years, and so might I. I got sick of it, and just rubbed on like the rest. If I had had my way, I'd have burned down the thundering old place long ago, and put up everything new at Steamboat Point. But you might as well talk to an old working bullock as to our trustees."

"What are the cattle like?" inquired Mr. Redgrave.

"Well, not so bad, considering there hasn't been a bull bought these ten years. It's first-class fattening country; I dare say you saw that if you noticed any mobs as you came along." Jack nodded. "When the country is real good cattle will hold their own, no matter how they're bred. There ain't much the matter with the cattle—a few stags and rough ones, of course, but pretty fair on the whole. I expect you're hungry after your journey. The hut-keeper will bring in tea directly."

In a few moments that functionary appeared, with a pair of trousers so extremely dirty as to suggest the idea that he had been permanently located upon a back block, where economy in the use of water was a virtue of necessity. Rubbing down the collection of slabs which did duty for a table with a damp cloth, he placed thereon a tin dish, containing a large joint of salt beef, a damper like the segment of a cart-wheel, and a couple of plates, one of which was of the same useful metal as the dish. He then departed, and presently appeared with a very black camp-kettle, or billy, of hot tea, which he placed upon the floor; scattering several pannikins upon the board, one of which contained sugar, he lounged out again, after having taken a good comprehensive stare at the new comer.

"We smashed our teapot last muster," said the manager, apologetically, "and we can't get another till the drays come up. This is a pretty rough shop, as you see, but I suppose you ain't just out from England?"

"I have been in the bush before," said Jack, sententiously. "Are the flies always as bad here?"

"Well, they're enough to eat your eyes out, and the mosquitoes too—worse after the rains; but they say it's worse lower down the river."

"Worse than this! I should hardly have thought it possible," mused Jack, as the swarming insects disputed the beef with him, and caused him to be cautious of shutting his mouth after enclosing a few accidentally. The bread was black with them, the sugar, the table generally, and every now and then one of a small black variety would dart straight into the corner of his eye.

When the uninviting meal was over, Jack walked outside, and, lighting his pipe, commenced to consider the question of the purchase of the place. With the sedative influences of the great narcotic a more calmly judicial view of the question presented itself.

He was sufficiently experienced to know that, whereas you may make a homestead and adjuncts sufficiently good to satisfy the most exacting Squatter-Sybarite, if such be wanting, you can by no means build a good run if the country, that is, extent and quality of pasture, be wanting. A prudent buyer, therefore, does not attach much value to improvements, scrutinizing carefully the run itself as the only source of future profits.

"It is a beastly hole!" quoth Jack, as he finished his pipe, "only fit for a black fellow, or a Scotchman on his promotion; but from what I saw of the cattle as I came along (and they tell no lies) there is no mistake about the country. They were all as fat as pigs, the yearlings and calves, as well as the aged cattle. I never saw them look like that at Marshmead, or even at Glen na Voirlich, which used to be thought the richest spot in our district. There is nothing to hinder me clearing out the whole of the herd and having ten or fifteen thousand ewes on the place before lambing time. There is no scab and no foot-rot within a colony of us. With fair luck, I could have up a woolshed in time to shear; and a decent lambing, say 70 percent, would give me—let me see, how many altogether after shearing?"

Here Jack went into abstruse arithmetical calculations as to the numbers, sexes, ages, and value of his possible property, and, after a very rapid subtraction of cattle and multiplication of sheep, saw himself the owner of fifty thousand of the last-named fashionable animals, which, when sold at twenty-five shillings per head, or even twenty-seven and sixpence (everything given in), would do very well until he should have visited Europe, and returned to commence operations upon a scale even more grand and comprehensive.

"I think I see my way," he said to himself, finally, knocking the ashes out of his pipe. "Of course one must rough it at first; the great thing in these large stock operations is decisiveness."

He accordingly decided to go to bed at once, and informed Mr. Hawkesbury, the overseer, that he should be ready as soon as they could see in the morning, and so betook himself to a couch, of which the supporting portion was ingeniously constructed of strips of hide, and the mattress, bed-clothing, curtains, &c., represented by a pair of blankets evidently akin in antiquity, as in hue, to Bob the cook's trousers.

Accepting his host's brief apologies, Jack turned in, and Mr. Hawkesbury, having disembarrassed himself of his boots, pulled a ragged opossum-rug over him, and lay down before the fire-place, with his pipe in his mouth.

The coach and mail travelling, continued during two preceding days and nights, had banged and shaken Jack's hardy frame sufficiently to induce a healthy fatigue. In two minutes he was sound asleep, and for three or four hours never turned in his bed. Then he woke suddenly, and with the moment of consciousness was enabled to realize Mr. Gulliver's experiences after the first flight of the arrows of the Liliputians.

He arose swiftly, and muttering direful maledictions upon the Warroo, and all inhabitants of its borders from source to mouth, frontage and back, myall, salt-bush, and cotton-bush, pulled on his garments and looked around.

It yet wanted three hours to daylight. Mr. Hawkesbury was sleeping like an infant. He could see the moon through a crack in the bark roof, and hear the far hoarse note of the night-bird. Taking his railway rug, he opened the door, which creaked upon its Egyptian hinge, and walked forth.

"Beautiful was the night. Behind the black wall of the forest."

And so on, as Longfellow has it in mournful *Evangeline*. The forest was not exactly black, being partly of the moderately-foliaged eucalyptus, and having a strip of the swaying, streaming myall, of a colour more resembling blue than black. Still there were shadows sufficiently darksome and weird in conjunction with the glittering moonbeams to appeal to the stranger's poetic sympathies. The deep, still waters of the lagoon lay like dulled silver, ever and anon stirred into ripples of wondrous brilliancy by the leaping of a fish, or the sinuous trail of a reptile or water rodent. All was still as in the untroubled æons ere discovery. In spite of the squalid surroundings and the sordid human traces, Nature had resumed her grand solitude and the majestic hush of the desert.

"All this is very fine," quoth Jack to himself. "What a glorious night; but I must try and have a little more sleep somehow." He picked out a tolerably convenient spot between the buttressed roots of a vast casuarina, which from laziness rather than from taste had been spared by the ruthless axes of the pioneers, and wrapping himself in his rug lay down in the sand. The gentle murmur of the ever-sounding, mournful-sighing tree soon hushed his tired senses, and the sun was rising as he raised himself on his elbow and looked round.

It was a slightly different sleeping arrangement from those to which he had been long accustomed. Nor were the concomitants less strange. A large pig had approached nearer than was altogether pleasant. She was evidently speculating as to the weak, defenceless, possibly edible condition of the traveller. Jack had not been conversant with the comprehensively carnivorous habits of Warroo pigs. He was, therefore, less alarmed than amused. He also made the discovery that he was no great distance from a populous ant-hill, of which, however, the free and enlightened citizens had not as yet "gone for him." Altogether he fully realized the necessity for changing front, and, rising somewhat suddenly to his feet, was about to walk over to the hut when the rolling thunder of horses at speed, rapidly approaching, decided him to await the new sensation.

Round a jutting point of timber a small drove of twenty or thirty horses came at a headlong gallop in a cloud of dust, and made straight for the stockyard in the direct track for which Jack's bedroom was situated. Standing close up to the old tree, which was sufficiently strong and broad to shield him, he awaited the cavalry charge. They passed close on either side, to the unaffected astonishment of an old mare, who turned her eyes upon him with a wild glare as she brushed his shoulder with her sweeping mane. Dashing into the large receiving-yard of the old stockyard, they stopped suddenly and began to walk gently about, as if fully satisfied with themselves. Following fast came two wild riders, one of whom was a slight half-caste lad, and the other, to Jack's great surprise, a black girl of eighteen or twenty. This last child of the desert rode *en cavalier* on an ordinary saddle with extremely rusty stirrup-irons. Her long wavy hair fell in masses over her shoulders. Her eyes were soft and large, her features by no means unpleasing, and her unsophisticated teeth white and regular. Dashing up to the slip-rails, this young person jumped off her horse with panther-like agility, and putting up the heavy saplings, thus addressed Mr. Hawkesbury, who, with Jack, had approached:—

"By gum, Misser Hoxbry, you give me that horrid old mare today I ride her inside out, the ole brute."

"What for, Wildduck?" inquired the overseer; "what's she been doing now?"

"Why, run away all over the country and break half-a-dozen times, and make me and Spitfire close up dead. Look at him." Here she pointed to her steed, a small violent weed, whose wide nostril and heaving flank showed that he had been going best pace for a considerable period. "That boy, Billy Mortimer, not worth a cuss."

Having volunteered this last piece of information, Wildduck pulled off the saddle, which she placed, cantle downward, against the fence, so as to permit the moistened padding to receive all drying influences of sun and air; then, dragging off the bridle to the apparent danger of Spitfire's front teeth, she permitted that excitable courser to wander at will.

"That one pull my arm off close up," she remarked, "all along that ole devil of a mare. I'll take it out of her today, my word! Who's this cove?"

"Gentleman come up to buy station," answered Hawkesbury; "by and by, master belong to you; and if you're a good girl he'll give you a new gown and a pound of tobacco. Now you get breakfast, and ride over to Jook-jook—tell'm all to meet us at the Long Camp tomorrow."

"Kai-i!" said the savage damsel, in a long-drawn plaintive cry of surprise, as she put her fingers, with assumed shyness, up to her face, and peered roguishly through them; then, hitching up her scanty and tattered dress, she ran off without more conversation to the hut.

"Good gracious!" said Jack to himself, "I wonder what old Elsie and Geordie Stirling would think of all this; Moabitish women and all the rest of it, I suppose. However, I am not here for the present to regulate the social code of the Lower Warroo. Have you got the tribe here?" he said, aloud.

"No, Wildduck ran away from a travelling mob of cattle," answered Hawkesbury. "She's a smart gin when she's away from grog, and a stunner at cutting out on a camp."

That day passed in an exhaustive general tour round the run. Mounted upon an elderly stock-horse of unimpeachable figure, with legs considerably the worse for wear, and provided with a saddle which caused him to vow that never again would he permit himself to be dissociated from his favourite Wilkinson, Jack was piloted by Mr. Hawkesbury through the "frontage" and a considerable portion of the "back" regions of Gondaree. It was the same story: oceans of feed, water everywhere, all the cattle rolling fat. Nothing that the most hard-hearted buyer could object to, if troubled with but a grain of conscience. Billowy waves of oat grass, wild clover (*medicago sativa*), and half-a-dozen strange fodder plants, of which Redgrave knew not the names, adorned the great meadows or river flats; while out of the immense reed-beds, the feathery tassels of which stirred in the breeze far above their heads, came ever and anon, at the crack of the stock-whip, large droves of cattle in Indian file, in such gorgeous condition that, as our hero could not refrain from saying, a dealer in fat stock might have taken the whole lot to market, cows, calves, bullocks and steers, without rejecting a beast.

Leaving these grand savannahs, when they proceeded to the more arid back country there was still no deterioration in the character of the pasturage. Myall and boree belts of timber, never known to grow upon "poor" or "sour" land, alternated with far-stretching plains, where the salt-bush, the cotton-bush, and many another salsiferous herb and shrub, betokened that Elysium of the squatter, "sound fattening country." John Redgrave was charmed. He forgot the dog-hole he had left in the morning, the fleas, the pigs, the evil habiliments of Bob the cook, the uninviting meal, all the shocks and outrages upon his tastes and habits; his mind dwelt only upon the great extent and apparently half-stocked condition of Gondaree. And as they rode home by starlight the somewhat perilous stumbles of the old stock-horse only partially disturbed a reverie in which a new wool-shed, a crack wash-pen, every kind of modern "improvement," embellished a model run, carrying fifty thousand high-caste merino sheep.

He demolished his well-earned supper of corned beef and damper that night with quite another species of appetite; and as he deposited himself in an extemporized hammock, above the reach of midnight marauders, he told himself that Gondaree was not such a bad place after all, and only wanted an owner possessed of sufficient brains to develop its great capabilities to become a pleasant, profitable, and childishly safe investment.

Wildduck's mission had apparently been successful. The old mare was making off from the men's hut in a comparatively exhausted state, while a chorus of voices, accented with the pervading British oath, told of the arrival of a number of friends and allies. High among the noisiest of the talkers, and, it must be confessed, by no means reticent of strong language, rose the clear tones and childlike laughter of the savage damsel. In the delicate *badinage* likely to obtain in such a gathering it was apparent that she could well hold her own.

"My word, Johnny Dickson," she was saying to a tall, lathy stripling, whose long hair protected the upper portion of his spine from all danger of sunstroke, "you get one big buster off that roan mare today; spread all over the ground, too. Thought you was goin' to peg out a free-selection."

"You shut up, and go back to old man Jack, you black varmint," retorted the unhorsed man-at-arms amid roars of laughter. "You ain't no great chop on a horse, except to ride him to death. I can back anything you'll tackle, or ere a black fellow between this and Adelaide. I'm half a mind to box your ears, you saucy slut."

"Ha, ha," yelled the girl, "*you* ride? that's a good un! You not game to get on the Doctor here tomorrow, not for twenty pound. You touch me! Why, ole Nanny fight you any day, with a yam-stick. *I* fight you myself, blessed if I don't."

"What's all this?" demanded Mr. Hawkesbury, suddenly appearing on the scene. "Have any of you fellows been bringing grog on the place? Because it's a rascally shame, and I won't have it."

"Well, sir," said one of the stockmen, "one of the chaps had a bottle, quite accidental like, and the gin got a suck or two. That's what set her tongue goin'. But it's all gone now, and nothing broke. Which way do we go tomorrow?"

"Well, I want to muster those Bimbalong Creek cattle, and then put as many as we can get on the main camp, just to give this gentleman here (indicating Jack) a sort of idea of the numbers. Daylight start, remember, so don't be losing your horses."

"All right," said the self-constituted spokesman, the others merely nodding acquiescence; "we'll short-hobble them tonight—they can't get away very far."

Considerably before daylight beefsteaks were frying, horses were being gathered up, and a variety of sounds proclaimed that when bent upon doing a day's work the dwellers around Gondaree could set about it in an energetic and business-like fashion. There was not a streak of crimson in the pearly dawn-light, as the whole party, comprising more than a dozen men and the redoubtable Wildduck, rode silently along the indistinct trail which led "out back." There was a good deal of smoking and but little talk for the first hour. After that time converse became more general, and the pace was improved at a suggestion from Mr. Hawkesbury that the sooner they all got to the scene of their work the better, as it was a pretty good day's ride there and back.

"So it is," answered a hard, weather-beaten-looking, grizzled stockman. "I never see such a part of the country as this. If it was in other colonies I've been to they'd have had a good hut, and yards, and a horse-paddock at Bimbalong this years back. But they wouldn't spend a ten pound note or two, those Sydney merchants, not for to save the lives of every stockman on the Warroo."

"*That* wouldn't be much of a loss, Jingaree," said the overseer, laughing, while a sort of sardonic smile went the round of the company, as if they appreciated the satire; "and I shouldn't blame 'em if that was the worst of it. But it's a loss to themselves, if they only knew it. All they can say is, plenty of money has been made on old Gondaree, as bad as it is. I hope the next owner will do as well—and better."

"Me think 'um you better git it back to me and ole man Jack," suggested Wildduck, now restored to her usual state of coolness and self-possession. "Ole man Jack own Gondaree water-hole by rights. Everybody say Gondaree people live like black fellows. What for you not give it us back again?"

"Well, I'm blowed," answered the overseer, aghast at the audacious proposition; "what next? No, no, Wildduck. We've improved the country." Here the stockmen grinned. "Besides, you and old man Jack would go and knock it down. You ain't particular to a few glasses of grog, you know, Wildduck."

"White fellow learn us that," answered the girl, sullenly, and the "chase rode on."

In rather less than three hours the party of horsemen had reached a narrow reed-fringed watercourse, the line of which was marked by dwarf eucalypti, no specimens of which had been encountered since they left the homestead.

Here they halted for a while upon a sand-ridge picturesquely wooded with the bright green arrowy pine (*callitris*), and, after a short smoke, Mr. Hawkesbury proceeded to make a disposition of forces.

"Three of you go up the creek till you get to the other side of Long Plain, there's mostly a mob somewhere about there. You'll see a big brindle bullock; if you get him you've got the leading mob. Jingaree, you can start; take Johnson and Billy Mortimer with you. Charley Jones, you beat up the myall across the creek; take Jackson and Long Bill. Four of you go out back till you come to the old Durgah boundary; you'll know it by the sheep-tracks, confound them. Waterton, you come with me, and Mr. Redgrave will take the Fishery mob. Wildduck, you too, it will keep you out of mischief, and you can have a gallop after the buffalo cows' mob, and show off a bit."

"All right," answered the sable scout, showing her brilliant teeth, and winding the stock-whip round her head with practised hand she made Spitfire jump all fours off the ground, and proceed sideways, and even tail foremost (as is the manner of excitable steeds), for the next quarter of a mile.

Every section of the party having "split and squandered" according to orders, which were, like those of a captain at cricket or football, unhesitatingly obeyed, Jack found himself proceeding parallel with the creek, with Mr. Hawkesbury as companion, followed by a wiry, sun-tanned Australian lad and Miss Wildduck aforesaid.

It was still early. They had ridden twenty miles, and the day's work was only commencing. Always fond of this particular description of station-work, John Redgrave looked with the keen eye of a bushman, and something of the poet's fancy, upon the scene. Eastward the sun-rays were lighting up a limitless ocean of grey plain, tinged with a delicate tone of green, while the hazy distance, precious in that land of hard outlines and too brilliant colouring, was passing from a stage of tremulous gold to the fierce splendour of the desert noon.

There was not a hill within a hundred miles. The level sky-line was unbroken as on the deep, or where the Arab camel kneels by the far-seen plumy palms. The horses stepped along briskly. The air was dry and fresh. The element of grandeur and unimpeded territorial magnificence told powerfully upon John's sanguine nature.

"I don't care what they say," he thought. "This is a magnificent country, and I believe would carry no end of sheep, if properly fenced and managed. I flatter myself I shall make such a change as will astonish the oldest and many other inhabitants."

Following the water, they rode quietly onward until, near a bend of the humble but enormously important streamlet, they descried the "Fishery," of which Hawkesbury had spoken. This was a ruinous and long deserted "weir," formed of old by the compatriots of Wildduck, for the ensnaring of eels and such fish as might be left disporting themselves in the Bimbalong after a flood of unusual height. At such periods the outer meres and back creeks received a portion of the larger species of fish which habitually reposed in the still, deep waters of the Warroo. Traces could still be seen of a labyrinth of artificial channels, dams, and reservoirs, showing considerable ingenuity, and distinct evidence of more continuous labour than the aboriginal Australian is generally credited with.

IV

"Ye seeken loud and see for your winninges."

—Chaucer

M y word," exclaimed Wildduck, jumping from her horse and gazing at the rare ruin of her fading race, "this big one fishery one time. Me come here like it picaninny. All about black fellow that time. Bullo—bullo."

Here she spread out her hands, as if to denote an altogether immeasurable muster-roll of warriors.

"Big one corrobaree—shake 'em ground all about; and old man Coradjee too."

Here she sank her voice into an awe-stricken whisper.

"Where are they all gone, Wildduck?" inquired Redgrave; "along a Warroo?"

"Along a Warroo?" cried the girl, mockingly. "Worse than that. White fellow shoot 'em like possum. That ole duffer, Morgan, shoot fader belonging to me."

"Come, come, Wildduck," said Hawkesbury, "we're after cattle just now—never mind about old Mindai. It wasn't one, nor yet two, white fellows only that *he* picked the bones of, if all the yarns are true."

"You think I no care, because I'm black," said the girl, reproachfully, as the tears rolled down her dusky cheeks. "I very fond of my poor ole fader.—Hallo! there's cattle—come along, Waterton."

"Changing the subject with a vengeance," thought Redgrave, as the mercurial mourner, with all the fickleness of her race, superadded to that of her sex, looked back a laughing challenge to the stockman, and closing her heels upon the eager pony, was at top speed in about three strides. Looking in the direction of Spitfire's outstretched neck, Redgrave and his companion could descry a long dark line of moving objects at a considerable distance on the plain, but whether horses, cattle, or even a troop of emu, they were unable to make out with certainty.

"Let's back her up quietly," said Hawkesbury. "She and Charley will head them; it's no use bustin' our horses. This is rather a flash mob, but they'll be all right when they're wheeled once or twice."

Keeping on at a steady hand-gallop, they soon came up with a large lot of cattle going best pace in the wrong direction. The accomplished Wildduck, however, flew round them like a falcon, Spitfire doing his mile in remarkably fair time. Being ably supported by Waterton, the absconders were rounded up, and were ready to return and be forgiven, when Hawkesbury and Mr. Redgrade joined them.

"By Jove!" cried our hero, with unconcealed approval, "what grand condition all the herd seem to be in! Look at those leaders." Here he pointed to a string of great raking five and six year old bullocks, whose immense frames, a little coarse, but well grown and symmetrical, were filled up to the uttermost point of development. "You don't seem to have drafted them very closely."

"No," said Hawkesbury, carelessly. "We never send anything away that isn't real prime, and we missed this mob last year. They get their time at Gondaree; and the last two seasons have been stunning good ones."

"Don't you always have good seasons, then?" asked Jack, innocently.

The overseer looked sharply at him for a moment, without answering, and then said—

"Well, not always, it depends upon the rain a good deal; not but what there's always plenty of back-water on this run."

"Oh! I dare say it makes a difference in this dry country," returned Jack, carelessly, thinking of Marshmead, where it used to rain sometimes from March to November, almost without cessation, and where a month's fine weather was hailed as a distinct advantage to the sodden pasturage. "But the rain never does anything but good here, I suppose."

"Nothing but good, you may say that, when it does come. This lot won't be long getting to camp. Ha! I can hear Jingaree's and the other fellows' whips going."

By this time they had nearly reached the camp at which the various scouting parties had separated. They had nothing to do but to follow the drove, which, after the manner of well-broken station herds of the olden time, never relaxed speed until they reached the camp, when they stopped of their own accord, and while recovering their wind moved gently to and fro, greeting friends or strangers with appropriately modulated bellowings.

Much about the same time the other parties of stockmen could be seen coming towards the common centre, each following a lesser or a greater drove. Jingaree had been fortunate in "dropping across" his lot earlier in the day, and was in peaceful possession of the camp and an undisturbed smoke long before they arrived.

Mr. Redgrave rode through the fifteen or sixteen hundred there assembled by himself, the stockmen meanwhile sitting sideways on their horses, or otherwise at ease, while he made inspection.

"I should like to have had a lot like this at the Lost Water-hole Camp, at poor old Marshmead," thought Jack to himself, "for old Rooney, the dealer, to pick from, when I used to sell to him. How he and Geordie would have gone cutting out by the hour. They would have almost forgotten to quarrel. Why, there isn't a poor beast on the camp except that cancered bullock."

When he had completed a leisurely progress through the panting, staring, but non-aggressive multitude, he rejoined Mr. Hawkesbury, with the conviction strongly established in his mind that he had never seen so many really fat cattle in one camp before, and that the country that would do that with a coarse, neglected herd would do anything.

Mr. Hawkesbury having asked him whether he wanted to see anything more on that camp, and receiving no answer in the negative, gave orders to "let the cattle go," and the party, proceeding to the bank of the creek, permitted their steeds to graze at will with the reins trailing under their feet, after the manner of stock-horses, and addressed themselves to such moderate refreshment, in the form of junks of corned beef and wedges of damper, as they had brought with them. Mr. Hawkesbury produced a sufficient quantity for himself and his guest, who found that the riding, the admiration, and the novel experience had whetted his appetite.

Fairly well earned was the hour's rest by the reeds of the creek. Hawkesbury had at first thought of putting together the greater part of the herd, but on reflection concluded that the day was rather far advanced.

They were twenty miles from home. It would be as well to defer the collection of the cattle belonging to the main camp until the following day. In a general way it might be thought that a ride of forty miles, exclusive of two or three hours' galloping at camp, was a fair day's work. So it would have appeared, doubtless, to the author of *Guy Livingstone*, who in one of his novels describes the hero and his good steed as being in a condition of extreme exhaustion after a ride of *thirty miles*. Whyte Melville, too, who handles equally well pen, brand, and bridle, finds the horses of Gilbert and his friend in *Good for Nothing*, or *All Down Hill*, reduced to such an "enfeebled condition" by sore backs, consequent upon one day's kangaroo-hunting, that they are compelled to send a messenger for fresh horses a hundred miles or more to *Sydney*, and to await his return in camp.

With all deference to, and sympathy with, the humanity which probably prompted so mercifully moderate a chronicle, we must assert that to these gifted writers little is known of the astonishing feats of speed and endurance performed by the ordinary Australian horse.

Hawkesbury, indeed, rather grumbled when the party arrived at Gondaree at what he considered an indifferent day's work. He, his men, and their horses would have thought it nothing "making a song aboot," as Rob Roy says, to have ridden to Bimbalong, camped the cattle, "cut out" or drafted, on horseback, a couple of hundred head of fat bullocks, and to have brought the lot safe to Gondaree stock-yard by moonlight. This would have involved about twenty hours' riding, a large proportion of the work being done at full gallop, and during the hottest part of the day. But they *had* done it many a time and often. And neither the grass-fed horses, the cattle, nor the careless horsemen were a whit the worse for it.

However, as Mr. Hawkesbury had truly stated in their first interview, the economy of time was by no means a leading consideration on the Warroo. So the next day was devoted to the arousing and parading of the stock within reach of the main camp. Mr. Redgrave's opinion, as to the number and general value of the herd after this operation, was so satisfactory that on the morrow he once more committed himself to the tender mercies of the Warroo mail, and proceeded incontinently to the metropolis, where he without further demur concluded the bargain, and became the first proud purchaser of Gondaree, and five thousand head of mixed cattle, to be taken "by the books."

Jack found the club a paradise after his sojourn in the wilderness. At that time comparatively few men had explored the *terra incognita* of Riverina with a view to personal settlement. Therefore Jack's fame as a man of daring enterprise and commercial sagacity rose steadily until it reached a most respectable altitude in the social barometer. He alluded but sparingly to the privations and perils of his journey, making up for this reticence by glowing descriptions of the fattening qualities and vast extent of his newly-acquired territory. He aroused the envy of his old companions of the settled districts, and was besieged with applications from the relatives of wholly inexperienced youths from Britain, and other youngsters of Australian rearing, who had had more experience than was profitable, to take them back with him as assistants. These offers he was prudent enough to decline.

His cash had been duly paid down, and the name of John Redgrave attached to sundry bills at one and two years—bearing interest at eight percent—the whole purchase-money being about twenty thousand pounds, with right of brand, stock-horses, station-stores, implements, and furniture given in. What was given in, though it cost some hard bargaining and several telegrams, was not of great value. Among the twenty stock-horses there were about two sound ones. The stores consisted of three bags of flour, half a bag of sugar, and a quarter of a chest of tea. There was an old cart and some harness, of which only the green hide portion was "reliable." Several iron buckets, which served indifferently for boiling meat and carrying the moderate supplies of water needed or, more correctly used on the establishment. Of the three saddles, but one was station property. The others belonged to Mr. Hawkesbury and the stockman.

Jack had decided to take the cattle at five thousand head without muster, being of opinion, from the "look of the herd," and from a careful inspection of the station-books, wherein the brandings had been carefully registered, and a liberal percentage allowed for deaths and losses, that the number was on the run. He knew from experience that a counting muster was a troublesome and injurious operation, and that it was better to lose a few head than to knock the whole herd about. He therefore made all necessary arrangements for going up and taking immediate possession of Gondaree.

His plan of operations, well considered and carefully calculated, was this: He had sternly determined upon "clearing off" the whole of the cattle. Sheep were the only stock fit for the consideration of a large operator. For cattle there could be only the limited and surely decreasing local demand. For sheep, that is, for wool, you had the world for a market. Wool *might* fall; but, like gold, its fashion was universal. Every man who wore a Crimean shirt, every woman who wore a magenta petticoat, was a constituent and a contributor; the die was cast. He was impatient of the very idea of cattle as an investment for a man of ordinary foresight. He was not sure whether he would even be bothered with a score or two for milkers.

To this end he now directed all his energies; and being able to work, as Bertie Tunstall had truly observed, when he liked, now that he was excited by the pressure of a great undertaking—an advance along the whole line of his forces, so to speak—he displayed certain qualities of generalship.

He first made a very good sale of all the fat cattle on the run (binding the buyer to take a number which would give the herd "a scraping") to his old acquaintance Rooney, the cattle-dealer. These were to be removed within two months from date of sale. He left instructions with his agents, Messrs. Drawe and Backwell, to sell the whole of the remaining portion of the herd (reserving only twenty milkers) as store cattle, to anyone who was slow and old-fashioned enough to desire them. He bought and despatched stores, of a quality and variety rather different from what he received, sufficient to last for twelve months; all the fittings and accessories for a cottage and for a wool-shed, including nails, iron roofing, doors, sashes—everything, in fact, except the outer timber, which could be procured on the spot. He had no idea of trusting himself to the war-prices of the inland store-keepers. A few tons of wire for preliminary fencing, wool-bales, tools, a dray, carts, an earth-scoop for dam-making, well-gearing and sixty-gallon buckets, a few tents, plough and harrow (must have some hay), a few decent horses, an American waggon with four-horse harness, and other articles "too numerous to mention," about this time found themselves on the road to Gondaree. All these trifling matters "footed up" to a sum which gave a temporarily reflective expression to Jack's open countenance. Necessaries for a sheep-station, especially in the process of conversion from cattle ditto, have a way of coming out strong in the addition department.

"What of that?" demanded Jack of his conscience, or that quiet cousin-german, prudence; "a sheep-station must be properly worked, or not at all. The first year's wool will pay for it all. And then the lambs!"

In order to manage a decent-sized sheep property (and nothing is so expensive as a small one), you must have an overseer. Jack was not going to be penny-lunatic enough to be his own manager. And the right sort of man must be thoroughly up to all the latest lights and discoveries—not a working overseer, a rough, upper-shepherd sort of individual who counted sheep and helped to make bush-yards, but a fairly-educated modern species of centurion, whose intelligence and knowledge of stock (meaning sheep) were combined with commercial shrewdness and military power of combination. A man who could tell you in a few minutes how much a dam displacing several thousand cubic yards of earth ought to cost; how many men, in what number of days, should complete it; what provisions they ought to consume; and what wages, working reasonably, they ought to earn. A man full of the latest information as to spouts and soda, hot water and cold, with a natural turn heightened by experience, for determining the proportionate shades of fineness, density, freeness, and length of staple which, in combination, could with safety be taken as a model for the ideal merino. A man capable of sketching, with accuracy and forethought, the multifarious buildings, enclosures, and "improvements" necessary for a sheep-station in the first year of its existence, or of conducting the shearing to a successful issue without them at need.

For subalterns so variously gifted a demand had of late years grown up, owing to the large profits and wonderful development of the wool-producing interest. Of one of these highly-certificated "competition-wallahs" John Redgrave had determined to possess himself.

In Mr. Alexander M'Nab, late of Strathallan, and formerly of Mount Gresham, he deemed that he had secured one of the most promising and highly-trained specimens of the type.

Sandy M'Nab, as he was generally called, was about eight-and-twenty years of age, the son of a small but respectable farmer in the north of Ireland, in which condition of life he had acquired an early knowledge of stock, and an exceedingly sound rudimentary education. Far too ambitious to content himself with the limited programme of his forefathers, he had emigrated at sixteen, and worked his way up through the various stages of Australian bush apprenticeship, until he had reached his present grade, from which he trusted to pass into the ranks of the Squatocracy.

Having secured this valuable functionary, and covenanted to pay him at the rate of three hundred per annum, his first act was to despatch him, after a somewhat lengthy consultation, to inspect a small lot of ten thousand ewes, and on approval to hire men and bring them to Gondaree. It was necessary to lose no time; lambing would be on in June, in August shearing would be imminent. And the cattle would require to be off, and the sheep to be on, somewhere about April, if the first year's operations were to have any chance of being financially successful.

The stores having been purchased, and Mr. M'Nab with his letter of credit having been shipped, that alert lieutenant, with characteristic promptitude, reporting himself in readiness to embark at six hours' notice, nothing remained but for Mr. Redgrave to "render himself" again at Gondaree in the capacity of purchaser.

He accordingly cleared out from the club with alarmingly stern self-denial, and, declining to risk his important existence in the Warroo mail, took the road in the light American waggon, with his spare horses and a couple of active lads accustomed to bush work.

After a journey of ordinary duration and absence of adventure, he once more sighted the unromantic but priceless waters of the Warroo, and beheld, with the eye of a proprietor, the "waste lands of the Crown"—most literally deserving that appellation—with the full right and title to which, as lessee, he stood invested.

Mr. Hawkesbury, in apparently the same Crimean shirt, with black and scarlet in alternate bars, stood smoking the small myall pipe in much the same attitude at the hut door as when Jack was borne off by two jibs and a bolter in the Warroo mail. Bob the cook, the dark hues of his apparel unrelieved by any shade of scarlet, appeared in his doorway with his hands in his pockets, but betraying unwonted interest as the *cortège* ascended the sandhill.

Ordering the boys to let go the horses, and to pitch the tent, which he had used on the journey, at a safe distance from the huts, Jack descended with a slight increase of dignity, as of one in authority, and greeted his predecessor.

"So you've bought us out," he said, after inspecting carefully the letter which Jack handed to him, "and I'm ordered to deliver over the cattle, and the stores,—there ain't much of them,—and the horses, and in fact the whole boiling. Well, I wish you luck, sir; the run's a good 'un and no mistake, and the cattle are pretty fair, considering what's been done for 'em. I suppose you won't want me after you've taken delivery."

"I shall be very glad if you will stay on," quoth Jack, whose honest heart felt averse to ousting any man from a home, "until the cattle are cleared off; after that I shall have another gentleman in charge of the sheep and place generally. By staying two or three months you will oblige me, if it suits your arrangements."

"All right," answered Mr. Hawkesbury: "I know the cattle pretty well, and I dare say I can save as many as will cover my wages. I think you'll find them muster up pretty close to their book-number."

The signal shot of the campaign was fired, so to speak, upon the arrival of Mr. John Rooney, who came in a few days by appointment to take the first draft of the Gondaree fat cattle.

Jack was sitting outside of his tent, like an Arab sheik, and thinking regretfully of the flower-laden evening breeze which he had so often inhaled at the same hour at Marshmead, when a tall, soldierly-looking man rode up on a tired horse and jumped off with an unreserved exclamation of relief.

"Hallo! Rooney, is that you, in this uncivilized part of the world? Rather different from the old place, isn't it! Come in, and I'll have your horse hobbled out. You mustn't expect stables or paddock or any other luxuries on the Warroo."

"Sure, I know it well—my heavy curse on the same river; there never was any dacency next or anigh it. Didn't they lend me a buck-jumper at Morahgil today, and the first place I found myself was on the broad of my back."

"What a shame! Did they give you another horse?"

"They did not. I rode the same devil right through. It's little bucking he feels inclined for now."

"So I should think, after an eighty-mile ride. When did you leave?"

"About twelve o'clock. I was riding all night, and got there to breakfast. The last time I took cattle from Morahgil I happened to knock down the superintendent with a roping pole, maybe that's why he treated me so—the mane blayguard."

"Well, he ought not to have let such a trifle dwell on his mind, perhaps. But take a glass of grog, Rooney, while the fellow gets your tea."

"Faith, and I will, Masther John; and it's sound I'll sleep tonight, fleas or no fleas. A man can't do without it for more than three nights at a time."

In a few days the muster was duly concluded, and three hundred prime bullocks secured in the ancient but massive stockyard. One of Rooney's drovers and a couple of road hands had arrived the evening before, to whom they were intrusted. Rooney was too great a man to be able to afford the time to travel with his own cattle, and had, indeed, a score of other mobs to meet, despatch, buy, or sell, to arrive in as many different and distant parts of the colony.

"Well, Masther John," said he, "I won't deny that I haven't lifted a finer mob this season. Isn't it a murthering fine run, when it puts the beef on them big-boned divils like that? If ye had some of those roan steers we used to get at the Lost Waterhole Camp, sure they wouldn't be able to see out of their eyes with fat. I'll be able to get the eight hundred out of these aisy enough. I'll send Joe. Best for the cows and the rest of the bullocks the moment he's shut of those circle-dot cattle.

I must be off down the river. I've a long ride before me. But, Masther John, see here now, don't be building too much on the saysons in these parts. It's not like Marshmead; I've seen it all as bare as a brickfield, from the Warroo to the Oxley; and these very cattle with their ribs up to their backbones, and dyin' by hundreds. D'ye hear me now? Don't be spending all your money before ye see how prices are going. I'm thinking we'll see a dale of changes in the next three or four years—all this racin' and jostlin' for breeding sheep can't hould out. Goodbye, sir."

And so the kindly, stalwart, shrewd cattle dealer went on his way, and Jack saw him no more for a season. But his warning words left an impression of doubt and distrust upon the mind of his hearer that no caution had previously had power to do. Was it possible that he had made a mistake, and an irrevocable one? Was such a change in the seasons credible, and could all his stretch of luxuriant prairie turn into dust and ashes? It was impossible. He had known bad seasons, or thought he had, in the old west country; he had seen grass and water pretty scarce, and had a lower average of fat cattle in some seasons than others; but as to any total disappearance of pasture, any ruinous loss of stock, such he had never witnessed and was quite unable to realize.

V

"So many days my ewes have been with young;
So many weeks ere the poor fools will ean;
So many years ere I shall shear the fleece."

—KING HENRY VI

J ack had soon quite enough upon his hands to occupy him for every
waking hour and moment, to fatigue his body, and, consequently, to
lay to rest any obtrusive doubts or fears as to the ultimate success of
his undertaking. The stores began to arrive, and he had to fix a site for
the new cottage and the indispensable wool-shed. The former locality
he selected at Steamboat Point, before alluded to by Mr. Hawkesbury,
which was a bluff near a deep reach of the river, shaded by couba trees
and river-oaks of great age, and at an elevation far above the periodical
floods which from time to time swept the lowlands of the Warroo, and
converted its sluggish tide into a furious devastating torrent.

Sawyers were engaged, carpenters, splitters, and labourers generally.
With these, as, indeed, with all the station *employés*, much conflict had
to be gone through as to prices of contract and labour. A new proprietor
was looked upon as a person of limited intelligence, but altogether of
boundless wealth, which, in greater or less degree, each "old hand"
believed it his privilege to share. It was held to be an act of meanness
and unjustifiable parsimony for one in his position to expect to have
work done at the same rate as other people. Jack had much trouble in
disabusing them of this superstition. Eventually it came to be admitted
that "the cove knew his way about," and "had seen a thing or two
before"; after which matters went more smoothly.

Then letters came from Drawe and Backwell stating that a large
operator, with a million of acres or so of new country, where "the blacks
were too bad for sheep," had bought the whole of the herd, after Rooney
had done drafting, and was ready to take delivery without delay.

In due time all this hard and anxious work was accomplished.
Mr. Joe Best returned and possessed himself of every fat bullock and
every decent cow "without incumbrance" on the place. And then the
long-resident Gondaree herd—much lowing, and fully of opinion,
judged by its demeanour, that the end of the world was come—was

violently evicted and driven off from its birthplace in three great droves by a small army of stockmen and all the dogs within a hundred miles.

So the cattle were "cleared off," at low prices too, as in after days Jack had occasion to remember. But nobody bought store cattle in that year except as a sort of personal favour. Nothing better could be expected.

"Well—so they're mustered and gone at last," said Hawkesbury, the day after the last engagement. "Blest if I didn't think some of us would lose the number of our mess. Those old cows would eat a man—let alone skiver him. The herd came up well to their number in the books, didn't they? There was more of those Bimbalong cattle than I took 'em to be. Well, there's been a deal of money took off this run since I came—next to nothing spent either; that's what I look at. I hope the sheep-racket will do as well, sir."

"I hope so, too, Hawkesbury," answered Jack. "One good season with sheep is generally said to be worth three with cattle. I had a letter today from M'Nab to say that he was on the road with the ewes, and would be here early next month."

"Well, then, I'll cut my stick; you won't want the pair of us, and I'm not much to do with sheep, except putting the dogs on old Boxall's whenever I've caught 'em over their boundary. You'll have to watch *him*, if you get mixed, or you'll come short."

"Every sheep of mine will be legibly fire-branded," said Jack, with a certain pride; "there's no getting over that, you know."

"He'll fire-brand too," said Hawkesbury, "in the same place, quick. And as his ear-mark's a close crop, and he's not particular what ear, his shepherds might easy make any stray lots uncommon like their own."

"By Jove!" said Jack, rather startled at the new light thrown on sheep management on the Warroo. "However M'Nab will see to that; he's not an easy man to get round, they say. Then, would you really prefer to leave? If so, I'll make out your account."

"If you please, Mr. Redgrave. I've been up here five years now; so I think I'll go down the country, and see my people for a bit of change. It don't do to stay in these parts too long at a time, unless a man wants to turn into a black fellow or a lushington."

On the very day mentioned in his latest despatch, Mr. M'Nab arrived with his ten thousand ewes; and a very good lot they were—in excellent condition too. He had nosed out an unfrequented back track, where the feed was unspoiled by those marauding bands of "condottieri," travelling sheep. Water had been plentiful, so that the bold stroke was successful. Pitching his tent in a sheltered spot, he sat up half the night busy with pen and pencil, and by breakfast time had every account made out, and all his supernumeraries ready to be paid off. The expenses of the journey, with a tabulated statement showing the exact cost per sheep of the expedition, were also upon a separate sheet of paper handed up to his employer.

From this time forth all went on with unslackening and successful progress. M'Nab was in his glory, and went forth rejoicing each day, planning, calculating, ordering, and arranging to his heart's content. The out-stations were chosen, the flocks drafted and apportioned, a ration-carrier selected, bush-yards made, while, simultaneously, the cottage walls began to arise on Steamboat Point, and the site of the wool-shed, on a plain bordering an ana-branch sufficient for water, but too inconsiderable for flood, was, after careful consideration, finally decided upon. The season was very favourable; rain fell seasonably and plentifully; grass was abundant, and the sheep fattened up "hand over hand" without a suspicion of foot-rot, or any of the long train of ailments which the fascinating, profitable, but too susceptible merino so often affects.

The more Jack saw of his new manager the more he liked and respected him. He felt almost humiliated as he noted his perfect mastery of every detail connected with station (*i.e.* sheep) management, his energy, his forecast, his rapid and easy arrangement of a hundred jarring details, and reflected that he had purchased the invaluable services of this gifted personage for so moderate a consideration.

"We shall not have time to get up a decent wool-shed this year, Mr. Redgrave," he said, at one of their first councils. "We *must* have a good, substantial store, as it won't do to have things of value lying about. A small room alongside will do for me till we get near shearing. We must knock up a temporary shed with hurdles and calico, and wash the best way we can in the creek. Next year we can go in for spouts, and all the rest of it, and I hope we'll be able to shear in such a shed as the Warroo has never seen yet."

"It's a good while to Christmas," said Jack. "How about the shed if we put more men on? I don't like make-shifts."

"Couldn't possibly be done in the time," answered Mr. M'Nab, with prompt decision. "Lambing will keep us pretty busy for two months. We *must* have shearing over by October, or all this clover-burr that I see about will be in the wool, and out of your pocket to the tune of about threepence a pound. Besides, these sawyers and bush-carpenters can't be depended upon. They might leave us in the lurch, and then we should neither have one thing nor the other."

"Very well," said Jack, "I leave that part of it to you."

All Mr. M'Nab's plans and prophecies had a fashion of succeeding, and verifying themselves to the letter. Apparently he forgot nothing, superintended everything, trusted nobody, and coerced, persuaded, and placed everybody like pawns on a chess-board. His temper was wonderfully under command; he never bullied his underlings, but had a way of assuring them that he was afraid they wouldn't get on together, supplemented on continued disapproval by a calm order to come in and get their cheque. This system was found to be efficacious. He always kept a spare hand or two, and was thereby enabled to fill up the place of a deserter at a moment's notice.

Thus, with the aid of M'Nab and of a good season, John Redgrave, during the first year, prospered exceedingly. His sheep had a capital increase, and nearly eight thousand gamesome, vigorous lambs followed their mothers to the wash-pool. The wool was got off clean, and wonderfully clear of dirt and seed; and just before shearing Mr. M'Nab exhibited a specimen of his peculiar talents which also brought grist to the mill.

It happened in this wise:—Looking over the papers one evening he descried mention of a lot of store sheep then on their way to town, and on a line of road which would bring them near to Gondaree.

"This lot would suit us very well, Mr. Redgrave," said he, looking up from his paper, and then taking a careful transcript in his pocket-book of their ages, numbers, and sexes. "Seven thousand altogether—five thousand four and six tooth wethers, with a couple of thousand ewes; if they are good-framed sheep, with decent fleeces, and the ewes not too old, they would pay well to buy on a six months' bill. We could take the wool off and have them fat on these Bimbalong plains by the time the bill comes due."

"How about seeing them?" quoth Jack; "they may be Queensland sheep, with wool about half an inch long. They often shear them late on purpose when they are going to start them on the road. 'They're a simple people,' as Sam Slick says, those Queenslanders."

"Of course I must see them," answered M'Nab. "I never buy a pig in a poke; but they will be within a hundred miles of us in a week, and I can ride across and see them, and find out their idea of price. Shearing is always an expensive business, and the same plant and hands will do for double our number of sheep, if we can get them at a price."

M'Nab carried out his intention, and, falling across the caravan in an accidental kind of way, extracted full particulars from the owner, a somewhat irascible old fellow, who was convoying in person. He returned with a favourable report. The sheep were good sheep; they had well-grown fleeces, rather coarse; but that did not matter with fattening sheep; they were large and would make good wethers when topped up. The ewes were pretty fair, and not broken-mouthed. They wanted eleven shillings all round, and they were in the hands of Day and Burton, the stock agents.

"Now, I've been thinking," said Mr. M'Nab, meditatively, "whether it wouldn't pay for me to run down to Melbourne by the mail—it passes tomorrow morning—and arrange the whole thing with Day and Burton. Writing takes an awful long time. Besides, I might knock sixpence a head off, and that would pay for my coach-fare and time, and a good deal over. Seven thousand sixpences are one hundred and seventy-five pounds. Thirty pounds would take me there and back, inside of three weeks."

"That will only allow you two days in town," said Jack, "and you'll be shaken to death in that beastly mail-cart."

"Never mind that," said the burly son of the "black north," stretching his sinewy frame. "I can stand a deal of killing. Shall I go?"

"Oh, go by all means, if you think you can do any good. I don't envy you the journey."

M'Nab accordingly departed by the mail next morning, leaving Jack to carry on the establishment in his absence, a responsibility which absorbed the whole of his waking hours so completely that he had no time to think of anything but sheep and shepherds, with an occasional dash of dingo. One forenoon, as he was waiting for his midday meal, having ridden many a mile since daylight, he descried a small party approaching on foot which he was puzzled at first to classify. He soon discovered them to be aboriginals. First walked a tall, white-haired old man, carrying a long fish-spear, and but little encumbered with wearing apparel. After him a gin, not by any means of a "suitable age" (as people say in the case of presumably marriageable widowers), then two lean, toothless old beldames of gins staggering under loads of blankets, camp furniture, spare weapons, an iron pot or two, and a few puppies; several half-starved, mangy dogs followed in a string. Finally, the whole party advanced to within a few paces of the hut and sat solemnly down, the old savage sticking his spear into the earth previously with great deliberation.

As the little group sat silently in their places bolt upright, like so many North American Indians, Jack walked down to open proceedings. The principal personage was not without an air of simple dignity, and was very different of aspect from the dissipated and debased beggars which the younger blacks of a tribe but too often become. He was evidently of great age, but Jack could see no means of divining whether seventy years or a hundred and twenty would be the more correct approximation. His dark and furrowed countenance, seamed with innumerable wrinkles, resembled that of a graven image. His hair and beard, curling and abundant, were white as snow. His eye was bright, and as he smiled with childish good humour it was apparent that the climate so fatal to the incisors and bicuspids of the white invader, had spared the larger proportion of his grinders. On Jack's desiring to know his pleasure, he smiled cheerfully again, and muttering "baal dalain," motioned to the younger female, as if desiring her to act as interpreter. She was muffled up in a large opossum-rug which concealed the greater part of her face; but as she said a few words in a plaintive tone, and with a great affectation of shyness, Jack looking at her for the first time recognized the brilliant eyes and mischievous countenance of his old acquaintance Wildduck.

"So it's you?" he exclaimed, much amused, upon which the whole party grinned responsively, the two old women particularly. "And is this your grandfather, and all your grandmothers; and what do you want at Gondaree?"

"This my husband, cooley belonging to me—ole man Jack," explained Wildduck, with an air of matronly propriety. "Ole man Jack, he wantim you let him stay long a wash-pen shearing time. He look out sheep no drown. Swim fust-rate, that ole man."

"Well, I'll see," replied Jack, who had heard M'Nab say a black fellow or two would be handy at the wash-pen—the sheep having rather a long swim. "You can go and camp down there by the water. How did you come to marry such an old fellow, eh, Wildduck?"

"My fader give me to him when I picaninny. Ippai and Kapothra, I s'pos. Black fellow always marry likit that. White girl baal marry ole man, eh, Mr. Redgrave?"

"Never; that is, not unless he's very rich, Wildduck. Here's a fig of tobacco. Go to the store and get some tea and sugar, and flour."

Old man Jack and his lawful but by no means monogamous household, were permitted to camp at the Wash-pen Creek, in readiness for the somewhat heavy list of casualties which "throwing in" always involves. A sheep encumbered with a heavy fleece, and exhausted by a protracted immersion, often contrives to drown as suddenly and perversely as a Lascar. Nothing short of the superior aquatic resources of a savage prevents heavy loss occasionally. So Mr. Redgrave, averse in a general way, for reasons of state, to having native camps on the station, yet made a compromise in this instance. A few sheets of bark were stripped, a few bundles of grass cut, a few pieces of dry wood dragged up by old Nanny and Maramie, and the establishment was complete. A short half-hour after, and there was a cake baked on the coals, hot tea in a couple of very black quart pots, while the odours of a roasted opossum, and the haunch of wallaby, were by no means without temptation to fasting wayfarers with unsophisticated palates. As old man Jack sat near the cheerful fire, with his eyes still keen and roving, wandering meditatively over the still water and the far-stretching plain, as the fading eve closed in magical splendour before his unresponsive gaze, how much was this poor, untaught savage to be pitied, in comparison with a happy English labourer, *adscriptus glebæ* of his parish—lord of eleven babes, and twelve shillings per week, and, though scarce past his prime, dreading increased rheumatism and decreasing wages with every coming winter!

For this octogenarian of one of earth's most ancient families had retained most of his accomplishments, a few simple virtues, and much of his strength and suppleness; still could he stand erect in his frail canoe, fashioned out of a single sheet of bark, and drive her swift and safely through the turbulent tide of a flooded river. Still could he dive like an otter, and like that "fell beastie" bring up the impaled fish or the amphibious turtle. Still could he snare the wild fowl, track the honey-bee, and rifle the nest of the pheasant of the thicket. Upon him, as, indeed, is the case with many of the older aboriginals, the fatal gifts of the white man had no power. He refused the fire-water; he touched not the strange weed, by reason of the magical properties of which the souls of men are exhaled in acrid vapour—oh, subtle and premature cremation!—or sublimated in infinite sneezings. He drank of the lake and of the river, as did his forefathers; he ate of the fowls of the air and of their eggs (I grieve to add, occasionally stale), of the forest creatures, and of the fish of the rivers. In spite of this unauthorized and unrelieved diet, lightly had the burning summers passed over his venerable pate. The square shoulders had not bowed, the upright form still retained its natural elasticity, while the knotted muscles of the limbs, moving like steel rings under his sable skin, showed undiminished power and volume.

VI

"Law was designed to keep a state in peace."

—CRABBE

The mail-trap arrived this time with unwonted punctuality, and out of it stepped Mr. M'Nab, "to time" as usual, and with his accustomed cool air of satisfaction and success.

"Made rather a better deal of it than I expected, sir," was his assertion, after the usual greetings. "There were several heavy lots of store sheep to arrive, so I stood off, and went to look at someothers, and finally got these for ten and threepence. We had a hard fight for the odd threepence; but they gave in, and I have the agreement in my pocket."

"You have done famously," said Jack, "and I am ever so glad to see you back. I have been worked to death. Every shepherd seems to have tried how the dingoes rated the flavour of his flock, or arranged for a 'box' at the least, since you went. I have put on Wildduck's family for retrievers at the wash-pen."

"Well, we wanted a black fellow or two there," said M'Nab. "Throwing in is always a risky thing, but we can't help it this year. There's nothing like a black fellow where sheep have anything like a long swim."

Jack re-congratulated himself that night upon the fortunate possession of the astute and efficient M'Nab, who seemed, like the dweller at the Central Chinese "Inn of the Three Perfections," to "conduct all kinds of operations with unfailing success." In this instance he had made a sum equalling two-thirds of his salary entirely by his own forethought and promptitude of action. This was something like a subaltern, and Jack, looking proud—

> *Far as human eye could see—*
> *Saw the promise of the future*
> *And the prices sheep would be.*

The season, with insensible and subtle gradation, stole slowly, yet surely, forward. The oat-grass waved its tassels strangely like the familiar hay-field over many a league of plain and meadow. The callow broods of wild fowl sailed joyously amid the broad flags of the lagoons, or in the deep pools of the creeks and river. The hawk screamed exultant as she floated adown the long azure of the bright blue, changeless summer sky. Bird, and tree, and flower told truly and gleefully, after their fashion, of the coming of fair spring; brief might be her stay, it is true, but all nature had time to gaze on her richly-tinted robes and form, potently enthralling in their sudden splendour, as are the fierce and glowing charms of the south.

Unbroken success! The new sheep arrived and were delivered reluctantly by their owner, who swore by all his gods that the agents had betrayed him, and that for two pins he would not deliver at all, but finally consented to hear reason, and sold his cart and horses, tent and traps—yet another bargain—to the invincible M'Nab, departing with his underlings by mail.

Shearing was nearly over, the last flock being washed, when one afternoon M'Nab came home in a high state of dissatisfaction with everything. The men were shearing badly; there had been two or three rows; the washers had struck for more wages; everything was out of gear.

"I've been trying to find out the reason all day," said he, as he threw himself down on the camp-bed in his tent, with clouded brow, "and I can think of nothing unless there is some villainous hawker about with grog; and I haven't seen any cart either."

"It's awfully vexatious," said Jack, "just as we were getting through so well. What the pest is that?" By this time, the day having been expended in mishaps and conjectures, evening was drawing on. A dark figure came bounding through the twilight at a high rate of speed, and, casting itself on the tent floor, remained in a crouching, pleading position.

"Why, Wildduck," said Jack, in amazement, "what is the matter now? You are the most dramatic young woman. Has a hostile brave been attempting to carry you off? or old man Jack had a fit of unfounded jealousy? Tell us all about it."

"That ole black gin, Nanny," sobbed the girl, lifting up her face, across which the blood from a gash on the brow mixed freely with her tears; "that one try to kill me, she close up choke me only for Maramie." Here she showed her throat, on which were marks of severe compression.

"Poor Wildduck!" said Jack, trying to soothe the excited creature. "What made her do that? I thought yours was a model happy family?"

"She quiet enough, only for that cursed drink. She regular debbil-debbil when she get a glass."

"Ay!" said M'Nab, "just as I expected; and where did you all get it? You've had a nip, too, I can see."

"Only one glass, Mr. M'Nab; won't tell a lie," deprecated the fugitive. "That bumboat man sell shearers and washers some. You no see him?"

"How should I see?" quoth M'Nab; "where is he now?"

"Just inside timber by the wash-pen," answered the girl; "he sneak out, but leave 'em cart there."

"I think I see my way to cutting out this pirate, or 'bumboat,' as Wildduck calls him," said Jack. "The forest laws were sharp and stern— that is, I believe, that on suspicion of illegal grog you can capture a hawker with the strong hand in New South Wales. So, Wildduck, you go and camp with the carrier's wife, she'll take you in; and, M'Nab, you get a couple of horses and the ration-carrier—he's a stout fellow—and we'll go forth and board this craft. We'll do a bit of privateering; ha, ha! 'whate'er they sees upon the seas they seize upon it.'"

With short preparation the little party set out in the cool starlight. Jack put a revolver into his belt for fear of accidents. Mr. M'Nab had fished out the section of the Licensed Hawkers' Act which referred to the illegal carrying of spirits, and, being duly satisfied that he had the law on his side, was ready for anything. The ration-carrier was strictly impartial. He was ready to assist in the triumph of capture, or to return unsuccessful with an equal mind, caring not a straw which way the enterprise went. He lit his pipe, and followed silently. As they approached the wash-pen they became sensible of an extraordinary noise, as of crying, talking, and screaming—all mingled. From time to time a wild shriek rent the air, while the rapid articulation in an unknown tongue seemed to go on uninterruptedly.

"Must be another set of blacks," said Jack, as he halted to listen. "I hope not; one camp is quite enough on the place at a time."

"It's that old sweep, Nanny, I'm thinking," said the ration-carrier. "When she has a drop of grog on board she can make row enough for a whole tribe. I've heard her at them games before."

As the miami of the sable patriarch came into view, dimly lighted by a small fire, an altogether unique scene presented itself. The old gin, called Nanny, very lightly attired, was marching backward and forward in front of the fire, apparently in a state of demoniac possession. She was crying aloud in her own tongue, with the voice at its highest pitch of shrillness, and with inconceivable rapidity and frenzy. In her hand she carried a long and tolerably stout wand, being, in fact, no other than the identical yam-stick to which Wildduck had referred as a weapon of offence, when proposing her as a fitting antagonist for the contumacious young stockman. With this she occasionally punctuated her rhetoric by waving it over her head, or bringing it down with terrific violence upon the earth. The meagre frame of the old heathen seemed galvanised into magical power and strength as she paced swiftly on her self-appointed course, whirling her shrivelled arms on high, or bounding from the earth with surprising agility. Such may have been the form, such the accents, of the inspired prophetess in the dawn of a religion of mystery and fear among the rude tribes of earth's earliest peoples—a Cassandra shrieking forth her country's woes—a Sibyl pouring out the dread oracles of a demon worship. The old warrior sat unmoved, with stony eyes fixed on vacancy, as the weird apparition passed and repassed like the phantasmagoria of a dream; while his aged companion, who seemed of softer mould, cowered fearfully and helplessly by his side.

"By Jove!" said Jack, "this is a grand and inspiriting sight. I don't wonder that Wildduck fled away from this style of thing. This old beldame would frighten the very witches on a respectable Walpurgis night. Great is the fire-water of the white man!"

"She'll wear herself out soon," said the ration-carrier. "Old man Jack wouldn't stand nice about downing her with the waddy, if she came near enough to him. He and the tother old mammy, they never touches no grog. They're about the only two people in this part of the country as I know of as doesn't. But the gins is awful."

"Polygamy has its weak side, apparently," moralized Jack, as still the frenzied form sped frantically past, and raved, and yelled, and chattered, and threatened; "not but what the uncultured white female occasionally goes on 'the rampage' to some purpose. Hallo! she's shortening stride; we shall see the finale."

Suddenly, as if an unseen hand had arrested the force which had so miraculously sustained her feeble form, she stopped. The fire of her protruding eyes was quenched; her nerveless limbs tottered and dragged; uttering a horrible, hoarse, unnatural cry, and throwing out her arms as in supplication and fear, she fell forward, without an effort to save herself, almost upon the embers of the dying fire. Old man Jack sat stern and immovable; but the woman ran forward with a gesture of pity, and, dragging the corpse-like form a few paces from the fire, covered it with a large opossum-skin cloak or rug.

"We may as well be getting on towards this scoundrel of a hawker," proposed M'Nab. "He ought to get it a little hotter if it were only for this bit of mischief."

"There's a deal of tobacky in the grog these fellows sell," observed the ration-carrier, with steady conviction, "that's the worst of 'em; if they'd only keep good stuff, it wouldn't be so much matter in this black country, as one might say. But I remember getting two glasses, only two as I'm alive, from a hawker once; I'm blest if they didn't send me clean mad and stupid for a whole week."

On the side furthest from the creek upon which the temporary wash-pen had been constructed, and midway between it and the plains, which stretched far to the eastward, lay a sand-ridge or dune, covered with thick growing pines. In this natural covert the reconnoitring party doubted not that the disturber of their peace had concealed himself. Riding into it, they separated until they struck the well-worn trail which, in the pre-merino days, had formed the path by which divers outlying cattle came in to water; following this, they came up to a clear space where a furtive-looking fire betrayed the camp of the unlicensed victualler. A store-cart, with the ordinary canvas tilt, and the heterogeneous packages common to the profession, were partly masked by the timber. As they rode up rapidly a man emerged from the shadow of a large pine and confronted them.

"Hallo! mates," he said, in a gruff but jocular tone; "what's the row? You ain't in the bushranging line, are you? because I've just sent away my cheques, worse luck."

"You'll see who we are directly," said Jack, jumping down, and giving his horse to the ration-carrier. "I wish to search your cart, that's all. I believe you've been selling spirits to my men. I'm a magistrate."

"What d'yer mean, then, by coming here on the bounce?" said the man, placing himself doggedly between Jack and the cart. "You ain't got a warrant, and I'll see you far enough before you touches a thing in that there cart. Why, my wife's asleep there."

"No she ain't," said a shrill voice, as a woman disengaged herself from the canvas, "but you don't touch anything for all that. We've our licence, ain't we, Bill, and what's the use of paying money to Government if pore people can't be purtected?"

"Perhaps you're not aware," said M'Nab, with cool accuracy, "that by the 19th and 20th sections of the 13th Victoria, No. 36, any magistrate or constable, on suspicion of spirits in unlawful quantities being carried for the purpose of sale, can search such hawker's cart and take possession of the spirits."

"That's the law," said Jack, "and we are going to search your cart; so stand aside, you cowardly scoundrel, making your ill-gotten profits out of the wages of a lot of poor fellows who have worked hard for them. Do you see this?" Here Jack suddenly produced his revolver, and giving the fellow a shove, which sent him staggering against a fallen tree, took possession of the vehicle, all unheeding the shrill tones and anything but choice language of the female delinquent.

"Ay!" said M'Nab, as he leaped actively into the cart, and turned over packages of moleskin and bundles of boots, bars of soap, and strings of dried apples, "this is all right and square; if you had only kept to a fair trade nobody could take ye. What's under these blankets?"

Lifting a pile of loosely-spread blankets, be suddenly raised a shout of triumph.

"So this was where the lady was sleeping, is it? Pity for you, my man, she didn't stay there; we should have been too polite to raise her. The murder is out." Here he drummed with his hand upon a new kind of instrument—a ten-gallon keg, half empty too. "What a lot the ruffian must have sold."

"What is your name?" asked Jack, blandly.

"William Smith," answered the fellow, gruffly.

"Alias Jones, alias Dawkins, I suppose; never mind, we shall have time to find out your early history, I dare say. Now, William, it becomes my duty to arrest you in the Queen's name, and, for fear of your giving us the slip, I must take the precaution of tying your hands behind your back."

Suiting the action to the word, he "muzzled" Mr. William so suddenly and effectually that, aided by M'Nab, there was no great difficulty in securing him by means of a stout cord which formed part of his own belongings.

"Keep off, Mrs. Smith, or we shall be under the necessity of tying you up too."

This was no superfluous warning, as with a considerable flow of Billingsgate, and with uplifted arms, the "bumboat woman" showed the strongest desire to injure Jack's complexion.

"You call yourselves men," she screamed, "coming here in the dead of night, three to one, and rummaging pore people's property like a lot of bushrangers. I'll have the law of ye, if you was fifty squatters—robbing the country, and won't let a pore man live. I've got money, and friends too, as'll see us righted. Don't ye lay a finger on me, ye hungry, grinding, Port Phillip Yankee slave driver"—(this to M'Nab)—"or I'll claw your ugly face till your mother wouldn't know ye."

"It's my opinion and belief," said M'Nab, "that she wouldn't be far behind old Nanny, if she had that yam-stick and another tot or two of her own grog. Here, Wilson, you catch this fellow's horse; there he is, hobbled under the big tree, and put him in the shafts. Mr. Redgrave and I will bring yours on."

The ration-carrier, much entertained, did as he was told, and Mr. William being ordered to enter his own vehicle, on pain of being attached to the tail-board, and compelled to walk behind, like a bullock-driver's hackney, the procession moved off, the ration-carrier driving, and the others riding behind. Mrs. Smith followed for some distance, disparaging everybody concerned, and invoking curses upon the innocent heads of all the squatters in Riverina, but finally consented to avail herself of the carriage.

In this order they reached Gondaree at an advanced hour of the night; and the next day Mr. William was safely lodged in the lock-up at the rising township of Burrabri, thirty miles down the river. Here he languished, until a couple of neighbouring Justices of the Peace could spare time from their shearing to try the case, when, the needful evidence being forthcoming, he was fined thirty pounds, with the alternative of three months' imprisonment in Bochara gaol.

Hereupon his faithful companion appeared in a new light, and made a highly practical suggestion—"You take it out, Bill," said the artful fair one; "don't you go for to pay 'em a red farden. You'll be a deal cooler in gaol than anywhere else in this blessed sandy country. I'll look arter the cart and hoss, and have all ready for a good spree at Christmas. You'll be out by then."

Mr. William looked at the blue sky through the open door of the public-house—the improvised court-house on such occasions—but finally decided to earn an honest penny—ten pounds per mensem, by voluntary incarceration.

When he *did* come forth, just before the Christmas week—alas that the chronicler should have to record one more instance of woman's perfidy!—the frail partner of his guilt had sold the horse and cart, retained the price thereof, and bolted with "another 'Bill,' whose Christian name was John."

The little episode ended, nothing occurred to mar the onward progress of events until the last bale of wool was duly shorn, packed, and safely deposited on a waggon *en route* for the steamer and a colonial market.

Then, with a clear conscience and a feeling of intense and cumulative satisfaction, Mr. John Redgrave betook himself once more to the busy haunts of men. Had he been Sir John Franklin, returning from a three-years' voyage to the North Pole, he could hardly have been more jubilant and grateful to a kind Providence, when he again ensconced himself in the up-train for the metropolis. He revelled and rioted in the unwonted luxuries of town life, like a midshipman at the Blue Posts. Bread and butter, decent cookery, and cool claret, the half-forgotten ceremonial of dinner, billiards, books, balls, lawn parties, ladies, luxuries of all sorts and kinds; how delicious, how intoxicating they were! Material advantages went hand in hand with this re-entrance to Eden. He had very properly agreed with M'Nab that it was well to sell this year's clip in the colony, as the washing and getting up were only so-so, and wool was high. Next year they might show the English and French buyers what the J R brand over Gondaree was like, and reasonably hope that every year would add to the selling price of that valuable, extensive, and scientifically got-up clip.

Jack looked bronzed, and thinner than of old, but all his friends, especially the ladies, voted it an improvement; he had the air of an explorer, a dweller in the wilderness, and what not. His wool, which followed him, sold extremely well. Assumed to be successful, he was more popular than ever. His bankers were urbane; he was consulted by some of the oldest and most astute speculators; men prophesied great things as to his ultimate financial triumphs. And Jack already looked upon himself as forming one of the congress of Australian Rothschilds, and began to think of all the munificent and ingeniously helpful things that he would do in such case; for he was of a kindly and sentimentally generous tendency, this speculative Jack of ours, and his day-dreams of wealth were never unmingled with the names of those who immediately after such realization would hear something to their advantage. Jack lingered in Paradise for a couple of months, during which time he received his wool money, and made arrangements with his bankers for the purchase of as much wire as would suffice to fence a large proportion of his run. His stores were commensurate with the future prestige of the establishment. He explained to Mr. Mildmay Shrood, his banker, that he might possibly put on a few thousand more sheep if he saw a good opportunity. Of course he could buy more cheaply for cash; and if they paid as well as the lot he had picked up this year, they would be very cheap after the wool was off their backs.

"My dear sir," said Mr. Shrood, with an air of friendly interest, "the bank will be most happy to honour your drafts up to ten thousand pounds. If you need more you will be kind enough to advise. I hear the most favourable accounts of the district in which you have invested, and of your property in particular. What is your own opinion—which I should value—upon the present prices of stock and stations? will they keep up?"

"I have the fullest belief," quoth Jack, with judicial certainty, "in the present rates being maintained for the next ten years; for five years at least it is impossible by my calculations, if correct, that any serious fall should take place. The stock, I believe, are not in the country in sufficient numbers to meet the rapidly enlarging demand for meat. Wool is daily finding new markets and manufacturers. I never expect to see bullocks above five pounds again; but sheep—sheep, you may depend, will go on rising in price until I should not be surprised to see first-class stations fetching thirty shillings, or even two pounds, all round."

"Quite of your opinion, my dear Mr. Redgrave," quoth the affable coin-compeller. "Happy to have my ideas confirmed by a gentleman of so much experience. Depend upon it, sheep-farming is in its infancy. Good morning. *Good* morning, my dear sir."

Jack saw no particular reason for hurrying himself, being represented at Gondaree by a far better man than himself, as he told everybody. So he spent his Christmastide joyously, and permitted January to glide over, as a month suitable for gradually making up his mind to return to the wilderness. Early in February he began to feel bored with the "too-muchness" of nothing to do, and wisely departed.

VII

"But he still governed with resistless hand,
And where he could not guide he would command."

—Crabbe

When Jack got back he was rather shocked at the altered aspect of the run. There had been no rain, except in inconsiderable quantity, during his absence, and the herbage generally showed signs of a deficiency of moisture. The river flats, which were so lush and heavily cropped with green herbage that your horse's feet made a "swish-swashing" noise as you rode through it, now were very parched up, dry, and bare, or else burned off altogether.

On mentioning this to Mr. M'Nab, he said—

"Well, the fact is that the grass got very dry, and some fellow put a fire-stick into it. Then we have had a great number of travelling sheep through lately, and they have fed their mile pretty bare. The season has been very dry so far. I sincerely trust we shall get rain soon."

"We may," said Jack. "But when once these dry years set in, they say you never know when it may rain again. But how do the sheep look?"

"Couldn't possibly look better," answered M'Nab, decisively. "There is any quantity of feed and water at the back, and I have not troubled the frontage much. I am glad ye sent the wire up. We were nearly stopped, as it came just as the posts were in. I have got one line of the lambing paddock nearly finished, and we shall have that part of the play over before long. No more shepherds and 'motherers' to pay in that humbugging way next year."

"And how are the other things getting on?" inquired Jack.

"Well, the cottage is nearly fit to go into. Your bedroom is finished and ready for you. I had a garden fenced in, and put on a Chinaman with a pump to grow some vegetables—for we were all half-way to a little scurvy. The wool-shed is getting along, though the carpenters went on the spree at Bochara for a fortnight. In fact, all is doing well generally, and I think you'll say the sheep are improved."

Jack lost no time in establishing himself in his bedroom in the new cottage, which he had judiciously caused to be built of "pise," or rammed earth, by this means saving the cartage of material, for the soil was dug out immediately in front of the building, and securing coolness, solidity, and thickness of wall, none of which conditions are to be found in weather-board or slab buildings. Brick or stone was not, of course, to be thought of, owing to the absence of lime, and the tremendous expense of such materials. The heat was terrific. But when Jack found himself the tenant of a cool, spacious apartment, with his books, a writing-table, and a little decent furniture, the rest of the cottage including a fair-sized sitting-room, with walls of reasonable altitude, he did not despair of being able to support life for the few years required for the process of making a fortune. The river, fringed by the graceful though dark-hued casuarinas, was pleasant enough to look on, as it rippled on over pools and sandy shallows, immediately below his verandah. And beyond all expression was it glorious to bathe in by early morn or sultry eve.

The garden, though far, far different from the lost Eden of Marshmead, with its crowding crops, glossy shrubs, and heavily-laden fruit trees, was still a source of interest and pleasure. Under the unwearied labour and water-carrying of Ah Sing, rows of vegetables appeared, grateful to the eye, and were ravenously devoured by the *employés* of the station, whom a constant course of mutton, damper, and tea—tea, damper, and mutton—had led to, as M'Nab said truly, the border-land of one of the most awful diseases that scourge humanity. Never before had a cabbage been grown at Gondaree, and the older residents looked with a kind of awe at Ah Sing as he watered his rows of succulent vegetables, toilsomely and regularly, in the long hot mornings and breezeless afternoons.

"My word, John," said Jingaree, who had ridden over from Jook-jook one day on no particular business, but to look at the wonderful improvements which afforded the staple subject of conversation that summer on the Warroo, "you're working this garden-racket fust chop. I've been here eight year, and never see a green thing except marsh-mallers and Warrigal cabbage. How ever do you make 'em come like that?"

"Plenty water, plenty dung, plenty work, welly good cabbagee," said Ah Sing, sententiously. "Why you not grow melon, tater, ladishee?"

"I don't say we mightn't," said Jingaree, half soliloquizing, "but it's too hot in these parts to be carrying water all day long like a Chow. Give us one of them cabbages, John."

"You takee two," quoth the liberal celestial. "Mr. Mackinab, he say, give um shepherdy all about. You shepherdy?"

"You be hanged!" growled the insulted stockman. "Do I look like a slouchin', 'possum-eating, billy-carrying crawler of a shepherd? I've had a horse under me ever since I was big enough to know Jingaree mountain from a haystack, and a horse I'll have as long as I can carry a stock-whip. However, I don't suppose you meant any offence, John. Hand over the cabbages. Blest if I couldn't eat 'em raw without a mossel of salt."

"Here tomala—welly good tomala," said the pacific Chinaman, appalled at the unexpected wrath of the stranger. "Welly good cabbagee, goodbye."

Jack being comfortably placed in his cottage, took a leisurely look through his accounts. He was rather astonished, and a little shocked, to find what a sum he had got through for all the various necessaries of his position.—Stores, wages, contract payments, wire, blacksmith, carpenters, sawyers, bricklayers (for the wash-pen and the cottage chimneys).—Cheque, cheque, there seemed no end to the outflow of cash—and a good deal more was to come, or rather to go, before next lambing, washing, and shearing were concluded. He mentioned his ideas on the subject to Mr. M'Nab.

That financier frankly admitted that the outlay *was* large, positively but not relatively. "You understand, sir," he said, "that much of this money will not have to be spent twice. Once have your fences up, and breed up, or buy, till you have stocked your run, and you are at the point where the largest amount of profit, the wool and the surplus sheep, is met by the minimum of expenditure. No labour will be wanted but three or four boundary riders. The wool, I think, will be well got up, and ought to sell well."

"I dare say," said Jack, "I dare say. It's no use stopping half way, but really, the money does seem to run out as from a sieve. However, it will be as cheap to shear 40,000 sheep as twenty. So I shall decide to stock up as soon as the fences are finished."

This point being settled, Mr. M'Nab pushed on his projects and operations with unflagging energy. He worked all day and half the night, and seemed to know neither weariness nor fatigue of mind or body. He had all the calculations of all the different contracts at his fingers' ends, and never permitted to cool any of the multifarious irons which he had in the fire.

He kept the different parties of teamsters, fencers, splitters, carpenters, sawyers, dam-makers, well-sinkers, all in hand, going smoothly and without delay, hitch, or dissatisfaction. He provided for their rations being taken to them, kept all the accounts accurately, and if there was so much as a sheepskin not returned, as per agreement, the defaulter was regularly charged with it. Incidentally, and besides all this work, sufficient for two ordinary men, he administered the shepherds and their charge—now amounting to nearly 30,000 sheep. Jack's admiration of his manager did not slacken or change. "By Jove!" he said to himself, occasionally, "that fellow M'Nab is fit to be a general of division. He never leaves anything to chance, and he seems to foresee everything and to arrange the cure before the ailment is announced."

The cottage being now finished, Jack began to find life not only endurable, but almost enjoyable. He had got up a remnant of his library, and with some English papers, and the excellent weeklies of the colonies, he found that he had quite as much mental pabulum as he had leisure to consume. The sheep were looking famously well. The lambs were nearly as big in appearance as their mothers. The store sheep had fattened, and would be fit for the butcher as soon as their fleeces were off. The shepherds, for a wonder, gave no trouble, the ground being open, and their flocks strong; all was going well. The wool-shed was progressing towards completion; the wash-pen would follow suit, and be ready for the spouts, with all the latest improvements, which were even now on the road. Unto Jack, as he smoked in the verandah at night, gazing on the bright blue starry sky, listening to the rippling river, came freshly once more the beatific vision of a completely-fenced and fully-stocked run, paying splendidly, and ultimately taken off his hands at a profit, which should satisfy pride and compensate privation.

He and Mr. M'Nab had also become accustomed to the ways of the population. "I thought at first," said Jack, "that I never set eyes on such a set of duffers and loafers as the men at the Warroo generally. But I have had to change my opinion. They only want management, and I have seen some of the best working men among them I ever saw anywhere. One requires a good deal of patience in a new country."

"They want a dash of ill temper now and then," rejoined M'Nab. "It's very hard, when work is waiting for want of men, to see a gang of stout, lazy fellows going on, refusing a pound and five-and-twenty shillings a week, because the work is not to their taste."

"But do they?" inquired Jack.

"There were five men refused work from one of the fence contractors at that price yesterday," said M'Nab, wrathfully. "They wouldn't do the bullocking and only get shepherds' wages, was the answer. I had the travellers' hut locked up, and not a bit of meat or flour will any traveller get till we get men."

"That doesn't seem unjust," said Jack. "I don't see that we are called upon to maintain a strike against our own rate of wages, which we do in effect by feeding all the idle fellows who elect to march on. But don't be hard on them. They can do us harm enough if they try."

"I don't see that, sir. The salt-bush won't burn, and they would never think of anything else. They must be taught in this part of the world that they will not be encouraged to refuse fair wages. Now we are talking about rates—seventeen and sixpence is quite enough to give a hundred for shearing. We must have an understanding with the other sheep-owners, and try and fix it this year."

Whether intimidated by the determined attitude of Mr. M'Nab, or because men differ in their aspirations, on the Warroo as in other places, the next party of travellers thankfully accepted the contractors' work and wages, and buckled to at once. They were, in fact, a party of navvies just set free from a long piece of contract, and this putting up posts, pretty hard work, was just what they wanted.

M'Nab fully believed it was owing to him, and mentally vowed to act with similar decision in the next case of mutiny. A steady enforcement of your own rules is what the people here look for, thought he.

The seasons glided on. Month after month of Jack's life, and of all our lives, fleeted past, and once again shearing became imminent. The time did not hang heavily on his hands; he rose at daylight, and after a plunge in the river the various work of each day asserted its claims, and our merino-multiplier found himself wending his way home at eve as weary as Gray's ploughman, only fit for the consumption of dinner and an early retreat to his bedroom. A more pretentious and certainly more neatly-arrayed artist—indeed, a *cordon bleu*, unable to withstand the temptations of town life—had succeeded Bob the cook. Now that the cottage was completed, and reasonable comfort and coolness were attainable, Jack told himself that it was not such a bad life after all. A decent neighbour or two had turned up within visiting distance—that is under fifty miles. The constant labour sweetened his mental health, while the "great expectations" of the flawless perfection of the new wool-shed, the highly improved wash-pen, and the generally triumphant success of the coming clip, lent ardour to his soul and exultation to his general bearing. M'Nab, as usual, worked, and planned, and calculated, and organized with the tireless regularity of an engine. Chiefly by his exertions and a large emission of circulars, the Warroo sheep-holders had been roused to a determination to reduce the price of shearing per hundred from twenty shillings to seventeen and sixpence. This reduced rate, in spite of some grumbling, they were enabled to carry out, chiefly owing to an unusual abundance of the particular class of workmen concerned. The men, after a few partial strikes, capitulated. But they knew from whence the movement had emanated, and were not inclined altogether to forget the fact. Indeed, of late M'Nab, from overwork and concentration of thought, had lost his originally imperturbable manner. He had got into a habit of "driving" his men, and bore himself more nearly akin to the demeanour of the second mate on board a Yankee merchantman than the superintendent of the somewhat free and independent workmen of an Australian colony.

"He's going too fast, that new boss," said one of the wash-pen hands one day, as Mr. M'Nab, unusually chafed at the laziness of one of the men who were helping to fit a boiler, had, in requital of some insolent rejoinder, knocked him down, and discharged him on the spot. "He'll get a rough turn yet, if he don't look out—there's some very queer characters on the Warroo."

And now the last week of July had arrived. The season promised to be early. The grasses were unusually forward, while the burr-clover, matted and luxuriant, made it evident that rather less than the ordinary term of sunshine would suffice to harden its myriads of aggressively injurious seed-cylinders. The warning was not unnoticed by the ever-watchful eye of M'Nab.

"There will be a bad time with any sheds that are unlucky enough to be late this year," he said, as Jack and he were inspecting the dam and lately-placed spouts of the wash-pen; "that's why I've been carrying a full head of steam lately, to get all in order this month. Thank goodness, the shed will be finished on Saturday, and I'm ready for a start on the first of August."

Of a certainty, everyone capable of being acted upon by the contagion of a very uncommon degree of energy had been working at high pressure for the last two months. Paddocks had been completed; huts were ready for the washers and shearers. The great plant, including a steam-engine, had been strongly and efficiently fitted at the wash-pen, where a dam sent back the water for a mile, to the great astonishment of Jingaree and his friends, who occasionally rode over, as a species of holiday, to inspect the work.

"My word," said this representative of the Arcadian, or perhaps Saturnian, period. "I wonder what old Morgan would say to all this here tiddley-winkin', with steam-engine, and wire-fences, and knock-about men at a pound a week, as plenty as the black fellows when he first came on the ground. They'll have a Christy pallis yet, and minstrels too, I'll be bound. They've fenced us off from our Long Camp, too, with that cussed wire. Said our cattle went over our boundary. Boundaries be blowed! I've seen every herd mixed from here to Bochara, after a dry season. Took men as knew their work to draft 'em again, I can tell you. If these here fences is to be run up all along the river, any Jackaroo can go stock-keeping. The country's going to mischief."

Winding up with this decided statement of disapproval, Mr. Jingaree thus delivered himself at a cattle muster at one of the old-fashioned stations, where the ancient manners and customs of the land were still preserved in an uncorrupted state. The other gentlemen, Mr. Billy the Bay, from Durgah, Mr. Long Jem, from Deep Creek, Mr. Flash Jack, from Banda Murranul, and a dozen other representatives of the spur and stock-whip, listened with evident approbation to Jingaree's peroration. "The blessed country's a blessed sight too full," said Mr. Long Jem. "I mind the time when, if a cove wanted a fresh hand, he had to ride to Bochara and stay there a couple of days, till some feller had finished knockin' down his cheque. Now they can stay at home, and pick and choose among the travellers at their ease. It's these blessed immigrants and diggers as spoils our market. What right have they got to the country, I'd like to know?"

This natural but highly protective view of the labour question found general acquiescence, and nothing but the absurd latter-day theories of the necessity of population, and the freedom of the individual, prevented, in their opinion, a return of the good old times, when each man fixed the rate of his own remuneration.

Meanwhile Mr. M'Nab's daring innovations progressed and prospered at the much-changed and highly-improved Gondaree. On Saturday afternoon Redgrave and his manager surveyed, with no little pride, the completed and indeed admirable wool-shed. Nothing on the Warroo had ever been seen like it. Jack felt honestly proud of his new possession, as he walked up and down the long building. The shearing floor was neatly, even ornamentally, laid with the boards of the delicately-tinted Australian pine. The long pens which delivered the sheep to the operator were battened on a new principle, applied by the ever-inventive genius of M'Nab. There were separate back yards and accurately divided portions of the floor for twenty shearers. The roof was neatly shingled. All the appliances for saving labour were of the most modern description, and as different from the old-world contrivances in vogue among the wool-sheds of the Warroo as a threshing-machine from a pair of flails. The wool-press alone had cost more as it stood ready for work than many a shed, wash-pen, huts, and yards of the old days.

VIII

"The crackling embers glow,
And flakes of hideous smoke the skies defile."

—CRABBE

There is accommodation for more shearers than we shall need this year," said M'Nab, apologetically, "but it is as well to do the thing thoroughly. Next year I hope we shall have fifty thousand to shear, and if you go in for some back country I don't see why there shouldn't be a hundred thousand sheep on the board before you sell out. That will be a sale worth talking about. Meanwhile, there's nothing like plenty of room in a shed. The wool will be all the better this year even for it."

"I know it has cost a frightful lot of money," said Jack, pensively, practising a gentle gallop on the smooth, pale-yellow, aromatic-scented floor. "I dare say it will be a pleasure to shear in it, and all that—but it's spoiled a thousand pounds one way or the other."

"What's a thousand pounds?" said M'Nab, with a sort of gaze that seemed as though he were piercing the mists of futurity, and seeing an unbroken procession of tens of thousands of improved merinos marching slowly and impressively on to the battens, ready to deliver three pounds and a-half of spout-washed wool at half-a-crown a pound. "When you come to add a penny or twopence a pound to a large clip, all the money you can spend in a wash-pen, or a shed, is repaid in a couple of years. Of course I mean when things are on a large scale."

"Well, we're spending money on a large scale," said Jack. "I only hope the returns and profits will be in the same proportion."

"Not a doubt of it," said M'Nab. "I must be off home to meet the fencers."

The shed was locked up, and they drove home. As they alighted, three men were standing at the door of the store, apparently waiting for the "dole"—a pound of meat and a pannikin of flour, which is now found to be the reasonable minimum, given to every wayfarer by the dwellers in Riverina, wholly irrespective of caste, colour, indisposition to work, or otherwise, "as the case may be."

Jack went into the house to prepare for dinner, while M'Nab, looking absently at the men, took out a key and made towards the entrance to the store.

"Stop," cried M'Nab, "didn't I see you three men on the road today, about four miles off? Which way have you come?"

"We're from down the river," said one of the fellows, a voluble, good-for-nothing, loafing impostor, a regular "coaster" and "up one side of the river and down the other" traveller, as the men say, asking for work, and praying, so long as food and shelter are afforded, that he may not get it. "We've been looking for work this weeks, and I'm sure, sliding into an impressive low-tragedy growl, the 'ardships men 'as to put up with in this country—a-travellin' for work—no one can't imagine."

"I dare say not," said M'Nab; "it's precious little you fellows know of hardships, fed at every station you come to, taking an easy day's walk, and not obliged to work unless the employment thoroughly suits you. How far have you come today?"

There was a slight appearance of hesitation and reference to each other as the spokesman answered—"From Dickson's, a station about fifteen miles distant."

"You are telling me a lie," said M'Nab, wrathfully. "I saw you sitting down on your swags this morning at the crossing-place, five miles from here, and the hut-keeper on the other side of the river told me you had been there all night and had only just left."

"Well, suppose we did," said another one, who had not yet spoken, "there's no law to make a man walk so many miles a day, like travelling sheep. I dare say the squatters would have that done if they could. Are you going to give us shelter here tonight, or no?"

"I'll see you hanged first!" broke forth M'Nab, indignantly; "what, do you talk about *shelter* in weather like this! A rotten tree is too good a lodging for a set of lazy, useless scoundrels, who go begging from station to station at the rate of five miles a day."

"We did not come far today, it is true," said the third traveller, evidently a foreigner; "but we have a far passage tomorrow. Is it not so, *mes camarades?*"

"Far enough, and precious short rations too, sometimes," growled the man who had spoken last. "I wish some coves had a taste on it themselves."

"See here, my man," said M'Nab, going close up to the last speaker, and looking him full in the eye, "if you don't start at once I'll kick you off the place, and pretty quickly too."

The man glared savagely for a moment, but, seeing but little chance of coming off best in an encounter with a man in the prime of youth and vigour, gave in, and sullenly picked up his bundle.

The Frenchman, for such he was, turned for a moment, and fixing a small glittering eye—cold and serpentine—upon M'Nab, said—

"It is then that you refuse us a morsel of food, the liberty to lie on the hut floor?"

"There is the road," repeated M'Nab; "I will harbour no impostors or loafers."

"I have the honour to wish you good-evening," said the Frenchman, bowing with exaggerated politeness; "a pleasant evening, and dreams of the best."

The men went slowly on their way. M'Nab went into the cottage, by no means too well satisfied with himself. A feeling of remorse sprang up within his breast. "Hang the fellows!" said he to himself, "it serves them right. Still I am going in to a comfortable meal and my bed, while these poor devils will most probably have neither. That Frenchman didn't seem a crawler either, though I didn't like the expression of his eye as he moved away. They'll make up for it at Jook-jook tomorrow. Why need they have told me that confounded lie? then they would have been treated well. However, it can't be helped. If we don't give them a lesson now and then the country will get full of fellows who do nothing but consume rations, and fair station work will become impossible."

Early next morning—it was Sunday, by the way—Jack was turning round for another hour's snooze, an indulgence to which he deemed himself fairly entitled after a hard week's work, when Mr. M'Nab's voice (*he* was always up and about early, whatever might be the day of the week) struck strangely upon his ear. He was replying to one of the station hands; he caught the words—"The shed! God in heaven—you can't mean it!" Jack was out of bed with one bound, and, half clad, rushed out. M'Nab was saddling a horse with nervous hands that could scarcely draw a buckle.

"What is it, man?" demanded Redgrave, with a sinking at the heart, and a strange presentiment of evil.

"The wool-shed's a-fire, sir!" answered the man, falteringly, "and I came in directly I seen it to let you know."

"On fire! and why didn't you try and put it out?" inquired he, hoarsely, "there were plenty of you about there."

He was hoping against hope, and was scarcely surprised when the man said, in a tone as nearly modulated to sympathy as his rough utterance could be subdued to—

"The men are hard at it, sir, but I'm afraid—"

ROLF BOLDREWOOD

Jack did not wait for the conclusion of the sentence, but made at once for the loose-box where his hack had been lately bestowed at night, and in a couple of minutes was galloping along the lately-worn "wool-shed track" at some distance behind M'Nab, who was racing desperately ahead.

Before he reached the creek upon which the precious and indispensable building had been, after much careful planning erected, he saw the great column of smoke rising through the still morning air, and knew that all was lost. He knew that the pine timber, of which it was chiefly composed, would burn "like a match," and that if not stifled at its earliest commencement all the men upon the Warroo could not have arrested its progress. As he galloped up a sufficiently sorrowful sight met his eye. The shearers, washers, and someother provisional hands, put on in anticipation of the unusual needs of shearing time, were standing near the fiercely-blazing structure, with fallen roof and charred uprights, which but yesterday had been the best wool-shed on the Warroo. The deed was done. There was absolutely no hope, no opportunity of saving a remnant of the value of five pounds of the whole costly building.

"How, in the name of all that's—" said he to M'Nab, who was gazing fixedly beyond the red smouldering mass, as if his ever-working mind was already busied beyond the immediate disaster, "did the fire originate? It was never accidental. Then who could have had the smallest motive to do us such an injury?"

"I am afraid I have too good a guess," answered M'Nab. "But of that by and by. Did you see any strange men camp here last night?" he asked of the crowd generally.

"Travellers?" said one of the expectant shearers. "Yes, there was three of 'em came up late and begged some rations. I was away after my horse as made off. When I found him and got back it was ten o'clock at night, and these coves was just making their camp by the receiving-yard."

"What like were they?"

"Two biggish chaps—one with a beard, and a little man, spoke like a 'Talian or a Frenchman."

"Did they say anything?"

"Well, one of them—the long chap—began to run you down; but the Frenchman stopped him, and said you was too good to 'em altogether."

"Who saw the shed first?"

"I did, sir," said one of the fencers. "I turned out at daylight to get some wood, when the fust thing I saw was the roof all blazin' and part of it fell in. I raised a shout and started all the men. We tried buckets, but, lor' bless you, when we come to look, the floor was all burned through and through."

"Then you think it had been burning a good while?" asked Jack, now beginning to understand the drift of the examination.

"Hours and hours, sir," answered the man; "from what we see, the fire started under where the floor joins the battens; there was a lot of shavings under the battens, and some of them hadn't caught when we came. It was there the fire began sure enough."

"Did anyone see the strange men leave?" asked M'Nab, with assumed coolness, though his lip worked nervously, and his forehead was drawn into deep wrinkles.

"Not a soul," said another of the hands. "I looked over at their camp as we rushed out, and it was all cleared out, and no signs of 'em."

John Redgrave and his manager rode back very sadly to Steamboat Point that quiet Sunday morn. The day was fair and still, with the added silence and hush which long training communicates to the mere idea of the Sabbath day.

The birds called strangely, but not unmusically, from the pale-hued trees but lately touched with a softer green. The blue sky was cloudless. Nature was kindly and serene. Nothing was incongruous with her tranquil and tender aspect but the stern, tameless heart of man.

They maintained for sometime a dogged silence. The loss was bitter. Not only had rather more money been spent upon the building than was quite advisable or convenient, but the whole comfort, pride, and perhaps profit, of the shearing would be lost.

"Those infernal scoundrels," groaned M'Nab; "that snake of a Frenchman, with his beady black eyes. I thought the little brute meant mischief, though I never dreamed of this, or I'd have gone and slept in the shed till shearing was over. I'll have them in gaol before a week's over their heads, but what satisfaction is there in that? It's my own fault in great part. I ought to have known better, and not have been so hard on them."

"I was afraid," said Jack, "that you were a little too sharp with these fellows of late. I know, too, what they are capable of. But no one could have foreseen such an outrage as this. The next thing to consider is how to knock up a rough makeshift that we can shear in."

"That doesn't give me any trouble," answered the spirit-stricken M'Nab; "we could do as we did last year; but the season is a month forwarder, and we shall have the burrs and grass-seed in the wool as sure as fate. But for that, I shouldn't so much care."

M'Nab departed gloomily to his own room, refusing consolation, and spent the rest of the day writing circulars containing an accurate description of the suspected ones to every police-station within two hundred miles.

Then it came to pass that the three outlaws were soon snapped up by a zealous sergeant, "on suspicion of having committed a felony," and safely lodged in Bochara gaol. There did they abide for several weary months, until the Judge of the Circuit Court was graciously pleased to come and try them.

The loss in the first instance was sufficiently great. The labour of many men for nearly a year; every nail, every ounce of iron contained in the large building had been brought from Melbourne; the sawyers' bill was considerable. Twice had the men employed to put on the shingles deserted, and the finishing of the roof was regarded by the anxious M'Nab as a kind of miracle. The sliding doors, the portcullises, the hundreds of square feet of battening, the circular drafting-yard; all the very latest appliances and improvements, united to very solid and perfect construction, made an unusual though costly success. And now, to see it wasted, and worse than wasted. "It is enough to make one believe in bad luck, Mr. Redgrave!" said Mr. M'Nab, who had just quitted his bedroom.

"I am afraid it means bad luck for this season," pursued he; "our wool will be got up only middling, and if prices take a turn downward it will be very puzzling to say what the damage done by this diabolical act of arson will amount to."

"We must hope for the best," said Jack, who, feeling things very keenly at the time, had a great dislike to the protracted torture which dwelling upon misfortunes always inflicts upon men of his organization. "The deed is done. Tomorrow we must rig up a second edition of last year's proud edifice."

The sheep were shorn, certainly. Mr. Redgrave did not exactly permit the crop of delicate, creamy, serrated, elastic, myriad-threaded material to be torn off by the salt-bushes, or to become ragged and patchy on the sheeps' backs. But the pleasure and pride of the toilsome undertaking, the light and life of the pastoral harvest, were absent. There was a total absence of rain; so there was a good deal of unavoidable dust. The men could not be got to take the ordinary amount of pains; so the work was thoroughly unsatisfactory. Then, in spite of all the haste and indifferent workmanship purposely overlooked by M'Nab, the grass-seed and clover-burr ripened only too rapidly, and the ewes and lambs, coming last, were choke-full of it. The lower part of every fleece was like a nutmeg-grater with the hard, unyielding, hooked and barbed tentacles. M'Nab groaned in spirit as he saw all this unnecessary damage, which he was powerless to prevent, and again and again cursed the hasty word and lack of self-control which, as he fully believed, had indirectly caused this never-ending mischief.

"A thousand for the shed, and another thousand for damage to wool," said he one day, as he flung one of these last porcupine-looking fleeces with a disgusted air into a rude wool-bin made of hurdles placed on end. "It's enough to make a man commit suicide. I feel as if I ought to walk to Melbourne with peas in my boots."

"Never mind, M'Nab," said Jack, consolingly; "as I said before, the thing is done and over, and we may make ourselves miserable, and so injure our thought and labour fund. But that won't build the shed again. Luckily the sheep are all right—they couldn't burn them. I never saw a better lot of lambs, and the numbers are getting up to the fifty thousand I once proposed as a limit. What's the total count we have passed through?"

"Forty-one thousand seven hundred and eighty," answered M'Nab, who always had anything connected with numerals at his fingers' ends. "We have bought several small lots since last year, and the lambing average was very high. Of course the lambs don't actually count till weaning time."

"Well, we must only hope for a good season," said Jack, "and for wool and prices to keep up. Then, perhaps, the loss of the shed won't be so telling. We ought to have a good many fat sheep to sell in the winter."

"So we shall," said M'Nab, "nearly ten thousand—counting the full-mouthed and cull ewes. Then we shall have lambs from nearly sixteen thousand ewes next year. I hope the season will not fail us, now the paddocks are all finished."

"Well, it *does* look rather dry," admitted Jack; "so early in the year too. But then it always looks dry here when it doesn't rain. I shall have to run away to Melbourne now, and arrange whether to sell or ship this only moderately well-got-up wool of ours. I must have another interview with Mr. Shrood. It has been all spending and no returns of late."

Shearing being over—how differently concluded to what he had fondly anticipated! Jack hied himself to town for his annual holiday. It did not wear so much the air of a festival this year. There seemed to be a flavour of stern business about it; much more than Jack liked.

The wool-market was by no means in so buoyant a condition as that of last year. The faces of his brother squatters, especially those of the more enterprizing among them, wore a serious and elongated expression. Ugly reports went about as to a probable fall in wool and stock. Jack found his indifferently got-up clip quite unsaleable in the colonial market. He therefore shipped it at once, taking a fair advance thereon. Freight, too, was unreasonably high that year. Everything seemed against a fellow.

He went in for the little interview with Mr. Mildmay Shrood, and thought that affable money-changer less agreeable than of yore. "He wanted to know, you know." He asked a series of questions, testifying a desire to have the clearest idea of Jack's stock, value of property, liabilities, and probable expenditure during the coming year. He dwelt much upon the unfortunate destruction of the wool-shed; asked for an estimate of the cost of another; looked rather grave at the account of the get-up of the clip, and the necessity for shipping the same. However, the concluding portion of the interview was more reassuring.

"Of course you will continue to draw as usual, my dear sir; but I may say, in confidence, that in commercial circles a fall in prices is very generally anticipated."

"There may be a temporary decline," rejoined Jack, candidly, "but it is impossible that it should be lasting. As for sheep, the stock are not at present in the country to enable us to keep up with the demand, especially since these meat-preserving establishments have commenced operations."

"Quite so, my dear sir, quite so," assented Mr. Shrood, looking paternally at him and rubbing his hands, "I am quite of your opinion; but some of our directors have doubts—have doubts. Would you mind looking in before you go—say in a week or two? Thanks. Good-day—good-day."

Jack attended the wool-sales pretty regularly, and saw the clips which were undeniably well got up sell at good prices, in spite of the general dullness of the market. The clip was an unusually heavy one, and everyday's train brought down trucks upon trucks of bales, as if the interior of Australia was one colossal wool-store, just being emptied at the command of an enchanter. But the "heavy and moity" parcels were not touched by the cautious operators at any price. So Jack groaned in spirit, doubting that he might come in for a low market at home, and knowing that he would have saved himself but for the woful work of the incendiaries. He did not derive much comfort from the daring spirits whose early and successful ventures had inspired him with the first ideas of changing his district. They walked about like people who owned a private bank, but upon which bank there happened to be, at present, a run. They were, as a rule, men far too resolute to give in during adversity, or the threatening of any, how wild soever, commercial tempest. Still they looked sternly defiant, as who should say—"to bear is to conquer our fate." Jack did not enjoy the probabilities. These were brass pots of approved strength for floating in the eddying financial torrents. Might not he, an earthen vessel, meet with deadly damage, fatal cracks, irrevocable immersion, in their company? *"Que diable allait-il faire dans cette galère?"*

He sent up his stores, making a close calculation as to quantity. There would not be so many men required after this shearing. The paddocks were all finished, and few hands would be needed. Then he had doors and windows, and hinges and nails, and tons of galvanized iron for roofing for the shed—all over again. Confound it! Just as a fellow was hoping to get a little straight. Jack *did* feel very unchristian. However, it was as necessary as tea and sugar—that is, if he ever intended to get a decent price for his wool again. Somewhat earlier in the season than usual, Jack commenced to revolve the question of a start. Then he bethought himself of Mr. Mildmay Shrood.

"I wonder what he wanted to see me for?" asked Jack of his inner consciousness; "very civil, friendly little fellow he is. I suspect my over-draft is pretty heavy just now. But the fencing is all done, that's a blessing. And forty thousand sheep and a first-class run are good security for more money than I'm ever likely to owe."

So Mr. Redgrave hied away to the grand freestone portals which guarded the palace of gold and silver, and the magic paper which gladdeneth the heart of man, who reflecteth not that it is but a fiction—a "baseless fabric"—an unsubstantial presentment of the potentiality of boundless wealth.

Mr. Shrood was examining papers when he was ushered into the sacred parlour, and looked rather more like the dragon in charge of the treasure than the careless, openhanded financier of Jack's previous experience, whose sole business in life seemed to be to provide cheque-books *ad infinitum* with graceful indifference. As he ran his eye down column after column of figures, his brow became corrugated, his jaw became set, and his face gradually assumed an expression of hardness and obstinacy.

Throwing down the last of the papers, and clearing his brow with sudden completeness, he shook hands affectionately with Jack, and gently anathematized the papers for their tediousness and stupidity.

"Awfully wearing work, Mr. Redgrave, this looking over the accounts of a large estate. I feel as fatigued as if I had been at it all night. How are you, and when do you leave?"

"I think the day after tomorrow," said Jack. "I'm really tired of town, and wish to get home again."

"Tired of the town, and of all its various pleasures," asked Mr. Shrood, "at your age? Well, of course you are anxious to be at work again—very creditable feeling. By the way, *by* the way, now I think of it—you haven't encumbered your place by mortgage or in any other way during the last year, have you?"

"Sir," replied Jack, with dignity, "I regard my property as pledged in honour to your bank, by which I have been treated hitherto with liberality and confidence. I trust that our relations may continue unaltered."

"Certainly, my dear sir, certainly," replied Mr. Mildmay Shrood, with an air of touching generosity. "Precisely my own view. I trust you will have no cause to regret your connection with our establishment. But I have not concealed from you my opinion that, financially, there exists a certain anxiety—premature in my view of events—but still distinct, as to the relations between stock and capital. I have been requested by my directors, to whose advice I am constrained to defer, to raise the point of security in those instances where advances, I may say considerable advances, have been made by us. You see my position, I feel sure."

"Oh, certainly," said Jack; "of course," not seeing exactly what he was driving at.

"You will not, therefore, feel that it amounts to any want of confidence on the part of the bank," continued Mr. Shrood, with reassuring explanation in every tone, "if I name to you the formal execution of a mortgage over your station, as a mere matter in the ordinary routine of business, for the support of our advances to you past and future?"

"Oh, no," replied Jack, with a slight gulp, misliking the sound of the strictly legal and closely comprehensive instrument, which he had always associated with ruined men and falling fortunes hitherto. "I suppose it's a necessary precaution when the mercantile barometer is low. I shall be able to draw for necessary expenses as usual, and all that?"

Mr. Shrood smiled, as if anything to the contrary was altogether too chimerical and beyond human imagination to be considered seriously for one moment.

"My dear sir," he proceeded, "I hope you have never had reason to doubt our readiness to follow your suggestions hitherto. We have unbounded confidence in your management and discretion. As we have reached this point, however, would you mind executing the deed which has been prepared in anticipation of your consent, and concluding this, I confess, slightly unpleasing section of our arrangements while we are agreed on the subject, to which I hope not to be compelled again to recur."

"Not at all," replied Jack, "not at all," feeling like the man at the dentist's, as if the tooth might as well be pulled out now as hereafter.

"Thank you; these things are best carried through at one sitting. Pray excuse me for one moment. Mr. Smith!" Here a junior appeared. "Will you bring in that—a—legal document, for Mr. Redgrave's signature, and a—attend to witness his signature? Your present liability to the bank, Mr. Redgrave," he explained, as the young gentleman disappeared, "amounts to, I think, fifteen thousand pounds in round numbers—that is, fourteen thousand nine hundred and eighty-seven pounds fourteen and ninepence. I think you mentioned forty thousand sheep as the stock, was it not, at present depasturing on the station?"

"Forty-two—some odd hundreds," answered Jack, "but that is near enough."

Here Mr. Smith reappeared, with an imposing-looking piece of parchment, commencing "Know all men by these presents," which was handed to Jack for his entertainment and perusal. Jack glanced at it. Nobody, save a North Briton or a very misanthropical person, ever does read a deed through, that I know of. But Jack knew enough of such matters to pick out heedfully the principal clauses which concerned him. It was like most other compilations of a like nature, and contained, apart from unmeaning repetitions and exasperating surplusage, certain lucid sentences, which Jack understood to mean that he was to pay up the said few thousands at his convenience, or in *default* to yield up Gondaree, with stock thereto attached, to the paternal but irresponsible "money-mill," under the wildly improbable circumstance of his being unable to clear off such advances in years to come—with principal and interest.

"Forty-two thousand sheep, and station, at a pound," said Jack to himself, "leave a considerable margin; so I needn't bother myself. Here goes. It will never be acted upon—that is one comfort."

So the name of John Redgrave was duly appended, and Mr. Smith wrote his name as witness without the least embarrassment. He regarded squatters who required accommodation as patients subject to mild attacks of epidemic disease, which usually gave way to proper medical, that is to say financial, treatment. Occasionally the patient succumbed. That however was not *his* affair. Let them all find it out for themselves.

He had many a time and oft envied the bronzed squatter lounging in on a bright morning, throwing down a cheque and stuffing the five-pound notes carelessly into his waistcoat-pocket. But, young as he was, he had more than once seen a careworn, grizzled man waiting outside the bank parlour, with ill-concealed anxiety for the interview which was to tell him whether or not he went forth a ruined and hopelessly broken man. Nothing could have been more soothing than the manner in which the whole operation of the mortgage had been performed. Still it *was* an operation, and Jack felt a sensation difficult to describe, but tending towards the conviction that he was not quite the same man as he had been previously. He was not in his usual spirits at dinner that evening, though of his two sharers of that well-cooked, yet not extravagant repast, Hautley had ordered it, and Jerningham was by odds the neatest talker then in town. The wine somehow wasn't like last week's. Must have opened a new batch. He had no luck at billiards. He sat moodily in an arm-chair in the smoking-room, and heard not some of the best (and least charitable) things going. He mooned off to bed, out of harmony with existing society.

"What the dickens is up with Redgrave?" asked little Prowler of old Snubham, of the Indian Irregular Force. "He looks as black as thunder, and hasn't a word to say for himself."

"A very fine trait in a man's character," growled Snubham; "half the people one meets jabber everlastingly, Heaven knows. What would be the matter with him? Proposed to some girl, and is afraid she'll accept him. A touch of liver, perhaps. Nothing else *can* happen to a man at the present day, sir."

"Must be a woman, I think; he was awful spoony on Dolly Drosera. He's too rich to want money," said Prowler, with a reverential awe of the squatter proper.

"Humph! don't know—wool's down, I believe. He pays up at loo. Beyond that I have no curiosity. Very ungentlemanlike thing, curiosity. Mornin', Prowler."

IX

"A perfect woman, nobly planned,
To warn, to comfort and command."

—WORDSWORTH

Jack's doubts and misgivings were written upon his open brow for twenty-four hours, but after that period they disappeared like morning mists. He awoke to a healthier tone of feeling, and determined to combat difficulty with renewed vigour and unshaken firmness.

"After all, I have not borrowed more than one good clip, and a little cutting down of the stock will set all right," said he to himself. "Where would Brass, Marsailly, and all these other great guns have been if they had boggled at a few thousands at the beginning? Next year's clip will be something like; and I never heard of anyone but old Exmore that had *two* wool-sheds burned running. He put up a stone and iron edifice then, and told them to see what they could make of that. There was no grass-seed in his country though. Well, there is nothing like a start from town for clearing out the blues. I wonder how fellows ever manage to live there all the year round."

These encouraging reflections occurred to the ingenuous mind of Mr. Redgrave as he was speeding over the first hundred miles of rail which expedite the traveller pleasantly on the road to the Great Desert. *Facilis descensus Averni*—which means that it is very easy to "settle one's self" in life—the "downtrain" being furnished with "palace-cars" of Pullman's patent, and gradients on the most seductive system of sliding scale.

Again the long gray plains. Again the night—one disjointed nightmare, where excessive jolts dislocated the most evil witch-wanderings, multiplying them, like the lower forms of life, by the severance. Then the long, scorching day, the intolerable flies, and lo! Steamboat Point. Gondaree, in all its arid, unrelieved glare and grandeur once more— Mr. M'Nab weighing sheepskins to a carrier, with as much earnestness as if he expected half-a-crown a pound for them. Everything much as usual. Ah Sing in the garden, watering cauliflowers. When Redgrave caught the last glimpse of him as he left for town he was watering cabbages Everything very dry. No relief, no shade. The cottage looked very small: the surroundings stiff and bare. "My eyes are out of focus just now," said Jack to himself. "I must keep quiet till the vision accommodates itself to the landscape; otherwise I shall hurt M'Nab's feelings."

"Well, how are you?" said Jack, heartily, as that person, having despatched his carrier, walked towards him. "You look very thriving, only dry; rather dry, don't you think?"

"Well, we have hardly had a drop of rain since you started. Might be just a shower. But everything is doing capitally. We are rather short-handed; I sent away every soul but the cook, the Chinaman, and four boundary-riders directly you left, and we are now, thanks to the fencing, quite independent of labour till shearing-time."

"How in the world do you get on?" inquired Jack, quite charmed, yet half afraid of M'Nab's sudden eviction.

"Nothing can be simpler. The dogs were well poisoned before the fences were finished. There's no road through the back of the run, thank goodness. We haven't any bother about wells because of Bimbalong. I count every paddock once a month, and that's about all there is to do."

"And who looks after the store?" inquired Jack.

"I do, of course," said M'Nab; "there is very little to give out, you'll mind. Two of the boundary-riders live at home here, and the other two at a hut at Bimbalong. Now you've come there will be hardly enough work to keep us going."

"Four men to forty thousand sheep," moralized Jack. "What would some of the old hands think of that? Oh! the weaners," cried he; "I had forgotten them. How did you manage them, M'Nab?"

"Well, we had a great day's drafting, and put them back in the river paddock. They are all as contented as possible, and as steady as old ewes—thirteen thousand of them."

"There's a trifle of bother saved by that arrangement. What a burden life used to be for the first three months after the weaning flocks were portioned out!"

Jack's spirits were many degrees lighter after this conversation. Certainly there was a heavyish debt—and this millstone of a mortgage hung round "his neck alway" like the albatross in the *Ancient Mariner*; but the compensating economy of the fencing was beginning to work a cure. If one could only tide over the shearing with the present reduced Civil List, what a hole would the clip and the fat sheep make in the confounded "balance debtor!" There is the wool-shed over again, to be sure. What a murder that one should have all those hundredweights of nails, and tons of battens, and acres of flooring, and forests of posts and wall-plates to get all over again! It was very bitter work in Jack's newly-born tendency to economy to have all this outlay added on to the inevitable expenditure of the season.

"As I said before," concluded Jack, rounding off his soliloquy, "I never knew any fellow but Exmoor undergo the ordeal by fire two seasons running, so it's a kind of insurance against the chapter of accidents *this* year."

Jack insensibly returned to his ordinary provincial repose of mind and body. He rode about in the early mornings and cooler evenings, and took his turn to convoy travelling sheep, to officiate at the store, and to relieve the ever-toiling M'Nab in anyway that presented itself. He kept up this kind of thing for a couple of months, and then—the unbroken monotony of the whole round of existence striking him rather suddenly one day—he made up his mind to a slight change. There was a station about fifty miles away, down the river, with the owner of which he had a casual acquaintance; so, *faute d'autre*, he thought he would go and see him.

"You can get on quite as well without me, M'Nab," he said. "I think a small cruise would do me good. I'll go and see Mr. Stangrove. One often gets an idea by going away from home."

"That's true enough," assented M'Nab, "but I doubt yon's the wrong shop for *new* ones. Mr. Stangrove is a good sort of man, I hear everyone say; but he hails from the old red-sandstone period (M'Nab knew Hugh Miller by heart), and has no more idea of a swing-gate than a shearing-machine."

"Well, one will get a notion of how the Australian Pilgrim Fathers managed to get a livelihood, and subdue the salt-bush for their descendants. There must be a flavour of antiquity about it. I will start tomorrow."

After a daylight breakfast, Mr. Redgrave departed, riding old Hassan, and, like a wise man, leading another hackney, with a second saddle, upon which was strapped his valise. "If you want to go anywhere," he was wont to assert, "you want a *few* spare articles of raiment." Sitting in boots and breeches all the evening is unpleasant to the visitor and disrespectful to his entertainers, whether he be what the old-fashioned writers called "travel-stained" in wet weather, or uncomfortably warm in the dry season. If you carry the articles alluded to you need a valise.

A valise is much pleasanter on a spare horse than in front of your own person; and all horses go more cheerily in company, particularly as you can divide the day's journey by alternate patronage of either steed. I think life in a general way passes as pleasantly during a journey *à cheval* as over any other "road of life." Then why make toil of a pleasure? Always take a brace of hacks, O reader, and then—

> *"Over the downs mayst thou scour, nor mind*
> *Whether Horace's mistress be cruel or kind."*

The sun was no great distance above the far unbroken sky-line; the air was pleasantly cool as Jack rode quietly along the level track which led to his outer gate, and down the river. The horses played with their bits, stepping along lightly with elastic footfall. "What a different life," thought he, "from my old one at Marshmead! How full of interest and occupation was everyday as it rose! Neighbours at easy distances; poor old Tunstall to go and poke up whenever John Redgrave failed to suffice for his own entertainment and instruction. Jolly little Hampden, with its picnics and parties, and bench-work, and boat-sailing, and racing, and public meetings, and 'all sorts o' games,' as Mr. Weller said. The bracing climate, the wholesome moral and physical atmosphere, the utter absence of any imp or demon distantly related to the traitor Ennui; and here, such is the melancholy monotony of my daily life that I find myself setting forth with a distinctly pleasurable feeling to visit a man whom I do not know, and very probably shall not like when our acquaintance expands. *Auri sacri fames,*—shall I quote that hackneyed tag? I may as well—the day is long—there is plenty of time and to spare on the Warroo, as Hawkesbury said. Fancy a fellow living this life for a dozen years and *making no money* after all. The picture is too painful. I shall weep over it myself directly—like that arch-humbug Sterne."

About half way to his destination was an inn—hostelry of the period; an ugly slab building covered, as to its roof and verandah, with corrugated iron. There was no trace or hint of garden. It stood as if dropped on the edge of the bare, desolate, sandy plain. It faced the dusty track which did duty as high road; at the back of the slovenly yard was the river—chiefly used as a convenient receptacle for rubbish and broken bottles. A half-score of gaunt, savage-looking pigs lay in the verandah, or stirred the dust and bones in the immediate vicinity of the front entrance. A stout man, in Crimean shirt and tweed trousers, stood in the verandah, smoking, and, far from betraying any "provincial eagerness" at the sight of a stranger, went on smoking coolly until Jack spoke.

"How far is Mr. Stangrove's place?" inquired he.

"What, Juandah?" said the host, in a tone conveying the idea that in ordinary social circles it was on a par, for notoriety, with London or Liverpool. "Well, say thirty mile."

"Do you take the back road, or the one nearest to the river?" further inquired Jack.

"Oh, stick to the river bank," answered the man; "at this time of year it is nearest."

"What in the name of wonder," inquired Jack of himself, as he rode away, "can a man do who lives at such a fragment of Hades *but* drink? He must be a Christian hero, or a philosopher, if he refrain under the utterly maddening conditions of life. Were he one or the other, he probably would not keep the grog-shop which he dignifies with the title of the Mailman's Arms." Of course he drinks—it is written in his dull eye and sodden face—his wife drinks, the barman drinks—the loafer who plays at being groom in the hayless, strawless, cornless stable drinks. The shepherd hands his cheque across the bar—and till every shilling, purchased by a year's work, abstinence, and solitude, disappears, drinks—madly drinks. The miserable, debased aboriginal—camping there for weeks with his squalid wives—drinks, and, perchance, when his wild blood is stirred by vile liquor, murders ere his fit be over. From that den, as from a foul octopus, stretch forth tentacula which fasten only upon human beings. Question them, and hear vain remorse, bitter wrath, agonized despair, sullen apathy—the name of one resistless, unsparing curse—*drink, drink, drink*!

The midday sun was hot. The stage was a fair one; but Jack pushed on, after receiving his information, for half-a-dozen miles further. Then, discovering a green bend, he unsaddled, and, taking the precaution to hobble his nags, lighted his pipe. They rolled and cropped the fresh herbage, while he enjoyed a more satisfactory noontide lounge than the horsehair sofa of Mr. Hoker's best parlour would have afforded, after a doubtful, or perhaps deleterious, repast.

The day was gone when Jack was made aware, by certain signs and hieroglyphics, known to all bushmen, that he was approaching a station. The pasture was closely cropped and bare. Converging tracks of horses, sheep, and cattle obviously trended in one direction. At some distance upon the open plain he could see a shepherd with his flock, slowly moving towards a point of timber more than a mile in advance of his present position. "I shall come upon the paddock fence just inside that timber," he remarked to himself, "and the house will probably be within sight of the slip-rails. It will not be a very large paddock, I will undertake to say."

This turned out to be a correct calculation. He saw the sheep-yard, towards which the flock was heading, as he reached the timber. He descried the paddock fence and the slip-rail in the road; and within sight—as he put up the rails and mustered a couple of temporary pegs, for fear of accidents—was a roomy wooden building surrounded by a garden.

Riding up to the garden gate, he was announced as "Mr. Stranger" by about twenty dogs, who gave the fullest exercise to their lungs, and would doubtless have gone even further had Jack been on foot. A tall, sun-burned man, in an old shooting-coat, appeared upon the verandah, and, making straight through the excited pack, greeted Redgrave warmly.

"Won't you get off and come in? I'll take your horses. (Hold your row, you barking fools!) Oh! it is you, Mr. Redgrave; from Gondaree, I think—met you at Barrabri—very glad to see you; of course you have come to stay? Allow me to take the led horse."

"I think I promised to look you up some day," said Jack. "I took advantage of a lull in station-work and—here I am."

"Very glad indeed you have made your visit out, though I don't know that I have much to show you. But, as we are neighbours, we ought to become acquainted."

The horses were led over to a small but tolerably snug stable, where they were regaled with hay previous to being turned out in the paddock, and then Jack was ushered into the house. Mr. Stangrove was a married man; so much was evident from the first; many traces of the "pug-wuggies, or little people," were apparent; and a girl crossing the yard with a baby in her arms supplied any evidence that might be missing.

"Will you have a glass of grog after your ride?" inquired the host, "or would you like to go to your room?"

Jack preferred the latter, being one of those persons who decline to eat or drink until they are in a comfortable and becoming state of mind and body; holding it to be neither epicurean nor economical to "muddle away appetite" under circumstances which preclude all proper and befitting appreciation.

So Redgrave performed his ablutions, and, having arrayed himself in luxuriously-easy garments and evening shoes, made his way to the sitting-room. He had just concluded "a long, cool drink" when two ladies entered.

"My dear, allow me to introduce Mr. Redgrave—Mrs. Stangrove, Miss Stangrove."

A lady advanced upon the first mention of names and shook hands with the visitor, in a kindly, unaffected manner. She was young, but a certain worn look told of the early trials of matronhood. Her face bore silent witness to the toils of housekeeping, with indifferent servants or none at all; to want of average female society; to a little loneliness, and a great deal of monotony. Such, with few exceptions, is the life of an Australian lady, whose husband lives in the far interior, in the *real* bush. Her companion, who contented herself with a searching look and a formal bow, was "in virgin prime and May of womanhood"—and a most fair prime and sweet May it was. Her features were regular, her mouth delicate and refined, with a certain firmness about the chin, and the *mutine* expression about the upper lip, which savoured of declaration of war upon just pretext. She had that air and expression which at once suggest the idea of interest in unravelling the character. Jack shook hands with himself when he thought of how he had persevered after the traitorous idea had entered his head that after all it was no use going, Mr. Stangrove wouldn't be glad to see him, or care a rush about the matter.

The evening meal was now announced, which circumstance afforded Jack considerable satisfaction. He had ridden rather more than fifty miles, and, whereas his horses had not done so badly in the long grass of the "bend," our traveller's lunch had been limited to a pipe of "Pacific Mixture." All the same, while the preparations for tea were proceeding he took a careful and accurate survey of his younger feminine neighbour.

Maud Stangrove was somewhat out of the ordinary run of girls in appearance, as she certainly was in character. Her features were regular, with a complexion clear and delicate to a degree unusual in a southern land. Her mouth, perhaps, denoted a shade more firmness than the ideal princess is supposed to require. But it was redeemed by the frank, though not invariable, smile which, disclosing a set of extremely white and regular teeth, gave an expression of softness and humour which was singularly winning. The eyes were darkest hazel, faintly toned with gray. They were remarkable as a feature; and those on whom they had shone—

in love or war—rarely forgot their gaze; they were clear and shining; but this is to say little; such are the everyday charms of that beauty which is in woman but another name for youth. Maud's eyes had the peculiar quality of developing fresh aspects and hidden mysteries of expression as they fell on you—calm, clear, starlike, but fathomless, glowing ever, and with hidden, smouldering fire. She was dressed plainly, but in such taste as betokened reference to a milliner remote from the locality. Rather, but very slightly, above middle height in her figure, there was an absence of angularity which gave promise of eventual roundness of contour—perhaps even too pronounced. But now, in the flower-time of early womanhood, she moved with the unstudied ease of those forest creatures in whom one notices a world of latent force.

Such was the apparition which burst upon the senses of Mr. Redgrave.

"Average neighbours!" said he to himself. "Who ever expected this—a vision of no end of fear and interest? This is a girl fit for anyone to make love to or to quarrel with, as the case might be. I think the latter recreation would be the easier. And yet I don't know."

"I don't think you have ever been so far 'down the river,' as the people call it, before?" said Mrs. Stangrove.

"I'm afraid I have not been a very good neighbour," said Jack, beginning to feel contrite at the *de haut en bas* treatment of the general population of the Warroo, in accordance with which he had devoted himself to unrelieved work at Gondaree, and looked upon social intercourse as completely out of the question. "But the fact is, that I have been very hard at work up to this time. Now the fences are up I hope to have a little leisure."

Here Jack paused, as if he had borne up, like another Atlas, the weight of the Gondaree world upon those shapely shoulders of his.

Miss Stangrove looked at him with an expression which did not imply total conviction.

"We have heard of all your wonders and miracles, haven't we, Jane? I don't know what we should have done in the wilderness here without the Gondaree news."

"I was not aware that I was so happy as to furnish interesting incidents for the country generally," answered Jack; "but it would have given me fresh life if I had only thought that Mrs. and Miss Stangrove were sympathetical with my progress."

"You would have been rather flattered, then," said Stangrove, who was a downright sort of personage, "if you had heard the lamentations of these ladies over your woolshed—indeed, Maud said that—"

"Come, Mark," said Miss Stangrove, eagerly, and with the very becoming improvement of a sudden blush, "we don't need your clumsy version of all our talk for the last year. Nobody ever does anything upon this antediluvian stream from one century to another, and of course Jane and I felt grieved that a spirited reformer like Mr. Redgrave should meet with so heavy a loss—didn't we, Jane?"

"Of course we did, my dear," said that matron, placidly; "and Mark, too, he said the wicked men who did it ought to be hanged, and that Judge Lynch was a very useful institution. He was quite ferocious."

"Thanks very many; I am sure I feel deeply grateful. I had no idea I had so many well-wishers," quoth Jack, casting his eyes in the direction of Miss Maud. "It comforts one under affliction and—all that, you know."

"How you must look down upon us, with our shepherds and old-world ways," said Maud. "You come from Victoria, do you not, Mr. Redgrave? We Sydney people believe that you are all Yankees down there, and wear bowie-knives and guns, and calculate, and so on."

"Really, Miss Stangrove," pleaded Jack, "you are indicting me upon several charges at once; which am I to answer? I don't look very supercilious, do I? though I admit hailing from Victoria, which is chiefly peopled by persons of British birth, whatever may be the prevailing impression."

"Well, you will have an opportunity of discussing the matter—the shepherds, I mean—with my brother, who is a strong conservative. I give you leave to convert him, if you can. We have hitherto found it impossible, haven't we, Mark?"

"Mark has generally good reasons for his opinions," said the loyal wife, looking approvingly at her lord and master—who, indeed, was very like a man who could hold his own in any species of encounter. "But suppose we have a little music—you might play *La Bouquetière*."

"The piano is not so wofully out of tune as might be expected," asserted Maud, as she sat down comfortably to her work, all things being arranged by Jack, who was passionately fond of music—a good deal of which, as of other abstractions, he had in his soul.

"Far from it," said he, as the shower of delicate notes which make up this loveliest of airy musical trifles fell on his ear like a melody of *le temps perdu*.

Jack had all his life been extremely susceptible to the charm of music. He had a good ear, and his taste, naturally correct, had been rather unusually well cultivated. With him the effect of harmony was to bring to the surface, and develop as by a spell, all the best, the noblest, the most exalted portions of his character. Any woman who played or sang with power exercised a species of fascination over him, assuming her personal endowments to be up to his standard. When Miss Stangrove, after passing lightly over *capriccias* of Chopin and Liszt, after a fashion which showed very unusual execution, commenced in deference to his repeated requests to sing *When Sparrows Build*, and one or two other special favourites, in *such* a mezzo-soprano! he was surprised, charmed, subjugated—with astonishing celerity.

However, the evenings of summer, commencing necessarily late, come to an end rather prematurely if we are very pleasantly engaged. So Jack thought when Mr. Stangrove looked at his watch, and opined that Jack after his ride would be glad to retire.

Jack was by no means glad, but of course assented blandly, and the two ladies sailed off.

"Shall we have a pipe in the verandah before we turn in?" asked his host. "You smoke, I suppose? We can open this window and leave the glasses on the table here within easy reach."

Taking up his position upon a Cingalese cane-chair on the broad verandah, and lighting his pipe simultaneously with his host, Jack leaned back and enjoyed the wondrous beauty of the night.

The cottage, unlike the Mailman's Arms, fronted the river, towards which a neatly-kept garden sloped, ending in a grassy bank.

"My sister belongs to the advanced party of reform, Mr. Redgrave, as you will have observed," said his entertainer. "She and I have numerous fights on the subject."

"I am proud to have such an ally," said Jack; "but, seriously, I wonder you have not been converted. Surely the profits and advantages of fencing are sufficiently patent."

"You must bear with me, my dear sir, as a very staunch conservative," answered his host, smoking serenely, and speaking with his usual calm deliberation. "There is something, I think much, to be said on the other side."

"I feel really anxious to hear your arguments," said Jack. "I fancied that beyond what the shepherds always say—that sheep can't do well or enjoy life without a bad-tempered old man and a barking dog at their tails—the brief against fencing was exhausted."

"I do not take upon myself to assert," said Stangrove, "that my reasons ought to govern persons whose circumstances differ from my own. But I find them sufficient for me for the present. I reserve the privilege of altering them upon cause shown. And the reasons are—First of all, that I could not enter into the speculation, for such it would be, of fencing my run without going into debt—a thing I abhor under *any* circumstances. Secondly, because the seasons in Australia are exceedingly changeable, as I have had good cause to know. And, thirdly, because the prices of stock are as fluctuating and irregular, occasionally, as the seasons."

"Granted all these, how can there be two opinions about an outlay which is repaid within two years, which is more productive in bad seasons than in good ones, and which dispenses with three-fourths of the labour required for an ordinary sheep-station?"

"I have no reason to doubt what you say," persisted Stangrove, "but suppose we defer the rest of the argument until we have had a look at the run and stock together. I can explain my meaning more fully on my own beat. I dare say you will sleep tolerably after your ride."

X

"Absence of occupation is not rest."

—Cowper

J ack went to bed with a kind of general idea of getting up in the morning early and looking round the establishment. But, like the knight who was to be at the postern gate at dawn, he failed to keep the self-made engagement; and for the same reason he slept so soundly that the sun was tolerably high when he awoke, and he had barely time for a swim in the river, and a complete toilet, before the breakfast-bell rang.

In spite of the baseless superstition that "there is nothing like one's own bed," and so on, it is notorious that all men not confirmed valetudinarians sleep far more satisfactorily away from home. For, consider, one is comparatively freed from the dire demon, Responsibility, you doze off tranquilly into the charmed realm of dreamland—with "nothing on your mind." Perfectly indifferent is it to you, in the house of a congenial friend or affable stranger, whether domestic disorganization of the most frightful nature is smouldering insidiously or hurrying to a climax. The cook may be going next week, the housemaid may have contracted a clandestine marriage. Your host may be sternly revolving plans of retrenchment, and may have determined to abandon light wines, and to limit his consumption to table-beer and alcohol. But nothing of this is revealed to you; nor would it greatly concern you if it was. For the limited term of your visit, the hospitality is free, smooth, and spontaneous. Atra Cura, if she does accidentally drop in by mistake, is a courteous *grande dame*, rather plainly attired in genteel mourning, but perfect in manner. Not a violent, unreserved shrew as she can be when quite "at home." A visit is in most instances, therefore, a respite and a truce. The parade, the review, the skirmish are for a time impossible; so the "tired soldier" enjoys the calm, unbroken repose in his own tent so rarely tasted.

The weather was hot, and there did not appear to be any likelihood of a change. Nevertheless, Jack could not but acknowledge that no detail had been omitted to insure the highest amount of comfort attainable in such a climate. The butter was cooled, the coffee perfect, the eggs, the honey, the inevitable chop, excellent of their kind. Everything bore traces of that thorough supervision which is never found in a household under male direction. Jack thought Miss Stangrove, charmingly neat and fresh in her morning attire, would have added piquancy to a much more homely meal.

"Just in time, Mr. Redgrave," said that young lady; "we were uncertain whether you were not accustomed to be aroused by a gong. Bells are very old-fashioned, we know."

"I doubt whether anything would have awakened me an hour since. I am a reasonably early riser generally; but the ride and the extreme comfort of my bedroom led to a little laziness. But where's Stangrove?"

"I blush to say he went off early to count a flock of sheep," said Miss Stangrove, with assumed regret. "You must accustom yourself to our aboriginal ways for a time. But is it not dreadful to think of? I hope you extracted a total recantation from him last night."

"We only made a commencement of the game last night," said Jack. "Your brother advanced a pawn or two, but we agreed to defer the grand attack until after a ride round the run, which I believe takes place today."

"I am afraid you will have a hot ride; but I don't pity you for that. Anything is better than staying indoors day after day, week after week, as we wretched women have to do. You might tell Mark if he sees my horse to have her brought in. I feel as if I should like a scamper. Oh! here he comes to answer for himself. Well, Mark, how many killed, wounded, and missing?"

"Good morning, Mr. Redgrave," said Stangrove, smiling rather lugubriously at his sister's pleasantry. "I am afraid you are just in time to remark on one of the weak points of my management. A shepherd came before daylight to say that his flock had been lost since the day before. I have been hunting for them these five hours."

"And have you brought any home?" inquired Mrs. Stangrove.

"None at all," he answered.

"Did you see any?" persisted the lady, who seemed rather of an anxious disposition.

"Yes—ten."

"And why didn't you bring them?" pursued the chatelaine, whose earnestness was in strong contrast with her sister's nonchalance.

"Because they were dead," replied Stangrove, laconically; "and now, my dear, please to give me some tea. 'Sufficient for the day'—and so on."

"Accidents will happen," interposed Jack, politely. "It is like more important calamities and crimes, a matter of average."

"Just so," said Stangrove, gratefully; "and though I can't help worrying myself at a small loss, such as this, I know that the annual expense from this cause varies very little."

"There were wolves in Arcadia, were not there?" demanded the young lady. "They ate a shepherd now and then, I suppose. If the dingoes would look upon it in that light, what a joy it would be, eh?"

"I could cheerfully see them battening upon the carcase of that lazy ruffian Strawler," he very vengefully made answer.

"My love!" said Mrs. Stangrove, mildly, "the children will be in directly—would you mind reading prayers directly you finish?"

"Well—ahem," said the bereaved proprietor, rather doubtfully; "perhaps you might as well read this morning, Mr. Redgrave and I have a long way to go—what are you laughing at, Maud, you naughty girl?"

"Don't forget to have old Mameluke got in for me, Mark, and tomorrow I will go sheep-hunting with you myself, if little Bopeep continues unsuccessful, and in an unchristian state of mind, unable to say his prayers. I didn't think the fencing question involved so high a moral gain before."

Breakfast over, two fresh hacks were brought up (Stangrove was a great horse-breeder, and Jack's eye had been offended as he rode up with troops of mares and foals), and forth they fared for a day on the run, and a contingent search for the lost flock.

Stangrove's run was about the same size as Gondaree, but, save the cottages and buildings of the homestead, there were no "improvements" of any kind other than the shepherds' huts. For stock, he had seventeen or eighteen thousand sheep, a herd of cattle, and two or three hundred horses. These last were within their boundaries in a general way, but were occasionally outside of these merely moral frontiers. So also the neighbouring stock wandered at will inside of the said imaginary subdivisions.

"You see," commenced Stangrove, in explanation, when they were fairly out on the plain, "that I came into possession here some ten years past, just after I had left school. My poor old governor, who was rather a scientific literary character, lived at one of those small comfortable estates near town, where a man can spend lots of money, but can't by any possibility make a shilling. Decent people, in those days, would as soon have gone out to spend a few years with Livingstone as have come to live permanently on the Warroo. We had a surly old overseer, of the old sort, who managed a little and robbed a great deal. When I came here, after the poor old governor died, you never saw such a place as it was."

"I can partly imagine," Jack said.

"Well, I worked hard, and lived like a black fellow for a few years, got the property out of debt, improved the stock, and here we are. I get a reasonable price for my wool, I sell a draft of cattle now and then, and some horses, and am increasing the stock slowly, and putting by something every year."

"No doubt you are," said Jack; "but here you have to live and keep your wife and family in this out-of-the-way place; and at the present rate of progress it may be years before you can make money or sell out profitably. Why not concentrate all the work and self-denial into three or four years—sell out, and enjoy life?"

"A tempting picture—but consider the risk. Debt always means danger; and why should I incur that danger? At present I don't owe a shilling, and call no man master. As for happiness, I am not so miserable now (if I could only find those sheep). I have a day's work to do everyday, or to decline, if I see fit; and I would just as soon be here—a place endeared to me by old association—as anywhere else."

"But your family?" asked Jack, rather insincerely, as he was thinking of Maud chiefly, and the stupendous sacrifice of *her* life. "But," he said, "your children are growing up."

"Yes, but only *growing* up. By the time they need masters and better schooling I shall be a little better off. Some change will probably take place—stock will rise—or it will rain for two or three years without stopping, as is periodically probable in New South Wales; and then I shall sell, go back to the paternal acres in the county of Cumberland, and grow prize shorthorns and gigantic cucumbers, and practise all the devices by which an idle man cheats himself into the belief that he is happy."

"By which time you will have lost most of the zest for the choicer pleasures of life."

"Even so—but I am a great believer in the 'in that state of life' portion of the catechism. I was placed and appointed here, and hold myself responsible for the safety and gradual increase of my 'one talent.' Maud, too, has a share. I am compelled to be a stern guardian in her interest."

"Well," returned Jack (after his companion had opened his mind, as men often do in the bush to a chance acquaintance—so rare ofttimes is the luxury of congeniality), "I am not sure that you are altogether wrong.

It squares with your temperament. Mine is altogether opposed to such views. I think twenty years on the Warroo, with the certainty of a plum and a baronetcy at the end, would kill me as surely as sunstroke. Isn't that sheep?"

As Jack propounded this grammatically doubtful query, he directed Stangrove's attention to a long light-coloured line at a distance. It was soon evident that it was sheep coming towards them. To Stangrove's great relief, they proved to be the missing flock, in charge of one of the volunteers sent out in all directions, if only they might perchance manage to drop across them. Upon being counted they were only fifteen short. Ten being accounted for by the domestic declaration of Mr. Stangrove, the other five were left to take their chance, and the flock sent back to a new shepherd, *vice* Strawler superseded.

Stangrove brightened up considerably after this recovery of his doubtfully-situated property. Byron asserts "a sullen son, a dog ill, a favourite horse fallen lame just as he's mounted," to be "trifles in themselves," but adds, "and yet I've rarely seen the man they didn't vex." So with lost sheep. You must lose a dozen or twenty—you hardly lose more than fifty, say from ten to five-and-twenty pounds—not a sum to turn the scale of ruin by any means. Yet, from the time that the announcement is made of "sheep away" until they are safely counted and yarded, rarely does the face of the proprietor relax its expression of weighty resolve and grave foreboding.

Jack found by his companion's avowal that at least one person besides Bertie Tunstall held the same unprogressive but eminently safe opinions. "Here's a man," said Jack, "with a worse climate, far less recreation and variety than I had, and see how he sticks to his fight! However, I *am* differently constituted—there's no denying it. If Stangrove's father had not been somewhat of the same kidney, he and I would have had little chance of discussing our theories on the banks of the Warroo."

"And so you won't be tempted into fencing?" demanded Jack, returning to the charge.

"Not just at present," rejoined Stangrove. "I do not say but that if I find myself surrounded by fencing neighbours, willing to share the expense and so on, in a few more years I may give in. But I am a firm believer in the Safe. I am now in a position of absolute security, and I intend to continue in it."

"But suppose bad seasons come?"

"Let them! I have no bills to meet. I can weather them again as I have done before, when on this very station we had to boil down our meat to a kind of soup; it was too poor to eat otherwise. We outlived that. Please God, we shall do so again."

"I suppose you had terrible losses?"

"You may say that; if another season came like it, the country would be 'a valley of dry bones,' literally. But even if I lost all my increase for a year, and a proportion of my old stock, it would only shake me, not break me. A man who is in debt it cooks altogether—that is the difference."

"Well, let us hope that such times won't come again," said Jack, beginning to be unpleasantly affected by the idea of an interview with Mr. Shrood, in which he should be compelled to inform him that the season had been fatal to his whole crop of lambs, and the greater part of his aged ewes. "Everyone says the seasons have changed, and that the climate is more moist than it used to be."

"I am not so sure of that," said his host, who was not prone to take much heed of "what everybody said." "I see no very precise data upon which to found such an assertion. *What has been may be again.* We shall have another dry season within the next five years, as sure as my name is Mark Stangrove. What do you think of those horses? That is rather a fancy mob. I see Maud's horse Mameluke among them. We must run them in."

"How do you reconcile it to your conscience to keep such unprofitable wretches as horses?" inquired Jack, "eating the grass of sheep and cattle, and being totally unsaleable themselves, unfit to eat, and hardly worth boiling down."

"I am grieved to appear so old-fashioned and ignorant," said Mark, "but I have a sentiment about these horses, and really they don't pay so badly. They are the direct descendants, now numbered by hundreds, of an old family stud. They cost nothing in the way of labour; they need no shepherd or stockman: they are simply branded up every year. You couldn't drive them off the run if you tried. And every now and then there springs up a demand, and I clear a lot of them off. It is all found money, and it tells up."

"Meanwhile, the grass they eat would feed ten thousand sheep."

"That is perfectly true; but of course I make no scruple of putting the sheep on their favourite haunts when hard up. Horses, you see, can pick up a living anywhere. Besides, I have always remarked that each of the great divisions of stock has its turn once or twice in a decade, if not oftener. You have only, therefore, to wait, and you get your 'pull.' My next 'pull' with the stud will be when the Indian horse market has to be supplied by us, as it must some day."

"You seem a good hand at waiting," said Jack. "I don't know but that your philosophy is sound. I can't put faith in it however."

"Everything comes to him who waits, as the French adage goes," said Stangrove. "I have always found it tolerably correct. However here we are at home. So we'll put this lot into the yard, and I'll lead up the old horse with a spare rein. We must have a ride out to Murdering Lake tomorrow; it's our show bit of scenery."

"Another eventful day over, Mr. Redgrave," said Maud, as they met at the tea-table. "Yesterday the sheep were lost; today the sheep are found. So passes our life on the Warroo."

"You're an ungrateful, naughty girl, Maud," said Mrs. Stangrove. "Think how relieved poor Mark must be after all his hard work and anxiety. Suppose he had lost a hundred."

"I feel tempted to wish sometimes that everyone of the ineffably stupid woolly creatures *were* lost for good and all, if it would only lead to our going 'off the run' and having to live somewhere else. Only I suppose they are our living, besides working up into delaines and merinos—so I ought not to despise them. But it's the *life* I despise—shepherd, shearer, stockman—day after day, year after year. These, with rare exceptions (here she made a mock respectful bow to Jack), are the only people we see, or shall ever see, till we are gray."

"You are rather intolerant of a country life, Miss Stangrove," said Jack. "I always thought that ladies had domestic duties and—and so on—which filled up the vacuum, with a daily routine of small but necessary employments."

"Which means that we can sew all day, or mend stockings, weigh out plums, currants, and sugar for the puddings—and that this, with a little nursing sick children, pastry-making, gardening, and *very* judicious reading, ought to fill up our time, and make us peacefully happy."

"And why should it not?" inquired Mark, looking earnestly at his sister, as if the subject was an old one of debate between them. "How can a woman be better employed than in the duties you sneer at?"

"Do you really suppose," said Maud, leaning forward and looking straight into his face with her lustrous eyes, in which the opaline gleam began to glow and sparkle, "that women do not wish, like men, to see the world, of which they have only dreamed—to mix a little change and adventure with the skim-milk of their lives—before they calm down into the stagnation of middle age or matrimony?"

"I won't say what I suppose about women, Maud," rejoined her brother. "Somethings I know about them, and somethings I don't know. But, believe me, those women do best in the long run who neither thirst nor long for pleasures not afforded to them by the circumstances of their lives. If what they desire should come, well and good. If not, they act a more womanly and Christian part in waiting with humility till the alteration arrives."

"What do you say, Mr. Redgrave?" asked the unconvinced damsel. "Is it wrong for the caged bird to droop and pine, or ought it to turn a tiny wheel and pull up a tiny pail of nothing contentedly all its days, unmindful of the gay greenwood and the shady brook; or, if it beat its breast against the wires, and lie dead when the captor comes with seed and water, is it to be mourned over or cast forth in scorn?"

"'Pon my word," answered Jack, helplessly, rather overawed by the strong feeling and earnest manner of the girl, and much "demoralized" by those wonderful eyes of hers, "I hardly feel able to decide. I'm a great lover of adventure and change and all that kind of thing *myself*; can't live without it. But for ladies, somehow, I really—a—feel inclined to agree with your brother. Sphere of home—and—all that, you know."

"Sphere of humbug!" answered she, with all the sincerity of contempt in her voice. "You men stick together in advocating all kinds of intolerable dreariness and nonsensical treadmill work because you think it good for women! You would be ashamed to apply such reasoning to anything bearing on your own occupations. But I will not say another word on the subject; it always raises my temper, and *that* is not permitted to our sex, I know. Did you see my dear old Mameluke today, Mark?"

"Yes, and he's now in the stable."

"Oh, thanks; we must have a gallop tomorrow and show Mr. Redgrave our solitary landscape. That will be one ripple on the Dead Sea."

Life seemed capable of gayer aspects, even upon the Warroo, as next morning three residents of that far region rode lightly along the prairie trail. The day was cool and breezy; a great wind had come roaring up from the south the evening before, crashing through the far woods and audible in mighty tones for many a mile before it stirred the streamers of the couba trees, as they all sat under the verandah in the sultry night. Then the glorious coolness of the sea-breeze, almost the savour of the salt sea-foam and of the dancing wavelets, smote upon their revived senses. Hence, this day was cool, bracing, with a clear sky and a sighing breeze. Jack was young, and extremely susceptible. Maud Stangrove was a peerless horsewoman, and as she caused Mameluke, a noble old fleabitten gray, descendant of Satellite, to plunge and caracole, every movement of her supple figure, as she swayed easily to each playful bound, completed the sum of his admiration and submission.

"Oh, what a day it is!" said she. "Why don't we have such weather more often? I feel like that boy in *Nick of the Woods*, when he jumps on his horse to ride after the travellers whom the Indians are tracking, and who shouts out a war-whoop from pure glee and high spirits. 'Wagh! wagh! wagh! wagh!' Don't you remember it, Mr. Redgrave?"

"Oh yes, quite well." Jack had read nearly all the novels in the world, and, if any good could have been done by a competitive examination in light reading, would have come out senior wrangler. "*Nick of the Woods* was very powerfully written—that is, it was a good book; so was the *Hawks of Hawk Hollow*. Dick Bruce was the boy's name."

"Of course. I see you know all about him, and Big Tom Bruce is the one that was shot, and didn't tell them that he had a handful of slugs in his breast till after the Indian town is taken, and then he falls down, dying. Grand fellow, is not he? Nothing of that sort in our wretched country, is there?"

"We had a little fighting at that Murdering Lake we are going to," said Mark. "Nothing very wonderful. But my horse was speared under me, and *he* remembered it for the rest of his life. Red Bob *was* killed; however, as he said before he died, it wasn't 'twenty to one, or anything near it.' He had shot scores of blacks, if his own and others' tales were true."

"And why were you engaged in your small war, Master Mark?" demanded Maud. "It's all very well to talk about Indians, and so on, but what had these miserable natives done to you?"

"They were not so miserable in those days," said her brother; "this tribe was strong and numerous. I would have shirked it if possible; but they speared a lot of the cattle and one of the men. We had to fight or give them up the run."

"The old story of Christianity and civilization? However I know *you* would not have hurt a hair of their red-ochred locks if you could have avoided it. Indeed, I wonder you kept your own scalp safe in those days. The most simple savage might have circumvented you, I'm sure, you good, easy-going, unsuspicious, conscientious old goose that you are."

Here another expression, which Jack preferred much to those more animated glances which opposition had called forth, came over her features; as she gazed at her brother a soft light seemed gradually to arise and overspread her whole countenance, till her eyes rested with an expression of deep unconscious tenderness upon the bronzed, calm face of Mark Stangrove. "I wonder if anything in the whole world could lead to her looking at me like that?" thought Jack.

"This is the place. 'Stand still, my steed,'" quoted Maud, as she reined up Mameluke upon a pine-crested sand-hill, after a couple of hours' riding. "There you can just see the water of the lake. Isn't it a pretty place? *The* pretty place, I should say, as it is the only bit with the slightest pretension upon the whole dusky green and glaring red patch of desert which we call our run."

It was, in its way, assuredly a pretty place. The waters were clear, and had the hue of the undimmed azure, as they gently lapped against the grassy banks. Around was a fringe of dwarf eucalypti, more spreading and umbrageous than their congeners are apt to be. On the further side was a low sand-hill with a thicker covering of shrubs. A drove of cattle were feeding near; a troop of half-wild horses had dashed off at their approach, and were rapidly receding in a long, swaying line in the distance. A blue crane, the Australian heron, flew with a harsh cry from the shallows, and sailed onward with stately flight.

"Oh for a falcon to throw off!" cried Maud, whose spirits seemed quite irrepressible. "Why cannot I be a young lady of the feudal times, and have a hawk, with silken jesses, and a page, and a castle, and all that? Surely this *is* the stupidest, most prosaic country in the world. One would have thought that in a savage land like this they would have devoted themselves to every kind of sport, whereas I firmly believe one would have more chance of hunting, shooting, or fishing in Cheapside. Why did I ever come here?" she pursued in a voice of mock lamentation.

"Because you were born here, you naughty girl," said Mark; "are you not ashamed to be always running down your native country? Don't I see a fire on the far point?"

They rode round the border of the lake, scaring the plover and the wild fowl which swam or flew in large flocks in the shallows. When they reached the spot where the small cape formed by the sand advanced boldly into the waters of the lake at the eastern side, they observed that the fire appertained to a small camp of blacks. Riding close up, the unmoved countenance of "old man Jack" appeared with his two aged wives, while at a little distance, superintending the boiling of certain fish, was the girl Wildduck. She turned to them with an expression of unaffected pleasure, and, rushing up to Miss Stangrove, greeted her with the most demonstrative marks of affection. Suddenly beholding Redgrave, she looked rather surprised; then, bestowing a searching look of inquiry upon him, she made her usual half-shy, half-arch, salutation.

"So Wildduck is a *protégée* of yours, Miss Stangrove," said Jack; "I had no idea she had such distinguished patronage."

"Maud is a bit of a missionary in her way," said Mark; "though perhaps you might not think it. Many a good hour she has wasted over the runaway scamp of a gin, and a little rascal of a black boy we had."

"Poor things!" said Maud, with quite a different tone from her ordinary badinage. "They have souls, and why should one not try to do them a little good! I am very fond of this Wildduck, as she is called, though Kalingeree is her real name. I remember her quite a little girl. Isn't she a pretty creature?—not like gins generally are."

"She is wonderfully good-looking," said Jack; "I thought so the first time I saw her—when she was galloping after a lot of horses."

"I am afraid her stock-keeping propensities have led her into bad company," said Maud; "and yet it is but a natural passion for the chase in the nearest approach the bush affords. I can't help feeling a deep interest in her. You wouldn't believe how clever she is."

"She looks to me very much thinner than she used to be," said Mark. "How large her eyes seem, and so bright. I'm afraid she will die young, like her mother."

"She has been ill, I can see," said Maud, as the girl coughed, and then placed her hand upon her chest, with a gesture of pain. "What has been the matter with you, Wildduck?"

"Got drunk, Miss Maudie; lie out in the rain," said the girl, who was as realistic as one of—let us say—Rhoda Broughton's heroines.

"Oh, Wildduck!" said her instructress; "how *could* you get tipsy again, after all I said to you?"

"Tipsy!" said the child of nature, with a twinkle of wicked mirth in her large bright eye—"tipsy! *me likum tipsy!*"

Mark and his guest were totally unable to retain their gravity at this unexpected answer to Miss Stangrove's appeal, though Jack composed his countenance with great rapidity as he noticed a deeply-pained look in Maud's face, and something like a tear, as she hastily turned away.

ROLF BOLDREWOOD

"Are the old miamis there still, Wildduck?" asked Mark, by way of turning the subject.

"Where you shoot black fellow, long ago?" asked she. "By gum, you peppered 'em that one day. You kill 'em one—two—Misser Stangrove."

"No, I think not, Wildduck. I fired my gun all about. Don't think I killed anybody. Black fellow spear Red Bob that day."

"Aha!" said the girl, her face suddenly changing to an expression of passion. "Serve him right, the murdering dog. He kill poor black fellows for nothing; shoot gins, too, and picaninnies; ask old man Jack."

Here she said a few words rapidly in her own language to the old man. The effect was instantaneous. He sprang up—he seized his spear—his eyes suddenly assumed a fixed and stony stare—with raised head he strode forward with all the lightness and activity of youth. He muttered one name repeatedly. Then his expression changed to one of horrible exultation.

"I believe old man Jack was there," said Mark. "Perhaps he threw the spear that hit me."

"Dono," said Wildduck; "might ha' been. He'd have done it quick if he had, I know that."

A spring cart with luncheon had been sent on at an early hour, and commanded to camp close by the deserted miamis, which had never been inhabited since the battle. Leaving their sable friends, with an invitation to come up and receive the fragments, they rode over to the spot indicated.

"Give me the hobbles," said Mark to the lad who drove the spring cart. "You can lay the cloth and set the lunch."

XI

"The Phantom Knight, his glory fled,
Mourns o'er the fields he heaped with dead."

—Scott

J ack had the privilege of lifting Maud from her horse, and then their three nags were unsaddled and hobbled. Rejoicing in this "constitutional freedom," they availed themselves of it to the extent of drinking of the lake, rolling in the sand, and cropping with relish the long grass which only grew on the lake-side.

"Here is the very spot—how strange it seems!" said Mark, "that we should be drinking bottled ale and eating *pâtés de foie gras* just where spears were flying and guns volleying. It was night, however, when we made our charge. We had been tracking all day, and were guided by their fires latterly."

"Did they make much of a fight?" asked Jack.

"They were plucky enough for a while. Our party had a few nasty wounds. They had some advantage in throwing their spears, as they were close, and we could not see them as well as they saw us. Poor old Bob! the spear that killed him was a long slender one. It went nearly through him. They took to the lake at last."

"And have they never inhabited these miamis since?" asked Maud.

"Never, from that day to this. Blacks are very superstitious. They believe in all kinds of demons and spirits. You ask Wildduck when she comes up."

They walked over the "dark and bloody ground" when the repast was over. There were the ruined wigwams just as their occupants had fled from them at the first volley of their white foes, nearly a generation since. Marks of haste were apparent. The wooden buckets used for water, and scooped from the bole of a tree, a boomerang or two, a broken spear, mouldered away together.

"The situation," said Jack, "is not without a tinge of romance. This isn't particularly like Highland scenery; and blacks always return and carry off their dead, if possible; otherwise Sir Walter's lines might stand fairly descriptive—

"A dreary glen—
Where scattered lay the bones of men,
In some forgotten battle slain,
And bleached by drifting wind and rain."

"It must be a terrible thing in a deed like this not to be *quite* certain whether one was in the right or not. Very likely some of those buccaneers of stockmen provoked this tribe, if you only knew it, Mark."

"Perhaps they did, my dear—more than likely. But we had only plain facts to go upon. They were killing our cattle and servants. We did not declare war. It was the other way. Injustice may have been done, but my conscience is clear."

"There comes old man Jack, and Mrs. old man Jack, collectively," said Redgrave. "Let us hear what they say about it."

Slowly, and with sad countenances, the little band approached, and sat down at a short distance from the luncheon. They were regaled with the delicacies of civilization. Maud administered port wine to Wildduck, and, guardedly, to old Nannie. The others declined the juice of the grape, but partook freely of the eatables.

"Now, then, Wildduck," said Redgrave, "tell us anything you know about this battle. Your people never lived here since?"

"Never, take my oath," said Wildduck, "never no more—too many wandings (demons). One black fellow sleep there one night, years ago; he frighten to death—close up. He tell me—"

"What did he tell you, Wildduck?" said Maud.

"Well," began the girl, sitting down on her heels in the soft grass, "he was out after cattle and tracked 'em here at sundown. So he says, 'I'll camp at the old miamis, blest if I don't. Baal me frighten,' he say. Well, he lie down long a that middle big one miami and go fast asleep. In the middle of the night he wake up. *All the place was full of blacks.* Plenty—plenty," spreading out both her hands. "They ran about with spears, and womrahs, and heilaman. Then he saw white fellows, and fire came out of their guns. Very dark night. Then a white fellow, big man with red hair, fire twice— clear light shine, and he saw a tall black fellow send spear right through him. He say," said the girl, lowering her voice, "just like old man Jack."

"This *is* something like the legitimate drama, Miss Stangrove," said Jack. "You see there is more good, solid tragedy in Australian life than you fancied."

"Go on, Wildduck," said she. "What a strange scene—only to imagine! What happened then?"

"When white fellow fall down, the tall black fellow give a great jump, and shout out, only he hear nothing. Then all the blacks make straight into the lake. He look again—all gone—he hear 'possum, night-owl—that's all."

"And do you believe he saw anything *really*, Wildduck? Come now, tell the truth," cross-examined Mark.

"Well, Charley, big one, frighten; I see that myself. But he took a bottle from the Mailman's Arms, and he'd never wait till he saw the bottom—I know that. Here come old man Jack; he look very queer, too."

The old savage had begun to walk up towards the spot where they had gathered rather closely together in the interest of Wildduck's legend. There was, as she had said, something strange in his appearance.

He walked in a slow and stately manner; he held himself unusually erect. From time to time he glanced at the old encampment, then at the lake. His face lit up with the fire of strong passion, and then he would mutter to himself, as if recalling the past.

"Ask him what he is thinking about, Wildduck," said Mark.

The girl spoke a few words to the old man. It was the philter that renews youth, the memory of the passionate past. He stalked forward with the gait of a warrior. Shaking off the fetters of age, he trod lightly upon the well-known scene of conflict, with upraised head and lifted hand. Words issued from his lips with a fiery energy, such as none present had ever witnessed in him.

"He say," commenced Wildduck, "this the place where his tribe fight the white man, long time ago. Misser Stangrove young feller then. Many black fellow shot—so many—so many (here she spread out her open palms). By and by all run into lake."

"Does he remember Red Bob being killed?" asked Maud.

"Red Wanding," cried the girl, still translating the old man's speech, which rolled forth in faltering and passionate tones, "he knew well; that debil-debil shoot picaninny belonging to him—little girl—'poor little girl' he say. (Here the gray chieftain threw up his arms wildly towards the sky, while hot tears fell from the eyes still glaring with unsated wrath and revenge.) He say, before that he always friend to white fellow—no let black fellow spear cattle."

"Ask him where *he* was himself that night," said Mark.

The inquiry was put to him. Old man Jack replied not for a few moments; then he walked slowly forward to a large hollow log of the slowly-rotting eucalyptus, which had lain for a score of years scarce perceptibly hastening on its path of slow decay. Stooping suddenly, he thrust in his long arm and withdrew a spear. It was mouldering with age, but still showed by its sharpened point and smoothed edges how dangerous a weapon it had been. He felt the point, touched a darkened stain which reached to a foot from the end, and, suddenly throwing himself with lightning-like rapidity into the attitude of a thrower of the javelin, shouted a name thrice with a demoniac malevolence which curdled the hearts of the hearers. He then snapped the decayed lance, and, throwing the pieces at Mark's feet with a softened and humble gesture, relapsed into his old mute, emotionless manner, and strode away along the border of the lake.

"He say," concluded Wildduck, with a half confidential manner, "that *he* spear Red Bob that night with *that one spear*. He hide 'em in log, and never see it again till this day."

"Some secrets are well kept," said Mark. "If it had been known within a few years after the fight, old man Jack would have been shot half a dozen times over. Now, no one would think of avenging Red Bob's death more than that of Julius Cæsar. After all, it was a fair fight; and I believe old man Jack's story."

"Well, I shall never laugh at bush warfare again," said Maud; "there is sad earnest sufficient for anybody in this tale."

"We may as well be turning our horses' heads homeward. Wildduck, you come up tomorrow and get something for your cough."

"Come up now," accepted Wildduck, with great promptitude. "Too much frightened of Wanding tonight to stop here."

A brisk gallop home shook off some of the influences of their somewhat eerie adventure. Maud strove to keep up the lively tone of her ordinary conversation, but did not wholly succeed. Her subdued bearing rendered her, in Jack's eyes, more irresistible than before. He was rapidly approaching that helpless stage when, in moods of grave or gay, a man sees only the absolute perfection of his exemplar of all feminine graces. From the last pitying glance which Maud bestowed on Wildduck, to the frank kiss which she so lovingly pressed on Mameluke's neck as she dismounted, Jack only recognized the rare combination of lofty sentiment with a warm and affectionate nature.

Next morning Jack was under marching orders. He had left M'Nab sufficiently long by himself, in case anything of the nature of work turned up. He had secured an extremely pleasant change from the monotony of home. He had, most undeniably, acquired one or more new ideas. How regretfully he saw Mark finish his breakfast, and wait to say goodbye, preparatory to a long day's ride after those eternal shepherds!

"You must come and see us again," said Mrs. Stangrove, properly careful to retain the acquaintance of an agreeable neighbour and an eligible *parti*. "You have no excuse now. We shall not believe in the use and value of your fencing if it won't provide you with a little leisure sometimes."

"You must all come and see me before shearing," rejoined he. "I shall make a stand on my rights in etiquette, and refuse to come again before you have 'returned my call,' as ladies say. I have several novelties beside the fencing to show, which might interest even ladies. I hope you won't give Stangrove any rest till he promises to bring you."

"We have a natural curiosity to see all the new world you are reported to have made," Maud said, "and even your model overseer, Mr. M'Nab. He must surely be one of the 'coming race,' and have any quantity of 'vril' at command. I suppose the land will be filled with such products of a higher civilization after we early Arcadians are abolished."

"You must come and see, Miss Stangrove. I will tell you nothing. M'Nab is the ideal general-of-division in the grand army of labour, to my fancy. But whether it is to be Waterloo or Walcheren the future must decide. *Au revoir!*"

He shook hands with Stangrove, and, mounting, departed with his brace of hackneys for the trifling day's ride between there and home. Truth to tell, he tested the mettle of his steeds much more shrewdly than in his leisurely downward course. It was nearer to eight hours than nine when he reined up before the home-paddock gate of Gondaree.

Returning to one's own particular abode and domicile is not always an unmixed joy, however much imaginative writers have insisted upon the aspect. "The watchdog's honest bay" occasionally displays a want of recognition calculated to irritate the sensitive mind. Evidence is sometimes forced upon the unwilling *revenant* of the proverbial and unwarrantable playing of mice in the absence of the lord of the castle, who is thereby unpleasantly reminded that he occupies substantially the position of the cat. Possibly he is greeted with the unwelcome announcement that an important business interview has lapsed by reason of his absence. It may be that he finds his household absent at an entertainment, thus causing him to moralize upon desolate hearthstones and shattered statuettes, while he is gloomily performing for himself the minor offices so promptly bestowed on more fortunate arrivals. Or fate, being in one of her dark moods—a subtle prescience of evil, only too true—meets him on the threshold, and he enters his home as chief mourner. "Happy whom none of these befall"; and in such cheer did our hero find himself when, after hurried inquiry, it transpired that "nothing had happened," that everything was going on as well as could be, and that Mr. M'Nab was out at the woolshed (No. 3), and had left word that he would be in at sundown.

"So everything has gone on well in my absence," said Jack to his lieutenant, as they sat placidly smoking after the evening meal. "I began to be a little nervous as I got near home, though why it should be I can't say."

"So well," answered M'Nab, "that if it were not for the woolshed there would be too little to do. Once a month is often enough to muster the paddocks, and the percentage of loss has been very trifling. The sheep are in tip-top condition. The clip will be good and very clean. I hope we are past our troubles."

"I hope so too," echoed Jack. "How many sheep are there in the river paddock?"

"Nine thousand odd. You never saw anything like them for condition."

"Isn't there a risk in having them there at this time of year? The river *might* come down; and Stangrove told me the greater part of that paddock is under water in a big flood."

"Plenty of time to get them out. If the worst came we could soon rig a temporary bridge over the anabranch creek."

"People about here say," objected Jack, "that when a *real* flood comes down all sorts of places are filled which you wouldn't expect; and sheep are the stupidest things—except pigs—that ever were tried in water and a hurry."

"You needn't be uneasy; I'll have them out of that hours before there is any danger," said M'Nab, confidently. "Meanwhile, if they don't use the feed the travelling stock will only have the benefit of it. What did you think of Mr. Stangrove's place, sir?"

"I was agreeably surprised," said Jack, with an air of much gravity. "The whole affair is old-fashioned, of course; but the stock are very good, in fine order, and everything about the place very neat and nice. Mr. Stangrove and his family are exceedingly nice people."

"So I've heard," said M'Nab. "So I believe (as if that was a point so unimportant as to merit the merest assent); but the *Run!*—the run is one of the best and largest on the river, and to think of its being thrown away upon less than twenty thousand sheep, a thousand head of cattle, and a few mobs of rubbishy horses!"

"Dreadful, isn't it?" said Jack, smiling at M'Nab's righteous indignation; "but Stangrove is one of those men who thinks he has a right to do what he wills with his own. And really he has something to say for himself."

"I can't think it, sir; I can't think it," asserted the stern utilitarian. "The State ought to step in and interfere when a man is clearly wasting and misusing the public lands. I'd give all the shepherding, non-fencing men five years' warning; if at the end of that time they had not contrived to fence and dig wells the country should be resumed and let by tender to men who would work the Crown lands decently and profitably."

"You're rather too advanced a land-reformer," said his employer. "You might have the tables turned upon you by the farmers. However, you can argue the point of eviction with Mr. Stangrove, who will be here with the ladies, I hope, before shearing. But he has fought for his land once, and I feel sure would do so again if need were. Still I think he will be rather astonished at our four boundary riders."

The first necessity was an inspection of the new wool-shed, which was raising its unpretending form, like a species of degenerate ph(oe)nix, from the ashes of its glorious predecessor. It was strong and substantial, full of necessary conveniences—good enough—but not the model edifice—the exemplar of a district, the pride of Lower Riverina.

Now befell a halcyon time of a couple of months of Jack's existence, during which the millennium, as far as Gondaree was concerned, seemed to have arrived.

The weather was perfect; there was just enough rain, not more than was needed to "freshen up" the pasture from time to time. There were ten thousand fat sheep; the lambing had commenced, and prospects were splendid.

Better than all, the reactionary reign of economy directly proceeding from M'Nab's well-calculated outlay had set in. With forty-two thousand "countable" sheep and twenty thousand lambing ewes, "in full blast," there were but the four boundary riders, M'Nab, the cook, and Ah Sing, plus the shed workmen. "This was something like," Jack said to himself. "Fancy the small army I should have billeted upon me if I were like Stangrove, and had the same proportion of hands to employ. The very thought of it is madness, or insolvency—which comes to the same thing."

"I really believe we could do with even fewer hands upon a pinch," said M'Nab. "Ah Sing is of course a luxury, though a justifiable one. The boundary-riders come in for their own rations, so a ration-carrier is unnecessary. The two that live at the homestead cook for themselves. There is next to no work in the store till shearing; you or I can give out anything that is wanted. The cook chops his own wood, and fetches it in once a week; water is at the door. If it were not for having to convoy travelling sheep, one man could watch and the rest go to sleep till shearing. There are no dingoes, and we have no township near us to breed tame dogs. Next year we must have thirty thousand lambing-sheep by hook or by crook, and then you may put Gondaree into the market with sixty thousand sheep as soon after as you please."

"What about these ten thousand fat sheep?" said Jack. "Isn't it time we were thinking of drafting and sending them on the road?"

"If I were you, Mr. Redgrave, I would not sell them, unless you were obliged, till after shearing. They are worth from twelve to fourteen shillings all round in Melbourne, let us say. Well, the wethers will cut six shillings' worth of wool, and the ewes five. It would pay you to shear them and sell them as store sheep."

"That's all very well; but if you don't sell at the proper time I always notice that it ends in keeping them for another year; by which you lose interest, and risk a fall in the market."

"Not much chance of sheep falling below ten shillings," rejoined M'Nab. "We can send them in very prime about March. We may just as soon make one expense of the shearing."

"Well," yielded Jack, "I dare say it won't make much difference. We shall have it—the clip—and if they only fetch ten shillings there will be a profit of five and twenty percent. They don't cost anything for shepherding, that's one comfort."

So matters wore on till July. To complete the astonishing success and enjoyment of the situation, Jack received a letter from Stangrove, to say that he was going to drive over, and would bring the ladies for a day's visit to Gondaree.

Jack's cup well-nigh overflowed. To think of having her actually in the cottage, under his very roof—to have the happiness of beholding her walking about the garden and homestead, criticising everything, as she would be sure to do. Perhaps even appreciating, with that clear intellect of hers, the scope and breadth of the system of management, of his life pleasures even. Could she be won to take an interest, then what delirious, immeasurable joy!

Preparations were made. A feminine supernumerary was secured from the woolshed camp. Fortunately the cook was undeniable, and he needed but a word to "impress himself" and execute marvels. The cottage was entirely given up to the ladies, and the bachelors' quarters made ready for occupation by Stangrove, M'Nab, and himself. So might they retire, and smoke and talk sheep *ad libitum*. The small flower-garden round the cottage, or rather at the side, as its verandah almost overhung the river, was made neat. Even M'Nab, though grumbling somewhat at a feminine invasion "just before shearing," looked out his best suit of clothes, and prepared to abide the onset. Had there ever been a lady at Gondaree before? Jack began to consider. It was exceedingly doubtful.

At the appointed day, just before sundown, Stangrove's buggy rattled up behind, as usual, a very fast pair of horses. He was a great man for pace, and, having lots of horses to pick out of, generally had something only slightly inferior to public performers. Indeed, his friends used to complain that he never could be got to stay a night with anyone on the road—being always bent upon some impossible distance in the day, and insisting upon going twenty or thirty miles farther, in order to accomplish it. However that might be, no man drove better horses.

"Here we are at last, Redgrave," said he, as Jack rushed out to satisfy himself that Maud was actually in the flesh at his gates. "We should have been here before, but the ladies, of course, kept me waiting. However, I think we've done it under seven hours—that's not so bad."

"Bad! I should think not—splendid going!" said Jack. "I must get you to sell me a pair of buggy horses; mine are slow enough for a poison cart. Mrs. Stangrove, how good of you to cheer up a lonely bachelor! Miss Stangrove, I throw myself and household on your mercy. Will you, ladies, deign to walk in? you will find an attendant, and take possession of my house and all that is in it. Stangrove, we must take out the nags ourselves; no spare hands on a fenced-in run, you perceive."

"All right, Redgrave, that's the style I like. Mind you keep it up."

The stable was well found, though the groom was absent. Abundance of hay had been supplied, and the buggy was placed under cover. The friends were soon sauntering down by the river, and of course talking sheep, in the interval before dinner.

"Saw a lot of your weaners as we came along," said Stangrove. "How well they look. Much larger than mine, and the wool very clean. It certainly makes a man think. How many are there in that paddock?"

"Nine thousand," answered Jack, carelessly. "They have been there since they were weaned."

"And how often are they counted?"

"Once a month, regularly."

"What percentage of loss?"

"Next to none at all; the fact is we have no dogs, and the season has been so far, glorious."

"Well, I have five shepherds for the same number," said Stangrove; "have had one or two 'smashes,' endless riding, bother, and trouble. It seems very nice to turn them loose and never have any work or expense with them—the most troublesome of one's whole flock—till shearing. However, as I said before, my mind is made up for the next couple of years—after that, I won't say—"

"I think I hear the dinner-bell," said Jack; "the ladies will be wondering what has become of us."

M'Nab having arrived about this time, looking highly presentable, the masculine contingent entered the cottage, and dinner was announced.

"Your housekeeping does not need to fear criticism," said Mrs. Stangrove, as she tasted the clear soup. This was a *spécialité* of Monsieur Jean Dubois, an artist who, but for having contracted the colonial preference for cognac, our *vin ordinaire*, would have graced still a metropolitan establishment.

"We women are always complimented upon our domestic efficiency, home comforts, and so on," said Maud. "It appears to me that bachelors always live more comfortably than the married people of our acquaintance."

"I don't think that is always the case," pleaded Mrs. Stangrove. "But in many instances I have noted that you gentlemen, who are living by yourselves, always seem to get the best servants."

"'Kinder they than Missises are,' Thackeray says, you know; but it must be quite an accidental circumstance. In by far the greater number of instances a lone bachelor is oppressed, neglected, and perhaps robbed."

"I am not so sure of that," persisted Maud. "You exaggerate your chances of misfortune. I know when I am travelling with Mark we generally find ourselves much better put up, as he calls it, at a bachelor residence than at a regular family establishment. Don't we, Mark?"

"Well, I can't altogether deny it," deposed Stangrove, thus adjured. "It may not last, and the bachelor may be living on his capital of comfort. But I must say that, unless I know a man's wife is one of the right sort, I prefer the unmarried host. You fling yourself into the best chair in the room as soon as you have made yourself decent. You are safe to be asked to take a glass of grog without any unnecessary waste of time. And you are absolutely certain that no possible cloud can cast a shade over the evening's *abandon*. Whereas, in the case of the 'double event,' the odds are greater that it won't come off so successfully."

"What *are* you saying about married people, Mark? You're surely in a wicked sarcastic humour. Don't believe him Mr. Redgrave."

"My dear! you are the exceptional helpmate, as I am always ready to testify. But there *may* be cases, you know, when the husband has just stated that he'll be hanged if he will have his mother-in-law for another six months, just yet; or the cook, not being able to 'hit it' with the mistress's slightly explosive temper, has left at a moment's notice, and there is nothing but half-cold mutton and quite hot soda-bread to be procured; the grog, too, has run out, which is *never* the case in a bachelor's establishment—and so—and so. Unless the lady of the house is partial to strangers (like you, my dear), give me Tom, or Dick, and Liberty Hall."

"So I say too," added Maud. "Of course being a single young person, I feel flattered by the respectful admiration I meet with at such houses. It's not proper, I suppose. I ought to feel more pleased to be under the wing of a staid, overworked, slightly soured mother of a family, who keeps me waiting for tea till all the children are put to bed, and gives me something to stitch at during the evening; but I don't—and so there's no use saying I do."

"I'm afraid your tastes border on the Bohemian, Miss Stangrove," said Jack. "I'm rather a Philistine myself, I own, in the matter of young ladies."

"Thinking, no doubt, as is the manner of men, that stupidity contains a great element of safety for women. I could prove to you that you are utterly wrong; but you might think me more a person of independent ideas—that is, more unladylike than ever. So I abstain. How nicely your verandah looks over the river. It is quite a balcony. Isn't it very unpleasantly near in flood-time?"

"The oldest inhabitant has never seen water cover this point," said Jack. "I ascertained that very carefully before I built here. If you look

ROLF BOLDREWOOD

over to those low green marshy flats on the other side, you will see that miles of water must spread out for every additional inch the river rises."

"Yes, Steamboat Point is all right," said Mark. "I've heard the blacks admit that. I've seen a big flood or two here too; but the water runs back into the creeks and anabranches in a wonderful way. Gets behind you and cuts you off before you can help yourself, sometimes, in the night. If I were you I would have every weaner out of those river paddocks before spring."

"We could have them out soon enough if there was any danger," here interposed M'Nab.

"You would find it hard, take my word for it," said Stangrove, "if the river came down a banker."

"I could whip a bridge over any back creek here in half an hour," said M'Nab, decisively, "that would cross every sheep we have there in two hours."

"There's a Napoleonic ring about that, Mr. M'Nab," said Maud; "but the Duke would have had all his forces—I mean his sheep—withdrawn from the position of danger in good time. One or two of Buonaparte's bridges broke down with him, you remember."

"It doesn't look much like a flood at present," said Jack; "though this is no warranty in Australia, which is a land specially dedicated to the unforeseen. Let us hope that there will be nothing so sensational at or before shearing this year."

"Not even bushrangers," said Maud. "What does this mean?" handing over to her brother the *Warroo Watch-tower and Down-river Advertiser*, in which figured the following paragraph: "We regret sincerely to be compelled to state that the rumours as to a party of desperadoes having taken to the bush are not without foundation. Last week two drays were robbed near Mud Springs by a party of five men, well armed and mounted. The day before yesterday the mailman and several travellers on the Oxley road were stopped and robbed by the same gang. They are said to be led by the notorious Redcap, and to have stated that they were coming into the Warroo frontage to give the squatters a turn."

Mrs. Stangrove turned pale, Maud laughed, while Mark devoted himself very properly to calm the apprehensions of his wife.

"Maud," he said, "this is no laughing matter. It is the beginning of a period, whether long or short, of great trouble and anxiety, it may be danger, I am not an alarmist; but I wish we were well out of this matter."

"It seems very ridiculous," said Jack; "every man's hand will be against them, and they *must* be run or shot down, ultimately."

"Nothing more certain," admitted Stangrove; "but these fellows generally 'turn out' from the merest folly or recklessness, and become gradually hardened to bloodshed. They are like raw troops, mere rustics at first. But they soon learn the part of 'first robber,' and generally lose some of their own blood, or spill that of better men, before they get taken."

"We have a dray just loading up from town. There is time—yes, just time," said M'Nab, consulting his pocket-book, "to write by mail. We can order revolvers, and a repeating rifle or two, and have them up in five weeks. Can we get anything for you?"

"Certainly, and much obliged," said Stangrove; "if they know that we are well armed, they will be all the more chary of coming to close quarters. You may order for me a brace of repeating rifles and three revolvers."

"With some of the neighbours we might turn out a respectable force, and hunt the fellows down," said Jack, who felt ready for anything in the immediate proximity of Maud, and only wished the gang would attack Gondaree then and there.

There was no such luck, however. The ordinary station life was unruffled. The ladies rode and drove about with cheerful energy. Maud admired the paddocks and the unshepherded sheep immensely, and vainly tried to extort her brother's consent to begin the reformed system as soon as they returned to Juandah.

Mark had said that he would defer the enterprise for two years, and he was a man who, slow in forming resolves, always adhered to them.

XII

"So farre, so fast the eygre drave,
The heart had hardly time to beat,
Before a shallow seething wave
Sobbed in the grasses at our feet;
The feet had hardly time to flee
Before it brake against the knee,
And all the world was in the sea."

—JEAN INGELOW

The days passed pleasantly in excursions to Bimbalong, to the back paddocks, and in rides and drives along the perfect natural roads peculiar to the locality. In the long excursions, the twilight was upon them more than once before they reached home. Jack did not altogether neglect his opportunities. When he rode close to Maud's bridle-rein, as they flitted along in the mild half-light between the shadowy pines, or the avenues of oak and myall, words would become gradually lower in tone, more accented with feeling, than the ordinary daylight converse.

"And so you think," said Jack, on one of these pleasant twilight confidentials—Stangrove, who was driving, being rather anxious to get home before the light got any worse—"that I am not playing too hazardous a game in spending freely now, with the expectation of being so largely recouped within a year or two."

"It is exactly what I should do if I were a man," said the girl, frankly. "How men can consent to bury themselves alive in this wearisome, never-ending, bush sepulchre I cannot think. I should perish if I were compelled to lead such a life without possibility of change. When we think of the glorious old world, the dreamland of one's spirit, the theatre of art, luxury, war, antiquity, which leisure would enable one to visit—how can *one* be contented?"

"I never thought *I* should feel contented on the Warroo," said her companion; "yet now, really, I don't find it so awfully dull, you know."

"Not just at present," answered Maud, archly. "Well, I am candid enough to own that, our families having joined forces since your visit, things are a shade more bearable. But fancy growing gray in this life and these surroundings. Twenty years after! Fancy us all at that date, here!"

"I can't fancy it. What should we be like, Miss Stangrove?"

"I can tell you," pursued the excited girl. "Mark much the same, gray and more silent—strongly of opinion that the Government of the day were in league with free selectors, and generally robbers and murderers. His opinions are pretty strong now. *Then*, of course, they would have ripened into prejudices. My sister-in-law, frail, worn out by servants and household cares; just a *little* querulous, and more indisposed to read."

"And yourself?" asked Jack.

"Oh! I should have been quietly buried under a couba tree before that impossible period. Or, if I unhappily survived, would have become eccentric. I should be spoken of generally as a 'little strong-minded,' slight dash of temper, and so on; very fond of riding, and, they say, can count sheep and act as boundary-rider when her brother is short of hands. How do you like the picture?"

"You have not paid me the compliment of including me on the canvas."

"I don't possibly imagine you within thousands of miles of Gondaree or Juandah at such a time. You will be dreaming among the 'Stones of Venice,' lounging away the winter in Rome, or settled in a hunting neighbourhood in a pleasant English county, making up your mind, very gradually, to return to Australia, and to devote the rest of your days to model farming and national regeneration."

"There is only one thing absolutely necessary to render my existence happy under the conditions which you have so accurately sketched,"—here he leaned forward, and placing his hand upon her horse's mane, saw a softened gleam in her marvellous eyes—as of the heart's farewell to unacknowledged hope—"and that is—"

"We are really riding shamefully slow," said she suddenly, as she drew her rein, and the free horse tossed his head and went off at speed. "Mark must have nearly reached home, and Jane, as usual, will be fancying all kinds of impossible accidents—that dear old Mameluke has tumbled down, positively tumbled down and broken my arm in three places. I tell her she'll suspect me of taking a 'bait' next. How still the plain looks, and how exactly the same—north and south, east and west! But even in this light you can distinguish the heavy, dark, winding line of the river timber."

In due time the guests departed, and Mr. Redgrave was left to the consideration of the loneliness of his condition, a view of life which had not presented itself strongly before his introduction to Miss Stangrove. He had been contented to enjoy the society of wife, widow, and maid in the most artless, instinctive fashion, without any fixed plan of personal advantage. Not that this unsatisfactory general approbation had escaped criticism by those who felt themselves to be sufficiently interested to speak. He had been called selfish, conceited, fastidious, fast, uninteresting, and mysterious. Many adjectives had in private been hurled at his devoted head. But he "had a light heart, and so bore up." Besides, he had a reserve of popularity to fall back upon. There were many people who would not suffer Jack Redgrave to be run down unreasonably. So up to this time he had eluded appropriation and defied disapproval.

Now matters were changed. The slow, resistless Nemesis was upon him. In his ears sounded the prelude to that melody—heard but once in this mortal life—in tones at first low and soft, then rich and dread with melody from the immortal lyre. At that summons all men arise and follow. Follow, be it angel or fiend. Follow, be the path over vernal meads, through forest gloom, or the drear shades of the nether hell.

No woman, Jack soliloquised, had ever before commended herself to his tastes, his senses, his reason, and his fancy. She was in his eyes lovely in form and face; original, cultured, tender, and true. He would make her his wife if his utmost efforts might compass such triumph, such wild exaggeration of happiness. She might not care particularly about him. She might merely have whiled away a dull week. Now, many a time had *he* done likewise, with apparent interest and inward tedium. Were it so, he felt as if he could bestow a legend on Steamboat Point by casting himself into the rapid but not particularly deep waters which flowed beneath. At any rate he would try. He would make the great hazard. He would know his fate after shearing. Meanwhile, there was nearly enough to do until that solemn Hegira to put the thought of Maud Stangrove out of his head.

Having made up his mind, Mr. Redgrave dismissed the fair Maud with philosophical completeness. Master Jack was extremely averse to holding his judgment in suspense, that process involving abrasion of his peculiarly delicate mental cuticle. He was prone, therefore, to a speedy settlement of all cases of conscience. Judgment being delivered, he bore or performed sentence unflinchingly. Yet his friends asserted that during any stay of proceedings he could amuse himself as unreservedly, as free from boding gloom, or "the sad companion, ghastly pale, and darksome as a widow's veil," as any sportive lambkin on his way to mint sauce and deglutition. Thus, having settled that the subjugation of Miss Stangrove could not be undertaken until after shearing, he went heart and soul into the arrangements for that annual agony, to the total exclusion of all less material considerations.

To a healthy man, in the full possession of all mental and bodily faculties, perhaps a state of perfect employment is the one most nearly approaching to that of perfect happiness. It is rarely conceded at the time; but more often than we wot of do men recall, when in the lap of ease, that season of comparative toil and strife, with a sigh for the "grand old days of pleasure and pain." Each nerve and muscle is at stretch. The struggle is close and hard; but there is the glorious sensation of "the strong man rejoicing in his strength." The very fatigue is natural and wholesome. The recovery is sure and complete; and, if only a reasonable meed of success crown those unsparing efforts, the heart swells with the proud joy of him round whose brow is twined the envied crown in the arena. Let who will choose the dulled sensation with which, in after life, the successful merchant notes his dividends, or the politician accepts the long-promised leadership.

Mr. Redgrave, then, having girded himself for the fight, in company with M'Nab, drank delight of battle with his peers, that is, with the shearers, washers, and knockabout men, who struck repeatedly, and gave as much trouble as their ingenuity could manage to supply during the first week of shearing.

SUDDENLY—AS IS THE CUSTOM of all Australian weather-wonders— clouds charged with heavy driving showers came hurtling across the fair blue sky. This abnormal state of matters on the Warroo was succeeded by a steady, settled rainfall, pouring down heavily, and yet more heavily on several successive days, as if heaven's windows were once more opened, and the dry land was again to be circumscribed. Without loss of time, down came the river, "tossing his tawny mane," foam-flecked, and bearing on his broad brown bosom all sorts of goods and chattels not intended for water carriage. The anabranch surrounding a large portion of the river paddock, wherein were the weaners, was simultaneously filled by the turbid torrent, which dashed into its deep but ordinarily dry bed from the brimming river. At the present level no danger was to be apprehended for the unconscious weaners; but M'Nab was unwilling to trust to the probabilities, and decided upon getting them out. A bridge was extemporised, of a sort laid away in the well-stored chambers of his practical brain, and thrown across the narrowest part.

With a heavy expenditure of patience, and the efficient leadership of certain pet sheep, which M'Nab had reared and trained for shearing needs, the whole lot were mustered and safely crossed over the newly-born water-course.

"I am not sure now," said M'Nab, "that we have not had all our trouble for nothing. I believe the river will be low again in a week."

"All the same," affirmed Jack, "it's well to be on the safe side, especially of a back creek in flood-time. Nobody knows what these confounded rivers are capable of doing when no one wants them."

"Well, they can have the No. 2 paddock, and the dry ewes can have No. 3. I wanted No. 2 for the shorn sheep, though. It's just a nuisance the water coming down now."

The mild excitement of the spate, as Mr. M'Nab called it, died away. The sun came out; the waters returned to nearly their former limits, and a wide, half-dried surface of mud, alone denoted where the deep and turbid waters had rolled over the broad channel of the anabranch.

The wool-shed and wash-pen had been correctly placed upon the borders of a creek so conveniently humble as never to attain to any measure of danger or discomfort in the highest flood. So, directly the rain ceased, the great yearly campaign went on rapidly and smoothly.

Weeks passed; the season was advancing; the sun became hotter; there was not a day of broken weather; everything was in capital gear, and worked with even suspicious smoothness.

"We are getting on like a house afire," said M'Nab; "that is," as he suddenly bethought himself of the awkwardness of the allusion, "much faster than I expected. We have a good lot of men. There is no dust. The wash-pen is just grand. I never saw wool cleaner and better got up, though I say so."

"Our luck has turned," said Jack; "no more accidents; though it's strange that, when all is unnaturally successful, something is sure to happen. If the engine was to smash, a valve or some small trouble to happen, I should feel that the ring of Polycrates had been thrown into the Warroo, and not returned by an officious codfish."

"I don't know about Polly Whatsyname's ring," said Mr. M'Nab, whose education had not included the classics; "but things couldn't be better. I shall put those weaners back into the river paddock again. The grass is all going to waste."

"Just as you like," said Jack, who had forgotten his caution now that the emergency was over. "I suppose we shall have the dust blowing in about a fortnight."

"By then we shall be done shearing. I don't care what comes after," answered the manager. "And now I must go back to the shed."

"THANK GOD, IT'S SATURDAY NIGHT!" said Jack, as they sat down to their dinner at the fashionable hour of nine P.M. "I enjoy a good bout of work; it's exciting, and pulls one together. But one wants a *little* sleep sometimes; likewise something to eat."

"This has been a middling hard week," graciously admitted M'Nab, who rarely would concede that any amount of labour constituted a *really* laborious term. "One more week, and every dray will be loaded up, and the wool off our hands."

"Do you think the weather will hold good? It had rather a lowering, hazy look today."

"That means that it's raining somewhere else," said M'Nab, uninterestedly. "It's very often our share of it on the Warroo here."

"Don't know—somehow I have had a queer feeling all day that I can't account for. Hard work generally goes to raise my spirits in view of the splendid appreciation of food and sleep that follows. But I have felt what the teller of tales calls a 'presentiment'—a foreshadowing of evil—if such a thing can be."

"Take a glass of grog extra tonight, sir; you've caught cold at the wash-pen, or the influenza the men had before shearing has fastened on you. Some of them got a great shaking with it, and lay about like a lot of old women."

"I suspect the vagabonds considered it a favourable time to be ill," laughed Jack, "as they were not paying for their rations, and thought we might put them on at a little gentle work. However, we won't pursue the subject."

No one can have an adequate comprehension of the value of the Sabbath as a day of pure rest who has not worked at high pressure, with brain or hand, the week-time through. Well and wisely was the Lord's Day ordained—well and wisely is it maintained—for the needful recovery of the wasted powers of the wondrous, miraculous machine called Man. In this age, above all others, it is vitally necessary that a weekly truce should be proclaimed, when the life-long conflict may cease and the fever-throbs of the "malady of thought" may be stilled.

But for this anodyne, how many a brow, hot with the electric currents that flash ceaselessly through the brain, would pass swiftly from pain to madness! How many a stalwart frame, the unguarded, yet precious, capital of the son of labour, would stagger and fall by the wayside of a life which was one endless, monotonous martyrdom of unrelieved toil! But the eve, the blessed herald of the coming holy day, arrives; the worn craftsman rests, enjoys, and sinks into a dreamless sleep. The modern Alchemist, he who painfully coins his brain into gold, relinquishing crucible and furnace, walks forth into the pure air of heaven, and thanks the Great Ruler for the respite—the sweet moments of a charmed, untroubled day.

John Redgrave, as he awoke at dawn, and turned over for an hour or two of rare repose, had some such glimmerings of thankfulness. He had nothing to do or to think about until late in the afternoon, when the sheep for Monday's shearing would have to be packed into the shed, and the next contingent due for the somewhat trying lavation by spout placed near their tubbing apparatus. All the morning—what an amazing quantity of time!—absolutely free. A leisurely calm breakfast, with the glorious "nothing to do" forever so long afterwards. It was the reign of Buddha, the classic Elysium. He would sit on high like broad-fronted Jove, and meditate, and read and write, and be supremely happy.

From the tenor of Mr. Redgrave's thoughts, it will not escape the acute reader that he had forgotten his presentiment. But scarcely had he concluded his solitary, luxuriously-lingering meal—(M'Nab of course was miles away on some indispensable work, which he kept for Sundays and holidays)—than the Eidolon stole forth from the curtains of his soul, and confronted him with disembodied but ghastly presentment. Down went the register of Jack's animal spirits—down—down. The very face of heaven darkened—the sky became overcast. The breeze became chill and moaned eerily, without any assignable reason—for what were clouds in Riverina but the heralds of prosperity, or its synonym, the Rain-King, but the lord and gold-giver of all the sun-scorched land?

Thus he reasoned. But his logic was powerless to dislodge the demon. The necessary evening work was formally proceeded with; but the sun set upon few more depressed and utterly wretched mortals than John Redgrave, as he moodily smoked for an hour, and retired early to an uneasy couch. More than once he half rose through the night, and listened, as a strange sound mingled with the blast which roared and raved, and shook the cottage roof in the frenzied gusts of the changeful spring. But an hour before dawn he sprang suddenly up and shouted to M'Nab, who slept in an adjoining room.

"Get up, man, and listen. I thought I could not be mistaken. The river has got us this time."

"I hear," said M'Nab, standing at the window, with all his senses about him. "It can't be the river; and yet, what else can it be?"

"I know," cried Jack; "it's the water pouring into the back creek when it leaves the river. There must be an awful flood coming down, or it could never make all that row. The last time it filled up as smoothly as a backwater lagoon. Listen again!"

The two men stood, half-clad as they were, in the darkness, ever deepest before dawn, while louder, and more distinctly, they heard the fall, the roar, the rush of the wild waters of an angry flood down a deep and empty channel. A very deep excavation had been scooped of old by the Warroo at the commencement of the anabranch, which, leaving the river at an angle, followed its course for miles, sometimes at a considerable distance, before it re-entered it.

"My conscience!" said M'Nab, "I never heard the like of that before—in these parts, that is. I would give a year's wage I hadn't crossed those weaners back. I only did it a day or two since. May the devil—but swearing never so much as lifted a pound of any man's burden yet. We'll not be swung clear of this grip of his claws by calling on *him*."

With this anti-Manichæan assertion, M'Nab went forth, and stumbled about the paddock till he managed to get his own and Jack's horse into the yard. These he saddled and had ready by the first streak of dawn. Then they mounted and rode towards the back of the river paddock.

"I was afraid of this," said Jack, gloomily, as their horses' feet plashed in the edge of a broad, dull-coloured sheet of water, long before they reached the ridge whence they usually descried the back-creek channel. "The waters are out such a distance that we shall not be able to get near the banks of this infernal anabranch, much less throw a bridge over any part of it. There is a mile of water on it now, from end to end. The sheep must take their chance, and that only chance is that the river may not rise as high as Stangrove says he has known it."

"I deserve to be overseer of a thick run with bad shepherds all my life," groaned M'Nab, with an amount of sincerity in his abjectly humiliated voice so ludicrous that Jack, in that hour of misery, could scarcely refrain from smiling. "But let us gallop down to the outlet; it may not have got that far yet."

They rode hard for the point, some miles down, where the treacherous offshoot re-entered the Warroo. It sometimes happens that, owing to the sinuosities of the watercourses of the interior, horsemen at speed can outstrip the advancing flood-wave, and give timely notice to the dwellers on the banks. Such faint hope had they. By cutting across long detours or bends, and riding harder than was at all consistent with safety to their clover-fed horses, they reached the outlet. Joy of joys, it was "as dry as a bone."

"Now," said M'Nab, driving his horse recklessly down into the hard-baked channel, "if we can only find most of the sheep in this end of the paddock we may beat bad luck and the water yet. Did the dog come, I wonder? The Lord send he did. I saw him with us the first time we pulled up."

"I'm afraid not," said Jack; "we've ridden too hard for any mortal dog to keep up with us, though Help will come on our tracks if he thinks he's wanted."

"Bide a bit—bide a bit," implored M'Nab, forgetting his English, and going back to an earlier vernacular in the depth of his earnestness. "The dog's worth an hour of time and a dozen men to us. Help! Help! here, boy, here!"

He gave out the canine summons in the long-drawn cry peculiar to drovers when seeking to signal their whereabouts to their faithful allies. Jack put his fingers to his mouth and emitted a whistle of such remarkable volume and shrillness that M'Nab confessed his admiration.

"That will fetch him, sir, if he's anywhere within a mile. Dash'd if that isn't him coming now. See him following our tracks. Here, boy!"

As he spoke a magnificent black and tan collie raised his head from the trail and dashed up to Jack's side, with every expression of delight and proud success.

Mr. Redgrave was one of those men to whom dogs, horses, children, and others attach themselves with blind, unreasoning confidence. Is it amiability? Has mesmerism any share in the strange but actual fascination? There were many far wiser than he unsought and unrecognized by the classes referred to. In his case the fact, uncomplimentary or otherwise, remained fixed and demonstrable. The sheep-dog in question was introduced to him by an aged Scot, who arrived one day at Gondaree followed by a female collie of pure breed and unusual beauty. Jack, always merciful and sympathetic, had comforted the footsore elder, who carried a large bundle upon his back, at which the dog cast ever and anon a wistful glance. Lowering the pack carefully to the ground before he drained the cheering draught, he wiped his lips, and, untying the knapsack, rolled out, to his host's wild astonishment, *five blind puppies*!

"Ye ken, sir, the auld slut here just whelpit a week syne, maist unexpectedly to me. I was sair fashed to make my way doon wi' sax doggies. But I pledged my word to Maister Stangrove to gang back to Juandah before shearing, and I wadna brak my word—no, not for five poond."

"But are you going to carry the whole litter another fifty miles?"

"Weel, aweel, sir, I'll not deny it's a sair trial; but I brocht lassie here from the bonnie holms o' Ettrick, where my auld bones will never lie. The wee things come of the bluid of Tam Hogg's grand dog Sirrah. Forbye they're maist uncommon valuable here. I never askit less than a pund for ilka ane o' them yet, and siller's siller, ye ken."

"I'll give you a sov," said Jack, "for the black and tan pup—him with the spot between the eyes. I suppose we could rear him with an old ewe?"

"He's the king of this lot, but ye shall have the pick of them a' even withoot the siller, for the kind word and the good deed you've done to the auld failed, doited crater that ance called himsel' Jock Harlaw of Ettrick. May the Lord do so to me and mair, if I forget it."

The next day the old man came up, and solemnly delivered over the plump, roly-poly dogling, which, being fostered upon an imprisoned ewe, throve and grew into one of the best dogs that ever circumvented that deceitful and wicked quadruped called the sheep, the measure of whose intelligence has ever been consistently underrated.

The judicious reader will comprehend that, even on a fenced run, a good sheep-dog is valuable, and even necessary. The headlong, reckless system of driving, the cruel, needless terrorising under which "shepherded sheep" have for generations suffered in Australia may be as strongly repudiated as ever. But under certain conditions, it is well known to all rulers of sheep stations that there is no moving sheep without the aid and conversation of a dog. Therefore, though much of the occupation of the ordinary half-trained sheep-dog be gone, a really well-bred and highly-trained animal is still prized.

The collie "Help," then, as he grew up, showed great hereditary aptitude for every kind of knowledge connected with the "working" of sheep. He was passionately fond of Jack, whom he recognized as his real and true master; but he would follow and obey M'Nab, appearing to know by intuition when work among the sheep was intended. From him, as a man of sheep from earliest youth, he learned all the niceties of the profession. At drafting and yarding he was invaluable. Lifted into a yard crammed with panic-stricken or unwilling sheep, he would run along on their bodies or "go back through them" in a manner wonderful to observe—this last practice being known to all sheep-experts as the only way hitherto invented for prevailing on sheep to run up freely to a gate. He would bark or bite (this last with great discretion) at word of command. He would stay at any part of the yard pointed out to him, and though among the station hands it was commonly, but erroneously, reported that he could "keep a gate," and had been seen drafting "two ways at once," still it was so far near the truth that he had many times been posted at the entrance of sub-yards, and had prevented any sheep from entering during the whole duration of the drafting. For the rest, he was affectionate, generous, and brave, a good watch-dog, and no mean antagonist. In his own branch of the profession he was held to be unequalled for sagacity and effectiveness on the whole river.

In the hour of sore need this was the friend and ally, most appropriately named, who appeared on the scene. With a wave of the hand from Jack, he started off, skirting the nearest body of sheep. The well-trained animal, racing round the timid creatures, turned them towards the outlet, and followed the master for further orders. This process was repeated, aided by M'Nab, until they had gone as far from the outlet of the creek as they dared to do, with any chance of crossing before the flood came down.

"We must rattle them in now," said M'Nab. "I'm afraid there is a large lot higher up, but there's five or six thousand of these, and we must make the best of it."

As the lots of sheep coalesced on their homeward route, the difficulty of driving and the value of the dog grew more apparent. Large mobs or flocks of sheep are, like all crowds, difficult to move and conduct. By themselves it would have been a slow process; but the dog, gathering from the words and actions of his superiors that something out of the common was being transacted, flew round the great flock, barking, biting, rushing, worrying—driving, in fact, like ten dogs in one. By dint of the wildest exertion on the part of the men, and the tireless efforts of the dog, the great flock of sheep, nearly six thousand, was forced up to the anabranch. Here the leaders unhesitatingly took the as yet dry, unmoistened channel, and in a long string commenced to pour up the opposite bank.

"Give it them at the tail, sir," shouted M'Nab, who was at the lead, "go it, Help, good dog—there is not a moment to lose. By George, there comes the flood. Eat 'em up, old man!—give it 'em, good dog!"

There was fortunately one more bend for the flood water to follow round before it reached the outlet. During the short respite Jack and M'Nab worked at their task till the perspiration poured down their faces—till their voices became hoarse with shouting, and well-nigh failed. Horses and men, dog and sheep, were all in a state of exhaustion and despair when the last mob was ascending the clay bank.

"Two minutes more, and we should have been too late," said M'Nab, in a hoarse whisper; "look there!"

As he spoke, a wall of water, several feet in height, and the full breadth of the widest part of the channel, came foaming down, bearing logs, trees, portions of huts and haystacks—every kind of *débris*—upon its eddying tide. The tired dog crawled up the bank and lay down in the grass. A few of the last sheep turned and stared stolidly at the close wild water. There was a hungry, surging rush, and in another minute the creek was level with the river, and the place where the six thousand sheep had crossed dryshod (and sheep resemble cats very closely in their indisposition to wet their feet) was ten feet under water, and would have floated a river steamer.

Jack returned to the homestead rather comforted by this present bit of success, and hopeful that the sheep left in the river paddock might yet escape. They had no further anxiety about those which they had plucked out of the fire—that is to say, the water—for they were in a secure high and dry paddock, and they were not likely to attempt to swim back again.

It was very provoking to think, however, that only a week previous the whole lot had been absolutely safe if they had been sufficiently cautious to let well alone till after shearing.

On the morrow such a sight met John Redgrave's eyes as they had not looked upon since he entered into possession of Gondaree. The cottage was built, as has been before related, upon a bluff, and was believed to be impregnable by the highest flood that ever came down the Warroo. When Jack walked into the verandah, and saw by the pale dawn-light the angry waters, deep, turbulent, and wide as his vision went, rushing but a few feet below the floor on which he trod, he felt as if he were at sea, and trusted that the older residents had made no miscalculation. It was certainly a novel experience in that dry and thirsty land to hear the "roar of waters" so closely brought home to one's bed and board. On the other side of the river, far as the eye could see, the vast flats were as an inland sea, the trees standing in the water like pillars in a vast aqueduct, their stems forming endless colonnades.

This augured badly for his own river-paddock, and, breakfast hastily concluded, he started down to see if any of the sheep were visible from the opposite bank of the anabranch. He managed to get near enough to sweep the flats with a field-glass, and at last made out the greater part of the weaners, huddled together upon a small rise, surrounded by water, and not much above the general level. Here, though cold and hungry, they might remain in safety till the flood fell, if the waters rose no higher. But there lay the danger. The waters surrounded them for a long stretch on every side. Even if they could get near them, nothing would induce young sheep to face a much less expanse of water. The current was too rapid to work any species of raft. If the river continued rising through the night, there would not be a sheep of these three thousand and more alive by daylight.

Jack turned sick at heart with the bare idea. Good heavens! was he to be eternally the sport of circumstance and the victim of disaster? Was there such a thing as Bad Luck, an evil principle, in which he had steadfastly disbelieved, but which he did not doubt in other cases had hunted men to their doom? Could it possibly happen in his own case? How rarely do men accept any of life's evils as possibilities in their own cases! Here, however, he was again face to face with an unsolved difficulty, a peril imminent, deadly, and well-nigh hopeless of escape. Three thousand some hundreds of beautiful young sheep, with fourteen months' wool on. Another two thousand pounds gone at one blow! It was enough to make a man hang himself.

He had a long consultation with M'Nab, who had settled in his own mind that nothing could be done, except drown a man or two, in trying conclusions with such a waste of water, with large logs and uprooted trees whirling madly down the stream, which indeed looked like a lake dislodged from its moorings, and mad for a view of the distant sea.

So he calmly waited the issue, hoping for a fall during the night, and cursing himself, as deeply as a sound Presbyterian could afford to do, for having brought this loss upon his employer by over-greed of grass. The river did not fall. Indeed, it rose so rapidly that on their last visit to the place of observation they could hear the continuous bleating of the hapless sheep—a token that they were alarmed and endangered by the rising tide.

All that night the sound was in Jack's ears as he listened at intervals, or tossed restlessly on an uneasy bed.

With the earliest dawn he was astir and down at the look-out. There had evidently been a considerable rise during the night. He saw that the water had made a clean breach over the spot occupied by the flock—of the whole number, there was not a solitary sheep to be seen. He would have been saved a few days of anxious expectation—a feeling between utter despair and trembling hope—had he known that his friends at Juandah, that very day, had seen scores of their carcases floating past their windows, but were happily unconscious of their particular ownership.

For nearly a week Jack was inconsolable—he took no interest in the remaining portion of the shearing, which M'Nab finished with his customary exactness, paying off the shearers, washers, and extra hands, and despatching every pound of wool and every sheepskin as if the last of the clip—like a cow's milk—was the richest and most valuable.

The floods had rolled away, and the sun shone out hotter than ever upon miles of blackened clover and mud-covered pasturage, entirely ruined for the year by the unseasonable immersion. When they rode over the paddock the sight was pitiable in the extreme. By far the greater proportion of the drowned sheep had been floated away bodily, as the "cruel, crawling tide" rose inch by inch in the darkness, till they were swept from footing. But many were found entangled in drift-wood, carried into large hollow trees—as many as fifteen or twenty, perhaps, in one cluster—black and decomposing, with the wool bleaching in great strips and masses. A miserable sight for John Redgrave, in truth, who, but a fortnight since, had considered that wool almost in his pocket, and every shorn weaner good value for half a sovereign all round. Then the confounded *fama clamosa* of the affair. The local papers had quick and fast hold of the tale:

"We are deeply grieved to hear that Mr. Redgrave of Gondaree, who has spared no cost in improving that valuable property, has lost ten thousand sheep in the late disastrous flood." Next week—"We have much pleasure in stating that Mr. Redgrave has had only five thousand sheep drowned, but we had not then learned that his wool-shed and wash-pen, with a portion of the clip, were entirely washed away." And so on.

The quickest way to escape condolences and local sympathy would be

ROLF BOLDREWOOD

to make tracks for Melbourne. This he accordingly did, having, like the preceding season, had a sufficiency of salt-bush life for a while. Matters in some respects were more favourable to his mental recovery than on his former visit. Wool was up. The season, bar floods, had been good on the whole. Everybody connected with sheep was disposed to be cheerful and make allowances. Most of the people he met had not heard of the trifling overthrow of the remote Warroo, and the incidental "natural selection" of his lamented weaners. Others, who had heard, did not care. The joyous squatters, on the strength of a good twopenny rise in the home market, made light of his sorrows. One man said, laughingly, that he knew of a station, about a thousand miles lower down, which the same flood had treated even more scurvily.

"Wallingford, you know, had overstocked that run of his with store cattle; all the back country dry as a bone; no rain for two years; five or six thousand head of cattle all but starving; poor as crows, give you my word. Everything depending upon the river and the lake flats for the clover, as soon as it was ripe. Well, the flood comes down, smothers his clover; river twenty miles wide for nearly a month; lake overflowed too. Droll predicament, wasn't it? Quite antipodean. Half the run too dry; t'other half too wet. No rain; clover of course black as your hat when the water went down. Wallingford heaps of bills to meet, too."

The salient points of humour which Mr. Wallingford's ingeniously complicated calamities evolved under artistic treatment served indirectly to comfort our victim. The misfortunes of others, especially of the same profession, are soothing, benevolists notwithstanding. Jack felt ashamed of howling over his few sheep, and recollected the still imposing numbers of the last count, and returned to his normal state of contentment with today, and rose-coloured anticipation of tomorrow.

His interview with Mr. Mildmay Shrood was pacific and encouraging. That gentleman congratulated him upon the name and fame to which the Gondaree clip had attained, prophesying even greater distinction. He listened with polite sympathy to the account of the loss of the weaners, but observed that such accidents must occasionally happen in wet seasons, and that, as he was informed, the country generally had received immense benefit from the late rains.

"Your clip is one of the best in the whole of Riverina, my dear Redgrave, and your number of sheep—'52,000,' thank you—has on the whole kept up admirably. Management, my dear sir, is everything—everything. Good-morning. Good-morning."

XIII

"Hope told a flattering tale."

Thus endorsed, Jack began to consider himself to be as fine a fellow as the rest of the world was bent upon making him out to be. He held up his head as in the old days, when debt and he were strangers, and gave his opinion with imposing decision upon all matters, pastoral, social, and political. He was glad now that he had followed M'Nab's advice, and shorn the fat sheep. Their wool told up noticeably in the clip, and he trusted that in the coming autumn he should be able to top the market with the first draft of fat sheep from the glorious salt-bush plains which skirted the lonely Bimbalong.

He received a certain amount of satisfaction from observing how reduced was the list of stores and necessaries with which he had been entrusted by M'Nab. "Why, it's next to nothing," said he, as he looked over it; "one would think we were providing for a cattle station except for next year's shearing requirements. If we have only another decent year or two, the debt will be wiped off, and hey for Europe!" Then, from that vision of the sea, arose the form—as of a Venus Anadyomene—of Maud Stangrove. Would she share his pilgrimage? How enchanting the thought! How divine the companionship! Together would they wander through the cities of the old world, as through the dream-palaces of his boyish days. Paris, with her mingled splendours and luxuries. Rome, calm and majestic, even amid her ruins, as befitted the Mother of Nations. Venice, with mysterious gondolas still floating adown her sea, which is "her broad, her narrow streets," which still, as in old days of regal pride, and power, and love, is "her black-marble stair." Switzerland, with her pure, white-robed, heaven-gazing Alps, receiving their crimson dawn-blush ere beholding the fresh day-birth of a world. Last of all, but how far from least, "Merrie England," the great land of their fathers—every legendary and historical feature of which had been graven in his mind from earliest childhood. Bound on such a pilgrimage as this, "with one fair spirit for his minister," how cheerfully would he abandon, for a season, the dull labours and prosaic thoughts with which his later years had been bedimmed! He thought of Maud's cultured and receptive mind; her keen spirit of observation; her unfailing cheerfulness; and the deep, unselfish tenderness which he

ROLF BOLDREWOOD

had remarked in her home intercourse. Could he but win this peerless creature to himself; could he but provide for this diamond of purest ray serene the costly setting which alone harmonized with its rank among "earth's precious things," he told himself that the sayings of cynics about the ills of humanity would be meaningless falsehoods.

This, perhaps, slightly exalted conception of the probabilities of matrimony, combined with the absence of the central figure, around which such roseate clouds softly circled, tended to abridge Mr. Redgrave's metropolitan sojourn. He made the novel discovery that ordinary modern society was worldly and frivolous—that club *viveurs* were selfish and dissipated—that his acquaintances, generally, were destitute of ennobling aims; and that it behoved any man, whose soul cherished a lofty purpose, to follow out a sustained plan unswervingly. To this end he determined, rather ungratefully, considering how powerful a tonic his visit had proved, to abandon the vain city, and betake himself incontinently to the majestic desert and to—Maud Stangrove.

He made an abrupt departure, somewhat to the surprise of that very small section of society which troubled itself with his weal or woe, and appeared suddenly before M'Nab, who, in his turn, was surprised also.

Mr. M'Nab was not only astonished at his employer's short stay in Melbourne, but also at his cheerful and animated demeanour.

"The trip has done you a world of good, sir," he said. "I thought when you went away that it would take you longer to forget our losses."

"Well, there's nothing like change of air, and the knowledge of what other people are doing, when you are low. If people spent more money in trains and coaches they would spend less on doctors, I believe. A man who is shut up with his misery broods over it till, like a shepherd, he goes mad some day. When I got to town, I found others had suffered even more heavily, and, of course, that comforted me."

"And the wool?" inquired M'Nab.

"Nothing but compliments," answered Jack. "Never expected to see wool got up like it on the Warroo, and so on. Mr. Shrood prophesied all kinds of triumphs and fancy prices next year. I might have had ten thousand sovereigns to take away in my hat, if I had asked for them. This flood seems to have done a world of damage, and such a trifle as the loss of two or three thousand sheep was voted not worth talking about."

"It was an awful sacrifice—just a throwing to the fishes of two thousand golden guineas, anyway ye look at it," said, slowly and impressively, the downright M'Nab. He could never be led to gloss over any shortcomings, losses, or failures, holding them as points in the game of life to be carefully scored, which no player worthy of the name would omit. "You're welcome to knock half of it off my wages," he continued, "as I shall always believe that I was to blame for want of care. But I hope we'll have profits yet that will clear off the score of this and other losses."

"I am fully confident that we shall, M'Nab," said Jack, hopefully; "and I have no notion of making my deficit good out of your screw, though it is manly of you to offer it. You work as hard and do as much as one man can. Whether things go right or wrong, I shall never blame you, be assured. I am free to admit that in your place I should not do half as well. And now, do you want any help for a week or two, for I think I shall ride down to Juandah?"

"I did not expect you back for a month more," said M'Nab, smiling to himself; "so I had arranged to do without you, you see. I can get on grandly till we begin to draft the fat sheep for market."

Thus absolved and conscience-clear, Mr. Redgrave immediately betook himself to Juandah, where he was received with frank and kindly welcome by everybody. It was fortunate that he had gone to Melbourne after the flood-disaster, as he was now able to treat that damaging blow in a much more light and philosophical fashion than would have been possible to him without the aid of his metropolitan experiences.

"It was rather a facer," he admitted to Stangrove, who had delicately described their grief at seeing the drowned weaners floating past their windows in scores and hundreds, "but when a fellow has a large operation in hand he must look at the progress of the whole enterprise, and not fix his mind upon minor drawbacks. A single vessel doesn't matter out of the whole convoy of East Indiamen. The loss of the *Royal George* had no perceptible influence on the rest of the British navy. I shall shear over sixty thousand sheep next year, with luck, and when I sell shall think no more of those poor devils of weaners than you do of the blacks—probably mythical—that Red Rob slew during your minority."

"With luck—with luck—as you say," said Stangrove, rather absently. "But, as we agreed before, luck seems necessary to the working out of your plan, which I admit, at present prices, looks feasible enough. But suppose we *don't* get our fair share of luck this year, what then? However, we needn't anticipate evil. Let's come in and see the ladies."

"'So behold you of return,' as dear old Madame Florac says," commenced Maud, looking up from *The Newcomes*. "How truly fortunate you men are, Mr. Redgrave, that you can get away to some decent abode of mankind every now and then under the pretence of business! Now we poor, oppressed women have to give reasons that will bear the most searching investigation before we are allowed to go anywhere. Men only say vaguely 'must go—important business,' and take themselves off."

"Really, Miss Stangrove, I don't see but that you, in this nice cool room, with nothing to do but to read about Ethel and Barnes, that grand old cat Lady Kew, and the dear old Colonel, are about as well off as anyone I have seen in my travels."

"That's all nonsense. We endure life here, of course, but look at the delightful change of scene, air, life, people, trees, bread and butter, everything new and fresh that you have had lately. Uniformity is death to some natures. That is why some unhappy individuals of my sex make dismal endings and horrid examples of themselves. Some girl marries the butler, or the stockman, or the music master periodically. Depend upon it, it is nothing but Nature's protest against the murderous monotony of their daily lives."

"Maud, Maud," interposed Mrs. Stangrove, "how can you say such dreadful things? Quite improper, I think. I declare Mr. Redgrave will be shocked and alarmed if you go on so. Really, my dear!"

Jack mildly combated these extreme and unconventional opinions, declaring that some of the most discontented, useless, and life-weary people he had ever seen had enjoyed no end of variety—passed their lives in sight-seeing—been everywhere—and yet were more utterly *ennuyés* than even Miss Stangrove on the banks of the Warroo.

"Well," said that young lady, "you see they had only been working out the vanity and vexation of spirit theory, and how dreary a result it was for the Wise King to come to! But I should like 'to see the folly of it too.' I think manufacturing one's own vanity and vexation is more satisfactory than acquiring it second-hand."

"I wonder if our black friends ever feel bored," said Jack; "before we came and gave them iron tomahawks it must have taken a fellow a week to chop out a 'possum; so I suppose constant employment conduced to cheerfulness. Still, of late years, food being plentiful, wars traditionary, and travel impossible, game perhaps a trifle scarcer, a sense of impatience of the 'slow, strong hours' *may* have crossed their unused intelligences."

"It may be, for all we know," said Mark, who had re-entered and thrown himself upon a sofa, "at the root of the frantic love for ardent spirits which all the younger natives have. The men of a generation or two back, like 'old man Jack,' don't drink. But all the middle-aged and younger ones, *more particularly those, by comparison, educated*, drink fearfully hard whenever they get the chance."

"So do all savages," said Jack; "likewise smoke furiously. Alcohol and tobacco seem particularly attractive to their organizations; and they have no power of moderation. 'Too much of anything is not good,' said the Red Indian, 'but too much rum is just enough.' That's their idea— all over the world."

"I suggest that we have exhausted the subject," mildly interposed Mrs. Stangrove, "and as it is getting cool we might all go for a drive in the break with Mark and the young horses. Can you take us, my dear?"

This was voted a first-rate suggestion. The evening, comparatively cool only, was approaching. So the ladies apparelled themselves suitably, and as Mark let the half-broken team out, without fear of stone or stump, along the glorious, level, sandy out-station track, the rushing air refreshed their senses, jaded by the long, breezeless midsummer day. It was twilight deepening into night as they returned, a very cheerful and animated party. Maud, with the changeful mood of her sex, declared herself again reconciled to existence, and even conscious of pleasurable anticipation as regarded tea.

Jack was catechised after that refection upon the balls, archery-parties, picnics, races, &c., to which he had been on his late visit to town. Maud sang a new song or two which she had managed to get up, buried alive as she assumed herself to be, and John Redgrave was more deeply enthralled than ever.

Stangrove asked him to stay a fortnight or so with them, if he could spare the time; and Jack declared it would be most uncomplimentary to M'Nab's management, and the fencing system generally, to suppose that a proprietor was pinned to his homestead like a mere shepherding squatter. So he gratefully accepted the invitation and the opportunity. In spite of the weather—and even the presence of the beloved object cannot render the month of January a pleasant one in Lower Riverina— the days passed in a dreamily luxurious tropical fashion. Jack had an early enjoyable swim in the capacious Warroo, now rippling over sand-bars and pebbles, as if it had never risen with death upon its angry tide. Then the breakfast in the cool darkened room, before the great and resistless glare of the day commenced, was very pleasant. After that period, and until the sun was down, I am free to confess that all the *dramatis personæ* might as well have been in Madras or Bombay. Outside the heat was awful, and the first effect on leaving the shelter of the cottage after ten o'clock A.M., was as if one had suddenly encountered the outer current of a blast furnace. Mark was out on the run, as a matter of course, pretty nearly all day and everyday. There were never-ending duties among the sheep, cattle, and horses which did not permit him to make any philosophical reflections upon the heat of the weather. He simply put it out of the question, as he had done from boyhood. Consequently he did not feel it half as much as those who tried by every means to evade it.

Jack did not feel himself called upon to offer to join his host in these daily expeditions. He occasionally, of course, volunteered when his assistance was likely to be useful. But generally he lounged about the house, and made himself generally useful by reading aloud to the ladies, irrigating Mrs. Stangrove's flower-garden, practising duets with Maud, and generally raising Miss Stangrove from that desolate and vacuous condition into which she had been in danger of falling before his opportune arrival. The riding and the driving parties were of course not abandoned. There was always some period arbitrarily defined as the cool of the evening, when such exercise, even walking by the Warroo under the sighing river-oaks, was suitable and satisfactory. He and Mark had long arguments about all kinds of subjects, in which the ladies now and then took part. Nothing could have been more generally agreeable than the whole thing. But the days wore on, and Jack felt that he had no decent excuse for staying longer; he therefore prepared to depart. He had not seen his way either, much as he longed for an opportunity, to put that very tremendous and momentous question to Maud, to which he had sworn to himself that he *would* receive a definitive answer before quitting Juandah. Truth to tell, their intimacy had not advanced so quickly as he had hoped. He saw, or thought he saw, that Maud liked his society. But she was so frank and unembarrassed that he mistrusted the existence of any deeper sentiment. He was not altogether without knowledge of the ways of womenkind; and he knew that this frank recognition of the pleasantness of his society was by no means a good sign. He did not feel inclined to ask any girl, obviously non-sympathetic, to marry him, trusting to the unlikeliness of her seeing any decenter sort of fellow in these wilds, and to her acknowledged distaste for life on the Warroo. "No, hang it," he said to himself, "that would be hardly generous. I'll wait till she shows some sign that she really cares for me— loves me, I mean. If she doesn't, John Redgrave is not the man to ask her. If she does, she can't hide it, nor can any woman that ever lived. I know so much of the alphabet."

Thus hardening his heart temporarily and strategically, Mr. Jack finished copying the last galop, put a finishing touch to the grand arterial system of irrigation borrowed from Ah Sing, which he had engineered for the benefit of Mr. Redgrave's roses and japonicas, gave Mark Stangrove a real good day's work at the branding-yard, showed him a new dodge for leg-roping which elicited the admiration of the stockmen, and went on his way, accompanied for a mile or two by his host.

XIV

"Soft! What are you?
Some villain mountaineers?
I have heard of such."

—CYMBELINE

Mrs. Stangrove and Maud were sitting in the drawing-room that morning, a little silent and distrait, we may confess, when a man's footstep was heard on the verandah. "I did not think that Mark would have returned so soon," said Maud, going to the French window and looking out. She stood there for an instant, and then, turning to her sister a face ashen-white and strangely altered, gasped out a single word—that word of dread, often of doom, in the far, lone, defenceless Australian waste—"Bushrangers!" Mrs. Stangrove gave a moaning, half-muffled cry, and then, obeying the irresistible maternal instinct, rushed into the adjoining apartment where her children were. At the same moment a tall man with a revolver raised in his right hand stepped into the room, and gazed rapidly round with restless eyes, as of one long used to meet with frequent foes. Behind him, closely following, were three other armed men, while a fifth was visible in the passage, thus cutting off all retreat towards the rear.

Maud Stangrove was a girl of more than ordinary firmness of nerve. She strove hard against the spasmodic terror which the feeling of being *absolutely in the power* of lawless and desperate men at first produced. Rapidly conning over the chances of a rescue, in the event of the working overseer and his men returning, as she knew they were likely to do, at an early hour, having been out at the nearest out-station since sunrise, accompanied by Mark, who had intended when leaving to cut across to them and inspect their work, she felt the necessity of keeping cool and temporizing with the enemy.

Steadying her voice with an effort, and facing the intruder with a very creditable air of unconcern, she said—"What do you want? I think you have mistaken your way."

The robber looked at her with a bold glance of admiration, and then, with an instinctive deference which struggled curiously with his consciousness of having taken the citadel, made answer—"See here,

Miss, I'm Redcap; dessay you've heard of me. You've no call to be afeared; but we've come here for them repeating rifles as Mr. Stangrove's been smart enough to get up from town."

"I don't know anything about them," said Maud, thankful to remember that she had not seen lately these unlucky celebrities in the small-arm way, which, for their marvellous shooting and rapidity of loading, had been a nine-days' wonder in the neighbourhood.

"Well," interposed a black-visaged, down-looking ruffian, who had ensconced himself in an easy chair, "some of you will have to know about 'em, and look sharp too, or we'll burn the blessed place down about your ears."

"You shut up, Doctor," said the leader, who seemed, like Lambro, one of the mildest-mannered men that ever "stuck up mails or fobbed a note." "Let me talk to the lady. It's no use your fencing, Miss, about these guns; we know all about 'em, and have 'em we will. Mr. Stangrove shot a bullock with the long one last Saturday. You'd better let us have 'em, and we'll clear out."

Maud was considering whether it would not be safer to "fess" and get rid of the unwelcome visitors, who, though wonderfully pacific, might not remain so. A diversion was effected. One of the younger members of the band suddenly appeared with the baby—the idolized darling of the household—in his arms.

"Here," he cried, "I've got something as is valuable. I shall stick to this young 'un to put me in mind of my pore family as I've been obliged to cut away from."

Mrs. Stangrove, poor lady, had been keeping close with the older children, flattering herself that this precious infant, then taking the air in his nurse's arms, was safe from the marauders. She was speedily undeceived by the piercing cry which reached her ears, as the affrighted babe, just old enough to "take notice" of the stranger, proclaimed distrust of his awkward, though not unkind, dandling.

Rushing in with frantic eagerness, and the "wrathful dove" expression which the gentlest maternal creature assumes at any "intromitting" with her young, as old Dugald Dalgetty phrases it, Mrs. Stangrove suddenly confronted the audacious intruder, and, seizing the child, tore it out of his arms with so deft a promptitude that the delinquent had no time for resistance. Looking half startled, half sullen, he stood in the same position for a moment, with so ludicrous an expression of defeat and mortification that his companions burst into a fit of unrestrained laughter, while Mrs. Stangrove, in the reaction from her unaccustomed ferocity, clasped the child to her bosom in a paroxysm of tears.

"This here's all very well," said Redcap, "but we didn't come for foolery. If these rifles ain't turned up in five minutes you'll be sorry for it. If some of 'em gets to the brandy, Miss," here he lowered his voice and looked significantly at Maud, "there's no saying what will happen. Better deal with us while we're in a good temper."

Maud believed that the coveted weapons were somewhere upon the premises, although she had spoken truly at the first demand when she averred that she was ignorant of their precise locality. She was aware that a moment might change the mood of the robbers from one of amused toleration to that of reckless brutality. Not wholly ignorant of the terrible legends, still whispered low and with bated breath, of wrongs irrevocable suffered by defenceless households, her resolution was quickly taken.

"Jane," she said to Mrs. Stangrove, who, helpless and unnerved, was still sobbing hysterically, "if you know where these guns are tell me at once, and I will go for them. It can't be helped. These men have behaved fairly, and as we can neither fight nor run away, we must give up our money-bags, or what they consider an equivalent. Where are the rifles?"

"Oh, what will Mark say?" moaned out the distracted wife. "If he were only here I should not care. And yet, perhaps, it's better as it is. If they do not hurt the dear children I don't care what they take. You know best. The rifles are in Mark's dressing-room, in the shower-bath."

Maud went out, and presently reappeared with the beautiful American repeaters, one of which had the desirable peculiarity of being able to discharge sixteen cartridges in as many seconds, if needful; the other was a light and extremely handy Snider—"a tarnation smart shooting-iron," as one of the station hands, who hailed from the Great Republic, had admiringly expressed himself.

Redcap's eyes glistened as he possessed himself of the "sixteen-shooter," and handed the Snider to the Doctor.

"All's well that ends well," growled that worthy, "we'll be a match for all the blessed traps between here and Sydney with these here tools; but for two pins I'd put a match in every gunyah on the place, just to learn Stangrove not to be in such a hurry to run in a mob of pore fellers as had got tired of being messed about by those infernal troopers."

"You'll just do what I tell you, Doctor," said Redcap, savagely, "and if I catch one of you burning or shooting without orders he'll have to settle with me. Hallo! it can't be dinner-time."

This last observation was called forth by the appearance of the parlour-maid with the table-cloth and a tray. She was a buxom country girl, without any of that hyper-sensitiveness of the nervous system common to town domestics. A bushranger to her was simply an exaggerated "traveller," and nothing more. One o'clock P.M. having arrived, it did not occur to her that the family would choose to omit the important midday meal on account of visitors, however unwelcome. She proceeded, therefore, with perfect coolness to lay the cloth, and observing no sign of objection from Maud, presently brought in the dishes, and set the chairs as usual. Maud, thinking that the less fear they showed the better it would be for them, called the children, and motioned to Mrs. Stangrove to take her accustomed place. Simultaneously, Miss Ethel, a quiet little monkey of nine years, being extremely hungry, then and there recited the customary grace, praying God to "relieve the wants of others, and to make them truly thankful for what they were about to receive."

Maud afterwards confessed that it cost her a strong effort to repress a smile as she noted the look of undisguised astonishment which came over the faces of Redcap and his men, who probably had not heard for many a year, if ever, that simple benediction.

The Doctor recovered himself first. "I feel confoundedly hungry," said he; "I suppose we may as well take a snack too."

"Then come along with me to the kitchen," said the maid, promptly, with the most matter-of-fact air, opening the door of the passage.

The men stared for a moment as if disposed for equal privileges in the region of communism which they now morally inhabited. But the old instinct was not entirely overpowered, and with one look at Maud's rigid countenance and the pale face of Mrs. Stangrove, Redcap followed the girl, and signed to his comrades to do likewise.

At this moment one of the bed-room doors opened, and a man entered the room, dressed in a full suit of black. His hair shone with pomatum, and he looked something between a lay reader and a provincial footman.

"Look out," roared the Doctor, "perhaps there's more of 'em coming," as he raised his revolver.

"Come, none of that, Doctor," said the new-comer; "don't you never see nothin' but a cove's clothes?"

A roar of laughter from the others and the returned Redcap apprised him of his mistake. It was the youngest member of their own band, who, being of a restless disposition, had managed to find his way to the spare room, where he had coolly appropriated a combination suit of John Redgrave's, and had further anointed himself with a pot of pomatum, which did not belong to that gentleman. This episode improved the spirits both of captors and captives, and, hustling one another like school-boys, the whole gang made their way into the kitchen, where, to judge from the sounds of laughter that issued therefrom, they enjoyed themselves much more than would have been the case in the dining-room.

In about half an hour Maud had the inexpressible gratification of seeing them mount and make off steadily along the road which led "up the river."

When they were fairly off Maud felt symptoms of having taxed nature severely. She turned deadly pale as she threw herself upon the sofa, covering her face with her hands, while her whole frame shook with convulsive sobs, as she tried with her full strength of will to control the tendency to "the sad laugh that cannot be repressed." However, as chiefly happens in those feminine temperaments where the reasoning powers are stronger than the emotional, she succeeded, and bestowed all her regained energy to the support and consolation of her sister-in-law.

While these wonderful things were happening, John Redgrave was peacefully riding along the up river road, thinking of the manifold perfections of his divinity, and little dreaming that she was at that very moment a distressed damsel, in the power of traitors and *faitours*.

"What a lovely morning!" soliloquized he, "not so warm as it has been; a breeze too. How peaceful everything looks! Really, this is *not* such a fearful climate as I thought it at first. With a decent house, and one fair spirit to be his minister, a fellow might gracefully glide through existence here for a few years—that is, if he were making lots of money. It would be almost too uneventful, that's the worst of it—nothing ever happens here. Hallo! what a pace the Sergeant is coming at, and old Kearney too!"

This exclamation was called forth by the sudden appearance of the whole police force which was thought necessary for the protection of a district about a hundred miles square. Jack knew their figures, and indeed their horses, the Sergeant's gray and the trooper's curby-hocked chestnut, to well to be mistaken. They raced up to him, and, pulling up short, both addressed him at once—a trifle out of breath.

"Have you seen any travellers on horseback, Mr. Redgrave?" asked the Sergeant.

"If it's purshuing them ye are, ye're going right wrong," blurted out trooper Kearney.

"Seen who? Pursuing what?" demanded Jack. "Why should I pursue anybody?"

"Then you haven't heard," said the Sergeant.

"The divil a hear," interrupted Private Kearney; "sure he doesn't look like it, and he ridin' along the road as peaceful as if there wasn't a bushranger betuxt here and Adelaide."

"Bushrangers!" quoth Jack, fully aroused. "I'd forgotten all about them, and near here? Where were they seen last, Stewart?"

"Constable Kearney, will you oblige me by keeping silence, and falling to the rear," said the Sergeant, majestically, while he proceeded to enlighten Jack as to the probable whereabouts of the gang "from information received."

"As far as I can make out, sir, and if that scoundrel of a mailman hasn't put me on the wrong track, they were at Mr. Stangrove's Ban Ban out-station last night, and have either gone down the river or over to his head-station today."

"His head-station! His head-station!" echoed Jack, in wild tones of astonishment—"no! surely not!"

"Very likely indeed, *I* think," said the Sergeant, "it's just about their dart from Ban Ban—they may be there now."

"What in the name of all the fiends are we wasting time here for, then?" answered he, in a voice so hoarse and strange that the Sergeant looked narrowly at him to note whether he had been drinking, all forms of eccentricity on the Warroo being referable, in his opinion, founded upon long experience, to different stages of intoxication. "Thank God, I brought my revolver with me—come on, there's a good fellow."

Sergeant Stewart had not, indeed, done more than slacken his pace for the time necessary to restore the wind of his horses, pretty well expended by a three-mile heat. He was a cool, plucky, good-looking fellow, and no bad sample of a crack non-commissioned officer of Australian police, a body of men inferior to none in the world for general light cavalry. He was as distinguished-looking in his way as his old namesake, Bothwell, in *Old Mortality*, whom he resembled in more points than one.

By the time Jack had concluded his sentence, his blood-hackney was pulling his arms off, neck and neck with the Sergeant's wiry gray, while Mr. Kearney and the doubtful chestnut were powdering away behind, at no great distance.

"It's lucky we met you," said the Sergeant; "there are five of them, I hear; three of us are a pretty fair match for the scoundrels."

"I see you have your rifles," said Jack; "you don't generally carry them."

"No; but this time we thought we were out for a week. I only saw the mailman, who gave me the office, early this morning, and came here as hard as we could split. Here comes another recruit, I suppose—by George! it's Mr. Stangrove."

So it proved. That gentleman, as unsuspicious as Jack himself, was cantering along a bush track which led into the main "frontage road" at right angles.

"Halloa, Redgrave! turned round since I left you, and our gallant police force too. What's the row—horse-stealers?"

"Worse than that, I'm afraid, old fellow," said Jack, going close up. "Redcap and his lot have been seen not far off."

He stopped—for the sudden spasm of pain which contracted Stangrove's features was bad to see.

"Good God!" he said, at length, gnawing his set lip; "my poor wife will be frightened to death, and Maud! Let us ride—pray God we are not too late."

Little was said. The horses, all tolerably well-bred, and possessing that capacity for sustaining a high rate of speed for hours together peculiar to "dry-country horses," held on, mile after mile, until they sighted a large reed-bed, which occupied a circular flat or bend of the river.

"By gad! here they are," said the sergeant, "camped on the bank! I can see their saddles; the horses are feeding in the reed-bed. Now if we can get up pretty close before they see us we have them."

"All right," said Jack, with the cheerfulness of a man whose spirits are raised by the near approach of danger. "You and Mr. Stangrove get round that clump of gums, and take them in the rear; Kearney and I will sneak along close to the bank, till we're near enough to charge. I'll bet a tenner I have the saddles first. Then they are helpless."

"I think you wouldn't make a bad general, sir," said the Sergeant. "Mr. Stangrove, I think we can't do better."

Stangrove handled his revolver impatiently, and, with something between a groan and a reply, rode silently on.

"Now, see here, Mr. Redgrave," said Pat Kearney—a *rusé* old veteran, who had put "the bracelets" upon many a horse and cattle stealer, and was not now about to have his first fray with bushrangers—"if we can snake on 'em before they have time to take to thim unlucky rade-bids—my heavy curse on thim for hiding villains—we have thim safe. They may fire a shot, but they're unsignified crathers, not like Bin Hall or Morgan."

"And why shouldn't these fellows fight?" asked Jack.

"Ye see, now, it's this a way. Just keep under the bank near thim big oaks—sure that's iligant. 'Tis a great ornamint to the force ye'd make intirely. Well, as I tould ye, that spalpeen of a Redcap—more by token I put a handful of slugs in him once—has never killed anyone yet—nor the others—d'ye see now?"

"I don't see, Kearney, that it makes much difference—they're outlaws."

"Ah! but there's a dale of differ between men that's fighting with a halter round their necks, and these half-baked divils that hasn't more than fifteen years' gaol to fear, with maybe a touch of Berrima, at the outside."

"I understand, then; you think that they are more likely to give in after the first flutter than if they were sure to be hanged when caught."

"By coorse they will; why wouldn't they? I knew Redcap when he'd think more of duffing a red heifer than all the money in the country. If he seen me, I believe he'd hold up his hands, from habit like."

"Then you don't think it a good plan to make bush-ranging the same as murder, and to hang a fellow directly he turns out?"

"Thim that wanted that law made didn't have their families living on the Warroo," said the old trooper, sturdily. "How can a couple of men like us thravel and purtect a district as big as Great Britain? And what would turn a raw lot like these devils let loose quicker than a blundering, over-severe law? By the mortial, they see us. Hould on, sir, and we'll charge them together, like Wellington and the Proosians at Waterloo."

The robbers had a good strategical position. Their base of operations was the reed-bed, a labyrinth of cane-like stalks which met overhead in the narrow paths worn by the feet of the stock. They were, however, divided in party and in purpose. Two of them had been detailed to fetch up the horses grazing in the reed-bed, and the remainder, having just sighted Redgrave and Constable Kearney, stood to their arms with sufficient determination.

On the very edge of the river bank, beneath which the stream ran in a deeper channel than ordinary, were the five saddles of the gang. They had evidently dismounted at this spot, and, after unsaddling, had gone to the edge of the reed brake, where an unusually shady tree afforded them an inviting lounge.

Thus it chanced that Jack's keen eyes discovered the state of affairs, as he and Kearney prepared to rival Waterloo, on a necessarily limited scale.

"Look here, Kearney," said he, as they commenced the grand charge, "I mean to throw those saddles into the river. The rascals are a good thirty yards from them. They can't do much without horses. So you blaze away, and cover me as well as you can."

"It's a great move intirely—but watch that divil Redcap; 'tis a mighty nate shot he is—and you'll be out in the open—bad cess to it."

Jack's blood was up, and he did not care two straws for all the Redcaps and revolvers in Saltbushdom. Racing frantically for the accoutrements, he jumped off, and emptied his revolver, save one barrel, at the enemy. Kearney, a cool and experienced warrior, drew off some little distance to the right, and opened business on his own account, not only with his revolver, but with his breach-loading rifle, while his trained horse stood as steady as a Woolwich gunner. Jack, stooping down, coolly threw one saddle after another into the swirling current, where they were swept off before the very eyes of the brigands. As he stood upright, after hearing the "ping" of more than one bullet unpleasantly close, he felt a sharp blow—an electric throb—in his left arm, and realized the fact that a bullet had passed through the muscles near the shoulder.

Inwardly congratulating himself that his right arm was unharmed, Jack drew himself up, and, facing the dropping shots which still hissed angrily around him, his eye fell upon the redoubtable Redcap, who, rifle in hand, had evidently been trying the range of Stangrove's late purchase in a manner not contemplated by that gentleman. Jack swung round, and lifting his revolver, as if at gallery practice, pulled the trigger with that deadly confidence of aim which some men say is never experienced save in snipe-shooting or man-shooting. Bar accidents, the career of William Crossbrand, otherwise Redcap, was ended. Not so, however, was he to be sped. There had been an old forcing-yard built at the spot for the purpose of swimming cattle and horses over the river. A few straggling posts were left. Behind one of these the robber adroitly slipped, and the bullet buried itself in the massive and twisted timber, just on a level with Mr. Redcap's unharmed breast.

"Sure it was the greatest murder in the world," said Mr. Kearney, afterwards, with apparent incongruousness. "'Twas a dead man he was, only for that blagguard of a post."

At this moment the Sergeant and Stangrove—who had been waiting till the two other outlaws came up, driving their hobbled horses before them—made a rush, which was the signal for an advance in line of the attacking party. A few scattered shots were exchanged on both sides. The shooting (let any of my readers try what practice they can make, with the best revolvers, from moving horses) was not anything to boast of. It was soon evident that the bushrangers were not going to fight to the last gasp. They began to slacken fire, and show signs of capitulation. Perhaps the most dramatic incident occurred just before the surrender. The Sergeant had ridden up, neck and neck, with Stangrove to their partially entrenched position, and had exhausted his ammunition in a sharp exchange, when the Doctor stepped forward from behind a tree, and took deliberate aim at him with the Snider.

There was no time to reload. Things looked critical. Stangrove and the others were engaged on their own account; but the Sergeant was equal to the situation; he fell back upon the moral force in which he so enormously excelled his antagonist. Raising his hand in a threatening attitude, and drawing himself up as if on parade, he fixed his stern eyes upon the audacious criminal and roared out—

"You infernal scoundrel, would you dare to shoot *me*?"

It was a strange and characteristic spectacle. The handsome, soldierly, comparatively refined man-at-arms, sitting upon his horse, affording a perfectly fair mark; the half-sullen, half-irresolute criminal, with the power of life and death in his wavering hands; but the mental pressure was too great. The old reverence for the representative of the Law was not all uprooted. A host of doubts and dismal visions of dock and judge, and manacled limbs, and the Sergeant sternly implacable, "reading him up" before a crowded court, rose before his overcharged brain. The conflict was too intense. With a muttered oath he flung down the historic Snider, and stood with outstretched hands, which the alert officer of police immediately enclosed in the gyves of the period.

"You've acted like a sensible chap," said Stewart, patronizingly, as the handcuffs clicked with the closing snap. "I'm not sure that you won't get off light. You have had the luck not to have killed anybody that I know of since you turned out."

About the same time Mr. Redcap and the other semi-desperadoes had lowered their flags to Stangrove, his late guest, and Constable Kearney. This last warrior had, like his superior officer, lost no time in securing the prisoners. Four pairs of handcuffs were available for the elder men. The youngest brigand had his elbows buckled together behind his back with a stirrup-leather.

"Bedad! ye're a great arr-my intirely," said Mr. Kearney, complacently. "Sure it's kilt and murthered I thought we'd all be with a lot of fine young men like yees forenint us. But the Docther there hadn't the heart to rub out the Sergeant; 'tis the polite man he always was."

"Well, they say taking to the bush is a short life and a merry one," grumbled out Redcap in a kind of Surrey-side tragedy growl. "I know our time's been short, and a dashed long way from merry. I'm thankful we ain't shed any blood—leastways not killed any cove as I knows of." Here he looked at Jack's wounded arm, the blood from which had considerably altered the hue of his shooting-jacket.

"Oh! the divil a hanging match there'll be, if that's what ye're thinking of," said Kearney. "Sure when they didn't hang Frank Gardiner why would they honour the likes of ye with a rope, and Jack Ketch, and a parson? Cock ye up with hanging indeed! Ye'll be picking oakum or chipping freestone, or learning to make shoes and mats, ten years from now."

"You have been at my station, I see by the rifles," said Stangrove; "was that all you took?"

"Nothing else, Mr. Stangrove," said Redcap, humbly, "as I'm a living man. We'd heard so much about them—that the big one could carry a mile and shoot all day—that we was bound to have 'em. But we done no harm, and the ladies wasn't much frightened—not the young lady anyhow."

"It's lucky for you they were not," said Stangrove, huskily; "and it may serve you something at your trial. Sergeant, what are you going to do with the prisoners? will you bring them to Juandah tonight?"

"No, sir, I propose to make straight for the gaol at Barrabri; we'll get to the 'Mailman's Arms' sometime before tomorrow morning. It's the first halt we shall make; so step out, you fellows. The sooner we get to Barrabri the sooner you'll be comfortably in gaol, where you'll have nothing to think of till the Quarter Sessions."

"Goodbye, Sergeant. Goodbye, Kearney. Redgrave, you had better come home with me and get that arm seen to. By the way, Sergeant, leave word at the 'Mailman's Arms' to send on Doctor Bateman, if he's anywhere about."

"So far so good," said Jack, as they turned their horses' heads towards Juandah. "They were not a very terrific set of ruffians, and had evidently not bound themselves by a dark and bloody oath never to be taken alive."

"The sharpest shooting seems to have come your way," said Stangrove, noticing that Jack's face was growing pale. "I heard a bullet or two whistle near me; but I believe they were sick of their life and anxious to yield decently. I feel mercifully inclined towards them, inasmuch as I believe they let us off cheap at Juandah; whereas, if it had been one of the old gangs—"

"Here we are," said Jack, as they reined up at the stable door. "Do you know I feel very queer." Here he dismounted, and moving with some difficulty, that mortal paleness overspread his face which, once seen, is indelibly associated with real or temporary lifelessness, and down went Mr. John Redgrave, helpless as a new-born babe, or a young lady menaced by a black beetle.

Stangrove let go his horse, and raised his prostrate guest in his arms (and a most awfully heavy burden be found him) when out rushed Mrs. Stangrove and Maud.

"Oh, my darling, we have had the bushrangers here, the horrid men; they took both the rifles; and one of them took dear baby in his arms and frightened me to death. Have you seen them? And who is that? Why, it's Mr. Redgrave. Is he wounded?"

"He was hit through the arm, but he is not desperately wounded. He lost some blood and fainted. Oh, you're coming to; that's right; sit up, old man, and we'll soon have you in bed."

Maud had come forward with a half-cry parting her lips, while her widely-opened eyes were expressive of pained yet warmest sympathy. She could not trust herself to speak, but, kneeling beside the insensible form, bathed Jack's face with her handkerchief dipped in water, with a woman's ready wit, and, loosening his neckerchief, watched with deepest earnestness the first faint signs of returning life.

"'Pon my word," said Jack, as he sat up and stared rather wildly around him, "I feel awfully ashamed of myself to tumble down and give trouble all from a scratch like this. But I suppose it has bled and Sangrado-ed one a bit. It will soon pass off."

"You have been fighting for us, Mr. Redgrave," said Maud, with involuntary tenderness in every tone of her voice; "and we must not be ungrateful. Try if you can walk inside now. Lean on me. I am ever so strong, I can tell you."

Jack did as he was bid, and felt it necessary to avail himself of the rude strength of which Miss Stangrove boasted. Without any great loss of time he found himself on a couch in the spare room, where, with the aid of Mr. and Mrs. Stangrove, he was turned into an interesting invalid, with his arm bound up, pending the arrival of Dr. Bateman.

Part of the evening was spent by the household in his bedroom, and a very pleasant evening it was. Mrs. Stangrove was gravely happy, but inclined to be tearful when recurring to the dear children. Maud and her brother took the humorous side of the adventure, and Jack laughed till his arm ached at Maud's description of the appearance of the younger bushranger as he turned out in part of Jack's raiment, and the remainder as left by a travelling agent for an orphan asylum.

"'All's well that ends well,'" said Stangrove. "I shall not have the same anxious feeling everytime the dogs bark now. It might easily have been worse; and, taking them as bushrangers, a decenter lot of fellows I never wish to meet."

Dr. Bateman came next morning, having fortunately looked in at the 'Mailman's Arms' on his way in from a back block, whither he had been called to set a stockman's leg, broken only the week before. Hearing of the casualty awaiting him at Juandah, he came on best pace, making running with his wiry iron-legged mustang from the start. The doctor, who had in a general way to minister to the indispositions and accidents of the population of a district about a hundred and fifty miles long and a hundred broad, required to possess the constitutional qualities of his favourite mare. Most of them he did possess, thinking as little of a ride of a hundred miles in a day and a half as she did of carrying him.

"So you managed to get hit, Mr. Redgrave?" quoth he, in a loud cheery voice, bustling in after breakfast. "Infernal scoundrels—never knew such a gang. *Never* in my life. Worst lot that have taken the bush since old Donohoe's time."

"But, doctor," protested two or three voices in a breath, "you surely mistake—they—"

"What I say I stick to," interrupted the doctor, with a twinkle in his shrewd gray eye. "Worst gang I ever knew—*for a medical man*. Why, you are, my dear sir, the only wounded man in the whole district. I'm ashamed of them—the country's going to destruction. No energy among the natives."

"Oh, that's it," said Stangrove; "I was going to stand up for my friend, the enemy—Mr. Redcap and his merry men; but from your point of view they did behave disgracefully; not a patch upon Morgan, or the Clarkes, or even the virtuous and politically celebrated Frank Gardiner. What do you think of your patient, doctor?"

"That he is in very good quarters. Pulse marks quicker time today than yesterday. Slight touch of fever, only natural; arm inflamed and painful. A week's quiet, not a day less, will set him right. Would have been a very pretty case had bullet perforated the humerus. As it is, merely amounts to laceration of muscles, minor vessels, and nerves."

"You'll stay tonight, doctor, of course?" asked Stangrove.

"No, must go after lunch; have to ride down the river as far as Emu Reach. Man drowned last night—inquest."

"How was that?"

"Oh, shepherd, of course; frightful amount of lunacy among them. Poor old Pott Quartsley got a great fright last week up Din Din. He went into a shepherd's hut at dusk and saw him standing just in front of the door. 'What are you staring at me like that for, you old fool?' he said. Gave him a slight push. The shepherd turned half round and slid into the same posture, silently, 'Great God!' said Quartsley, rushing frantically out, 'what is all this?'"

"And what was it?" asked Stangrove.

"Why, the man *had hanged himself* the day before with his bridle-rein fastened to the tie-beam. His feet just touched the ground, and his hat was on his head, so that he looked, in the half-light, exactly like a man standing upright. It had a great effect on old Quartsley."

"What direction will the result take?"

"That of fencing, I believe. Says he can't afford to keep expensive luxuries like shepherds any longer. That they're extravagances are sure to injure the finest property—the soundest constitution in the long run. Says he shall repent, economize, and fence—for the future."

"Bravo!" said Jack, a little feebly; "if old Quartsley begins to fence you won't be left behind, Stangrove?"

"I said two years," answered he, "and in two years I'll consider the question, not an hour before that time. In the interval don't you excite yourself. The doctor and I are going to the men's hut. I'll send Maud with some cold tea for you."

XV

"A little cloud as big as a man's hand."

It is not half a bad thing to "be laid up," as it is called, for a reasonable and moderate fraction of one's life—more especially if a "bright particular star" is impelled to beam softly and brilliantly upon one in consequence. Jack, after the inflammation, which gave him "fits" the first day or two, had subsided, began to enjoy himself after a subdued fashion. Though food was restricted by the despotic doctor, and liquor, other than tea, altogether interdicted, there was no embargo laid upon tobacco. Mr. Redgrave, therefore, used to get over the window which "gave" into the garden, and have many a soothing and delightful pipe in the afternoons and the long, clear, bright nights.

He was, I firmly believe, perfectly well able to read; but he pretended that it made his head ache, so Maud fell into the trap and volunteered to read Macaulay's *Essays*, the *Saturday Review*, *Macmillan's Magazine*, Market Harborough, and even some choice bits from Tennyson and Browning. What pleasant mornings these were! Stangrove was out; Mrs. Jane deep in housekeeping and nursery details; so these two people were able for a brief season to taste uninterruptedly the charm of pure intellectual enjoyment, unalloyed by the jar of small duties or the regretful sense of unperformed work. Convalescence, that regal state and condition, evades all ordinary responsibilities. It is above duty, blame, arithmetic and grammar—the scourges and penances of this toiling pilgrimage we call life. It was joy unspeakable to lie back with half-closed eyes and hear Maud's fresh, clear young voice ringing out in accents of love, or laughter, or denunciation, or sounding strangely unnatural in the bitterness of the *Saturday's* sarcasms.

There was much reviewing of reviewers too, poetizing upon poets; philosophizing upon philosophers. Arguments and comments were plentifully superinduced by the variety of texts. A week on board ship is equal to a year on land—a day's tending of an invalid involves a feeling of dominancy and ownership, which renders the experience equal in completeness to a week on shipboard. According to this scale of reckoning, Maud Stangrove and John Redgrave had protracted opportunities of knowing each other's characters, amounting in all to such duration of time as fully justified them in contracting that morally indissoluble betrothal called an "engagement." This unlimited liability they actually had the temerity to enter into, and in the usual solemn manner sign, seal, and ratify, before John Redgrave left Juandah, perfectly recovered and unutterably happy.

He, of course, immediately acquainted Stangrove with the stupendous and miraculous fact, which that unimaginative personage received with his usual coolness.

"Maud is of age," he remarked, "and is fully entitled to choose for herself. She could not have chosen a better fellow; but I wish that confounded mortgage of yours was sold for sewing guards, or whatever the women buy obsolete deeds for. I was quite startled by seeing 'Know all men by these presents' glaring at me on Jane's work-table the other day. I hate the look even of one; it's like the skin of a dead serpent."

"Pooh! pooh!" said Jack, "you don't think the trifle of debt I owe upon 60,000 sheep—which they will be and more by lambing time—worth thinking seriously about. Why, Mildmay Shrood told me when I was down—"

"Just what he wished you to believe, I dare say. He's a good fellow, as men of money go, I grant you; but he would put his thumb or his foot on you if the money market fell with as little compunction as I feel for this fellow here." And Mark trod savagely upon a large brown flat insect, which was making its way in a blundering, purblind fashion from a decayed log to the wood-pile.

"I'm sorry that I can't show as clear a sheet as I could have done once upon a time, old fellow," said Jack. "But, on the other hand, nothing venture nothing have. If things turn out as I expect, please God, Maud shall have everything in the wide world that she can frame a wish for."

"And if not—you must pardon me for looking on the dark side of things—I have so much more often seen that colour come up—"

"If not," said Jack, "if not—I will never ask her or any woman to share my poverty. Our engagement must remain as it is till I can tell with some show of accuracy how things are likely to go. You may trust me not to hurry her."

"I trust you in that and in far more important matters," returned Mark, as he wrung his hand. "Henceforth you are our brother, save in name—let things go as they will—but I must do my best for Maud."

"Do you think I shall place a single obstacle in your way? If I thought I could not add some colour and richness to her life, which—pardon me—it lacks here, I would turn away now and never see her face more."

WHEN JACK RETURNED TO HIS home and his duties he displayed an amount of interest in the statistics and general progress of the station which amazed and delighted Mr. M'Nab. That energetic personage had been toiling away by himself since the news, much exaggerated, of Mr. Redgrave's adventure with his ordinary conscientious regularity. Everything was in apple-pie order. The minimization of labour had been carried out almost to a fault, as Jack thought, when he had to unsaddle and feed his own horse, and, Mr. M'Nab being absent, and Monsieur Dubois gone for a load of wood, the place looked desolate enough after the home-like, old-fashioned Juandah. However, Jack comforted himself with thinking that this was the straight road to clearing off the mortgage—to a triumphant sale of a fully stocked run, and to the final possession of a "kingdom by the sea," or beyond sea, in which Maud Stangrove should reign, when "the happy princess followed him."

Day after day he accompanied M'Nab in long rides from one end of the run to the other. With him he counted the sheep wherever such counting might be necessary. He took his turn at weighing of rations, and in every way worked with hand and head as hard (so M'Nab, with grim humour, asserted) as if he had been his own overseer.

In the rare intervals of leisure, when that embodiment of concentrativeness permitted his thoughts to dwell upon any subject other than sheep, he could not avoid the inference that the proprietor of Gondaree was a changed man. Up to this turning-point of his life John Redgrave had been content to work fairly, sometimes fiercely, with head or hand; but, in any case, to accept success or failure with undisturbed serenity. Now it was otherwise. He examined searchingly the whole working of the establishment, and satisfied himself, much to M'Nab's gratification, of the condition and well-being of each division of the stock, of the plant, and machinery of the place. He went carefully through the account-books, and verified the debits and credits, with an accuracy which his lieutenant had not believed to be in him, as he afterwards said. He compiled a statement of the financial position of Gondaree, which, after various testings and corrections, was agreed between them to be arithmetically, mathematically, indisputably exact. He had fully decided to sell. The sheep were in fine condition, severely culled, and originally well chosen. The run was of the best possible quality, in full working order, and capable of yet greater development. He could not imagine its fetching less than the highest market price. At that time such a run, so stocked, so improved, was held to be good value for twenty-five shillings per head. It was not impossible or even unlikely that two competing buyers might run it up to twenty-seven and sixpence. The lesser price would pay off the mortgage—he had no other debts in the world—and leave him, say, forty or fifty thousand pounds.

This was the account current he had ciphered out many and many a time. It was written upon sheets of paper, large and small, upon blotting-pads, upon stray leaves of journals, and pretty well engraven upon a less perishable, more retentive, material—the heart of John Redgrave.

Something in this wise were the figures:—

10,000 fat sheep, now ready for market at, say, 15s.		£7,500
50,000 sheep, with station, stores, furniture, implements, horses, drays, &c., all given in at, say, 25s.		£62,500
		£70,000
Mortgage due Bank of N. Holland	£25,000	
Interest, commission, incidentals, and expenses overlooked, say	£5,000	
		£30,000
		£40,000

As far as anyone could make out, judging from the present prices, Gondaree was as safe to sell at this estimate as Mr. Stangrove's fast, handsome buggy horses—young, sound, and a dead match—were to bring fifty pounds in any sale-yard in the colonies. Here was a magnificent surplus. Say, forty thousand pounds. That was enough, surely. A large proportion would of course remain on mortgage, and, as he would receive one-third or one-half cash, it could not be better placed, receiving, as he would, eight percent interest, the ordinary tariff between squatter and squatter. Should he not sell before shearing, and realize this Aladdin's Palace, into which the Princess was ready to step, at once and without delay?

He could not exactly afford the train of slaves, with diamonds as big as pigeons' eggs, and rubies and emeralds to match; but on three or four thousand a year a decent approximation to rational luxury might be reached. Should he decide at once, and, as with poor, dear, old, despised *little* Marshmead, scribble off the fatal advertisement and abide the issue?

He took up his pen. But why do so few people sell out mining shares, railway debentures, seductive scrip of all sorts, at exactly the maximum of profit? He wavered. Then he concluded to reap the profit of the last, *really* the last shearing; wait till the 20,000 lambs were fit to count, and thus make sure—of course it was a moral certainty—of an additional twenty thousand pounds. Prices would keep up at least another couple of years—that would be long enough for him.

So he decided to see his shearing over, and to have everything fit to deliver, at a week's notice, by the time the coming crop of lambs should be weanable and countable. While this great resolve was maturing, the fiercely bright summer days, each about sixteen hours long, were gliding by. The stars burned nightly in the unclouded heavens, in which so pure was the atmosphere, so free from the slightest hint of mist or storm, that the most distant denizen of the thought-untravelled stellar waste shone golden-clear. Even in the sultry monotony of that changeless sea-like desert summer is not endless. Autumn, with an earlier twilight, a keener breath of early morn, a shorter, scarce less burning day, advanced, followed with slow but firm step the fading summer-time.

"So the fat sheep are drafted, tar-branded, and fairly on the road at last," said Mr. Redgrave, after a week's tolerably sharp work. "They look very prime. I hope they will meet as good a market as they deserve."

"Never a better lot left the Warroo," said M'Nab; "the wethers are very even, and extraordinary weights. Better sheep I never handled. The drover is a good steady fellow; and I'll catch them up before they get near the train."

"The season has been dry the last month or two," remarked Jack; "after those unlucky floods one felt as if it never would be too dry again; but it looks like it now for all that."

"The feed is not so good as it might be on the road, they say," agreed M'Nab; "but six weeks' steady driving will take them to the train; and they will lose very little condition in that time. If we don't top the market we ought to do."

Within a few weeks after this conversation Jack found himself sole denizen of Gondaree, M'Nab having taken himself off by the mail, allowing just sufficient time for him to catch the sheep and organize the order in which they should be "trained" for the Melbourne market. With the first mail after his departure, Jack discovered to his great vexation that a sudden and serious fall had taken place in fat stock. The season had, without any great demonstration of dryness, been consistently free from rain. It was cool and breezy—a hopeful condition, Jack thought. It was a very bad sign with the older residents.

It has been remarked, by persons of lengthened Australian experience, that the sudden fluctuations in price which have occurred with a curious periodicity since there has been stock enough in the colonies to found theories upon, have usually as little warning as the alarm of fire in a theatre. One person, scenting the coming danger, rises and steals quietly out, a few more follow with ill-concealed haste, then with sudden terror starts up every creature in the building, and the resistless agony of the panic is in full operation.

So, apparently, is it with those mighty and disastrous changes in the value of live stock, which have ever, in the history of Australia, pulled men's houses about their ears, like those of cards. They have whelmed alike the grizzled pioneer after a life of toil, the youthful capitalist in the first year of his first purchase, the hoary merchant, and the gambling speculator in one tidal wave of ruin. Before such an under-current sets in the apparent dearth of stock, in a land full of sheep and cattle, from Cooktown to the county of Cumberland, is curiously noticeable. Nobody will sell their oldest ewes, their most decrepit cows; it pays so much better to hold on. Bills, when times and credit are good, are renewed (with, of course, interest added), and every financial accommodation is resorted to rather than that the sanguine stockholder should be compelled to slay the goose which (in his opinion) is so prolific of the golden eggs, in the guise of wool and increase.

So the game goes on, until some fine day the money-market tightens, after its deadly, unforeseen, boa-constrictor fashion. The ominous cry of fire, or its financial synonym, is raised. A few wary or fortunate operators "get out"; but for the rank and file, who have been trusting to continuous good luck, high prices, and a "change in the climate for the better," the stampede of the panic is their only portion. In all lost battles of life, more than once has it chanced that "the brave in that trampling multitude had a fearful death to die."

Similar storm-signals now smote upon Jack's unaccustomed ear.

"We are sorry to note that all our correspondents speak of continued absence of rain in their particular localities. A drought is beginning to arouse the fears of stockholders, and prices of fat and store stock have fallen rapidly." Such was the utterance of the *Warroo Watchman*.

This was the letter from his town agents, to whom he had entrusted the sale of the much-considered fat sheep:—

Dear Sir,

If you haven't started your fat sheep, keep them back till you hear again from us.

Market glutted—all stock down.

Yours faithfully,
Drawe & Backwell

This looked bad. What a nuisance it was! For the last two years he couldn't have gone wrong, at whatever time he had despatched them; a fair average price had been always obtainable; and now, just when everything was marked out, the whole arrangements incapable of failure in anyway—here the confounded demand breaks down, and upsets all a man's calculations!

Something after this fashion ran Jack's thoughts. What should he do? Bringing the sheep back again was expensive, undignified, and would by no means aid in decreasing the debt, which had lately become rather a *bête noir* in his daily imaginings. The Warroo was not sufficiently advanced for the telegraph, or he might have held converse with the ready-witted M'Nab, who would have been certain to strike out the most favourable line of action. He had nothing for it but to write to Drawe and Backwell, to say that he *had* sent forward the sheep; that they must communicate with M'Nab, in charge, and do the best they could under the circumstances.

Up to this period of the enterprise John Redgrave, in despite of the episodes of the wool-shed and the flood, had suffered from no anxiety as to the ultimate success of the great venture. The prices of wool and sheep, store, fat, ewes and lambs, culls—everything that could be counted and could run out of a yard—had been firm and adamantine, as the bullion in the vaults of the Bank of England. Every sort, kind, and condition of sheep was worth half-a-sovereign, two to a pound, minimum; one pound a head with station; without, ten shillings.

Now there seemed a danger of the citadel being undermined, of the great fabric of investment and adventure—built up by a free expenditure of capital and energy during the last five years—melting away like an iceberg before the south wind. With such a thaw—resolving into primitive elements the gilded temple—down would go the fame and fortune of John Redgrave, and, for aught he cared, down might go his life, and stilled forever might be those restless heart-beats. Thus, when by a sudden intuitive forecast the shadow of misfortune fell athwart the sunlight of his soul, did he for an instant feel the dull agony of despair—thus spoke he to his saddened spirit.

With the first mail that was due after M'Nab's departure, allowing him time to reach the sheep, came a letter, as thus—"Sheep-market is bad—decidedly bad, with no hope of getting better. I can keep the sheep about Echuca till I get your answer. Shall I send them on, or return? My advice is to sell at all hazards."

Jack returned answer that he was to do whatever he thought best, and to use his own discretion unreservedly.

The sheep were sold accordingly. They brought eight shillings and tenpence all round, which just returned, clear of all expenses, eight shillings net. A magnificent price truly, and a terrible come-down from the fourteen or fifteen shillings which had been the regular price, for years past, of large, aged, prime sheep, as were the Gondaree lot.

M'Nab was back in remarkably quick time after this untoward outcome of so much care and forethought, and planning and contriving.

"The sheep were beautifully driven; I never saw a lot better looked after; they showed first-rate in the yards at Newmarket. All the drovers, butchers, and agents said there hadn't been a lot in like them this season. They topped the market, but what sort of a market was it?—rushed and glutted with all kinds of half-fat stock, going for nothing. And cattle down too—regular store prices; a most miserable sight."

"And what's said about wool and stations?" inquired Jack.

"That there's going to be the devil to pay; there's a tremendous commercial panic in England. Discount up to war figures. The great dissenting bankers—Underend, Burney & Co.—gone for any sum you like to mention. Run on the Bank of England. Panic on the Stock Exchange. The end of the world, as far as accommodation is concerned!"

"By Jove!" said Jack, "could anything have been more unlucky? I wish to heavens that I had sold out three months since, though that might only have landed someother unlucky beggar in the same fix. There's no chance of selling now at any price?"

"Sell!" answered M'Nab, and here he looked kindly and almost pitifully at Jack, on whose face there was a dark and troubled look, such as he had never seen there in bygone mishaps. "There won't be a station sold for the next three years, except at prices which will leave the owners the clothes they wear, and not a half-crown to put in the breeches-pocket either."

"What in the world shall I do?" groaned Jack. "I would have given much to have cleared out after shearing."

"Well, sir," said M'Nab, sitting down and putting on a calm, argumentative look, "let us look at the matter both ways. No doubt the outlook is gloomy; but here we have the place and the stock. There's not a station in the colonies that can be worked at a less annual expense. Surely we can carry on and pay interest on the mortgage till times come round."

"Perhaps," said Jack, disconsolately. "But suppose times *don't* come round; and suppose the Bank presses for their money?"

"The times *will* change and improve," said M'Nab, impressively, "as surely as the sun will shine after the next stormy day, whenever that may be. And as for the Bank, they seldom push any customer in whom they have confidence, and who has a real good property at his back."

"I trust so. But how in the world shall I ever grub on for three or four years more in this infernal wilderness, waiting for better seasons, and a rise in the market, which, for all we know, may never come?"

"My dear sir," said M'Nab, "nothing but patience and doggedness ever did any good in stock matters yet. It's the men that stick to their runs and their cattle and sheep, in spite of losses and danger, and discouragement and misery, that have always come out in the end with the tremendous profits that from time to time have always been realized in Australia, and *will again*. Look at old Ruggie M'Alister, coming back to his place one day, after counting out his two flocks to a person sent up to take charge by his agents, finding the place burnt down, the hut robbed, the cook speared, and a big black fellow swimming the Murray with his best double-barrelled gun in his mouth. There was cause for despair for ye, if ye like!"

"And what did your friend do?"

"Shot the black fellow with his carbine; dived for the double-barrel. Lived under a dray with the bailiff till after shearing; got the run out of debt, and is worth ten thousand a year, and has a villa near Melbourne this minute."

"I could have done that *once*," answered Jack; "but whether I am growing old, or have only one supply of energy, which is exhausted, I know not; I can't face the idea of all the work, and daily drudgery, and endless monotony—over again—over again!"

"There's nothing else to be done, sir. You'll think better of it tomorrow. And you needn't bother about my salary. We'll work together, and I'll never ask you for a penny of it till better times come."

Next day, as was his custom, Jack did not find the storm-signals so unmistakable or portentous. As M'Nab had very properly pointed out, there were still the first-class, fully-improved run, the sixty thousand sheep. The clip would be large and well got up, in spite of the fall in the value of the carcase.

Underend, Burneys, might totter and fall, crushing under the ruins of a long-decayed house, tunnelled and worm-eaten with usury, the trusting friend, the confiding public; but unless mankind and womenkind abandoned those garments, delicate, indispensable, and universally suitable from India to the Pole, the demand for wool, like that for gold, might slacken, but could not cease. This confounded American war would come to an end. Why the deuce could they not put off this insane, suicidal contest for a year or two? The season would improve—even that was against a man. It looked drier, and yet more dry, everyday he got up. Whereas, at Marshmead—ah! why, why did he ever leave that lovely (though flattish—but never mind), cool, green, regularly raining Eden? "Sad was the hour and luckless was the day"—as Hassan the camel-driver said. But if he had never left it he would never have seen Maud. "So, after all, it is Kismet. The will of Allah must be done!"

With this rather unorthodox consolation Jack ended his soliloquy, and prepared to march sternly along the path of duty, though the flowerets lay withered by the wayside, the surges of the shoreless sea of Ruin sounded sullenly in his ears, and though the illuminating image of Maud Stangrove, smiling welcome with eyes and brow, was hidden by mists and storm-rack.

ALL THINGS WENT ON MUCH as usual; but it was like the routine of a household in which there has been a death. Jack's favourite of all the Lares and Penates had always been Hope. Her image was not shattered; but the light and colour had faded from the serenely glowing lineaments. The calm eyes that had looked forth over every marvel of earth and sea and sky—resting on the far mountains, illumined by golden gleams from the Eternal Throne—were now rayless.

Hope-inspired, John Redgrave was and had proved himself capable of bodily and mental labour of no mean order—of self-denial severe and enduring. But severed from the probability of attainment of success, of eventual triumph, he was prone to a state of feeling as of the cheetah that has missed the prey, and after a succession of lightning-like bounds retires sullenly to hood and keeper.

As soon as he could assure himself that he was in a proper and befitting state of mind, he rode down to Juandah, making the journey in a very different tone and temper from the last. He did not find that his altered prospects had made his friends less cordial; on the contrary, it seemed to him that never before was he so manifestly the *bien-venu* as on this occasion. Maud sang and played, and talked cheerily, and with a slight preference for the minor key, which harmonized with the sore and bruised spirit of the guest. Mrs. Stangrove, too, exerted herself to the extent of sprightliness wonderful to behold. When a man is suffering in mind, body, or estate, the sympathy of sincere, unworldly women—and all women are unworldly with those they love—is soothing, tender, and inexpressively healing. As the dark-souled physician in the *Fair Maid of Perth* was enabled by the perfection of his art to apply to the severed hand of the knight the unguent which stilled his raging torment at a touch, so the sweet eyes and the soft tones of Maud Stangrove cooled and composed his fevered soul. Mark Stangrove, also, was unusually genial, even hilarious.

"This insatiable Warroo is going to have another dig at us," he said. "We have just *not* escaped a flood, and now we are in for a drought. That means a few years more of the mill for us. Well, we're all in the same boat; we must stick to the oars, keep a good look out, and weather it out together."

"A good look out!" echoed Jack. "I see nothing but rocks and breakers."

"Come, come, old fellow; a capful of wind, or even a heavy gale, doesn't mean total wreck always. We shall, of course, have to take in sail, throw cargo over, and all that. Seriously, things are going to be bad in more ways than one. I'm not altogether taken by surprise; I've seen it before; but I don't wish to crow over you for all that. I think in some ways you are better off than I am."

"How do you make that out?"

"Why, though I am a good deal under-stocked, this drought will put me ever so much about. I shall lose a lot of my lambs and calves, have to travel all the sheep, and, generally, be compelled to spend money and lose stock right and left till rain comes again."

"You can afford it," said Jack, "and I can't; it will be the straw that breaks the camel's back. A long drought means unsaleable stock—which means increase of debt, interest, and principal—which means ruin."

"You go too fast, my dear fellow. I used to tell you that you were going to be rich rather more quickly than I fancied probable; and now you are determined to be ruined with equal rapidity. I must tell Maud to read you a sermon upon patience and perseverance."

"I deserve no quarter from her or from you either," professed Jack, who was now *en pénitence* all round, "for dragging her into this uncertain, anxious life of mine."

"Well, accidents will happen, you know. I blame those rascally bushrangers and your gun-shot wound for it all; no woman can nurse any fellow, under a hundred, without appropriating him. But I'll take care that you are not married till you are something more than a bank overseer, which is a different thing from a bank manager, you know."

"Hang all banks and bank officials, from the board of directors to the junior messenger," fulminated Jack, "though, as they only sell money to fools like me, who choose to buy, they are scarcely to blame either. And now, old fellow, as I've relieved my mind, we'll go in and be civil to the ladies. Even if times are bad, one must not quite forget to be a gentleman. Thank you, once and for all, old fellow, for your true kindness."

After this Jack put away his Skeleton gently, though firmly, into his closet, and, turning the key, compelled him there to abide, only permitting him to come out and sit by the fire with him occasionally when no one was present, or to walk cheerfully round the room when he was dressing in the morning—or to wake him before earliest dawn and whisper in his ear till he rose desperately at the first faint streak of day. But these being the regularly allotted periods and interviews, lawfully to be claimed and recognized by all well-bred skeletons and their proprietors, Jack could not with any conscience grumble.

He explained the whole state of affairs to Maud, who, to his surprise, took it coolly, and, like Mark, said "that things might not turn out so badly. That everyone agreed that his station was very well managed, and that probably he might overrate the probability of loss. That, whether or no, she knew he would fight it out manfully—and that she would wait—oh, yes! years upon years—as long as he would promise to think of her, and for her, now and then."

So they parted, Jack thinking how difficult it was to understand women. He would have sworn that the fiery girl, whose petulances had so often amused him, would have been as deeply disappointed, as intolerant of the delay, as himself. And now here she was calmly looking forward to years of stocking-mending and child-nursing on the Warroo before they could be married, as if she had never dreamed of a higher life, to be realized in a few short months.

John Redgrave had never experienced, and therefore had not realized, the most deeply-rooted attribute of woman's manifold nature—the capacity for self-sacrifice. Rarely can he who is blessed with her first pure love overtax its wondrous endurance—its angelic tenderness.

With right down hard work, as with the conscientious performance of military duty, in the trenches or otherwise, before the enemy, much of the darker portion of the spirit's gloom disappears. Man is a working animal—civilization notwithstanding; and an undecided mental condition, combined with bodily inaction, has ever produced the direst forms of misery to which our kind is subjected here below.

So day after day saw Jack and his faithful subject fully occupied from dawn to sunset in the ordinary routine of station work. The personal labour devolving upon each was tolerably severe, but the exact number of hands allotted to the place by the inexorable M'Nab was rigidly adhered to, and not an extra boy even would he hear of until the inevitable month before shearing, when all ordinary labour laws must perforce be suspended.

The four boundary-riders, all active, steady men, young or in the prime of life, well-paid and well-housed, did their duty regularly and efficiently. It was part of M'Nab's creed that, if you kept a man at all you should pay him well, and otherwise minister to his well-being. In cheap labour there was no economy; and for anything like indifferently-performed work he had a dislike almost amounting to abhorrence. He and Jack transacted all the business that of right appertained to the home station. They by turns convoyed the increasingly numerous and hungry flocks of travelling sheep; took out the rations; laid the poisoned meat, which, spread over the run in cartloads, was daily returning an equivalent in dead eagles, dogs, and dingoes; counted the sheep regularly; and all this time there was not a sheep-skin unaccounted for—not a nail or a rail out of order in the whole establishment.

So fared all things until the time for shearing drew nigh. Jack felt quite delighted at the first engagement of washers, the first appearance of three or four shearers, with their big swags and low-conditioned horses, having journeyed from far land where winter was not wholly obsolete as a potentate, and did not stand for a mere section of the year between autumn and spring. The changed appearance of the long-silent huts was pleasant to his eye; the daily increase of strange voices and unembarrassed, careless talk; the giving out of rations; the arrangement of the steam-engine; the arrival of teamsters—all these things heralded the cheerful, toilsome, jostling shearing-time, half festive, half burdensome, yet still combining the pains and pleasures of harvest.

XVI

"And did she love him? What and if she did?
Love cannot cool the burning Austral sands,
Nor show the secret waters that lie hid
In arid valleys of that desert land."

—Jean Ingelow

The season had not been a good one for grass. It was a very good one for wool. Save a little dust, no exception could be taken to anything. The clip was well grown; the washing simply perfection. The lambing had been a fortunate one. Counting these aspirants for the trials and triumphs to which the merino proper is foredoomed, the count stood well over sixty thousand sheep, of all ages. But a few months since, what a comfortable sum of money did they represent; whereas now—but it would not bear thinking of! The shearers even seemed to be unnaturally good and easy to manage now that no particular benefit could accrue from their conduct. Everything was right but the one important fact, which lay at the root—the price of stock. Even if that had improved, the season was going to turn and evilly entreat them; the "stars in their courses fought against Sisera"; and Jack began to consider himself as his modern exemplar—the prey of the gods!

He sent off his wool, but this year he determined not to go to town himself; with the present prices and a fast-coming drought staring him in the face, what could a man do in the Club or in Collins Street but advertise himself as an incipient insolvent? Better stick to his work, save a little money, now that it was too late, and spend the summer pleasantly in staving off bush fires, following in the dusty wake of endless hordes of starving travelling sheep, and watching the desolation of the grass famine, already sore in the land, deepen from scarcity into starvation. A pleasant programme truly, and considerably altered from that one dreamily sketched out for himself and Maud so short a year agone—ah, me!

He wrote to his agents, desiring them to sell or ship the clip at their discretion, and to pour the proceeds into the lap of the Bank of New Holland, so to speak, by the hands of Mr. Mildmay Shrood. From that gentleman he, by and by, received a missive, very soothing and satisfactory, as times went—"The wool had been sold very well, and had maintained the high reputation of Gondaree both for quality and condition. Mr. Redgrave was empowered to continue to draw upon the bank for expenses, though (he might, perhaps, be pardoned for suggesting, in the present severe financial pressure) the bank trusted that their constituents would use every effort to keep down expenses to the lowest limit consistent with efficient working. It was thought by gentlemen of experience that the present untoward season would soon break up. In the meanwhile, however, the utmost care and caution were necessary to prevent loss and depreciation of valuable securities."

"All this is very reassuring," said Jack, grimly, to himself, as he marked the allusion to the securities—doubtless now regarded as the property of the bank, or something nearly akin. "However, we are not quite sold up yet, and if the season would change and a little rally come to pass in the market we might snap our fingers at the men of mortgage yet. There is a chance still, I believe. The wool fetched the best price on the river; everything will depend upon the season, and how we get through the summer."

When poor Tom Hood once wrote that the "summer had set in with its usual severity," little thought the great humorist that he was describing the sad simple earnest of the far land, to him a *terra incognita*.

All places have their "hard season"—that portion of the year when the ordinary operation of the weather has power to inflict the greatest amount of damage upon dwellers or producers. In one country it is winter, which is the foe of man with unkind frosts, cruel snow-storms, hurtling blasts, or dark and dreary days. In another land it is the hurricane season, when every vessel goes down at anchor, or is lifted high and dry over bar and beach, when the town totters above the shrinking inhabitants, and when, perchance, the more awful earthquake gapes for the wretches whom the great tempest has spared. But in Australia, more especially in that great interior system of sea-like plains, where for hundreds of miles the level is unbroken, and where, doubtless, at no very distant period the surges of ocean resounded, the hard season there is the summer, more particularly the periodically recurring oppression of a dry summer following a dry winter. In that land, where the brief spring is a joy and a luxury only too transient, where the winter is a time of rejoicing—mild, fair, verdant—where autumn is the crown and utter perfection of sublunary weather, the sole terror is of the slow, unnatural, gradual desiccation which—as in the olden Pharaoh days—eats up every green herb, and, if protracted, metamorphoses plain and forest and watercourse into similitudes of the "valley of dry bones."

Such *has* happened aforetime in the history of Australia. Such may, at the expiration of any aqueous cycle, happen again.

A term of dread was apparently settling down upon the land when John Redgrave resolved to stay at home the summer-time through. Such were the prospects which confronted him as he rode from paddock to paddock, among the tens of thousands of sheep, and watched from day today the pasturage shrivel up and disappear; the water retire into the bosom of the sun-baked earth.

The days were long, even dreary, and as the summer wore on they seemed longer and more dreary still. Hot, glaring, breezeless—there was no change, no relief—apparently no hope. There was no sign of distress among the Gondaree flocks. In that well-watered, well-pastured, well-fenced, and subdivided station the stock scarcely felt the pressure of the death-like season which was decimating the flocks in less-favoured localities. But everything that was heard, said, or thought of in that melancholy time tended to depression and despair. "This man had lost ten thousand sheep, having made too late a start for the back country, and been unable to reach water from the intervening desert. They—fine, strong, half-fat wethers—had gone mad with thirst—obstinately refused to stir—as is the manner of sheep in their extremity, and had perished to the last one. Then someone had sold three thousand weaners for ninepence a head, a well-grown lot too."

As the panic and the season acted and reacted upon one another, by the time the summer had passed, and the autumn and the cold nights, but still dry, stern, merciless as the summer, had come, the value of stock and stations had come to be nominal.

People of imaginative temperaments began to ask themselves whether they could have been sane when they in cool blood set down 20,000 sheep and a station as value for £20,000 or £25,000. Had such prices been actually paid?

Yes, actually paid! Not in golden sovereigns, perhaps, but in good cheques upon perfectly solvent bank accounts, and in bills of exchange, which were legally strong enough to extract the last penny of their value from him whose name was written under the talismanic word "accepted." The money had been there, doubtless; and now it seemed as if it had turned into withered leaves, like the fairy gold in the old legends.

So mused Jack on his daily rounds, as wearily he rode day after day, often on a weak and tired horse, for grass was none, and hay and corn were considerably dearer than loaf sugar; or when he lighted his pipe at night, and sat staring at the stars, while M'Nab wrote up his accounts, and generally bore himself as if droughts were merely passing obstacles to the prosperity which *must* eventually attend the proprietor of well-classed sheep and a fenced-in run.

The famine year dragged on. Long will that season be remembered throughout the length and breadth of the great island-continent. Its history was written in the hearts of ruined men—in the dangerously-tasked minds of many a proprietor whom "luck and pluck" carried through the ordeal. Still the drought grasped with unrelenting gripe the enfeebled flocks—the thirst-maddened and desperate herds. The great merchants of the land were beginning to grow accustomed to the sound of the terrible word "bankruptcy." All bank shares had fallen, and were falling, to prices which showed the usual cowardly distrust of the public in the time of trial. Rumour began to be busy with the names of more than one bank, including the Bank of New Holland, which had, it was asserted, made stupendous advances to the squatters. "Hadn't they lent old Captain Blockstrop a quarter of a million, and even that wouldn't do? Everyday the directors met, old Billy used to talk to the manager in much the same tone of voice that he had been accustomed to use to his first mate, and demand ten, twenty, or thirty thousand pounds, as the case might be. 'I must have it, Mr. Shrood,' the old man would roar out, 'if I'm to carry on, or else, sir, the house of William Blockstrop and Co. will have the shutters up tomorrow morning.' And he got the money of course."

"And suppose he didn't get it?" might remark an inquiring bystander, innocent of the mighty system of involuted financial machinery.

"Not get it!" would Croker, or Downemouth, *flaneurs* informed in all the monetary diplomacy of the day, say—"Do you suppose *that* bank can afford to let old Blockstrop drop? No, sir; rotten as the commercial and pastoral interests are, they know better than to cut their own throats just yet. Other fellows may have to sell their sheep for half-a-crown a head, and take to billiard-marking, or 'pies all hot,' for all the bank cares; but once you're in like old Blockstrop they *can't* let you go."

Autumn passed over, winter commenced—that is, the month of June arrived. The rain seemed as far off as ever. One day Jack smiled grimly as he observed the anachronism of a tolerably smart bush-fire, which was burning away merrily, not the grass, good wot, but the dried forest leaves which lay inches deep on the bare bosom of the tranced and death-like earth.

Up to this time hope had prevailed among the sore disheartened stock-owners that the weather *must* change. It would be unnatural, impossible, that such a season could last over the next three months. There would be some rain, and even a little rain in that strange country, where most of the trees and shrubs are edible and even fattening for stock, counts for much. Were it to last for three months more millions of sheep and hundreds of thousands of cattle would be lying dead on the bare, dusty, wind-swept wastes, which had formerly been considered to be pastures.

Could this thing be? The old colonists shook their heads. They remembered 1837–38–39—during which memorable years but little rain fell, when flour was £100 per ton, when rice even was too expensive for consumption, when more than half of the handful of stock then in New South Wales perished for lack of food. With the present heavily-stocked runs what manner of desolation might be expected now?

In the midst of this "horror of a great tempest—when men's hearts were failing them for fear"—John Redgrave received this letter, lying innocently, *anguis in herbâ*, among the ordinary contents of his Monday morning's mail-bag:—

BANK OF NEW HOLLAND,
June 30th, 1868
John Redgrave, Esq., Gondaree, Warroo.
My dear Sir,
I have been instructed by the Board of Directors to draw your attention to the amount of your over-draft, amounting, at date, with interest, to £30,114 12s. 9d., which I am to request that you will reduce at your earliest convenience.

I remain,
Yours faithfully,
MILDMAY SHROOD

Jack's face turned nearly as white as when he fell fainting at the Juandah gate. He set his teeth hard as he crushed the fateful missive in his hand; and leaning back, growled out a savage oath, such as seldom passed his lips. "This was to be the end, then, of all his hopes, and plans, and work, exile, and anxiety. To be sold up now, in the very vortex of the unabated panic, in the worst month of the year, in the most depressing period of the worst drought that had been known for thirty years! No warning, no hint of such an impending stroke. The sword of Damocles had been suspended financially above his head, in his daily musings, in his nightly dreams, for many a month. But strong in sanguine anticipation of a change in the season, in a rise of the market, he had become accustomed to its presence. It had come to be as harmless as a punkah; and now—it had fallen, keen, deadly, inevitable, full upon his defenceless head."

For he knew his position to be utterly hopeless. "Reduce his overdraft!" What a world of irony lay in the request! Even could he sell without the consent of the bank—to which abstraction every sheep, lamb, and fleece was mortgaged—how was he to realize, when best fat sheep were selling under five shillings, and ewes, as well-bred and classed as his own, were offering in any number at half a-crown a head, and unsaleable at that? God in heaven! he was a ruined man—not in the sense of those whom he had known in mercantile life, who seemed in some wonderful fashion to fail, and come forth again with personal belongings hardly curtailed to ordinary observation, but really, utterly, tangibly ruined— left without home, or household goods, or opportunity to commence afresh. A beggar and a byword for rashness, extravagance, utter want of discretion, purpose, energy, what not. Who has not heard the chorus of cant which swells and surges round a fallen man? M'Nab was away; he would tell him the news next day. Meanwhile, he must go to town and see what could be done. Matters might be arranged somehow, though of what the "somehow" was to be composed he had not the faintest conception, even after a night cap wherein the proportion of "battle-axe" was not very closely calculated—"To bed, to bed, to bed!" Banquo, his ghost, did not more effectually murder sleep than in Jack's case did the delicate, deadly caligraphy of Mildmay Shrood.

On the morrow he told M'Nab what had happened, and betook himself on horseback to the stage which the mail could reach on the following day, choosing the distraction of a long ride rather than the slow torture of a whole day's waiting.

M'Nab was moved, though not altogether surprised, at the intelligence. He knew that the interest must have been running up upon the bank account, when all was necessarily going out and nothing, since the clip of wool, coming in. He held as firmly as ever to his opinion that stock and stations must rise again after a time. The ship would right herself, though water-logged and dipping bows under with every sea. The thing was to know how long the storm would rage. He cautioned Jack to be cool and cautious in his dealing with the bank, and at whatever cost to procure further accommodation—time being the all-important matter in such a season. Three days' rain would send up the value of all stock fifty percent at least, to rise another cent. percent within the year.

JOHN REDGRAVE REACHED MELBOURNE AFTER a journey over five hundred miles of a country which, in all but the essential features of camels and Arabs, would seem to have been translated bodily from the great desert of Sahara. Nor leaf, nor grass, reed nor rush relieved the bare, dusty, red-brown wastes. The stations, deserted by their travelling stock, looked as if built by a past generation of lunatics upon a "waste land, where no one comes or hath come since the making of the world."

From time to time columns of dust, moving cloud-pillars, met or passed them on their way, the abodes of evil Genii, as the Bedouins told. Evil spirits were abroad, doubtless Jack thought, in sufficient numbers. The land looked as if not only there never had been any herbage whatever, but, from the total absence of the roots, as if there could by no possibility be any in the future. The mail horses were worn and feeble, threatening to leave them stranded in the midst of some endless plain. At the mail-station, no fresh animals being forthcoming, it seemed as if their journey must then and there end, or be performed on foot. But the driver, a man of resources, lounged over to the pound, and seeing therein two comparatively plump nags, *one* of which had certainly worn harness, set up a claim, and promptly released them upon payment of sustenance fees. With these equivocal steeds the journey was prosecuted to the railway terminus, and once more, after nearly two years' absence, Mr. Redgrave found himself in the great city which has grown up in little more than a generation.

Pleasant would have been the change from the lone waste, in process of change into a charnel-house, but for the great overshadowing dread which dwelt with John Redgrave day by day. The fresh breezes of ocean fanned his bronzed cheek, but awoke not, as of old, the joyous pulsations of a heart free to respond to every tone of the grand harmony of Nature. The slave who feels at every step the galling of his heavy chain thanks not God for the blue sky, or the song of the soaring bird; and he who is the thrice fettered bond-slave of Debt bears a spirit steeled against all softening and ennobling influences.

Some transient gleams of the joy of new sensation and old friendship were permitted even to his hopeless condition. But even amid the welcome and the talk of old associates there ran depressing announcements.

"Times were incredibly bad. As for stock, no one would take them at a gift. Wool was down, lower than for years, and (of course) never would rise again. Hugh Brass was gone. Estate in liquidation. The Marsalays, Moreland, ditto; Heaven only knew for what amount—not that it mattered much, in these days, whether a man stopped for one hundred thousand or three. Fellow went one day to bank-manager, and actually wanted advances on a good run and twenty thousand sheep. Manager, new appointment, inquired if he had *any other liabilities*? Shut him up, rather. Times' changed, eh, old boy?"

Jack admitted that they were—indeed!

The day after his arrival, Jack hied him to the portals of the enchanted castle, at which he had so confidently blown the horn in the days of careless youth. Changed, alas! was the Knight; dimmed was his armour; hacked his morion; and shorn the waving plume that had nodded to the breeze. After entering the antechamber he was compelled to wait. That purgatorial apartment was tenanted by an elderly man of the squatter persuasion, as Jack could see at a glance. He, doubtless, was awaiting his turn in the *folter-kammer*, and by the fixed and anxious look of the worn face his anticipations were strongly tinged with evil. A different species of pioneer this from Jack, from Stangrove, from Hugh Brass, from Tunstall. He was more akin to the Ruggie M'Alister type. His sinewy hand and weather-beaten frame were those of a man who by long years of every kind of toil, risk, and privation had built up a modest property—a home and a competency— no more. He was the father of a family, possibly with boys at school receiving a better education than their parent, a brood of merry girls disciplined by a much-enduring governess. There would be an ancient orchard at such a man's homestead—no doubt it was in or near the settled districts—and a large "careless-ordered" flower-garden in which the masses of bloom compensated in picturesqueness and splendour for lack of neatness. Jack could have sworn he had only incurred debt by compulsion to buy a few thousand acres immediately round his house, when the free-selectors came swarming over the flats he had discovered in old dangerous days, and ridden over as his own, winter and summer, for twenty years. He had trusted (so he told Jack) to a good season or two pulling him through, whereas now, the strong man's voice trembled as he said—

"If they sell me up, I shall have to go out a beggar. Yes, a beggar, sir, after thirty years' work. I could bear it, very like; but my wife and the children. Great God! what will become of us?"

Out of the inner room came a plump, well-shaven townsman. He was evidently in good spirits; he hummed a tune, rubbed his hands, looked benevolently at Jack and the older bushman, and passed forth into the atrium. He was a stockbroker; his paper was all right till the fourth of next month. What could man wish for more? It was an eternity of safety. What changes in the market might take place by that time! He lit a cigar, looked at his watch, and lounging over to the *café*, ordered a somewhat luxurious lunch, to which, and to a bottle of iced moselle, he did full and deliberate justice. About the time when the broker had finished his soup, and was dallying with his amontillado, the door of the bank sanctum opened, and forth walked, or rather staggered, the pioneer squatter, with clenched teeth and features so ghastly in their expression of hopeless woe that Jack involuntarily rushed to his aid, as to a man about to fall down in a fit. The old man looked at him with eyes so awful in their despair that he shuddered—his lips moved, but no sound came from them. Waving his hand, with a gesture as deprecating remark, the unhappy man, like one in his sleep, passed on.

Jack walked in with a quick, resolute step, and an appearance of composure he was far from feeling, and saluted the man of doom.

There was a flavour of bygone cordiality in Mr. Shrood's greeting, but his face instantly assumed an expression of decorous gravity, mingled with the stern resolution of irresponsible power. Jack at once crossed swords, so to speak, by producing the fatal letter. "I received this from you a week since, Mr. Shrood. What am I to understand from it?"

Before this momentous interview proceeds further we may let our readers into a secret which was necessarily hidden from John Redgrave and the outside world—as the discussions of the terrible conclave preceding the dread fiat at the *Vehmegericht*.

The bank directors had held a general meeting, with the president in the chair, having in view the circumstances of the country and the securities and liabilities of the bank. Among those present were some of the best financial intelligences of the day, men of ripe experience, keen calculation, and sound logical habit of mind. Many were the pros and cons. There was some difference of opinion as to the mode of operation; none whatever as to the fact of the danger of the position. One of the oldest directors had opened the proceedings. He asserted that never before in the history of the colony had the indebtedness of all classes of constituents been so large. It had coincided with an altogether unparalleled period of financial loss and depression in England—he might add, in Europe; and, with a heavy fall in the price of wool, stock, and stations, a war of stupendous magnitude in the new world had not been without effect upon previous monetary relations. From all these causes had the great pastoral interest of Australia suffered, and the suffering was more intensified by the operation of a drought, still unbroken, and of a severity unknown for thirty years. He felt the deepest sympathy for the pastoral interest, for the gentlemen who had invested their capital—he might almost say their lives—in these mighty and fascinating adventures. He trusted he might not be accused of sentimentalism—but the pastoral tenants had paid in health, strength, and all the powers of manhood, to the credit of this account, and spent their blood freely in its support.

He knew that the liability of the bank connected with the indebtedness of this class of constituents—was very great. But so, likewise, were the resources of their old, stable, and securely-founded establishment. The squatters had, on the whole, been their best, their most solvent customers. Let all be helped now, in their hour of need, except those who were manifestly unreliable, incapable, or too deeply involved. A favourable change might take place within the year. If so, the bank would always receive the praise of having stood firm in danger, and having helped to save from ruin a deserving, an honourable, and an indispensable class of producers. Here Mr. Oakleigh paused, and a murmur as nearly resembling approbation as could be expected to emanate from the august assembly, came from the listeners. One would have concluded that the advocate of mercy and continuous accommodation had carried his point. But a still more reverend senior, no other than the president himself, during the debate, left his place with the deliberation of age, and, adjusting his spectacles, thus spoke:

"He had listened with great pleasure to the lucid statement of facts presented to the Board by their friend and valued director, Mr. Oakleigh. His suggestions did him honour. They might congratulate themselves upon the possession of such an intellect, so high a tone of feeling,

ROLF BOLDREWOOD

in their council. But," and here the speaker changed his position, and inserted one hand into his ample white waistcoat, "he must be pardoned for representing to gentlemen present that the laws which governed sound banking institutions, such as their own, did not admit of consideration for individuals or for classes of constituents, however deserving of sympathy. The logic of banking was inexorable. Economic laws were unvarying; they had stood the test of years, of generations. By them, and them only, could he consent to be governed." Here he applied himself to his snuff-box, and proceeded. "It would be clearly apparent to all now present that the liabilities of the bank were unusually large; they were daily increasing. The reserve fund was being seriously, he might say dangerously, lowered. If such a course were persevered with, in the present state of the money market, but one result could be looked for. The credit of the bank would be endangered; even worse might follow, to which he would not at present allude. Such being the case, and it could not in his opinion be denied, what was their plain, undoubted, inevitable course of action? He had had many years of experience as a merchant, and as director and president of the Bank of New Holland, which latter position he had had the honour to hold for a term exceeding the lifetime of some present. From the teaching of these long and chequered years, not unmarked by financial tempests, such as they were now contending with, he submitted his opinion, which was fixed and unalterable. The bank must close *all pastoral accounts under a certain amount*. They must realize upon such securities promptly, and without respect to persons. It would be for the directors to fix the sums, but obviously the larger accounts must be called in. But this course, once decided upon, must be inflexibly adhered to. Cases of great individual hardship would occur; it was unavoidable in the operation of all such acts of policy. No one, speaking as an individual, felt more deeply such consequences of a protective policy than he himself. But he would remind gentlemen present that they owed a justice to families of shareholders in the bank, rather than what might be considered mercy to those who had assumed a voluntary indebtedness. The action he had indicated comprehended safety to the bank, to the shareholders, and to the more important constituents. Temporizing would, in his opinion, involve the bank and all concerned in eventual ruin."

The president took off his spectacles, wiped them carefully with a spotless handkerchief, and sat solemnly down. His arguments were felt to be incontrovertible. His great age, his long experience, his unfailing success in the management of all affairs with which, for half a century, he had been connected, his high character, added weight to his arguments, of themselves not easily to be controverted. But little more was said, and that chiefly in a conversational manner. Before the Board separated, a motion was carried that the manager be instructed to close all pastoral accounts under thirty-five thousand pounds. In the event of non-payment to realize upon securities without delay.

Such had been the preliminary debate—such had been the bill before the oligarchs of the Council of Currency—the potentates who coerce kings and resist nations, who render war possible or truce compulsory—with whom peace and prosperity or "blood and iron" are matters of exchange.

Such was the court, such the gravely-debated proposition, such the irreversible verdict arrived at, before Jack reached Melbourne. All "unconscious of his doom," though full of intuitive dread, did he then demand of Mr. Mildmay Shrood what he was to understand by the letter he had received. That gentleman might have saved many words, and some anxiety to his interlocutor, by simply replying "Ruin!?"— but an answer so laconic would not have justified the reputation for politeness which the manager of the Bank of New Holland, in common with managers of banks generally deservedly held.

He used no insincerity when he answered that it gave him much pain to be compelled to state that the bank felt it necessary to call upon him to reduce, or indeed, to extinguish his liability to them without delay.

"And, if I am unable—in the teeth of this detestable season and this infernal panic, which the London money-mongers seem to have got up on purpose to take away our last chance, what then?" demanded Jack, commencing to boil over.

"I must again express my unfeigned regret," said Mr. Shrood, "but I cannot disguise from you that the bank will at once realize upon the security which it holds for your advances."

"In plain words, your bank, without warning of any kind, demands a very large sum of money, advanced during several years, and sells me up without mercy, in the midst of a grass famine and a money famine."

"I am afraid, though you put it strongly, and perhaps not altogether fairly as regards the bank, that your view of their action as regards yourself is correct."

"And can *you* talk of fairness?" said Jack with quivering lip and blazing eyes, as he stood up and faced the calm, decorous man of business. "Was I not led to imagine when this money was advanced with such apparent willingness, that I should have time, accommodation, all reasonable assistance if required, for the repayment? All the money has been faithfully invested in stock and permanent improvements. No run in the country, at this moment, is in better order or more cheaply managed. Can anyone say that I have been extravagant in my personal expenses? It is hard—devilish hard—and unfair to boot."

Mr. Shrood was quite of the same opinion. He was a man of kindly though disciplined impulses, and what men call "a good fellow," underneath his armour of caution and official reserve. He did not intend to explain the policy of the bank. It was his to obey, and not to criticize, though within certain well defined limits he had much discretionary power. But he had always liked Jack, and was as sorry as he could afford to be, with so many unpleasantnesses of similar character to deal with, for his gravitation towards the bad, which he doubted could not be arrested.

Still, he thought he would make one effort with the directors in favour of John Redgrave, whose property he knew was thoroughly good of its kind, and whose particular case he felt to be one of "real distress."

"I can but reiterate my expressions of regret, my dear Mr. Redgrave," returned he; "nothing but the extreme, the unprecedented financial disorganization could have led the bank authorities to countenance so harshly restrictive a policy. I cannot speak of it in any other terms. But I will make a special effort to obtain further accommodation for you, though I do not advise you to rest any great hope upon a favourable response. On Wednesday the Board sits again. If you will call on Monday morning next, I will inform you of their ultimatum."

Jack thanked the banker from his heart, and went forth to spend two or three days after a rather less melancholy fashion. We know that John Redgrave was so enthusiastic a votary of the present that, unless that genius was manifestly overshadowed by the awful future, he was apt to cry ruthlessly—"Stay, for thou art fair."

So he ate of the unaccustomed, and drank of the choice, and otherwise solaced himself, carrying a good hope of the success of Mr. Mildmay Shrood's intercession, the prestige of which he overrated sadly, until Monday morning.

His heart commenced to register a low tide of electricity—dark doubts, akin to despair, began to throng and rise; there was "a whisper of wings in the air," altogether non-angelic, as he stood once more in the presence of Mildmay Shrood, and of—Fate. One look at the fixed expression of the features of the manager was sufficient to settle the question of concession. All hope and expectation died out of Jack's heart. He nerved himself for the blow.

"I regret more deeply than I can express—" commenced Mr. Shrood.

"It is not worth while to go on," interrupted Jack. "I believe that you have tried to do what you could for me, and I thank you sincerely for it. The question is now, what time can I have to make arrangements with another bank, or a mercantile firm, to carry me on—if such an unlikely thing comes to pass?"

"The bank will take no action for one month—so much I can guarantee; at the end of that period no further cheque will be paid, and the bank will sell or take possession of the stock and station, as mortgaged to them."

"What about current expenses?"

"They will be paid as usual—if not exceeding ordinary amounts."

"Well, thank God," said Jack, "my people, the few there are of them, are paid up. I shall not have to trouble you for much. I wish you good morning."

The banker walked over to him, and looked full in the face of the man who was going forth, as he believed, to utter, inevitable ruin. *He* knew that only by a miracle could anyone obtain assistance in the present state of finance. All the other banks, all the great mercantile squatting houses, bankers themselves in all but name, had been throwing over dead weight, dropping small, doubtful, or not vitally necessary accounts, for months past.

John Redgrave's quest would be that of a drowning man who solicits the inmates of dangerously laden boats, in the worst possible weather, out of sight of land, to have pity upon him and to risk their lives, manifestly for his sake. He might not encounter the precipitate phraseology of the British tar, but a crack with an oar-blade would, metaphorically, represent his reception.

Mr. Shrood was not, of course, anymore than the officer of any other service, likely to divulge the inner workings of official action; but he wrung Jack's hand with an emphasis not all conventional, as he wished him success, and bade him a genuine farewell.

"It is precious hard upon that young fellow, I must say," said he, half aloud. "I really did not think I could be so unbusinesslike as to flurry myself about a single account, with the half-yearly balance coming on too. It must be near lunch-time."

Mr. Mildmay Shrood opened an inner baize-embellished door, and disappeared into a long passage, which led to his private suite of apartments. He then and there threw himself into a game of romps with his daughters, aged six and eight years respectively, and informed his wife that there would be a flower-show on the following Saturday, to which, if nothing materially affecting his health, or the weather, took place in the interval, he intended to have the honour of escorting her.

Mrs. Shrood expressed her high approval of this announcement, and at the same time stated her opinion that he looked rather fagged, asked if the affairs of the bank were going on well, and if he would like a glass of sherry.

"What bank, my dear? Yes, thank you; the brown sherry, if you please. What bank do you allude to?"

"Nonsense, Mildmay! Why, our bank, of course."

"Madam," replied the husband gravely, draining the glass of sherry with zest and approbation, "I have before had the honour to remark to you that, once inside that door, I know of the existence of *no* bank, either in New Holland or New Caledonia. And further, O partner of my cares and shares—I was about to say—but suppose we say Paris bonnets, *àpropos* of one that's just come in, unless, madam, you wish to come and see me periodically at Gladesville, you will not mingle my private life, in anyway or form, with my existence in that—other place."

Here Mr. Shrood, who had in his earlier days been a staunch theatre-goer, waved his wine glass, and, putting himself in the attitude of "first robber," scowled furiously at his wife.

That sensible matron first threw her arms round his neck, and told him. not to be a goose, and then, after arranging her ruff, rang the bell for lunch, to which Mr. Shrood, having by this time, like a wise man, got Jack's stony face and gloomy eyes out of his thoughts, did reasonable justice.

Mr. Redgrave, with his customary hopefulness, recovered from the first misery of his position sufficiently to go about to all likely places, and to test the money-market most exhaustively, as to the accommodation needed for a squatter with an undeniable property and a heavy mortgage. His agents, Drawe and Backwell, were first applied to. They had nothing to learn, as his relations with them had always been of a confidential nature, since the old, the good old days of Marshmead. They had always given him good advice, which he did not always want, and money, which he always did. They had always helped him to the limit of safety, and would have done anything in reason for him now; but, like many others, they were not able. Their capital and reserve fund were strained to the fullest extent. Times and the seasons were so bad that no one without the resources of the Count of Monte Christo, combined with the business talents of a Rothschild, could have done the pastoral community much good in that year. They had a smoke over it in the back office; but nothing, in the shape of relief, was found to be practicable.

"You see, old fellow," said Backwell, who, as old squatter himself, understood every move in the game, "we could find four or five thousand pounds for you, but what good would that be? You would have to sell twenty thousand of your best sheep to meet the acceptances, and, of course, the bank won't stand your reducing the stock much. Then—though that would have been a good payment to account a year or two back—they won't thank you for it now. They want the whole of their advances to you, and less won't do. There are plenty more in the same boat. People say they are shaky themselves. They have some fearfully heavy accounts—old Blockstrop and others—we all know. They can't afford to show any mercy, and they won't. What stock will come to, unless the drought breaks up, no man can say. We are not what I should call a very solvent firm at present; and so I tell you. They must have some fellows to sell stock, you know, or we should have a note to settle our little account in quick sticks. Let me drive you out to St. Ninian's tonight, and we'll have a taste of the sea-breeze, and look at Drawe's dahlias; they're all he has to live for now, he says."

XVII

"But dreary though the moments fleet,
O let me think we yet shall meet."

—Burns

Jack came back next morning rather "picked-up" after Mrs. Backwell's kindly talk, and Drawe's dahlias, and a stroll by the "loud-sounding sea," which looked to him as if it belonged in its glory and freshness to another world which he should soon quit and never revisit. He was sufficiently invigorated to try all the banks—the Denominational, the London Bartered, the Polynesian, the Irish, Welsh, and Cornish, the Occidental, the Alexandra, the United, and so on. It was of no avail. At the majority he was informed that the bank was not prepared to take up fresh squatting accounts at present. At some he was requested to call after the next Board day; but the answer, varied and euphemized, was "No," in all cases. Then he tried the mercantile firms, the old-standing English or Australian houses, which, in spite of the assumed supposed American domination in all things in the colony of Victoria, had held the lead, and kept their pride of place since the pre-auriferous days. With them, and the great wool-dealing firms, the same answer only could be obtained. They would advance anything in reason upon the coming clip, or on any given number of sheep, at market rates; but, as to "taking-up" a fresh account of that magnitude, they were "not prepared."

Tired out, disappointed, and disheartened, Jack left town, after writing a brief note to Mr. Shrood, intimating that the bank might sell Gondaree as soon as that remorseless corporation pleased. He recommended Messrs. Drawe and Backwell as auctioneers; they knew the property well, and would probably get as much for it as any other firm.

Then was the wearisome return journey commenced. In former days there had always been some glimmer of hope or expectation wherewith to gild the excessive neutral tints of the landscape. Now there was no hope, and the expectation was evil. He would have likened himself to an Indian chief going back to deliver himself up to the torture. At Gondaree was the stake to which he would have to be attached on arrival. The fire would be lighted, and the roasting would begin and continue till he should receive the *coup de grâce*, by being tacitly directed to leave his own station, and go forth into the wilderness—a beggar and a broken man.

M'Nab did not ask many questions; it was not his wont except when he wished to lower the spirits of an owner of store sheep, with a view to a slight concession in price. But he gathered from Jack's visage and listless air that no success of any kind had attended his efforts.

"Gondaree is to be sold," said he, with the recklessness of despair, "sometime next month. You will soon see an advertisement headed 'Magnificent salt-bush property on the Warroo,' and so on."

"And ye were unable to get any assistance from the bank?"

"No more than brandy and soda out of an iceberg," responded Jack, helping himself to the first-named restorative. "Whether they want money, and have to recoup themselves out of us poor devils, I don't know. But you would think that other than cash payments had been unknown since Magna Charta. Shall have to carry our coin in leather bags soon."

"Ay, that's bad, very bad! I didn't realize things would be just that bad. Surely the banks might have just a trifle of discrimination; if Gondaree is sold now, they're just making someone a present of thirty thousand pounds out of your pocket."

"I am much of your way of thinking, M'Nab; I am just as sure as that we shall see the sun tomorrow that I am going to be sold off at the edge of a rising market. It's hard—too hard; but a man's life, more or less, can't matter."

"Could you not have sold half, and held on with the rest?" suggested M'Nab, still restlessly cogitating every conceivable scheme. "The place could divide first-rate opposite the Point. If you had sent me down, I'll warrant I would have knocked up a deal, or a put-off, in some fashion."

"I shouldn't wonder if you had," assented Jack. "I ought to have sent you down with a power of attorney—only that one has a mistaken preference for mismanaging one's own affairs. Well, it can't be helped now. Cursed be the stock and station. Cursed be the whole concern."

Jack was fully a week at home before he could nerve himself for the inevitable last visit to Juandah—his farewell to Maud Stangrove. It was a cruel word; it would be a bitter parting; but he must tell her in his own speech that his fate had but suffered him to win her heart, had but lured him to the contemplation of the unutterable happiness that should have been theirs, to drop the veil forever, to shatter the goblet in which the draught had foamed and sparkled with unearthly brilliancy.

He had thought once that perhaps, pledged as they were to each other, a mutual understanding to await the events of the next few years might have still existed between them. But he cast out the tempting idea, with even added bitterness, as he thought of the lots of other men and other women whom he had often pitied and despised.

What, he told himself, could compensate her for the long weary years of waiting and watching, the gradual extinction of youth in form, in mind, in soul, to be repaid, after youth had passed by, with a sombre union, which poverty should divest of all grace, joy, and romance. No—they must part—and forever! Maud, with her youth and beauty, would soon find a mate more worthy than he of the treasure of her love. He, with all his faults, was not the man to drag those light footsteps into the mire of poverty and obscurity. As for him, he would carve out fame and another fortune for himself—or fill a nameless grave.

Juandah was suffering, like all the rest of the country from the withering drought, which still denied water to the dusty fissures, verdure to the earth, and had apparently closed up the windows of heaven. Still there was a look of homely comfort about the place, which showed the garrison to be trusty and bold—fierce though the siege had been, and close the blockade.

"Come in, old fellow, and we'll see if we can find you something to eat," called out Mark Stangrove, who, with a very old shooting-coat on, had just ridden in on a very lean steed, and with a general air of having finished a hard day's work. "I'm not very sure of it. Maud and the missus have been very hard set of late—no eggs, no butter, little milk, no vegetables, indifferent meat, and a great flavour of rice in all the dishes. I've been pulling weak sheep out of a water-hole all day. Pleasant work and inspiriting."

Jack walked in, and it was fully explained to him by the unspoken kindness of the ladies of the house that they knew pretty well the measure of his misfortune. Somehow, one is not always sufficiently grateful for the delicate and generous consideration that one meets with in time of trouble. It is like the deference accorded when people are too sick, or too old, or too generally incompetent to enter into active competition with the talents of the world militant. It is kindly meant, but there is a savour of accusation of weakness. So John Redgrave felt partly grateful, and partly savage with himself, at being in a condition to be morally "poor-deared" by Maud and her sister. All his life, up to this time, he had been from earliest boyhood as one in authority. He had said, since he could recollect, "to this man, go here," and so on. Now was it to be that he should have to descend from his pride of place, to suffer pity, to endure subordination, to live as the lowly in spirit and in fortune? With the suddenness of the levin-bolt it would sometimes flash across him that such might be his doom. And with the thought would come a passionate resolve to end his fast-falling, narrowing existence, ere it were swept away amid the melancholy and ignoble circumstances which had terminated other men's lives.

It may have been gathered from these and other faithful impressions of the inner workings of John Redgrave's mind, that, though a careless, kindly, easy-going species of personage, he was naturally and unconsciously proud. To his pride was just now added the demon of sullen obstinacy.

He was unable, however, after a few moments, to withstand the influence of the unaffected kindness and sympathy of his friends. When he looked at the two women, and remarked that they looked pale and careworn, as having had privations of their own to bear in this most miserable season, he hated himself for having entertained any selfish feeling.

"You have come back from your travels," said Maud; "it seems to me that you are always going and returning. I always have envied you your wanderings."

"I am afraid I have come to the stage when I shall go—but, in the words of the Highland Lament, 'return nae mair,'" answered he, sadly.

"You mustn't talk like that," said Mrs. Stangrove. "People who, like us, have lived so long in this country, know all about the ups and downs of squatting. Why shouldn't you begin again, like others, and do better with a second venture than the first? Look at Mr. Upham, Mr. Feenix, and Cheerboys Brothers; they have all been ruined, at least once, and how thriving they are now."

"I hope to show my friends, and the world too, my dear Mrs. Stangrove," said Jack, standing up and squaring his broad shoulders, "that one fall has not taken all the fight out of me. But it is an uphill game, and I may, like many a better man, find the odds too heavy. But, whatever happens, you may believe that I shall not forget my friends at Juandah, who have proved themselves such in my hour of need."

"I have heard," at length Maud said, in low faltering tones, "that people in—in their dark hours—and we all have them at sometime of our lives—should walk by the counsel of their friends if they know them to be good and true. We are too apt to be led by our own wayward spirits, and sorrow warps our better judgment. I know Mark will be glad to give you his best advice. And oh! do—do talk matters over with him. He is cool, and sure judging, and is seldom mistaken in his course."

Mrs. Stangrove had slipped out "on household work intent."

"Maud," he said, "dearest, loveliest, best-beloved, why has fortune, so kind though unsought for many a year, deserted me now, when for the first time in my life I had prized her with a miser's joy for your dear sake, and for yours alone? My heart will break—is broken—at the thought of leaving you. But—"

"Why should you leave us—me, if you will have it so?" interrupted she passionately; "stay with us for a time till your wound be healed, as in the first dear time when I nursed you, and knew the joy of lightening your weary hours and soothing all your pain. Do you think mine a fair-weather love, given in assurance of ease, and pleasure, and fairy summer-time—or did I yield my heart to be yours in weal or woe? You dishonour me by an implied mistrust—and yourself by such faint-hearted fears of the future."

She had risen, and laid her hand on his shoulder as she spoke with all the aroused magnetic energy of tender, yet impetuous womanhood, ere yet experience has quenched the open trust of youth, or sorrow smirched the faint delicate hues of beauty.

"Promise me that you will talk your plans over with Mark. And oh! if you *would* but follow his advice."

Jack groaned aloud, but his face was set unyieldingly, as he took her hand in both of his, and looked pityingly and mournfully in the sweet pale face, and loving, tear-brightened eyes.

"My darling, my darling," he said, hoarsely, "it cannot be. I must tread my path alone. For good or for evil, I will confront my fate sole and unfriended, and either make a name and another fortune, or add mine to the corses on life's battle-field. If I live and prosper I will return to my love. But here I release her from the pain and the lowliness of a life linked to so ill-starred a destiny as that of John Redgrave."

THE EVENING WAS NOT DREARY. Mark and his wife exerted themselves to dispel the gloom that threatened to enshroud the little party. Maud was again outwardly calm and self-possessed, as women often are, in the supreme hours of life. Jack exhibited the recklessness of despair, and appeared to have dismissed from his mind the misery of his position. Stangrove recounted the many shifts and contrivances rendered necessary by the exigencies of the season.

"Did you ever taste milk, old fellow," he said, "distilled chiefly from water-lilies? I assure you our two melancholy milkers have consumed no other food for weeks. There is not, of course, a particle of grass, or so much as an unstripped salt-bush or cotton-bush for miles. Well, the big lagoon (quite a lake it looks in winter) has not dried up yet. You may see the cows standing up to their backs in it all day long. Even the lilies are not on the surface. An occasional flower is all that they get there, but from time to time you may notice one of the amphibious creatures put her head deeply under water like a diving duck, and raise it after a longish interval, filled with a great trailing bunch of roots and esculent filaments. Great idea, isn't it? I wonder how long they would take to Darwinize into webbed feet and a beaverly breadth of tail."

"They manage to live, and give us milk besides, on this blanc-mange, or whatever it is," said Mrs. Stangrove. "I don't know what the poor children would have done but for these submarine plantations."

"My dear old Mameluke has copied their idea, then," joined in Maud, with a brave attempt at light converse, which ended in a flickering, piteous smile; "for I saw him in the cows' water party yesterday, with very little but his head visible. He has lost all the hair from his knees down, either from the leeches or the water."

"We are living in strange times," remarked Jack; "it is a pity we can't get a few hints from the blacks, who must have seen all the dry seasons since Captain Cook. What have you done with all your sheep, Mark?"

"We are eating the few that are left," said Mark.

"And very bad they are," interposed Mrs. Stangrove. "We are all so tired of mutton, that I shall never like it again as long as I live."

"The beef would be worse, if we had any," resumed Mark. "The sheep are just eatable, though I agree as to the indifferent quality. All the flocks are in the mountains in charge of my working overseer, old Hardbake, as well as the cattle. Here is the last letter: 'The sheep is all well, and the wool will be right if so be as you get rain by the time the snow falls here. We must cut and run then for fear of haccidence. The cattle is pore but lively. Send some more baccy. Yours, to command, Gregory Hardbake.' Curious scrawl, isn't it?"

The ladies having retired, Mark Stangrove and his guest adjourned to the veranda for the customary *tabaks parlement*, and for sometime smoked silently under the influence of the glorious southern night. All was still save the faint but clearly-heard ripple of the stream, and the low, sighing, rhythmical murmur of the river oaks. Cloudless was the sky; the broad silver moon hung in mid firmament, with splendour undimmed, save by a wide translucent halo—in happier times suggestive of rain. In this hopeless season, the denizens of the Warroo had learned by sad experience to distrust this and all other ordinary phenomena.

"Glorious night," said Mark at length, breaking the long silence, "but how infinitely we should prefer the wildest weather that ever frightened a man to his prayers! Strange, how comparative is even one's pleasure in the beauty of nature, and how dependent upon its squaring with our humble daily needs. When I read such a passage as—'the storm beat mercilessly in the faces of the wayfarers, with heavy driving showers,' &c.—when the author has exhausted himself in this endeavour to elicit your sympathy for the unlucky hero and heroine—I feel madly envious, which I take it is *not* the feeling intended to be produced. So you are going to clear out, old fellow, for good and all? You know, I am sure, how sorry we all are. Will you pardon me if I ask what your plans are for the future?"

"I have no plans," answered Jack. "I shall make a fresh start as soon as I am sold up. I must do as other shipwrecked men, I suppose—go before the mast, or take a third-mate's berth, and work up to a fresh command—if it's in me."

"That's all very well in its way. I admire pluck and independence; but without capital it's a long, weary business."

"How have the other men fared?" demanded Jack. "I am not the first who has been left without a shilling, but with health, strength, and—well—some part of one's youth remaining, it is a disgrace to such a man, in this country above all others, to lie down or whine for assistance at the first defeat."

"Granted, my dear fellow; though I confess I take your proposition to apply more strictly to the labourer proper than to him who starts weighted with the name and habits of a gentleman. There is no track open to him that he could not travel with tenfold greater speed with the aid of capital to clear the way."

"That I cannot have without laying myself under obligations to friends or relatives, and nothing would induce me to ask or accept such help," quoth Jack, with unwonted sternness. "I have lost a fortune and the best years of my life—as I believe by no fault of my own. I will regain it, as I have lost it, without help from living man; or the destiny which has robbed me of all that makes life worth having may take a worthless life also."

"It strikes me that you are hardly just, not to say generous," rejoined Mark, "to speak of your life as entirely worthless; but I am not going to preach, old fellow, to a man in your hurt and wounded state. I have been near enough to it myself to understand your chief bitternesses. Now listen to me, like a good fellow, as if I were your elder brother or somebody in the paternal line. You know I am a heap of years older, besides having the advantage of being a spectator, and a *very* friendly one, of your game."

Jack nodded an affirmative, while Stangrove, refilling his pipe, sent forth a contemplative cloud and recommenced:

"When a man is ruined—and I have seen a whole district cleared out in one year before now—one thing, almost the chief thing, he has to guard against is, a wild desire springing mainly from mortification, wounded pride, and a kind of reactionary despair, to get away from the scene of his disaster and from his previous occupation, whatever it may be. Now this feeling is perfectly natural. All the same it should not be indulged. When a man has done nothing worse than the unsuccessful, he should calmly review his position, and above all take the advice of his friends. If he have plenty of them—as you have—he may rest assured that their verdict as to his plans and prospects is far more likely to be correct than his own. When he disagrees with the whole jury of them, he generally is in the position of the proverbial person who found eleven most obstinate jurymen entirely opposed to *his* way of thinking."

"But surely a man must know his own capacity, and can gauge the measure of his own powers more correctly than any number of friends," pleaded Jack.

"I am not sure of that. I believe in several heads being better than one, especially where the latter has just come out of the thick of the conflict, and has not escaped without a hard knock or two. To pursue my lecture on adversity—don't take it so seriously, Redgrave, or I must stop. A good fellow, with staunch friends, is invariably helped to one fresh start, often to two. So you may look upon it as a settled thing. Sheep are cruelly low now—"

"What! begin with *another sheep station*, and a small one?" interrupted Jack. "Let me die first."

"There, again, allow me to differ with you, and to state another peculiarity of misadventure. A fellow always insists upon changing his stock. A cattle-man takes to sheep, after a knock-down, and *vice versâ*. Whereas, it is just the thing he should *not* do. He knows, or fancies he knows, all the expenses and drawbacks of one division of stock farming; of the peculiar troubles of the other he is ignorant, and so over-estimates the advantages. By this shuttle-cocking, he abandons one sort when their turn for profit is at hand, and generally gets well launched into the other as their turn is departing. Besides, all the accumulation of experience—a fair capital in itself—is thus wasted."

"Hang experience," swore Jack, with peculiar bitterness; "it's the light that illumines the ship's wake, as some unlucky beggar like me must have said; and which leaves the look-out as dim as ever."

"You persist in doing yourself injustice," continued his patient friend; "everybody will concede that you have had very hard luck; you have lost by one fluke—you may get your revenge by another, if you have the wherewithal to put on the card; not otherwise though. As I said before, sheep are down to nothing—at that painful price you are compelled to sell. Why not buy someother fellow's place at the same figure? When the tide rises, as it surely will, you will float into deep water with the rest of them."

"What do you fancy the real value of runs to be?"

"From six to ten shillings for sheep and stations, according to quality, not a halfpenny more." Jack could not repress a groan. "Well, with five thousand pounds you ought to be able to buy a good property with twenty thousand sheep—half cash, half at two years."

"Where's the money to come from?" demanded Jack, from the depths of his beard.

"My dear fellow," Stangrove said, getting up and walking over to him, "you don't think me such a beast as to have bored you all this time if I had not intended to act as well as talk. I will find the money; you know I have always been a screwing, saving kind of chap. You can relieve your conscience by giving me a second mortgage till you pay up."

Jack grasped the hand of his entertainer till the strong man half flinched from the crushing pressure.

"You are a good fellow, true friend, and worthy to be the brother of the sweetest girl that ever gladdened a man's heart. But I cannot accept your offer, noble and self-sacrificing as it is. I am an unlucky devil; I have no faith in my future fortune; and I will not be base enough to run the risk of dragging down others into the pit of my own poverty and wretchedness."

"But, my dear fellow, hear reason; don't decide hastily. You don't know to what you are, perhaps, condemning yourself, and—others besides yourself."

"It is because I *am* considering others," answered Jack, as he stood up and looked, half pleadingly, at the silver moon, the silent stars, the clear heavens, the wonder and majesty of night, as who should strive to win an answer from an oracle. "It is for the sake of others, for the sake of *her*, that I reject your offer. I should only blend your ruin with my own— foredoomed, it may be, like much else that happens in this melancholy, mysterious life of ours. And now, God bless you. I will start early. I could not say farewell to Maud. Tell her my words, and—to forget me."

The two men grasped each other's hands silently, and without other speech each went to his own apartment.

Before sunrise Jack left an uneasy pillow, and, dressing hastily, walked quietly out of the house, and into the horse-paddock, or an enclosure so designated, which in former days had contained adequate nutriment for all inmates. He found his attenuated steed, and caught him without much difficulty. The unlucky animal was standing by a box tree, staring vacantly upwards, and refreshing himself from time to time with a vigorous bite at the bark, which he chewed with evident relish. Saddling up at the stable, he walked towards the outer sliprails, intending to avoid the dismounting at that rude substitute for a gate, about which he had often rallied Mark. He had just concluded the taking down and replacing of these antiquated entrance-bars, and, with an audible sigh, was about to mount, when he saw Maud coming along the short-cut footpath from the house, which led to the garden gate. She waved her hand. He had no choice—no wish, but to stop. She was his love. She was before his eyes once again. He had tried to spare her—perhaps himself. But it was not to be.

She came swiftly up this dusty path, in the clear warm morning light, her hair catching a gleam of the level sun, her cheek faintly tinted with a sudden glow, her lips apart, her eyes burning bright. She looked at him, for one moment, with the honest tenderness of a woman, pure from the suspicion of coquetry—loving, and not ashamed though the world should witness her love.

"John," she said, in a tone of soft, yet deep reproach, "were you going away, forever perhaps, and without a word of farewell?"

"Was it not better so?" he murmured, taking her hand in both of his, and looking into her eyes with mingled gloom and passion, as though he had been Leonora's lover, doubting, pitying, yet compelled to bid her forth to the midnight journey on the phantom steed.

"Better! why should it be better?" said she, with a wild terror in her voice and looks. "Have you no pity for yourself—for me—that you despise the advice of your best friends, and insist upon dooming yourself to poverty and obscurity? I knew Mark was going to speak to you, and he told me that he would help—like a good fellow as he is—you or—us—why should I falter with the word?—to make a new commencement. Why, why are you so proud, so unyielding, so unwilling to sacrifice your pride for my sake? You cannot care for me!"

Here the excited girl flung herself forward, as if she would have humbled herself in the dust before him, while a storm of sobs shook her bosom, and caused her whole form to tremble as if in an ague fit.

Jack raised her tenderly in his arms, and, pouring forth every name of love, strove to soothe and pacify her.

"Darling," he said, "have pity upon me, and trust me a little also. All that a man should do would I do for your dear sake; and if I do not at once consent to accept Mark's generous offer, or that of any friend for the present, why will you not let me try my chance, single-handed, with fortune, like another? When the Knight returns to his Ladye-love after such a combat, is he not doubly welcome, doubly dear? Why should you insist upon my being defended from the rude blasts of adversity, as if I were unable to prove myself a man among men!"

"You deceive yourself," she said, in sad, serene accents; "you will not yield yourself to the counsels of those who are cool and prudent. Will you not let me tell you that, though you are the dearest, greatest of mortal men in my eyes, I do not think prudence is a marked gift of yours?"

"You are a saucy girl," he said, as she smiled sadly through her tears; "but you are only telling me what I knew before. Still, but for imprudence, or what the world calls such, conquests and splendid discoveries would never have been made. I have something of the 'conquestador' in me. It must have space and opportunity for a year or two, or I shall die."

"Will you make me one promise before you go?" said she, looking earnestly into his face, "and I can then wait—for, trust me, I shall wait for you till I die—with a heart less hopelessly despairing."

"I will, if—"

"Then promise me this—that if, in two years, you have not succeeded, as you expect, you will return to me, and will not then refuse Mark's proffered aid."

He hesitated.

"Think this," she said, as she raised herself slightly on tiptoe, and whispered in his ear. "It is my life that I am asking of you; I feel it. If you love your pride—yourself more—"

"I promise," he said hastily. "I promise before God, if in two years I have made no progress, I will return and bow myself at your feet. You shall deal with me as you list."

Their lips were pressed convulsively together in one lingering kiss. Then she released herself with mute despair.

She stood for one moment gazing upon him with all the ardour of her love and truth shining out of her wondrous eyes. Her face became deadly pale. Its whole expression gradually changed to one unutterably mournful and despairing. Then, turning, she walked slowly, steadily, and without once turning her head, along the homeward path. Jack watched her till she passed through the garden gate and entered the veranda. Mounting his horse, he rode along the river road at a pace more in accordance with the condition of his emotions than the condition of his hackney.

ROLF BOLDREWOOD

XVIII

E vents were following in quick succession across John Redgrave's life, like the presentments of a magic lantern; and it seemed to him at times with a like unreality. But reason, in hours of compulsory attention, proved with cold logic that they were only too harshly true.

A little while, as he could not help owning to himself, and he would be driven forth from the Eden of "the potentiality of wealth" and luxury, into the outer world of dreary fact, poverty, and labour. Fast sped the melancholy, aimless, half-anxious, half-despairing days, following upon the advertisement which took all the pastoral and commercial world into his confidence, and stamped him with the stigma of failure. Thus, one fine day, a stranger, a shrewd-looking personage, redolent of capital, from his felt wide-awake to his substantial boots, arrived by the mail, and presented the credentials which announced him a Mr. Bagemall (Bagemall Brothers and Holdfast) and the *purchaser of Gondaree*. It was even so. That "well-known, fattening run, highly improved, fenced and subdivided, with 65,794 well-bred, carefully-culled sheep, regularly supplied with the most fashionable Mudgee blood, the last two clips of wool having averaged two shillings and ninepence per lb.," &c., &c., as per advertisement, had been sold publicly, Messrs. Drawe and Backwell auctioneers. Sold, and for what price? For eight shillings and threepence per head, half cash and half approved bills at short dates!

Well, he had hoped nothing better. In the teeth of such a season, such a panic, such a general loosening of the foundations alike of pastoral and commercial systems, what else was to be expected as the proceeds of a forced sale, with terms equal to cash? The murder was out. The hazard had been played and lost—let the stakes at least be handed over with equanimity.

So Mr. Bagemall was received with all proper hospitality, and courteously entreated, he being apparently bent more upon the refreshment and restoration of the inner man, after a toilsome and eventful journey, than upon information regarding his purchase. He made no inquiries, but smoked his pipe and enjoyed his dinner, talking in a cheery and non-committal manner about the state of politics, and the last European news by the mail. He went early to bed, pleading urgent want of a night's rest, and postponed the serious part of the visit until the morrow.

When the morning meal and the morning pipe had been satisfactorily disposed of, he displayed a willingness, but no haste, to commence business.

"I suppose we may as well take a look round the place, Mr. Redgrave," said he; "everything looks well in a general way; nothing like fencing to stand a bad season. Monstrous pity to put such a property in the market just now. Can't think what the banks are about. Sure to be a change for the better soon, unless rain has ceased to form part of the Australian climate, and then we shall all be in the same boat."

"I shouldn't have sold if I could have helped it, you may be sure," answered Jack; "but the thing is done, and it's no use thinking about it. The sooner it's over the better."

"Just as you please—just as you please," said the stranger. "You will oblige me by considering me in the light of a guest during my short stay. I must go back the end of the week. I don't know that I need do anything but count the sheep, in which our friend here (turning to M'Nab) perhaps will help me. Everything being given in, I sha'n't bother myself or you by inspecting the station plant. The wash-pen and shed speak for themselves."

"Thank you very much," said Jack; "delivering over a station is generally a nuisance, especially as to the smaller matters. I remember being at Yillaree, when Knipstone was giving delivery to old M'Tavish. They had been squabbling awfully about every pot and kettle and frying-pan, all of which Knipstone had carefully entered—some of them twice over. To complete the inventory he produced a brass candlestick, saying airily, 'The other one is on the store table.' 'Bring it here, then, you rascal,' roared M'Tavish. 'I wouldn't take your word for a box of matches.'"

"The purchase-money was somewhere about eighty thousand pounds," remarked Bagemall, who seemed to remember what every station had brought for the last ten years. "A paltry fifty pounds couldn't have mattered much one way or the other."

The next morning the counting began in earnest. A couple of thousand four-tooth wethers had been put in the drafting yard, for some reason or other, and with this lot they made a commencement.

Now, except to the initiated, this counting of sheep is a bewildering, all but impossible matter. The hurdle or gate, as the case may be, is partially opened and egress permitted in a degree proportioned to the supposed talent of the enumerator. If he be slow, inexperienced, and therefore diffident, a small opening suffices, through which only a couple of sheep can run at a time. Then he begins—two, four, six, eight, and so on, up to twenty. After he gets well into his tens he probably makes some slight miscalculation, and while he is mentally debating whether forty-two or fifty-two be right, three sheep rush out together, the additional one in wild eagerness jumping on to the back of one of the others, and then sprawling, feet up, in front of the gate. The unhappy wight says "sixty" to himself, and, looking doubtfully at the continuous stream of animals, falls hopelessly in arrear and gives up. In such a case the sheep have to be re-yarded, or he has to trust implicitly to the honour of the person in charge, who widens the gate, lets the sheep rush out higgledy-piggledy, as it seems to the tyro, and keeps calling out "hundred"—"hundred" with wonderful and almost suspicious rapidity. Yet, in such a case, there will rarely be one sheep wrong, more or less, in five thousand. Thus, when arrived at the yard, M'Nab looked inquiringly at the stranger, and took hold of one end of the hurdle.

"Throw it down and let 'em rip," said Mr. Bagemall. "You and I will count, and Mr. Redgrave will perhaps keep tally."

Keeping tally, it may be explained, is the notation of the hundreds, by pencil or notched stick, the counter being supposed only to concern himself with the units and tens.

M'Nab, who was an unrivalled counter, relaxed his features, as recognizing a kindred spirit, and, as the sheep came tearing and tumbling out, after the fashion of strong, hearty, paddocked wethers, he placed his hands in his pockets and reeled off the hundreds, as did Mr. Bagemall, in no time. The operation was soon over. They agreed in the odd number to a sheep. And M'Nab further remarked that Mr. Bagemall was one of those gifted persons who, by a successive motion of the fingers of both hands, was enabled (quite as a matter of form) to check the tally-keeper as well. Paddock after paddock was duly mustered, driven through their respective gates, and counted back. In a couple of days the operation, combined with the inspection of the whole run, was concluded.

Sitting in the veranda after a longish day's work, all smoking, and Jack looking regretfully at his garden, which, small and insignificant compared with the exuberant plantation of Marshmead, was very creditable for the Warroo, and indeed was just about to make some small repayment for labour in the way of fruit, Mr. Bagemall remarked—

"I didn't know you had any blacks about the place. Does this lot belong here?"

"It must be old man Jack and his family," answered M'Nab. "I have been wondering what had become of them forever so long. I heard Wildduck was very ill. Yes, this is our tribe, sir; not a very alarming one, but all that brandy and ball-cartridge have left."

"What has the old fellow got on his back?" inquired Mr. Bagemall; "the men carry nothing if they can help it."

"Poor Wildduck," said Jack, half to himself, "I had forgotten all about her of late, with the allowable selfishness of misfortune. By Jove! it's she that the old man is carrying. She must be ill indeed."

The old savage, followed by his aged wives at humble distance, marched on in a stately and solemn manner, until he reached a mound near the garden gate. Here the little procession halted; one of the gins placed an opossum rug upon the earth, and upon this the old man, with great care and tenderness, placed the wasted form of the girl Wildduck. She it was, apparently in the last stage of consumption, as her hollow cheeks testified, and the altered face, now lighted by eyes of unnatural size, brilliant with the fire of death. The three men walked over.

"Ah, Misser Redgrave," said she, while a dreamy smile passed over her wan countenance, "stockman say you sell Gondaree and go away. Old man Jack carry me from Bimbalong—me *must* say goodbye." Here a frightful fit of coughing prevented further speech, while the old man and the gins made expressive pantomime, in acquiescence, and then, seating themselves around, took out sharp-edged flints, and, scooping a preliminary gash on their faces, prepared for a "good cry." Strangely soon blood and tears were flowing in commingled streams adown their swart countenances. Wildduck lay gasping upon her rug, and from time to time sobbed out her share of the lament for the kind white man who was about to leave their country.

Jack leaned over the ghastly and shrunken form of what had once been the agile and frolicsome Wildduck. The dying girl—for such unquestionably she was—looked up in his face, with death-gleaming and earnest gaze.

"You yan away from Gondaree, Misser Redgrave?" she gasped out. "No come back?"

Jack nodded in assent.

"Me yan away too," she continued; "Kalingeree close up die, me thinkum; that one grog killum, and too much big one cough, like it white fellow. You tell Miss Maudie, I good girl long time."

"Poor Wildduck," said Jack, genuinely moved by the sad spectacle of the poor victim to civilization. "Miss Maudie will be very sorry to hear about you. Can't you get down to Juandah? I'm sure she would take care of you."

"Too far that one place, now. Me going to die here. Old man Jack bury me at Bimbalong. My mother sit down there, long o' waterhole—where you see that big coubah tree. Misser Redgrave!" she said, with sudden earnestness, trying to raise herself; "you tell me one thing?"

"What is it, my poor girl?"

"You tell me"—here she gazed imploringly at him, with a look of dread and doubt piteous to mark in her uplifted face—"where you think I go when I die?"

"Go!" answered Jack, rather confused by this direct appeal to his assumed superior knowledge of the future. "Why, to heaven, I believe, Wildduck. We shall all go there, I hope, some day."

"I see Miss Maudie there; she go, I know. You go too; you always kind to poor black fellow."

"I hope and trust we shall all go there some day, if we're good," said he, unconsciously recalling his good mother's early assurances on that head. "Didn't Miss Maudie tell you so."

"Miss Maudie tell me about white man's God—teach me prayer every night—say, 'Our Father.' You think God care about poor black girl?"

"Yes, I do; you belong to Him, Wildduck, just the same as white girl. You say prayer to Him. He take care of you, same as Miss Maudie tell you."

"She tell me she very sorry for poor black girl. She say, why you drink brandy, Wildduck? that wicked. So me try—no use—can't help it. Black fellow all the same as little child. Big one stupid."

"White fellow stupid too, Wildduck," said John Redgrave; "you have been no worse than plenty of others who ought to have known better. But perhaps you won't die after all."

"Me die fast enough." Here the merciless cough for a time completely exhausted her. "I believe tomorrow. You think I jump up white fellow?"

"I can't say, Wildduck," answered he. "We shall all be very different from what we are now. You had better cover yourself up and go to sleep."

"I very tired," moaned the girl, feebly; "long way we come today. You tell new gentleman he be kind to old man Jack. You say goodbye to poor Wildduck." Here she held out her attenuated hand. It had been always small and slender, as in many cases are those of the women of her race. In the days of her health and vigour, Jack had often noticed the curious delicacy of her hands and feet, and speculated on the causes of such conformation among a people all ignorant of shoe and stocking. But now the small brown fingers and transparent palm were like those of a child. He held them in his own for a second, and then said, "Goodnight, Wildduck."

"Goodbye, Misser Redgrave, goodbye. You tell Miss Maudie, perhaps I see her some day, you too, long big one star." Here she pointed to the sky. Her eyes filled with tears. Jack turned away. When he looked again, she had covered her face with the rug. But he could hear her sobs, and a low moaning cry.

"Strange, and how hard to understand!" said Jack to himself, as he strode forward in the twilight towards the cottage. "I wonder what the extent of this poor ignorant creature's moral responsibility may be. What opportunities has she had of comprehending her presence on this mysterious earth? Save a few lessons from Maud, she has never heard the sacred name except as giving power to a careless oath. As to actual wickedness she is a thousand-fold better than half the white sinners of her own sex. Her sufferings have been short. And perhaps she lies a-dying more happily circumstanced than a pauper in the cold walls of a work-house, or a waif in a stifling room in a back slum of any given city. As far as the children of crime, want, and vice are concerned, all cities are much on a par, whether Australian, European, or otherwise."

The night was boisterous, yet, mingled with the moaning of the blast, Jack fancied that at midnight he heard a cry, long-drawn, wailing, and more shrill than the tones of the wind-harp, or the sighing of the bowed forest.

The pale dawn was still silent, ghostly gray. No herald in roseate tabard had proclaimed the approach of the tyrant sun—lord of that stricken waste—when John Redgrave walked over to the camp. He saw at once, by the attitudes of the group, that they were mourners of the dead. Each sat motionless and mute, gazing with grief-stricken countenances towards the fourth fire—in the equally divided space—by which lay a motionless figure, covered from head to foot with furs. He looked at old man Jack, but he moved not a muscle of his disfigured countenance, while in his eyes, fixed with a strong glare, there was no more speculation than in those of the dead.

The women sat like ebon statues; down their shrivelled breasts and bony arms the dried rivulets of blood made a ghastly blazonry. Jack knew enough of the customs and ceremonies of this fast-fading people to be aware that no speech, or even gesture, was possible during the two first days of mourning. He walked over and raised the covering from the face of the dead girl. Her features, always delicate and regular (for, though rarely, such types unquestionably do exist among most aboriginal Australian tribes), were composed and peaceful. The closed eyes were fringed with lashes of extraordinary length. The heavy waving locks, rudely combed back, were not without artistic effect. The pallor of death bestowed a fairer hue on the clear brown, not coal-black, skin. The lingering shadow of a smile remained upon the scarcely closed lips, which half recalled the arch expression of the merry forest child, dancing in the sunshine like the swaying leaflets. Now, like them in autumn-death, she was lying on the breast of the great earth-mother. One hand pressed her bosom, in the shut fingers of which was a small cross, hung round the neck by a faded ribbon, which he remembered to have been a present from Maud Stangrove. "He whose word infused with life this ill-starred child of clay will He not recall the parted spirit?" thought Jack, as he reverently replaced the fur cloak. "God bless her," he said, softly.

He turned and looked back as he entered his dwelling. There sat the three figures—rigid, sorrow-denoting, motionless as carvings on a mausoleum. For two days they watched their dead—soundless, sleepless, foodless. Ere the third day broke, the mourners and their charge had disappeared.

GONDAREE HAD BEEN SOLD. THE stock and station had been "delivered," in squatting parlance; the meaning of which is, that the purchaser had satisfied himself that the actual living, wool-bearing sheep coincided in number, sex, age, and quality with the statement of Messrs. Drawe and Backwell. Also that the run comprised about the specified number of square miles; that the fences were tangible, and not paper delineations; that the wool-shed and wash-pen were not ideal creations of the poet, or that synonymous son of romance, the auctioneer; lastly, that the great Warroo itself was a perennial summer-defying stream, and not a dusty ditch—a river by courtesy, full-tided only in winter, when everybody has more water than he knows what to do with. In the great pastoral chronicles it is written that serious mistakes as to each and all of these important matters have been made ere now.

None of these encounters between the real and the probable had occurred with respect to Gondaree. Mr. Bagemall had expressed himself in terms of unbusinesslike approval of the whole property both to Mr. Redgrave and M'Nab. The run was, in his opinion, first class; the improvements judicious and complete; the stock superior in quality, and in condition really wonderful, considering the season.

"Nothing the matter, my dear sir," said he to Redgrave, "but want of rain and want of credit. Both of these complaints have become chronic, worse luck. I remember, some years since, when we were nearly cleaned out from the same causes. However, if I had not bought the place, someone else would. I feel ashamed, though, of getting it such a bargain. Fortune of war, you know, and all that, I suppose. Horses? Certainly—not mentioned in terms of sale. But any two of the station-hacks you choose. I suppose you will go in for back blocks. Take my advice, don't be down-hearted. This is the best country that ever was discovered for making fresh starts in life. As long as a man is young and hearty, there are chances under his feet all day long. Think so? Know it. Why, look at old Captain Woodenwall, turned sixty when he was stumped up ten years ago, and look at him now. Warm man, member of the Upper House, drives his carriage again. Got everyone's good word too. Never give in. *Nil* whatsy-name, as the book says. Goodbye, sir, you have my best wishes. I have made my arrangements with your super-smart fellow, quite my sort, rising man. Sha'n't be here for years, I hope. Goodbye, sir."

After this somewhat lengthened address, protracted beyond his custom, Mr. Bagemall departed by the mail. He had previously entered into an arrangement with M'Nab, continuing to that energetic personage, whose talent for organization he fully appreciated, the sole management of Gondaree. He had furthermore admitted him to a partnership, the estimated value thereof to be "worked out" of future profits. Mr. Bagemall had not now to learn that this was the cheapest and surest way of securing the permanent services and uttermost efforts of a man of exceptional brain and energy, as he very correctly took Alexander M'Nab to be.

"Well, all is over now," said Jack to his late manager; "everything seems to be much as it was before—except that Hamlet will be played without the unlucky beggar of a prince. I'm glad Bagemall took you in—he showed his sense; he's not a bad fellow by any means."

"I'm glad, and I'm sorry, Mr. Redgrave. It was too good an offer for me to refuse; but I've saved a couple of thousand pounds, and I had a notion that if you could have raised as much more—which would have been easy enough—I should say we might have gone in together for some back country with a little stock on it. There are lots of places in the market, and it's a grand time for investing. There will never be a better, in my opinion."

"Thank you very much, old fellow," said Jack, moved by the generosity of his ex-lieutenant, the more so as M'Nab was very careful of his money, all of which he had hardly earned; "but I intend to make tracks, and go on my path alone. I have hardly settled what I shall do yet. I think I shall travel and look about me for a few months. I am heartily tired of this part of Australia."

"Better by far nip in now, while the chance is good," argued the shrewd, clear-sighted M'Nab. "Depend upon it, there will be no such opportunities this time next year. The first forty-eight hours' rain will make a difference. All kinds of good medium runs are hawked about now, and if Mr. Bagemall hadn't been so quick I should have been in Collins Street this week with half-a-dozen offers in my pocket. But what I want to say is this—there's two thousand lying to my credit in the London Bartered. Take my advice, run down to Melbourne and get two or three more to put to it, and Drawe and Backwell will give you a dozen runs to pick from. It's heartily at your service. If you don't like the saltbush, there's Gippsland, a splendid country, with good store cattle-stations going at three pounds a head."

John Redgrave grasped the hand of the speaker and wrung it warmly.

"You're a good fellow, M'Nab," said he, "and you have justified the opinion which I formed of you at the beginning of our acquaintance. I shall always remember you as a true friend, and a much cleverer fellow than myself. I should almost have felt inclined to have gone in with you as managing partner, but I cannot take your or any other friend's money, to run the risk of losing it and self-respect together. It cannot be; but I thank you heartily all the same."

XIX

"Strong is the faith of our youth to pursue
The path of its promise."

—FRANCES BROWN

On the following morning John Redgrave quitted forever the place in which he had spent five of the best years of his life, all his capital, and, measured by expenditure of emotional force, as much brain-tissue as would have lasted him to the age of Methuselah at quiet, steady-going Marshmead. He had packed and labelled his personal belongings, which were to be sent to Melbourne by the wool-drays. They would reach their destination long ere he needed them, doubtless. He mounted his favourite hackney, leading another, upon the saddle of which was strapped a compact valise. The boundary-riders had come in, apparently for no reason in particular. But it had leaked out that the master was to clear out for good on that day. They were all about the stable-yard as he came out of the garden gate, attended by M'Nab.

They made haste to anticipate him, and one of them led out the half-Arab gray, while another held his stirrup, and a third the led horse.

"We want to say, sir," said the foremost man, "that we are all sorry as things have turned out the way they have. All the country about here feels the same. You've always acted the gentleman to every man in your employ since you've been on the river; and every man as knows himself respects you for it. We wish you good luck, sir, wherever you go."

Jack tried to say a word or two, but the words wouldn't come. Something in his throat intercepted speech, much as was the case when he last said goodbye to his mother after the holidays. He shook hands with M'Nab and with the men all round. Mounting his horse, and taking the led horse by the lengthened rein, he rode slowly away along the Bimbalong track. The men raised a cheer, he waved his hand in response, and the small world of Gondaree went on much as usual, like the waters of a pond after the widening circles caused by a transient interruption.

After riding at a foot-pace for an hour, Jack began to press on a little, intending to put a fair day's journey at nightfall between him and his late home. Turning in his saddle for a moment, to take a last

ROLF BOLDREWOOD

look at the well-known landscape, with the winding, dark-hued line of the river timber cutting the sky-line, he saw that he was followed by the dog 'Help.' This astute quadruped, who, as Jack was wont to assert, "knew in a general way as much as other folks," had evidently considered the question of his master's departure, and had adopted his line of action. Aware from experience that if he exhibited an intention to go anywhere, or do anything, not comprehended in instructions connected with sheep, he was liable to be chained up till further orders, he had taken good care to keep out of the way at Jack's leave-taking. His master had no intention of taking him with him, but had wished to pat him for the last time, and great whistling and calling had taken place in consequence. "But Gelert was not there."

As the dog, therefore, upon Jack's discovering him, came sidling forward, wagging his tail apologetically, and bearing in his honest eyes an expression partly of joy and partly of confession of wrong-doing, Jack felt a sensation of satisfaction more considerable than some people would have thought the occasion warranted.

"So you've come after me, you old rascal," said he—upon which Help, divining that he was forgiven, set up a joyous bark, and careered wildly over the plain. "Do you know that you are not showing as much sense as I gave you credit for, in leaving a rich master to follow a poor one? You're only a provincial, it seems, not a dog of the world at all. However, as you *have* come, we must make the best of it. Come to heel—do you hear, sir?—and we must get a muzzle at the first store we come to."

The Bimbalong boundary, now a long line of wire fence, with egress only by a neat gate on the track, was reached in due time. Here Jack's memory, unbidden, recalled the day of their first muster of the cattle—the glorious day, the abundant herbage, the free gallop after the half-wild herd, in which poor Wildduck had distinguished herself; and, fairer than all, the glowing hope which had invested the unaccustomed scene with brightest colours. How different was the aspect of the spot now! The bare pastures, the prosaic fence-line—the Great Enterprise carried through to the point of conspicuous failure; the reckless, joyous child of these lone wastes lying in her grave, under the whispering streamers of the great coubah tree yonder. And is every hope as cold and dead as she? He was faring forth a wanderer, a beggar. Better, perhaps, thought he, in the bitterness of his spirit, that I had dropped to the bushranger's bullet. Better to have fallen in the front of the battle than to have survived to grace the triumph and wear the chain.

The landless and dispossessed proprietor rode steadily on along the well-marked but unfrequented track which led "back"—that is, into the indifferently-watered, sparsely-stocked, and thinly-populated region which stretched endless at the rear of the great leading streams. In this desolate country, compared with which the frontage properties on the Warroo, slightly suburban as they might be deemed, were as fertile farms, lay grand possibilities—the Eldorado which always accompanies the unknown. Here were still tenantless, as wandering stockmen had told, enormous plains to which those on the Warroo were as river flats, fantastic, isolated ranges, full of strange metallic deposits and presumably rich ores. Immense water-holes, approaching the character of lakes, where curious tribes of aboriginals hunted, some of which were entirely bald, others bowed in the limbs from the continuous chase of the emu and kangaroo. From time to time Jack had listened to these tales of Herodotus; had, with some trouble, verified the localities indicated, and seen a pioneer or two who had explored this *terra incognita*.

Full of eager anticipation of the new untrodden land, in which wonders and miracles might still survive, leading to fortune by a triumphant short cut—a new run with limitless plains and hidden lakes, a copper mine, a gold mine, a silver mine, a navigable river—all these were possible in the unknown land, waiting only for some adventurer with purse as empty and need as desperate as his owner. Lulled by these glorious phantasies, John Redgrave gradually recovered his spirits—they were elastic, it must be confessed; and as the horses, poor but plucky, like their master, stepped cheerily along the level trail, he caught himself more than once humming a half-forgotten air. He had proposed to himself to make for a small township about forty miles distant, the inhabitants of which were composed in equal proportions of horse-stealers, persons "wanted," and others, these last lacking only the courage, not the inclination, to turn bushrangers. Gurran—this was the name of this delectable settlement—of course boasted of two public-houses.

About an hour before sundown Jack calculated that he was about ten miles from his destination. He had of course not been pressing his horses, and had plodded steadily on without haste, but without halt, since the morning. He could not, as he calculated, reach Gurran by Sundown, but an hour's travelling along the smooth, broad trail by the clear starlight would be pleasant enough. He did not want, Heaven knows, to get to the beastly hole too early. A simple meal, hunger sweetened, a smoke by the fire, and then to bed, with a daylight start next morning. Such were his intentions.

As he thought over and arranged these "short views of life," he became aware that the sky was overclouded. Clouds were by no means rare on the Warroo, but no one had been in the habit of connecting them with rain for many a month past. And so Jack rode on carelessly, while the sky grew blacker, the air more still and warm, bank after bank rose in the south, and at length—no, surely, it never can be, by Jove! it is—a drop of *rain*!

"I shouldn't wonder, now I think of it," said Jack, sardonically, "if it were to rain cats and dogs, just when I am regularly cleaned out. A month ago it might have made a difference." He unfastened an overcoat which he threw over himself, and as the rain commenced in a gentle but continuous drizzle (*he* knew the sign) paced gloomily forward.

His cynical anticipations were but too literally fulfilled. At first light and almost misty, then a steady downpour, in twenty minutes it was half a shower-bath, half a water-spout. Every shred of Jack's clothing was soaked and resoaked, till the feeling was as if he were clad in wet brown paper. The horses slipped, and boggled, and stumbled, and laboured in the black soil plain which alternated with the sand, and which has the peculiar and vexatious quality of balling, or gathering on hoof or wheel, when thoroughly moistened. The air changed, the temperature was lowered, the night became dark, so that Jack more than once lost his way. The thunder pealed, and the lightning in vivid flashes from time to time showed a watery waste, with creeks running, and all the usual Australian superabundance of water immediately succeeding the utter absence of even a drop to drink. It was nine o'clock when, tired, soaked to the skin, with beaten horses, and temper seriously damaged, John Redgrave pulled up before the "Stock-horse Inn" at Gurran. The person who kept the poison-shop came out, with his pipe in his mouth, and, seeing a traveller, expressed mild surprise, but did not volunteer advice or assistance.

"Have you any hostler here?" demanded Jack, with pardonable acerbity.

"Well, there is a chap, but he's on the burst just now, as one might say. Are you going to stop?"

"Yes, of course," said Jack; "why don't you look a little more lively! If you were as wet and cold as I am you'd know what I want."

"I should want a jolly good nip to begin with," said the unmoved landlord; "but you can let your horses go, and put your saddles and swags in the ferendah, can't ye?"

"Haven't you got a stable?" asked Jack, furious at this reception after such a ride.

"Well, there's a stable at the back, but the door's off, and there's nothing in it."

"No corn? no chaff?"

"No—there ain't nothin'. How am I to get it up here?"

"And what is there for my horses to eat, if I let them go?"

"Well, there's a bit of picking down by the crick. It's all our horses has to live on."

Jack reflected for a while; then, considering that the other inn couldn't possibly be worse than this, and might be better, he concluded to try it, and telling the astonished innkeeper that he was an uncivil brute, and deserved to lose his license, he headed straight for the light of the rival hostelry.

Here he met with a decided welcome and abundant civility. His horses were unsaddled, and put into a building which, if rude, possessed the essentials of equine comfort. And when he found himself before a good fire in a small parlour adorned with wonderful prints, with a glass of hot grog in possession, and a supper of eggs and bacon in prospect, he felt that there were extenuating circumstances in the lot even of that ill-fated and persecuted individual John Redgrave, late of Gondaree.

He awoke next morning early, and, dressing hastily, went straight to the stable, which to his exceeding wrath and despair he found empty. The badly-fastened door was open; there was no means of knowing at what hour the nags had escaped or been *taken out*. Here was a pleasant state of matters; all the misery of the position, intensified by the state of his nerves, rushed upon him. He knew well what a nest of robbers he was among. If not stolen, the horses had been "planted" or concealed until a reward, consonant with the ideas of the thieves, was forthcoming. He would do anything rather than go back to Gondaree. He had a few pounds left, and he could, at worst, buy a mustang of the neighbourhood and pursue his journey. Turning back sullenly to the inn, he saw his host ride up, who stated that he had been out since daybreak after the absentees without success, but that he had sent a young man after them, who, if this here rain didn't wash out the tracks, would find 'em "if they was above ground." With this meagre consolation Jack proceeded to attack his uninviting breakfast.

The rain was still falling; the dismal, dusty, thinly-timbered flat, which stretched for miles in unbroken dulness, with a shallow, unmeaning, dry creek winding tortuously through, was now converted into a sea of black mud. Jack knew that in a week it would be carpeted with green, as would indeed be the whole of Gondaree, and the Warroo generally. He groaned as he thought that all this "unearned increment" would be of not a shilling's-worth of value to him. Mr. Bagemall and Mr. M'Nab would reap the benefit of it—it was a clear fifty percent upon the price of every sheep on the place to begin with. Gregory Hardbake would be on the way down from the mountains rejoicing. All the world would be joyful and prosperous, while he was left on his beam-ends, a stranded wreck, and not even allowed to pursue his lonely voyage in peace. It was hard; but Fate should break, not bend, him. His friends, if he had any left, should see that. All that day he was compelled to pace up and down the narrow verandah of the melancholy wooden box, comforted by the assurances of the host that his 'osses would be safe to be got within the week, that the "young man as was after 'em" had never been known to miss finding such runaways. Unless—added he, meditatively—they've gone and made back to where they came from.

However, that night the much-vaunted "young man," a long-legged, brown-faced, long-haired son of the soil, of the worst type of pound-haunting, gully-raking bush native, returned without the horses. When Jack, in the course of the evening, mentioned that thirty shillings for each horse would be forthcoming on delivery, he brightened up, and declared his determination to have another try next morning.

As Jack, about noon on the following day, was observing gloomily that the rain had stopped, to his intense delight the young man before eulogized was observed approaching, driving the lost horses before him. Perhaps no sense of gratification is keener for the moment than that of the traveller in Australia, who in a strange, possibly evil-reputed locality recovers the favourite steed. The agonizing anxiety, the too probable fear of total loss, the delay, expense, and inconvenience of remount—all these doubts and dreads vanish at the moment when the well-known outline appears. Like wrathful passengers upon reaching the end of the voyage, all previous offences are condoned. The despotic captain, the surly second officer, become almost popular, and a general amnesty is proclaimed.

So, as old Pacha, with his high shoulder and flea-bitten grey skin, followed by his companion, walked into the stable yard, about two panels square of rickety round rails, Jack thought the much-suspected "young man" not such a bad fellow after all. He perhaps reciprocated the compliment after receiving the reward, though his conscience ought to have troubled him if, as is too probable, he had "shifted" Jack's horses the first night, and left them at a convenient distance from the inn on the second.

Their owner concluded not to tempt misfortune further.

Saddling up promptly, he once more took the road, glad to leave behind Gurran and all its belongings.

That night John Redgrave reached a station where, of course, he was hospitably received, and where he rested secure from the machinations of persons to whom fresh horses and "clean-skinned" cattle presented an irresistible temptation.

Keeping a northerly course, he gradually passed the boundaries of the comparatively settled country, and entered the legendary and half-explored region that skirted the great desert of his dreams. Here rose, like polar meteors, fresh gleams of hope irradiating the sunless cloud-land in which his spirit had dwelt of late—glimpses of that garden of the Hesperides—anew discovery—fortunate isles—a land of gold and gems, were on the cards. Like the garden of old, there was the Dragon—a dragon to be fought or circumvented, as circumstances might direct.

Did he lose the faint track which led between the solitary outposts of the pioneers, there was the certainty of death by thirst. A few days' anxious wandering, twenty-four hours of delirious agony, and the bones of John Redgrave and his weary steeds would lie blanching on the endless plains and sand-ridges, until the next lost wayfarer or questing tracker fell across them.

Did he escape the famine-fiend, were there not the prowling patient human wolves of the melancholy waste ready to surround and do to death that enemy of all primeval man, the wandering, insatiable white man? Little, however, did John Redgrave reck of Scylla and Charybdis. The barque must float him onward and still onward to fortune and to fame, or must lie deep amid ocean's treasures, or a stranded wreck upon the inhospitable shore. He was in no mood to be frightened at aught which other men had dared. With the demon of poverty astern, what to him was the terrible deep, fanned by the wildest storm that ever blew? Still he pressed onward; not heedlessly, but with wary patience, as beseemed an experienced bushman, whose life might depend upon the strength and speed of the good horse between his knees. The influence of the great drought in this unstocked country became fainter and less unfavourable. The gray tufted grasses and salsolaceous bushes, uncropped by stock, remained nutritive and uninjured year after rainless year in that strange Australian desert. Their strength untaxed by the moderate journeys, old Pacha and his companion, with the wonderful hardihood of Australian horses, improved in condition.

Now it chanced that at one of the most distant stations, of which the proprietor had been able to say, like Othere, "no man lies north of me," Jack picked up a partner, who volunteered to join in his adventure, sharing equally in the expenses of the modest outfit and in the profits, such as they might be. Guy Waldron was a big, ruddy-faced, jovial young Englishman, scarce a year from his father's hall in Oxfordshire. An insuperable disgust for the slow gradation of English fortune-making, combined with the true dare-devil Norse temperament, had driven him forth with his younger son's portion to make or mar a colonial career. The two men took to one another with sudden strength of liking.

The quiet resolution and utter disdain of danger which Jack exhibited after a course of highly discouraging anecdotes volunteered by Mr. Blockham, the proprietor of Outer Back Mullah, attracted the younger son.

"I am horribly tired," he said to Jack, "of doing colonial experience with this old buffer. It's tremendously hard work and no pay, and, as I've been here for a year, I fancy we're quits. I know as much bullock as I'm likely to learn for the next five years. I got a tip from home the other day. What do you say if I go run-hunting with you? You're just the sort of mate I should like, and I believe there is some grand country to the north-west, in spite of what old Blockham says."

Jack looked at the cheerful, pleasant youngster, full of mirth, and with the eager blood of generous youth, unworn and sorrow free, coursing through every vein. Much as he hungered after congenial fellowship in his lonely quest, he yet spoke warningly.

"It's a risky game enough, Waldron, you know. I'd say, if you take my advice, stay where you are for another year. You'll get your money out then, and be *sure* of investing it properly. You have a little to learn yet, excuse me, like all new arrivals."

"Oh, yes, I dare say, that's all very prudent, and so on. There are new chums and new chums. Look at my arms, old fellow."

Here he rolled up his jersey and showed his muscular fore-arm, bronzed and well-nigh blackened by exposure to the unrespecting sun.

"I've not had my coat on much, as you see. I can ride, brand, leg-rope, split, fence, milk, and draft with any man we've ever had here. A year or two more Jackerooing would only mean the consumption of so many more figs of negro-head, in my case. No! take me or leave me, as you like, but I'm off exploring on my own hook if you don't."

"In that case," assented Jack, "we may as well hunt in couples. We can back up one another if the niggers are as bad and the water as scarce as your friend says."

"He be hanged!" said the impetuous youth. "He's not a bad old chap, but he tells awful yarns, and, like all old hands, he thinks nobody knows anything but himself."

"Then it's settled. Can you get a couple of horses?"

"Yes, and a stunning black boy. The young scamp is awfully fond of me, and as a tracker he's a regular out-and-outer. By Jove! won't it be jolly—Redgrave and Waldron, the intrepid explorers! I feel as if we could go to Carpentaria."

Jack smiled at the boy's joyous readiness for the battle. Once he had been as wild in delight at feast or foray; but those days had gone.

"We must wait till we come back," said he, gravely, "before we begin to arrange the fashion of the chaplet. If the black boy is plucky, and really wants to go with us, bring him by all means."

Mr. Waldron, for whom remittances had lately arrived, spent the next day in getting in his horses, packing his effects, the half of which were condemned by Jack as being overweight, and questioning and lecturing the boy Doorival as to his special "call" for the enterprise. This sable waif was not the particular property of anyone, so he was permitted to risk his valueless life without remark or remonstrance. He had been captured in a somewhat indiscriminate reprisal upon a wild tribe by a neighbour of Mr. Blockham's, with his foot sticking out of a hollow log, in which, like a dingo puppy, he had instinctively hidden. Dragged forth by that member, he had been chained up till he grew tame, and well flogged from time to time till further "civilized." After a few years of this stern training he had become sufficiently civilized to run away, and had arrived at Outer Back Mullah some months since, a shade more than half dead with fear and thirst. Travelling through hostile country, where his kidney fat wouldn't have been worth an hour's purchase after discovery by his countrymen, he had had necessarily but little leisure and less refreshment. Guy Waldron had taken him in hand as he would a bull-terrier pup, and, finding him game and sharp, had adopted him as personal retainer. On the third morning after the treaty, therefore, Doorival appeared on an elderly but well-conditioned screw, leading a pack-horse, and showing in his roving black eyes and gleaming teeth the strongest satisfaction at his promotion.

Mr. Blockham did by no means disguise his sentiments when he bade farewell to his quondam pupil and his adventurous guest.

"Well, Waldron, goodbye. I wish you both luck, I'm sure; but I'm blest if I don't believe a warrigal will be picking some of your bones before this day six months. I've no opinion of exploring; I don't believe in running after new country; let other fellows, if they're fools enough, do all that bullocking. Wise men buy their work afterwards—and cheap enough too. I didn't take up Outer Back Mullah; quite the contrary. I gave a chap two hundred pounds for it, and where's he now?"

"Somebody must find the runs," said Guy, "and a good run, with permanent water, or say a dozen or twenty blocks, are worth more than two hundred or two thousand pounds either."

"That's all very well," returned the cynical senior; "but how do you know there's any country where you're going, let alone water? Besides, excuse me, sir, but you're a-goin' with a man that's been unlucky, by his own word, with everything he's touched before. I don't believe in a man as is unlucky. I've seen a deal of life, and I never go in with one of that sort; not if I know it. No offence to you, sir." This to Jack. "*You* can't help it, I know. As for you, you young black bilber, what are you grinnin' and lookin' so pleased at? You'll wish old Driver was a lickin' ye with the dog-chain again, when some of them myalls gets round ye a little before daylight."

The little expedition set forth, maugre the boding utterances of Mr. Blockham. The equipment was not costly, but it was sufficient; and two of the party at least had a "letter of credit" good for all the drafts which they were likely to draw upon it for sometime to come.

What says the wise, sad humorist?—

> *"Our youth! our youth! that spring of springs,*
> *It surely is one of the blessedest things*
> *By Nature ever invented.*
> *When the rich are happy in spite of their wealth,*
> *When the poor are rich in spirits and health,*
> *And all with their lot contented."*

Guy Waldron, full of hope, and thirsting for wild life and adventure, rode side by side with Jack, carolling as he went, like Taillefer singing the song of Rollo in the fore-front of the Battle of Hastings.

Doorival followed at a short distance, accompanied by the dog Help, whom he had managed to propitiate, and to whom he from time to time addressed all kinds of pretended inquiries and suggestions.

"By Jove!" said Guy, "I feel quite a new man now I've got away from that confounded dull place, and that dismal old growler Blockham. He's like the man in Marcus Clarke's ballad, who 'Did nothing but swear and smoke.' It's a luxury to have a Christian to talk to again. Talk of Englishmen!—Doorival's a king to him."

"It's all luck," said Jack; "even in this rather distant region you might have found a chum who got the periodicals by every mail, and went in for decent reading at odd times."

"That's true enough," said the representative of "Young England," "for I went over one day to get our mail—sixty-mile ride too—and Haughton's cousin had just come down from India, such a jolly chap he was too—had been in Cashmere lately, and told us no end of yarns. But I was fool enough to think all squatters were alike, and let my agents send me anywhere they liked."

"Well, you'll know better next time," said Jack, "after we've discovered this new country, and sold a few blocks to buy a couple of thousand store cattle with. You can pick up an Indian swell, or any sort of partner you fancy, if that works out."

"*You'll* suit me down to the ground, old fellow," said Mr. Waldron, enthusiastically. "We're in 'for better for worse,' as they say in the christening service, or the matrimonial questions and answers, or whatever it is."

"It doesn't concern us at present," said Jack, gravely. "Possibly you'll be better informed on that subject likewise, some day. In the meantime, how long shall we be getting through this cursed scrub?"

"I believe we shall have a week of it, if old Blockham is to be believed. He always used to swear that the scrub on this side of Mullah was more than a hundred miles thick, and that beyond that was a sandy desert, which ran right into the middle of the continent."

"Probably his geographical information was defective," answered Jack. "He is evidently one of that order of pioneers whose watchword is 'no good country beyond me.' We must keep a due north-west course, take our chance of water, and if Australia keeps true to her past character the worse country we pass through the better our chance of dropping on to something astoundingly good."

"You think so really?" asked Waldron.

"Sure of it—look at the Won-won country, the Matyara, and half-a-dozen other choice districts I could name. The first explorers must have been perfectly desperate with the awful jungles and barren tracts they had to pass through. Then one fine morning a fellow climbs up the last iron-bark range, or tears his garments in pushing through the last thicket, and lo! the Promised Land lies stretched out before him."

"By George! you raise a fellow's spirits awfully," said Guy. "I suppose you have been in this funny country ever so many years?"

"I wasn't born in it, if that is what you mean," answered his companion; "but I have been in Australia ever since I could speak; so I have had the benefit of sufficient colonial experience at any rate."

Thus conversing, sometimes idly enough, at times with a strong tinge of earnestness, the day wore on. At sundown they reached a fairly commodious spot, and there they made their simple dispositions for passing the night.

Here Mr. Doorival began to demonstrate his quality, and to establish the soundness of the reasoning which led to his being promoted to his present position. He it was who discovered the water, made the fire, helped to unpack the cooking utensils, and to hobble out the horses—the whole under the watchful eye of the dog Help, who lay under a bush and watched the proceedings with great interest.

One horse was tethered, so as to be at hand in case of need; the others were permitted to range within moderate bounds. Only a small fire was made, as, once within the boundaries of the real wild blacks, it would be hazardous to run the chance of attracting them to the camp. And it was thought *en règle*. The nights were mild, as rarely in that region is it otherwise, the occasional storms and fierce rainfalls excepted.

After the evening meal and the *postc(oe)nal* smoke, each one wrapped himself in his blanket and lay down separately, and at some distance from the fire; so in case of attack their antagonists would be less likely to surround them, or to discover the precise locality from which the deadly discharge of the white man's firearms might be expected. Help deserted his youthful acquaintance of the day, and, curling himself up beside his master, dozed all watchfully, as is the manner of his kind.

XX

"Oh, for a lodge in some vast wilderness."

—Cowper

For five days the explorers pursued their toilsome journey. The scrub was dense; the travelling was monotonous and discouraging; but the leader was too old a bushman to expect other than difficulty and privation at the onset, while the temperament of Guy Waldron soared easily in its first essay of conflict with the wilderness above such trifles as scarcity of water and a dangerous route. The boy Doorival managed to jack up a little game from time to time, which materially aided their unpretending *menu*. Once, indeed, the horses went back a whole day's journey; the situation was far from reassuring while they waited in camp for their scout. But at sundown the unerring and patient tracker returned triumphantly with the truants; and that night in camp was so full of satisfaction that it might be considered to approach a condition of actual pleasure so lightly flow or ebb the currents of mental circulation which we characterize as joy or sorrow.

"By Jove!" said Guy, "I've often thought it was jolly enough dozing before the fire on a great ottoman at Waldron Hall, after a good day's shooting, before it was time to dress for dinner, but I really believe I feel more real pleasure at this moment as we lie here smoking and seeing these rascally nags of ours short-hobbled and safe again for a start. I thought we were up a tree several times today, for exploring on foot is *not* inspiriting exercise, anyhow you look at it."

"Doorival is a trump," assented Jack. "He was a happy thought; here's his health in this flowing bowl of 'Jack the Painter.' I wish Mr. Blockham's stores had been a little more *recherché*."

"He believes in the great doctrine of cheap and t'other thing," answered Waldron. "I never could have imagined that sugar of such exceeding blackness was manufactured as we always had there. I used to tell him that some planter distantly related must have worked up his spare niggers in it. He was always giving me lessons in economy. One night he said solemnly, as we were smoking, 'Look here, Waldron, you'll never make no money if you use matches to light your pipe when there's a fire right before you;' whereupon he placed a coal on the bowl of his and puffed away like a man who had saved a sovereign. Fancy saving the fractional part of a farthing, and then paying a shilling for a glass of bad grog."

"It sounds absurd," agreed Jack, "but with colonists of his stamp the grog is exceptional, while the penny wisdom is invariable. And I must say in justice that the Blockhams of our acquaintance generally die rich, having burrowed their way to wealth, mole-blind to the pleasures of the intellect, the claims of sympathy, and the duties of society."

"Well, we'll go in for the severest screwing," said Guy, "when we get hold of this new run, with which we shall make a colossal fortune and a European reputation. I *should* like to crow over my old governor, bless his old soul!—he always delicately hinted that I should never do any good out here, or anywhere else. Wanted me to take a farm. A farm! Fancy three hundred acres in Oxfordshire, with a score or two of bullocks, and twice as many black-faced Down sheep. Regular cockatooing. I didn't see it then. Now I'd almost as soon 'keep a pike.'"

"You're an adventurous, crusading kind of fellow, I know, Master Guy," said Jack, reflectively, "and I'm very glad to find another knight-errant. But I'm not sure, all the same, whether both of us might not have gone into the Master of Athelstane business advantageously, and grown heavier and fussier every year, while we looked after our own green fields and these same despised short-horned beeves. However, it's Kismet, I suppose, that such land and sea rovers should exist, and either plant their standards or fill the breach for other more cautious combatants to walk over. Now, every man to his blanket. Goodnight."

The scrub was passed at length, and, as Jack had prophesied, they descried open country so superior to the character of the district generally as to warrant the expectation of still more splendid discoveries.

The watercourses were larger and the occasional lagoons deeper, and beyond all question permanent. The plains were immense, and though not richly grassed were covered with the best kinds of salsolaceous herbage, known to bushmen as affording better and healthier food for stock than the more enticing-looking green sward.

However, with the insatiable greed of their kind, they were not disposed to content themselves with anything short of the magnificent and exalted standard which they had set up for themselves. So onward and onward still they pressed, though from time to time the existence of "Indian sign" began to be pressed upon their attention by the watchful, uneasy Doorival.

"My word, plenty wild black fellow sit down here," he exclaimed one day. "Big one tribe—plenty fighting men—you see um track." Here he pointed to some perfectly invisible imprint upon the hard dry soil. "We better push on, these fellows sneak 'long a camp some night."

"Then they'll get pepper," answered Guy, with his customary contempt of danger. "I could knock over as many of your countrymen, Doorival, with this Terry-rifle as would keep them corroboreeing for a month. All the same, I'd rather they didn't tackle us just yet."

"I think we must take rather longer stages," proposed Jack, "and get out of this hostile country. We haven't seen the track of cattle or sheep for nearly a week. I suspect we are beyond the furthest-out people."

However, it would appear that Jack had under-estimated the enterprise of his countrymen, for next day Doorival came tearing in full of excitement to announce that he had seen cattle tracks, "all about—all about"; and by a patient system of induction the gradually concentric tracks brought them before the light had wholly faded within view of the actual encampment.

It *was* an outside station, in every sense of the word. As they rode up across the long, ever-lengthening plain to the speck in the shifting wavelets of the mirage which they knew to be a hut, a strangely characteristic reception awaited them.

In front of a small mud-walled cabin, thatched with wiry tussock grass which grew sparsely by the great lagoon on the bank of which it was constructed, sat a ragged individual, whose haggard features displayed pain and anxiety in equal proportions.

Before him were two crossed sticks, upon which were arranged a brace of double-barrelled rifles, much after the fashion of the disabled soldier in *Gil Blas* who levied contributions from the charitable on the roadside.

Perceiving as they advanced that the sentinel hoisted a flag of truce, so to speak, by waving a tattered handkerchief, they rode up and dismounted.

"By George! this is a droll homestead," said Mr. Waldron, with his usual impetuosity. "May I ask if you are the survivors of Leichhardt's expedition, or the Spirits of the Inner Desert, or Robinson Crusoe *redivivus*? At any rate I'm proud to make your acquaintance, sir. Allow me to introduce my friend, Mr. Redgrave; my own name, Waldron."

An unaccustomed smile distorted the stranger's features. He retained his sitting position, as if, like the prince in the greatest of all fairy tales, he was composed of black marble below the waist.

"We're very glad to see you and your friend too—pleasure decidedly mutual. Name of our firm, Heads and Taylor. We made out from Burnt Creek. I've been at death's door with rheumatism—can't walk a yard to save my life. Taylor is just recovering from fever and ague. He's in bed in the humpy."

"I am sorry to hear that," said Jack, sincerely. "But what is the idea of this battery?"

"Blacks!" said the rheumatic gentlemen. "I believe we have the greatest lot of devils on this run anywhere this side of Carpentaria. They've tried to rush the hut several times—once at night, luckily when the stockmen were at home, and we potted seven. They're away all day, and I have to mount guard, as you see. However, turn out your horses, and we'll enjoy ourselves for once in a way. It's no compliment, unfortunately, to say that the longer you stay the better shall we be pleased."

"Thanks, very much," said Jack; "we won't trespass on your rations; but we'll camp alongside of you for a few days, and perhaps we may be able to be of mutual assistance."

"Likely enough," said the prince with the black marble legs, moving uneasily on his form. "I suppose you are looking out for country?"

"That is our object. Have you a notion of anything first class?"

"If you wait till the stockmen come in, I believe one of them knows of some wonderful country close by, that is within fifty miles. He lost himself, and got out there when we first came up; and he has ever since wanted us to move over and take it up; but this place is good enough and large enough for all the stock we shall have for the next ten years. So Taylor and I refused to budge. It will be the very thing for you. Perhaps you won't mind helping me into the hut. I should like to see if Taylor wants anything. It is quite a luxury to feel safe."

They lifted their afflicted brother pioneer carefully, and deposited him upon the edge of a rude stretcher in the hut. On the other bed lay the wasted form of a man, who raised his eyes beseechingly as they entered.

"Poor chap," said Mr. Heads, "he's past the worst stage, but he's awfully weak, and generally very thirsty about this time. I was just wondering whether I could drag myself in when you hove in sight. Of course I knew it was all right when I saw your horses. Horses denote respectability, always."

"Except when mounted by bushrangers," said Jack.

"I didn't think of that. There's nothing to steal out here, and an off-chance of being walked into by the blacks. We haven't attained to a sufficiently high stage of civilization to support white Indians. Meanwhile, 'sufficient for the day,' &c."

"I should say so," said Waldron, lost in admiration of the courage and coolness of these dwellers in the wilderness. "*You* have had your share of evils, and something over."

"It's all a lottery—the fellows at Burnt Creek used to call us 'heads and tails,' and say we ought to toss up who would be first eaten by the niggers. I didn't think it would be such a close thing, however."

At nightfall the two stockmen came home, and the history of the establishment was fully disclosed. The overland journey with the stock had been unusually toilsome, and in swimming a river and remaining in wet clothes Mr. Heads had contracted an illness which had taken the form of acute rheumatism, and threatened to cripple him for life. Fever and ague had fastened their *remitting* fangs upon Taylor, and here in this lonely outpost, in the midst of hostile savages, hundreds of miles from medical or other aid, had the wayworn pioneers to brave their fate—to recover if their constitutions proved sufficiently strong, or to die and be buried in the waste. Such are the risks, however, which Englishmen have ever been found willing to dare for fame or for fortune.

And such, as long as "proud England keeps unchanged the strong hearts of her sons," will they still continue to brave. Fortunately the stockmen were resolute, active young men, or a very Flemish account of the cattle would have been rendered. Of course they rode armed to the teeth with carbine and revolver, and made but little scruple of using both on occasion.

"I'm blowed if I know how the boss stands it, sitting up there like an image, day after day. He's a good shot, and these warrigal devils knows it, or they'd have rushed the place long enough before now. I'm that afraid of seeing the hut burned, and them lyin' cut up in bits outside, that I hardly durst come home of a night."

"How are the cattle doing?" asked Jack.

"Well—they can't help doing well; and they'd do better if these black beggars would let 'em alone. Better fattening country no man ever see. Pity you gentlemen don't sit down handy and be neighbours for us."

"I'm not sure that we won't," said Jack, in a non-committal tone of voice; "but we sha'n't go in for any but real, first-class country, and plenty of it. We want run for ten or fifteen thousand head of cattle, at least."

"Come, Mick," said Mr. Heads, "you may as well lay this gentleman on to that Raak country that you saw when you were lost beyond the range, if you were not too frightened to know what it was like."

"Well, I don't say but I will," said Mick, slowly. "I dare say he'll sling me a tenner if it turns out all right. It *is* country, and no blessed mistake. This here run ain't a patch on it."

"Is there plenty of it?" inquired Jack, with commendable caution. "We don't want a mulga scrub and a plain or two. We must have a whole country side; good water, and twenty-five-mile block. Something in that line. And I'll give you—"

"Twenty pounds, after we've seen and approved," broke in Waldron, who was impatiently chafing to clench the bargain. "So it's a bargain, eh?"

"Done—and done with you, sir," said the stockman heartily. "You're one of the right sort; and I'd give a trifle out of my own pocket to have you alongside of us. I'll go a bit of the way tomorrow, and put you up to the lay of the country—there's room enough and water enough for half the cattle in Queensland."

This important stage reached, the rest of the evening was spent in comparatively cheerful and abstract talk. Mr. Heads took a more cheerful view of his situation and surroundings, and stated that when Messrs. Redgrave and Waldron had arrived and fairly put down stakes, he should look upon themselves as residents in a settled district. "They had not had a beast speared for a week. Matters were decidedly improving. If Taylor would only get stronger, he believed he would be on his legs again in no time. Couldn't say how cheered up they all felt. Don't you, Taylor?" Here the periodical chills came on the sick man, and he began to shiver as if he would shake his teeth out soon.

It was held, after due consultation, to be only consistent with the exercise of Christian charity to remain for a few days, and to comfort the garrison of this *garde douloureuse*. The horses profited by the respite; and when the journey was recommenced the explorers had the satisfaction of leaving their hosts in a state of mental and bodily convalescence. Mr. Taylor, having passed over the shaking stage, began to recover strength, while Mr. Heads, still much restricted as to locomotion, was hopeful as to ultimate recovery, and inclined to believe that the heathen would be confounded in due time, and the persecuted cattle be permitted to eat their cotton-bush unharmed, free from spears and stampedes.

Detailed information as to route and water-courses was obtained from Mick Mahoney, the stockman, a New South Welshman of Irish extraction, who was loud in praise of the grand country he was, in his own phrase, "laying them on to." Altogether, matters wore a more hopeful and encouraging appearance to Jack's mind than at anytime since the "hegira" from Gondaree. The horses were fresh and in good heart; their arms and ammunition were carefully looked to. Some slight addition was made to the commissariat; and Mr. Waldron, as he rode forth, all *adieux* having been made, declared himself to be "as fit as a fiddle," and ready to fight all the blacks in the glorious new territory of Raak if it was half as good as Mick Mahoney had made out.

"I feel like one of the Pilgrim Fathers," he was good enough to remark, "just unloaded from the *Mayflower*, and all ignorant of Philip of Pokanoket, Tecumseh, and the rest of the Red Indian swells. I suppose we shall not have any of their weight to do battle with. A spear like an arrow is a mild kind of weapon enough unless it hits you. I propose if we get this country, to be kind to these Austral children of Ishmael, against whom is, apparently, the hand of every man."

"The worst possible policy," said Jack; "after the place is settled, well and good, but as long as ill-blood lasts you can't be too careful."

"I think you are disposed to be hard on them," answered Guy; "but of course you're the commanding officer, and I give in. Only, I have a strong feeling in favour of a genuine patriarchal reign. The whole tribe, gradually convinced of the good feeling and firmness of the new ruler, bowing down to the beneficent white stranger, and, while toiling for him with passionate devotion, insensibly creating for themselves a higher ideal."

"Dreams and phantasies of youth, my dear Waldron, frightfully exaggerating the good qualities of human nature, never by any chance realized. There's always some scoundrel of a stockman who undoes all your teaching, or some long-headed crafty pagan who convinces his brethren of the very obvious fact that stealing is a cheaper way of procuring luxuries than working for them."

"It may be so," said the boy (another name for enthusiast, unless the nature be precociously cold or corrupt); "but all the same, if we get this country, I should like to do something for these pre-Adamite parties, or whatever they are. I think they are very improvable myself."

"Up to a certain point, but not a peg further; like all savages, they lack the power of continuous self-denial; that's where the lowest known specimens of the white races immeasurably excel them. Out of any given hundred of the most debased whites you may get an individual infinitely susceptible of development by culture. You may take the continent through, and from the whole aboriginal population you shall be unable to cull such a one."

"Well, I know that is the general creed about niggers, as we comprehensively call all men a few shades darker than ourselves; but when we annex this kingdom of Raak I will certainly try the experiment. In the meanwhile, when shall we get to it? I feel most impatient to gaze on this land of the Amalekites. They have no walled cities at any rate."

"If we have luck we may get there tomorrow," said Jack, "and camp on our own run, or runs, for we shall have plenty to sell as well as to keep."

Steering precisely by the directions given, and a rough chart manufactured for them, they found themselves quartered for the first night in a barren and unpromising scrub. However, this was the description of country described, being, indeed, the occasion of Mick Mahoney losing his tracks and eventually blundering into the astonishing land of Raak.

Next morning they were all on the alert, and for the greater part of the day toiled through a most hopeless and apparently endless scrub. Evening approached and found them still in the jungle. Guy began to think that they had missed their course; or that Mick Mahoney had lied; or that they were going deeper and deeper into one of the endless waterless thickets which occur "down there." Doorival, who by no means relished this description of travelling, and who had found his pack-horse most vexatious and hard to manage, suddenly ascended a high tree, and soon as he reached the top began to gesticulate and call out.

"All right, Misser Redgrave," he cried out, as soon as he had deposited himself, with some breathlessness, on the ground; "me see 'um that one new country, big waterhole, and big hill, like't Mick tell you. Plenty black fellow sit down; I believe me see 'um smoke all about."

"They be hanged!" said Guy, throwing up his hat; "let us push on and camp on the edge of it. I don't want to stop another night in the wilderness."

Fired with new hope, they redoubled their exertions, and as the sun fell in broad banners—"white and golden, crimson, blue"—he lighted up the welcome panorama of a vast pyramidal mass of granite, throwing its shadows across a silver-mirrored lake, while, far as eye could see, stretched apparently endless plains.

The comrades looked at each other for a moment, and then Guy burst into a wild hurrah, and, taking Jack's hand, shook it with unacted fervour.

"By Jove, old fellow," said he, "this is a moment worth living for, worth a whole long life in Oxfordshire, with all the partridge and pheasant shooting, fishing and hunting, dressing for dinner, and all the other shams and routine of recreation. This is life! pure and unadulterated; travel, adventure, anxiety, and now Success! Triumph! Fortune!"

"Don't make such a row, my dear fellow," said Jack, more philosophical, but inwardly exultant, "or else we shall have the whole standing army of Raak upon our backs. You may depend upon it the fellows are pretty well fed in this locality; and when that is the case they are apt to become very ugly customers in a skirmish. We may as well take off the packs."

"What, camp here?" demanded Waldron, in a most aggrieved tone.

"Why not? You would not have us go on to the lake before we know whether the tribe is not in force there. No! here we have the scrub at our backs, and if attacked—and we must keep that possibility uppermost in our minds—we have a capital cover to fight or fly in, whichever may be most expedient."

So they abode there, warily abstaining from making any but the smallest fire, and deferring possession of the new world till the morrow.

They had been long on their way to the lake—to *their* lake—concerning the name of which they had already held discussion, before the sun irradiated the virgin waste which lay unclaimed, untrodden, save by the foot of the wandering savage, before and around them. The pyramid of fantastically piled rocks rose clear and sharp in outline on the shore of the lake. The distance, as is usual with such landmarks in a perfectly level country, was greater than they had supposed. It was midday when they loosed their tired horses among the luxuriant herbage at its base, and wandered to the edge of the gleaming waters, doubly gracious from their rarity in that land of fierce heat and infrequent pool and stream. Amid the caves which deeply tunnelled the foundation of this wonder-temple of Nature they found traces of burial and tribal feast, and the strange, gigantic Red Hand, the symbol of forgotten rites, traced rudely but indelibly upon the dim cavern walls. Doorival gazed with wondering and troubled looks upon these tokens of an older day—a more powerful organization of the fast-fading tribes.

"I believe big one black fellow sit down here," he said, with some appearance of awe and perturbation, a most unusual state of mind with him, a full-blooded wolf cub that he was, and curiously devoid of fear; "one old man Coradjee come every moon and say prayer along a that one murra. By and by wild black fellow run track belonging to us, and sneak up 'long a camp."

"We must keep a good look out, then, Doorival," said Redgrave, sanguine and fearless in the presence of the great discovery. "Keep your revolver in good order, and Mr. Waldron and I will pick them off with our rifles like crows. Help will tell us when they are coming, won't you, old man?"

That intelligent quadruped, conscious that he was being appealed to, but not, let us say, fully understanding the whole of the conversation, looked wistfully at his master for a minute, and then relieved his feelings by a series of loud barks and a rush down to the lake, in the erroneous expectation of catching some of the water-fowl that thronged the shallows.

They concluded to camp at the lake that day, and on the next to try and discover the river which they doubted not divided at some point this magnificent tract of country. The one fact established of a permanent watercourse, and their prize was gained. They had nothing more to do but to put in their tenders for as many five-mile blocks as they pleased of the Raak country. Their fortune was made; they could easily dispose of a third part of it; stock up another third with breeding cattle, and after three or four years of very easy squatter-life—*pace* the blacks—might consider themselves to be wealthy men.

XXI

"The brown Indian marks with murderous aim."

—GOLDSMITH

L ate next day they fell upon converging tracks and indications that the wild creatures of the region walked steadily in one direction, mostly discovered and collated by Doorival. Keeping the average direction, they came towards evening upon a noble, full-fed flowing stream, running north-easterly, and abounding in fish and wild-fowl.

"Hurrah!" shouted Guy Waldron, "this is something like a river. What a glorious reach that is! We ought to christen it, for I swear no white man ever saw it before; what shall we call it? I make you a present of the lake, by which to immortalize any of your fair friends; but I should like to name this river; or I'll toss up, whichever you like."

"I will accept the lake, which I hereby call Lake Maud—we will provide the champagne on a future occasion. What shall you call the river?"

"I shall call it the Marion, after my dear old mother. Heaven knows whether she will ever see her wild boy again. I should like to have my head in the old lady's lap again, as I used to do when I was a schoolboy, and she used to talk to me in her gentle way, and charm all the perversity out of me. I wonder what sets me thinking of the blessed saint now."

"It won't do you any harm, Guy," said Jack, kindly. "Mine died when I was a little chap, but I shall never forget her, it seems like yesterday. And now, what about making tracks for civilization—save the mark— the day after tomorrow? We may run the river down tomorrow to see if the country gets worse or better, and then we must head for the nearest place the mail passes and send in our tenders—the sooner the better."

"All right. I should like a month here; but one can't be too spry about the tenders; there are always such a lot of rascally landsharks on the look-out for anything like good new country. They might have got a scrap or two of information out of old Blockham, from which basis they are quite capable of tendering for all the available country within a thousand miles of him."

"Quite true," said Jack. "I'm glad you see it in that light. I've heard of many a pioneer who has had the hard work of years snatched away from him by tenders suspiciously close to, but little in advance of, his own. How the information was supplied Heaven only knows, but it has been done before now. Didn't old Ruthven get Yap-yap and Marngah, all that country side? and didn't Westrope, who discovered it, lose heart and migrate to California, disgusted with Australia, and wroth with the whole civil service from the messengers to the minister?"

Their exploration fully confirmed the previous high estimate of the quality of the country. Following the river downward, they came from time to time upon unusually broad, deep reaches, equal to a three years' drought without serious diminution. The plains retained their character, and were rich in saline herbage, intermingled with the best kinds of fattening grasses. There was room for half-a-dozen stations of the largest size; and as far as they could see there was no appearance of the country "falling off"—that is, changing into the apparently verdant but utterly worthless spinifex, or the endless scrubs which multiply labour and decrease profits. No; the Raak country was as good as good could be, perfect in quality, and more than sufficient in quantity. They rested contented, and decided to make back to the settlements with morning light. With that end in view they shaped their course in such fashion as to strike the Great Scrub, which they had penetrated after leaving Mr. Blockham's, at a point more in the direct line to the settled country, whence they might send in their tenders for their principality with the smallest possible loss of time.

By cutting off corners, and making use of their previous experience, they managed to reach the border of this jungle tract late on the following evening.

All that day and the previous night the boy Doorival had been uneasy and watchful. Had they not known his exceptional courage, they would have attributed his uneasiness to the causeless fear and general apprehension so often exhibited by aboriginals when in strange territory. More than once he pointed out a thin column of smoke rising at no great distance from them. Sometimes one was observable on one flank, sometimes on the other, or in their rear. And as they rode forward it seemed that these tiny vaporous phenomena were rather less distant than in the earlier part of the day.

"You see that one?" said the boy, in a low, broken voice, indicative of dread. "Black fellow talk along that one smoke. One black fellow 'long a hill see you, _he_ make smoke. 'Nother one black fellow see that one smoke, _he_ make 'um smoke, tell 'nother one black fellow 'all right.' By and by, I believe, we see 'um, and no mistake. I think keep watch, all hands, 'long a camp tonight."

"Very well, Doorival," said Jack, "we shall all sleep with one eye open. Help will tell us when they are pretty close up, and we have plenty of cartridges all ready for the first round."

They had approached within a couple of miles of a long cape of scrub which stretched out into the open country, as a promontory into the sea, when it suddenly became apparent that they had entered upon a different description of travelling. They found a wide expanse of deep sand, level as the blown beaches of the sea, embellished in large patches here and there with the pink flowering mesembryanthum, which looked like a great bright flag cast down on the mimic shore, but deep and toilsome for the horses, so that an active footman could have run as fast as the struggling, floundering quadrupeds. Here, in this unexpected trap, suddenly appeared two large bodies of blacks, who converged, as if by preconcerted signal, and followed closely upon their tracks. They did not make any pretence of attack, but followed patiently in the wake of the party, as if more in the hope that the horses might sink exhausted in the sand, and so place the party at their mercy, than with the intention of forcing an engagement.

John Redgrave and his companions had ridden hard that day in order to reach the point now in front of them, and, ignoring the possibility of any change of country, had not perhaps exercised sufficient caution in so doing. Now they saw their error. The horses toiled, stumbled, and staggered in the deep, yielding sand, while nearer and still nearer came the savage horde, following up, with wolf-like obstinacy, their faltering footsteps. At length, when the timber was distant about a mile, the expedition held a council of war.

"I wonder, if we get into the cover, whether there is any chance of the fellows following us further," said Waldron. "My horse is nearly done, thanks to my unfair weight; but I don't like to leave him behind."

"Plain black fellows never go 'long a scrub," asserted Doorival; "we get 'long a timber they stop and turn round. Too much afraid of debil-debil; but I believe they catch us before that; they close up now."

"How can we stop them?" demanded Guy. "I can't go faster to save my life."

"I'll show you," said Jack, dismounting; "you lead my horse on slowly, and be ready to wait for me as I come up. I'll manage to stop them."

"But you are going to certain death," said Waldron. "I can't stand that."

"Not at all," said Jack, coolly; "you take my orders: I'm first officer, you know. Walk on quietly, and leave me here."

Jack remained where he was, and permitted Waldron and Doorival to go slowly forward. He looked carefully to his rifle, and as the array of natives came rather confusedly along he picked out a conspicuous-looking personage in the lead and fired. The unfortunate savage threw up his arms and dropped dead in his tracks. Another fell, desperately wounded, and yet another to the third shot. The mass of pursuers became confused at this sudden onslaught. They halted, appeared irresolute, and finally made a flank movement, and suffered our travellers to pursue their way in peace.

Jack quickly rejoined his men, who had stopped at the first shot; they then dismounted, and, leading their weary horses, made good their way to the cover, where they found firm ground and a sheltered nook, wherein they rested for the night, thankful to believe that they would remain unmolested by the dismayed contingent of the tribes of Raak.

"It was unfortunate that we should be compelled to draw first blood," said Jack, as they kept midnight watch, "but it was unavoidable. If one horse had fallen we should have had the whole mob upon us at once, without the faintest chance of escape."

"What made you think of that particular style of defence?"

"I happened to know two explorers," answered Jack, "who saved themselves in a similar emergency long ago. Only that they were in very wet, marshy country. Shirley told me he had never known it fail; and he being an unquestioned authority I determined to try it."

"Well, there's nothing like experience," said Guy, reflectively. "I should never have thought of it, though I was just preparing to sell my life dearly, as the writing fellows call it. Tomorrow we shall be well across this belt of scrub, and I suppose we may consider the war-path business over."

"I trust so," answered his comrade; "we have plenty of obstacles and troubles before us yet without that. I must say I shall be glad to see the first bush inn again, unsatisfactory halting-places as they are, notwithstanding."

"That tribe give us fits when we go back to Raak again," observed Doorival, with decision. "How many men you take, Misser Redgrave?"

"Plenty of men, plenty of guns, Doorival," said Guy Waldron; "don't you be afraid. You must tell them all about that if they don't touch the cattle we'll be the best friends they ever had."

"I not afraid," said the boy, proudly. "You nebber see me frighten, Misser Waldron!"

"Well, I never did," admitted Guy; "you are as plucky a little beggar as I ever saw of your age, white or black."

For three days they pursued their course through the interminable scrub, occasionally suffering for want of water, and at other times rendered anxious by the idea that they had mistaken their course, and perhaps struck the barren, waterless thicket at a point where it was broader than they had imagined, in which case they might be a week or even a fortnight before they threaded its ofttimes fatal maze. On the fourth day they sent Doorival ahead to see if he could find any indication of a change of landscape, which would fortify them in the idea that they had not been mistaken in their calculations.

To their great joy their messenger returned before sunset with the welcome intelligence that he had seen open country ahead, and they would reach it early next morning.

A small supply of water being discovered, the little party camped, full of sanguine anticipation of the morrow, looking upon the worst of the journey as past, and already fancying themselves restored to civilization and free to enter upon the first stage of their successful discovery.

Their camp-fire was rather larger than usual that night. Some of the minor precautions were dispensed with. No sign of native trails had been seen lately, and after their repulse of the Raak army they felt themselves equal to any ordinary skirmishing party.

The partners talked long as they sat and smoked by the fire. Guy was unusually excited with the confirmation of their reckoning and the expectation of a trip to the metropolis for the presentation of their tenders, in the names of Redgrave and Waldron, for so many blocks upon either bank of the river Marion, with others, including, of course, Lake Maud and Mount Stangrove.

"It's full of magnificent sensations, this *rôle* of successful explorer, Redgrave," he said. "Nothing comes up to it that I ever felt before, especially when you see plainly before you the unmistakable profits and advantages. It comprehends so much beside discovery; it's the creation, as it were, of a colony of one's very own."

"It's a grand thing in its way," agreed Jack, with less enthusiasm, recalling one great enterprise which had looked as fair and yet failed so fatally. "But, as I said before, many things have to be done yet; and I'm getting old enough, I fear, to dread the proverbial slip."

"I know," interrupted Guy, with eager scorn; "but there *can't* be a break-down in our case—it's morally impossible. They *must* accept our tenders. We can't have any difficulty in selling some of our spare blocks for cash enough to put on store cattle. How glorious it will be to see them pitching into that lovely saltbush by the lake! I know my governor would send me out two or three thousand pounds if he knew I had a real partner and a real station—a country-side of my own."

"It all looks very well, old fellow," said Jack, "and I feel with you that nothing in the ordinary run of events can prevent our forming a fine property out of our discovery, which is entirely confined to our own knowledge. You had better go straight in with the tenders as soon as we reach the region of her Majesty's mails, and I will stay at any convenient township till I hear from you."

"But why not come down with me?" demanded Guy. "I have lots of tin to carry us on for a few months, and a spell in town would do you no harm."

"I have made no vow," said Jack, "but I have taken a solemn resolution"—and a strange light came into his eyes as he spoke, and into his heart a thrill as he thought of Juandah and his last words to Maud Stangrove—"a resolution not to resume my position in society until I do so as the man who has achieved a success; I must return a leader, a conqueror, or my old comrades shall see me no more. My barque must sail up the harbour with flags flying and prizes towed astern, or lie a battered hull for wind and wave to hold revel over."

"Ha!" said Guy, "stands the case thus? So we are too proud to bend to the breeze until the wind changes? Well, I understand the feeling; only you must put me up to all the ways of your Lands Department, or else I shall get sold or nobbled, or 'had,' and then where will the prize-money come from?"

"It is all simple enough," said Redgrave. "You will leave with everything cut and dry, and in writing. You will be able to manage advances and so on down below, and I shall be all the more handy to go and take delivery of the first lot of store cattle."

"By Jove!" said Waldron, excitedly, "I feel as if I were behind them at this very moment."

As he spoke the dog Help rose slowly and, looking out into the darkness, growled in a low, fierce tone, while Doorival, converted suddenly into a statue, expressive of the act of listening, with an intensity apparent in every nerve and muscle, raised his hand in silent warning. Each man felt for his arms, and placed himself in full and perfect readiness for the reception of whatever enemy might appear. The night was intensely dark. Within a few feet of the fire the thicket was altogether composed of Egyptian darkness. It might have been solitary as the great desert, it might have contained an army with banners, for all that could be seen: still evil was abroad, they doubted not. The dog, whose tongue never lied, growled yet more menacingly. From Doorival at length came the interpretation of the faint sounds of the desert.

"Hang that fire," he said, at last, "I think we big fools for making it; black fellow coming to rush the camp; I hear 'em stick break just now."

Not a sound had fallen upon the less delicate organs of the two men, and Redgrave, but for the corroboration of Help's evidence, would have felt almost inclined to discredit Doorival's information.

"Sticks break all night in the bush," he said, "still there's something up by the old dog's bristles. If it were a dingo he would walk out to meet it; but you see he cowers close by us. Listen again."

"Your hear 'em now?" said Doorival, in a hoarse whisper, as a very faint but continuous murmur of voices came in on the breeze. "Black fellow—no mistake."

"Every man to his tree," said Guy. "I vote we clear out to the rear of the fire, so that we may deliver a converging fire upon the scoundrels when they come near the light. I call it devilish unhandsome to try and pot us now we are so near civilized society. However, they'll get it hot, that's one comfort."

"It was a strange experience," Redgrave thought, as he coolly picked out the largest available tree where none were very big, and with Guy awaited the attack. In utter desolation of that nameless solitude, with the hour midnight, and the faint but distinct sounds as of the light tread and hushed voices of the advancing savages, Redgrave felt as if they were enacting a scene in some weird drama, and were awaiting the Demon with whose intercourse their fate was interwoven.

That they would come off victorious, with the advantage of preparation and the immense superiority of fire-arms, he never doubted. Still the blacks had the advantage of numbers, and of that instinctive cunning which renders the savage man no mean antagonist.

The noises ceased; for some minutes, an unpleasant period of suspense, they awaited the onset. Then the dog suddenly burst into a loud, fierce bark, as the still, warm midnight air was rent by a storm of yells; and a shower of spears, apparently from every point of the compass, covered the fire and every foot of ground within some distance with thirsty spear-points.

A double volley, fired low and carefully in the direction of the thickest spears apparently had some effect, as a sudden cry, promptly checked, implied. For sometime this curious interchange of missiles took place. Whenever the blacks pressed forward, desirous of discovering the exact hiding-place of the daring white men, a steady discharge repulsed them. The whites were well supplied with ammunition, and the rapidity with which they loaded and fired deceived the attacking party. More than one man of note had fallen, and they became less eager in the attack upon a party so well prepared, so skilled in defence. Apparently a last attack was ordered. Some kind of flank movement was evidently arranged, and some of the boldest of the fighting men of the tribe ordered to the front. The spears commenced to fall very closely among the resolute defence corps. They appeared as if thrown from a shorter distance. Guy could have sworn that the spear which whizzed so closely by his head, as he leaned over to fire in the direction of a suspiciously opaque body, was thrown from behind yon small clump of mulga. With the decision of intelligence, or the recklessness of despair, the dog Help suddenly rushed out and assaulted what appeared to be a man at the base of the clump referred to. Guy dashed forward to the smouldering fire, and seizing a fire-stick threw it in the direction of the combat where the dog was baying savagely, and occasional blows and spear-thrusts showed that a fight *à l'outrance* was proceeding. The brand blazed up for a moment, just sufficient to display the burly form of a savage warrior engaged in the ignoble contest. With practical quickness Guy took a snap shot and sent a bullet through the broad chest, the arms of which at once collapsed.

In the excitement of the moment Guy moved forward, displaying the whole of his grand and lofty figure in the uncertain light. A score of spears from the concealed enemy hurtled around him with the suddenness of a flight of arrows. One of the puny-looking missiles— they were reed spears, tipped with bone—pierced his arm, another struck him in the side. Snapping the former short off, and carelessly drawing forth the other, the wounded man stalked back to his cover, from whence he, with Jack and Doorival, kept up a ceaseless fusillade. So deadly was the fire that their assailants dared not approach more nearly the desperate strangers, who fought so hard and shot so straight. From time to time a yell, a smothered cry, proclaimed that a shot had taken effect.

The explorers took advantage of a pause in the attack to draw together and hold converse.

"Redgrave, old fellow," said Guy, in tones which were strangely altered, "I fancy that I've lost more blood than shows, or else I'm hard hit, for I feel deuced faint and queer."

"You don't mean it, Guy; surely you can't be serious in thinking those two needle punctures could stop you."

"The one in the arm *is* only a scratch, though it makes one wince; but this confounded one in the flank has bitten more deeply, and I don't know what to say about it."

"Then there is nothing for it," said Jack, decisively, "but to beat a retreat. If these black devils think you are badly hurt nothing will stop their rush when they choose to make it. We must take stars for our guide, and move steadily back, keeping our course as well as we can."

"And what about the horses?"

"They must be left to their fate; we should risk our lives, and perhaps lose them, if we attracted notice now by trying to catch them."

"Pacha and all?" asked Guy, incredulously.

"I believe I could almost suffer my hand to be hacked off rather than lose him if it were optional," confessed Jack; "but we must choose between life and death: the time is short."

Having communicated the decision to Doorival, and pointed out the direction, that young person selected a star, and, marching with eyes steadfastly fixed upon it, the others followed him.

They were not pursued, probably because they were near the boundary of the tribe that had assailed them. No people while unmolested are more punctilious in preserving a proper attitude to friends and foes than the untaught aborigines. They respect the hunting-grounds of their neighbours in the most conscientious manner, and are always ready to hunt up an outlaw or criminal who has taken refuge in the territory of a foreign tribe. Such was one element of safety upon which the little party reckoned, and by great good fortune it did not fail them.

By the merest chance it happened that the spot where the unlucky camp-fire had been lighted was within a short distance of the ancient and scarcely-observed tribal boundary. So that when John Redgrave with his wounded comrade and their henchman abandoned their position they were unwittingly in perfect safety before they had left the scene of the conflict three miles behind them. It afterwards transpired that the second chief of the tribe had been mortally wounded in the last

ROLF BOLDREWOOD

volley. The excitement and grief caused by his fall aided the retreating party in their silent flight.

All the night through they travelled slowly but steadily onward, having for their pilot the untiring Doorival, and for their guidance one friendly star.

As day broke, and the red dawn stole soft and blushing over the gray plain and duller foliage, they found themselves upon a pine-clothed sand-hill, from whence they could survey the landscape in all directions. By the clear dawn-light each man was enabled to scan the face of his comrade. The pale and changed countenance of the once gay and volatile Guy Waldron struck Redgrave with a feeling of wonder and dread.

"Well, it seems that we are clear of these highly patriotic 'burghers of this desert city,'" said he, with an attempt at his old manner, though the pained and fixed expression of his features belied the jesting words. "Do you think there is a medical practitioner within hail, Redgrave? though I fear me he would come late."

"Good God!" said Jack, "you don't say—you can't think, old man, you are *really* hurt. I thought it was a mere scratch. Let us look and see; surely something can be done."

"'Tis not 'as deep as a draw-well, or as wide as a church-door,' as Mercutio says, but I am really afraid that I shall see the old hall no more, not even the modified home of a club smoking-room. It's hard—deuced hard, isn't it, to die by the hand of miserable savages, in a place only to be vaguely guessed at as within certain parallels; just when we had hit the white too."

"Don't think of that, my dear old boy," said Jack, gently, "you lie down and have a sleep, and perhaps we shall find that you have over-rated the damage."

They made a fire; Jack and the boy Doorival kept watch, while the sore-fatigued and wounded man slept. No sound of fear or conflict smote upon their ears, as toil-worn and saddened, they passed the mournful hours. Towards evening Guy Waldron stirred, but moaned with fresh and increasing pain.

"Where am I?" he asked, as he looked around, with eyes which incipient delirium had begun to brighten. "Oh, here, on this miserable sand-hill—and dying—dying. Yes, I know that I am going fast. Do you know, Redgrave, that I dreamed I was back in the old place in Oxfordshire, and I saw my mother and the girls. I wish—I wish you could have met my people, but that's over—as plain as I see you and

Doorival. Don't cry, you young scamp. Mr. Redgrave will look after you, won't you? Well, I thought the governor looked quite gracious, and said I was just in time for the hunting season. Everyone was so jolly glad to see me, and then I woke and felt as if another spear was going slap through me. Oh, how hard it is to die when a fellow is young and has all the world before him! I don't want to whine over it; but it seems such awful bad luck, doesn't it now?"

"I wish I had been hit instead," groaned Jack. "I'm used to bad luck, and it seems only the order of nature with me. Try and sleep again, there's a good fellow."

"I shall never sleep again—except the long sleep," answered Guy, mournfully. "I feel my head going, and I shall begin to rave before long. So we may as well have our last talk. When I'm gone send my watch and these things—they are not of any great value—to my agents in Sidney, and ask them to send them to my people. They know my address—and, Doorival, come here."

The boy came, with deepest sorrow in every feature, and knelt down by his master's side.

"Will you go home to my father, my house across the big sea, and tell them how I was struck with a spear in a fight, and all about me."

"I go, Misser Walron," said the boy, cheerfully. "I tell your people."

"You not afraid of big one water, and big canoe?"

"Me not afraid," said the boy, proudly. "I go anywhere for *you*—you always say, Doorival afraid of nothing."

"All right, Doorival; you were always a game chicken. I should have made a man of you if I had lived. Mr. Redgrave will give you new clothes when you go down the country, and put you on board ship. Mind you are a good boy, and remember what I told you, when you go to my country, and see father belonging to me. Now goodnight."

The boy threw himself on his face beside the dying man, and with many tears kissed his hand, and then, raising himself, walked to a tree at some distance and sat with his head upon his knees, in an attitude of the deepest dejection.

"Look here, old fellow," continued Guy, "there's a hundred or two to my credit at the agents'. I'll scrawl an order in your favour. You take it and do what you can for the honour of the firm, and my share of the profits, if there be any, in time to come, can go to my sisters. It will remind them of poor Guy. I shall die happier if I think they will get something out of it when I'm gone. Let the boy take all my traps home in the ship with him. It will comfort the girls and the old people at home, who have seen the last of their troublesome Guy. I wish you all the luck going; and some day, when you are thinking of the first draft of fat cattle, remember poor Guy Waldron, who would have rejoiced to knock through all the rough work along with you; but it cannot be. Somebody gets knocked over in every battle, and it's my luck, and that's all about it. Goodbye, Redgrave, old fellow. I'm done out of my share of hut-building, stock-yard-making, and all the rest of it. I feel that as much as anything. Give me your hand—my eyes are growing dim."

All the long night John Redgrave and the boy watched patiently and tenderly by the dying man. Shortly before daylight there was a period of unusual stillness. Jack lighted a torch and took one look at the still face which he had learned to love. The features still wore the calm air habitual to the man. The parted lips bore recent traces of a smile. The square jaw was set and slightly fallen—Guy Waldron was dead!—dead in this melancholy desert, thousands of miles from anyone of his own name or kindred.

John Redgrave closed the fearless blue eyes, which still bore unchanged their steadfast look of truth or challenge. He covered the still face, placed by his side the arm, carelessly thrown, as in life's repose, above the head, and, casting himself on the sand beside the dead, was not ashamed to weep aloud.

How well-nigh impossible to realize was it that, but one short night before, that clay-cold form had been full of glowing life, high hope, and generous speech. A fitting representative of the old land, which has sent forth so many heroes, conquering and to conquer. The darling of an old ancestral home—the deeply-loved son of a gallant father. The long-looked-for, dreamed-of wanderer, a demi-god in the eyes of his sisters. And now, there lay all that was left of Guy Waldron— lonely and unmarked in death amid that solitary waste, as a crag fallen from the brow of their scarce-named peak, as a tree that sways softly but heavily to its fall amid the crashing undergrowth of the desert woodlands.

That night John Redgrave and the wailing Doorival buried him at the foot of a mighty sighing pine, covering up their traces as completely as the boy's woodcraft enabled them to do, and marking the spot in a sure but unobtrusive manner, so that in days to come the burying-place of Guy Waldron should not be suffered to remain undistinguished. This duty being performed, Jack gathered up the small personal treasures of the dead man, and long before dawn, steering by the southern stars, they pursued their mournful progress towards the settlements.

XXII

"I loved him well; his gallant part,
His fearless leading, won my heart."

—Scott

For several days they had an average measure of privation only. The resources of Doorival were found equal to supplying them with food and water. From the course pointed out to him he had never varied, and Jack was, from observation and calculation, perfectly certain that it would bring them, if carried out, well within the line of the settled districts.

But as to one condition of success he felt undecided. For some weeks there had been no rain, and a stretch of country lay yet before them in which, according to the rainfall, they might, or might not, find water; in the language of explorers, signifying that they might, or might not, perish. Desperate from the death of Guy Waldron, he had been too reckless to take this risk into the account. He would dare the hazard, and put his last chance upon the die.

So it fared that, after leaving the last watercourse and entering upon the wide untrodden system of plain, scrub, and sand-hill—scrub and sand-hill and plain—which divided the rivers, Jack was compelled to admit, after two days' short allowance of water, and one with none at all, that he had been foolhardy. The third day passed without the slightest appearance of moisture. It was inexpedient to diverge from the line for more than a short distance in search for fear of wasting their failing strength. The boy, strong in passive courage, held out unflinchingly. John Redgrave had the fullest faith in the accuracy of his reckoning. They must, without the shadow of a doubt, strike the waters of the Wondabyne, *if they could hold out*. But that was the vital question. By his closely-examined and re-examined calculation they should sight the great eucalypti that towered above those deep and gleaming waters (oh, thought of Paradise!) hurrying beneath the carved limestone cliffs on the following sunset, or at least before midnight. Were but one day longer necessary, then were they both lost. The boy was failing now in spite of his courage. For himself, he would not, could not, consciously yield as long as he could stand or crawl on hands and knees. Yet a certain swelling of his parched throat, a murmur in his ears, a disposition to talk aloud and unbidden, all these signs announced to him, as a practised bushman, that the fourth day, if passed without water, would find them delirious and dying. Shutting out these thoughts as far as his volition availed, he strode on, followed feebly by the boy, during the long terrible day.

At sunset they halted for a few minutes upon the inevitable sand-hill, with pine and shrub and long yellow grass, the exact fac-simile of scores which they had crossed since they had left Raak. Jack faced the west and gazed for a few moments upon the gorgeous blazonry of scroll-like clouds, the rolling wavelets of orange, splashed with crimson and ruddy with burning gold, which rose and fell in shifting masses, as if rent by Titans from the treasure-house of Olympus. Far away northward, far as the eye could see, lay the dim green desert, measureless, lifeless, and life-denying.

"It is the last sunset that I shall see, possibly. It seems hard, as poor Guy said; but when he and better men had gone on the battle-field and elsewhere with the sound of victory in their ears, John Redgrave may well go too. It is a fitting end of the melodrama of life. Doorival, shoot that crow."

This highly inconsequent concluding remark was occasioned by the alighting of the bird of ill-omen, which had been following them since dawn with the strange instinct of its kind, on a branch almost immediately above them. The boy, wayworn almost to the death, and looking well-nigh lifeless as he lay at Jack's feet, could not resist the irony of the situation, and, noiselessly sliding his carbine into aim, sent a bullet through the breast of the unlucky "herald of the fiend," who dropped down before them, like the raven at the feet of Lucy Ashton and her fateful, fascinating companion.

> *"To tear the flesh of princes*
> *And peck the eyes of kings."*

Murmured Jack, "If one ever could smile again, it would be at this transposition of situations. A minute since this unprejudiced fowl had a well-grounded expectation that he was about to dine or sup upon us. Now we are going to eat *him*."

"Stupid fellow this one waggan," said Doorival, taking a long and apparently satisfactory suck at the life-blood of the incautious one; "he think we close up dead."

"He wasn't far wrong either," answered Jack, grimly. "Now light a fire, and let us roast him a little for the look of the thing."

Stimulated by even this unwonted repast, the forlorn creatures struggled on till midnight. The night was comparatively cool, and with parched throats and fevered brain John Redgrave judged it better, in spite of the increasing weakness of the boy, to press forward and make their last effort before dawn.

The Southern Cross, burning in the cloudless azure, with, as it appeared to the despairing wayfarer, a mocking radiance and intensity of lustre, had shown by its apparent change of position that the night was waning, when the boy, who had been going for the last hour like an over-driven horse, fell and lay insensible. Jack raised him, and after a few minutes he opened his eyes and spoke feebly.

"Can't go no furder, not one blessed step. You go on, Misser Redgrave, and leave me here. I go 'long a Misser Waldron." Here his dark eyes gleamed. "He very glad to see Doorival again. I believe Wondabyne ahead; you make haste."

Jack's only reply to this was to pick the boy up and to stagger on with him across his shoulder. For some distance he managed by frantic effort and sheer power of will to support the burden; but his failing muscles all but brought him heavily to the earth over every slight obstruction. He was compelled to halt, and, placing the lad at the foot of a tree, he extemporized a sort of couch for him of leaves and branches.

"Now look here, Doorival," he said; "you and I are not dead yet, though close up, I know. I will go on, and if I get to the water before daylight I will come back and bring you on. I will keep the same track till I drop. I know the river is ahead, perhaps not very far. I break the branches and leave track. You come on tomorrow morning if you don't see me. Now, goodnight. I'll leave Help with you."

The boy's dull eye glistened as he placed his arm round the neck of the dog, who, with the wondrous sympathy of his race, sat in front of the exhausted lad, looking wistfully into his face. Famishing as was the brute himself, he had made no independent excursions for the water he so sorely needed, but had followed patiently the feeble steps of his comrades in misfortune. At his master's word he lay down in an attitude of watchfulness by the fainting boy, and remained to share a lingering death, as Jack's steps died away in the distance.

John Redgrave shook the boy's hand, parting as those who, in a common adventure, have been more closely knit together by the presence of danger and of death. Then he strode on—weak, weary, alone, but still defiant of Fate. For more than two hours he pressed forward unwaveringly, though conscious of increasing weakness of mind and body. The timber became more dense, and his progress was retarded by small obstacles which still were sufficient to entangle his feeble feet. Then his brain began to wander. Sometimes he thought he was at Marshmead. He heard plainly the musical cry of the swans in the great meres, and the shrill call of the plover, circling and wheeling over the broad marshes. If he could only get through this timber he would see the reed-brake ahead, and, falling into the knee-deep water, would lap and lave till his fevered soul was cooled. Then a white shape walked beside him, and extended a hand pointing towards that bright star. It was Maud Stangrove, though her face was turned away—and the Shape was misty, transparent, indistinct—he knew every curve and outline of that faultless figure, the poise of her head, the swaying grace of her step. She had come to tell him that her pure spirit had passed from earth, that *his* hour was come—that they would be united forever beyond yon fair star—that toil and weariness, hope, fear, and mordant anxiety, the fierce pangs, the evil dreams of this vain life, were over. Be it so—he was content. Let the end come.

Then the fair shape floated onward, gazing on him with sad, luminous eyes, as of farewell. The look of despairing fondness, of unutterable pity, was more than his overwrought senses could bear. He threw up his arms, and calling on the name of his lost love dashed madly through the dense undergrowth. Suddenly he was sensible of a crushing blow, of intense pain, then of utter darkness, and John Redgrave fell prone, and lay as one dead.

He awoke at length to full consciousness of his position and surroundings, more clear, perhaps, from the loss of blood which had followed the blow against his brow from the jagged limb of a dead tree against which he had staggered and fallen. The moon shone clearly, the night was cool almost to coldness. He felt revived, but full of indignation. It was the ingenious cruelty which restores the fainting man to the dire torments of the rack. His swollen tongue, which all that day his mouth had been unable to contain, was covered, as were his face and throat, with ants. His throat was parched still, but his brain was revived. He rose to his feet, sternly obstinate while life yet flickered. Onward still. He would die with his face to the river. He would crawl when he could no longer walk. He would die as a man should die.

Onward—still onward; he remembered his course, and the star which Doorival called Irara. Weak at first, but gradually rallying, he walked steadily and more cautiously forward. An hour passed. The temporary feeling of excitement has subsided, and overpowering, leaden drowsiness is pressing heavily upon his brain. Again he sinks to the earth, half fearing, half wishing to rise no more. Suddenly he hears the whistling wings of a flight of birds which sweep overhead. His languid senses are aroused; he watches mechanically the dark, swift forms cleave the air in relief against the clear sky. They are wild-fowl, on their way, no doubt, to distant waters. His gaze follows them as they glide forward in swaying file, and suddenly, with the plummet-like fall, drop and disappear.

Merciful Heaven! can it be? Versed in all the habits of fur and feather, as becomes a sworn sportsman, well he knows that when such birds drop they drop in water, in *water*! He staggers to his feet, and stumbling, reeling, tottering like a drunken man, makes for the place where they became invisible. One glance, one hoarse broken cry of joy, pain, rapture mingled in one utterance, and he is on his knees beside a gleaming, rushing stream. He hears the gurgling, whistling note of the delighted birds that are diving and splashing and chasing one another in ecstasy of enjoyment. It is the Wondabyne! He remains upon his knees looking for some seconds at the starry heavens; then, slowly and sparingly, he drinks at intervals; he laves his brow and parched and bleeding lips again and again in the cool waters. Then he carefully fills the tin cup which hangs from a leather strap at his waist, and turns on his track to the boy Doorival. Him he finds still sleeping, with the dog beside him, who barks joyously at his approach. He wakes him, and pointing to the tin cup, of which the boy drinks eagerly, repeats but the single word "Wondabyne."

It is enough; Doorival arises, staggers off with him, as one risen from the dead.

Once more he sees the reedy shore—the gleaming river into which Help plunges incontinently. He has much difficulty in preventing Doorival from "drinking himself to death." Both assuage the fiery thirst which has been burning up brain and marrow. Both throw themselves upon the warm sandy turf, and sleep till the sun is far on his path on the morrow.

The battle is won—the standard is planted—all is plain and easy journeying for the future. They are close to the mail track; another day's journey will bring them to the actual settled country.

On the morrow, just before sunset, they reach The Pioneers' Royal Hotel, a palatial weather-board edifice, apparently dropped down like an aerolite upon the bare red soil of the plain. If it has no other advantages, it possesses the inestimable one of being the mail depot. That invaluable custodian of her Majesty's correspondence, the mailman, passes the door daily. Tomorrow, if need be, John Redgrave may put himself, his followers, and his tenders "on board" of this unpretending express waggon, which bears the fortunes, the passions, the emotions, the whole abstract life of the interior, to the metropolis.

XXIII

"I, the sport of Fortune."

—Duke Charles of Orleans

Jack, "ragged and tanned," half-starved, and a "footman" (as a person not in possession of a horse is termed in Australian provincial circles), was not for the moment regarded with special favour by the landlord of the Royal Pioneer.

However, the first few words led to immediate "class legislation." The landlords of Australian inns, I may observe, are tolerably good judges of "who's who," and, to their honour, are more regardful of gentlemanlike bearing than of money and good clothes.

So Jack was inducted into the front parlour, and invited to repair the inroads upon his outward man in a bedroom of comparative grandeur. He first of all arranged for the purchase of an entirely new rig-out from the affiliated store, also in possession of the landlord, and a bath. After indulgence in the latter luxury, he made up the whole of his former wearing apparel in a package, and desired that they might be given to the poor, or otherwise disposed of. He then decided that he would transact the imposing ceremony of dinner, and afterwards draw up his tenders for twenty five-mile blocks on the River Marion, and be ready for a start to the metropolis next morning.

Entering the parlour in a suit of rough tweed, he felt much more like a shepherd king of the future than the death-doomed pioneer—half hunter, half savage—of the preceding few days. As he came in, a well-dressed, strongly-jewelled personage arose from the sofa on which he had been sitting, and greeted Jack with much cordiality.

"Mr. Redgrave, I believe, I have the honour of addressing. I've heard of your heroic feats, sir. I hope you will give me the pleasure of your company at dinner. Took the liberty of ordering it the moment I heard of your arrival. No denial, sir, if *you* please. You are Frank Forestall's guest tonight, whatever happens."

There was no resisting the dash and pertinacity of his entertainer, so Jack quietly subsided into the position, and permitted the strange gentleman to make himself happy in his own way. The dinner, after a rather unreasonable delay, arrived, by no means so indifferent as to cuisine as might have been imagined. Mr. Forestall insisted on "Piper, No. 2," and pressed Jack to do him justice in huge glasses, which he seemed to have magical powers of emptying.

It must be remembered that Jack had been many months without the taste of spirits, much less of decent wine. His recent experiences, the total change of scene, the hope of a happy sequel, now near and tangible, to the volume of his life, all these things tended to produce a general feeling of exhilaration, tending, as the evening wore on, to entire loss of caution and self-control. Mr. Forestall described himself as an extensive mail-contractor, who visited the far interior from time to time with a view to comprehensive contracts, in which he intended, at no distant period, to rival, if not to overshadow, the foreign element, as represented by the potentate Cobb. He artfully led the conversation to explorations, privations, and the adventures of Jack and his hapless comrade, mingling sympathetic flattery with acute inquiries, until, after successive beakers of "hot stopping" and pipes of negrohead, Jack was in no humour to conceal any portion of his intentions and discoveries. How and when he had retired for the night John Redgrave was, next morning, unable to remember; but awaking, long after sunrise, with a splitting headache and a disordered system, he had a confused recollection of having imparted much information which he had never intended to reveal except in the sealed tenders of Redgrave and Waldron, passing in due course through the Department of Lands.

Dressing and shaking himself together with no inconsiderable effort, he found by inquiring of the landlord that the mail had come and gone, and that his genial host of the preceding evening had departed with it. Wroth with himself for the loss of even one day, he adhered sternly to the drawing out of the tenders in proper form.

After a subdued and decorous meal, he retired early, and at the appointed hour deposited himself, Doorival, and Help in the unpretending conveyance which bore the toilers of the midmost plateaux to the breeze-swept cities of the "kingdom by the sea."

Here, in due time, he was deposited as one who re-enters Paradise, after rejoicing in the as yet unforgiven outer world, amid the rayless toil of ungrateful labour, amid the briars and thorns of Earth—accursed and unreclaimed.

He lost not an hour after his arrival in despatching the inestimable "Tenders for (20) twenty five-mile blocks, situated on the River Marion, west of Daar Creek, and bearing south-west from the Camp No. XL. of Mr. Surveyor Kennedy."

Having done this, Jack awaited impatiently the time when a reply might reasonably be expected to arrive. He sought the agents of Guy Waldron, and deposited with them the relics and the few lines in which the dying man had traced the record of his last wishes. He found these gentlemen kindly disposed, and grateful to him for the manifest sympathy which he exhibited.

"How the old squire will bear it I can't think," said the senior partner. "I am the son of a tenant on his estate, and I can remember him since I was that big. He was a terrible man when he was crossed, and Mr. Guy was always a wild youngster, but he was prouder of him, I used to think, than of all the rest put together. It will be a comfort to them all to see this lad here. I dare say he wrote about him; and as he saw him at the very last, it may please them to hear of his last moments."

So the heroic Doorival was despatched, accompanied by poor Guy's big outfit in a chest full of all his unused property, books, papers, &c., and arriving safely in Oxfordshire was installed as prime favourite, and second in command to the butler. Let us hope that he behaved better than one anglicised aboriginal, who was for some slight offence chastised by the butler. That official was solemn and awe-inspiring of aspect. But the wolf-cub had grown and strengthened; he turned fiercely to bay, and smote suddenly and so shrewdly his superior officer that a coroner's inquest appeared imminent. Sentence of deportation went forth against him, afterwards commuted. But the son of the waste was respected after this outbreak, and in the servants' hall was permitted to possess his soul in peace.

There was a balance of something over £300 remaining in the hands of Guy Waldron's agents, and this sum, in the terms of his note, they paid over to Jack, as representative of the firm of Redgrave and Waldron. He had nothing now to look forward to but the acceptance of his tenders. He found that with the weighty and responsible task before him he was unable to interest himself in the ordinary frivolities of town life. He was deeply anxious to get his first lot of store cattle on the way; and to this end these tenders must be accepted and returned to him with but little delay.

Day after day he haunted the Lands Office, and by dint of pertinacity and daily application he managed to get his papers "put through" that excellent and long-suffering department. It is hinted that from press of work or other causes delay has become chronic in that much-maligned, calm-judging branch of the public service. Whether they pitied his manifest impatience, or whether the lives of certain officials were made a burden to them during the passage of the papers, certain it is that some weeks before the ordinary routine Jack had reason to believe that an acknowledgment of his communication would reach him in advance of the ordinary official period. Before the impatiently expected official communication arrived, Jack had made several important arrangements depending upon this contingency, so that no more time than was absolutely necessary might be lost. He was feverishly anxious to be again on the war-path.

He thought of joyous Guy Waldron lying beneath the solitary pine-tree, on the far sand-hill, swept now in the advanced season by the burning desert blast; and he pined for the moment when he could recommence his labour, and make some progress in fulfilment of his pledge to his dead comrade.

He thought of fair Maud Stangrove, lonely, weary with vigil and orison, enduring her prosaic, unrelieved life at Juandah; and his heart stirred with an unaccustomed throb as he pictured her wild joy upon receiving his letter, telling of the acceptance of the tenders, and his departure to stock the Wonder-land so dearly-bought, so hardly wrested from Nature and from man. He had arranged with certain stock and station agents for the placing of a certain number of the blocks in their hands for sale, upon the receipt of which security they were willing to advance the cash necessary for the purchase of a couple of thousand head of cattle.

In pursuance of these plans he had determined, after extracting a solemn pledge from one of the higher officials that within a very short space of time he should receive the necessary reply to his proposals, to proceed at once to the station where the cattle were on approval. He authorized the momentous despatch to be delivered to his agents, to be by them forwarded to him at the cattle-station.

The cattle were mustered, counted, and approved of. The price was very low, the quality reasonable—it was not necessary to be too fastidious under the circumstances. The time Jack had calculated upon expending had just expired, when lo! the expected despatch, "On Her Majesty's Service," with her Majesty's envelope and her Majesty's Lion-and-Unicorned seal, arrived.

"Just as I calculated, to a day," quoth Jack. "This reminds one of old times, when I used to be rather proud of 'fitting my connections' in business matters, as Americans phrase it. Now for the first Act of Victory in Westminster Abbey!" He opened the missive hastily. How neat and decided were the characters of this long-looked-for epistle! Jack read it twice over, as his vision after one glance was temporarily obscured.

This was the wording of the important document:—

DEPARTMENT OF LANDS,
October 15, 186—

SIR

I have the honour to acknowledge the receipt of tenders for unoccupied Crown lands, as noted in the margin, bearing date September 10th *ultimo*, and to inform you that tenders on the part of F. Forestall and Co. and others, which would appear to be for the same blocks, were received at this office upon the 9th September *ultimo*.

I have the honour to be, sir,
Your obedient servant,
J.M. INGRAM,
Under Secretary

John Redgrave, Esq.,
Care of Messrs. Thornbrook and Bayle,
Stock and Station Agents

Jack read more than once the fatally clear and concise announcement, with the blank, expressionless countenance of a man perusing his death-warrant, unexpectedly received. Was it credible, possible, that an overruling Providence could permit such hellish treachery? Now he understood all the artful inquiries, the feigned *bonhomie* and hospitality, the sudden departure of the double-dyed traitor Forestall. Was this to be the recompense for the deadly perils, the hunger, the thirst, the blood of Guy Waldron, his own passage through the Valley of the Shadow? It could not be! Again and again he showered wild curses upon his own weakness, on the heartless villain who had taken advantage of him, the feeble survivor of the desperate conflict waged with the malign powers of the desert.

Again he assured himself that such monstrous injustice before high Heaven could not be carried out. He would return at once to the metropolis, and if such base theft, worse a thousand times than the comparatively straight-forward and manly robbery under arms by the wandering outlaw, who risked his life upon the hazard, were confirmed, he would shoot Forestall in midday, in the public streets, before he would submit to be mocked and plundered of the prize for which he and his dead comrade had shed their blood. He felt compelled, to his deep mortification, to explain to the owner of the partly-purchased herd that unforeseen circumstances prevented his completing his bargain, and necessitated his instant presence at head-quarters. Deeply disappointed, and with a host of doubts bordering upon despair preying upon his very vitals, he abjured rest and sleep, almost food, until he once more found himself in the streets of—.

Without an instant's delay he presented himself at the office of Messrs. Thornbrook and Bayle, to whom, haggard and fierce of mien, he at once presented the official letter.

"I see the whole thing," said the senior partner, "and I feel as indignant as yourself at the vile deception which has been practised upon you. I know the scoundrel well, and it is far from his first crime in the same direction. I will go with you to the Minister for Lands, and we will see what we can do. But first have some breakfast, and calm down your excitement a little. We may manage to arrange matters, surely."

Jack took the well-meant advice, and before long they were in the ante-chamber of the Minister for Lands, the arbiter of fate, he who gives or withholds fortune, decreeing affluence or ruin, "according to the Regulations under the Land Act."

After waiting about an hour for the return of a glib gentleman who went in just before them, with the assurance that his business could be settled in ten minutes, they passed into the presence of the great man. They found a quiet-looking personage seated before a very comfortable writing-table, on which lay piles of official-looking papers in envelopes of every gradation of size, some of them apparently constructed to receive a quire or two of foolscap without inconvenience. They were received with politeness, and Mr. Thornbrook introduced Jack, who at once stated his grievance.

"Your tenders were sent to this department on or about the—?"

"The tenth of September," said Jack. "I came down at once, after returning from the new country applied for."

The minister rang a bell, and a clerk appeared.

"Send up the tenders, signed John Redgrave for Redgrave and Waldron, for unoccupied Crown lands, and any others for the same blocks."

In a few minutes several large envelopes were laid upon the table, upon one of which was marked "Redgrave and Waldron.—Tenders for Raak new country."

"I understand you to complain," said the minister, blandly, but not without a tone of sympathy, "that, whereas you and your partner—since dead, I regret to hear—were the actual discoverers and explorers of this Raak country, other persons have put in tenders for apparently the same blocks."

"That is my complaint," said Jack; "and not an unreasonable one either I should fancy. My partner and I, at the risk of our lives, he, poor fellow, did lose his, found and traversed this country, never seen or heard of by white men, with the sole exception of the stockman who told us. I came to town with hardly a day's loss of time, put in formal tenders, and now, to my utter astonishment, I find that tenders for the same country are in before mine. I certainly did speak unguardedly about the affair to a fellow named Forestall, and he, it appears, has planned to rob me of my very hardly-earned right to the run."

"It appears to be a very bad case," answered the minister; "but you will, I am sure, concede that the department can only deal with tenders or applications for pastoral leases of unoccupied Crown lands as brought before it, without reference to the characters or motives of applicants. I may point out to you that these tenders (here he gathered up a sheaf of the octavo envelopes) appear to have been put in on the ninth of September, one day before yours. You and your friend can examine them."

Jack and Mr. Thornbrook did look over them. There were a large number. They were prepared evidently by skilled and experienced hands. Some were in the name of Francis Forestall and Co., many in other names, of which Jack had no knowledge. They offered a shade above the yearly rental and premium which Jack had put down, never dreaming of a competitor. Then, again, they were geographically most accurate. Close calculations evidently had been made, charts studied, and the nearest possible approximation as to latitude and longitude around it. Nor was this the worst. Every square mile of the Raak country was of course included. But the tenders in the strange names took in the whole available country above, below, around that desirable oasis, so that there it was hopeless, if the hostile tenders were accepted, to find even a decent-sized run anywhere within a week's ride of Mount Stangrove and Lake Maud.

Jack turned from the accursed papers to the minister and demanded whether the mere accident of priority was to override his unquestionable claims as discoverer.

"Did the matter rest wholly with me," he replied calmly—for hundreds of difficult cases, passionate appeals, and wild entreaties had educated his mind, during his term of office, to a judicial lucidity and decision—"I have no hesitation in saying that I should at once direct that your tenders be accepted; but I am compelled to decide all cases of this nature entirely by certain regulations made under the Crown Lands Occupation Act. One of these specifically states that the order of priority, other things being equal, must rule the acceptance of tenders; with no other fact or consideration can I deal. The tenders of Forestall, Robinson, Andrews, Johnson, and Wade are apparently for the identical and adjacent blocks. They were received in this department twenty-four hours before yours."

"Of course, of course, we allow that," said Mr. Thornbrook. "But can nothing be done for my friend here? It is the hardest of all hard cases. It will ruin him. I speak advisedly: he has already entered into engagements that I fear, if this matter goes adversely, he cannot meet. My dear sir," said Mr. Thornbrook, warming with his client's wrongs, "pray consider the matter; you must see the equity of the case is with us; try and prevent such a palpable wrong-doing and perversion of justice."

"My dear sir," said the minister, rising, "the matter shall have the most serious and minute consideration of myself and my colleagues. There will be a cabinet meeting on Thursday, at which the affair can be appropriately brought up. I will order a letter, containing the final decision of the Government, to be sent to Mr. Redgrave, whom I now beg to assure of my deep sympathy. Good morning, gentlemen."

In the course of ten days Jack received another official letter, in the handwriting which he had come to know, and also to dread. He had passed a wretched, anxious time, and now he was to know whether he was to be lifted up afresh to the pinnacle of hope, or to be hurled down into an *inferno* of despair, lower than he had ever yet, dark as had been his experiences, unmerciful his disasters, been doomed to endure. He read as follows:—

ROLF BOLDREWOOD

Department of Lands,
October 30, 186—

Sir

I have the honour to inform you, by direction of the Minister for Lands, that, after the fullest consideration of your case, it has been finally decided to accept the tenders of Messrs. Forestall and others for the blocks noted in margin, as having been received prior to those of Messrs. Redgrave and Waldron.

I have the honour to be, sir,
Your obedient servant,
J.M. Ingram,
Under Secretary

John Redgrave, Esq.

XXIV

DE PROFUNDIS

J ack hardly knew how and in what fashion he left the city. Mechanically, and all aimlessly, as he steered his course, some old memories helped to guide his footsteps towards the desert, towards the great waste amid which he had joyed and sorrowed, toiled and endured, in which the palm-fringed fountains had been so rare, whence now the simoon had arisen which had whelmed all the treasures of his existence. From time to time as he wandered on, ever northward, and trending towards the outer bush-world, he accepted the rudest labour, working stolidly and desperately until the allotted task was concluded. In truth his mind was stunned; he had no hope, no plan. What was the use of his trying anything? Was he not doomed? Did not Mr. Blockham warn poor Guy against having anything to do with an unlucky man? He tried to forget the past and to avoid thoughts of the future by hard work and continual exertion. When he walked it was not in his accustomed leisurely pace, but as if he were walking for a wager, trying to get away from himself.

But this could not last long. One day, after he had left a lonely bush inn, he felt attacked with dizziness, which for a few moments would obscure his sight. From time to time he felt as if a mortal sickness had seized him, but he disregarded the warnings of Nature and obstinately continued his course, until all at once his powers failed him, and, sick to death in body and in mind, he flung himself down by the side of a sheltering bush and scarcely cared whether he lived or died. Faithful to the last, patient of hunger and of thirst, strong in the blind, unreasoning love of his kind, with a fidelity that exceeds the friendship of man, and equals the purest love of woman, the dog Help, with silent sympathy, lay by his side.

The form of the wanderer lay beneath the forest tree, which swayed and rocked beneath the rising blast. With the moaning of the melancholy shrill-voiced wind, wailing all night as if in half-remembered dirges, mingled the cries of a fever-stricken man. John Redgrave was delirious.

With recovered consciousness came a wondering gradual perception of a hut, of the limited size and primitive design ordinarily devoted to the accommodation of shepherds. A fire burned in the large chimney;

and the small resources of the building had been carefully utilized. By the hearth, smoking on a small stool, sat an elderly man, whose general appearance Jack seemed hazily to recall.

As Jack moved, the man turned round, with the watchful air of one who tends the sick, and disclosed the white locks and rugged lineaments of the old Scotch shepherd whom he had relieved at Gondaree, and to whose gratitude he had owed the gift of the dog Help.

"Eh! mon!" exclaimed the ancient Scot, "ye have been mercifully spared to conseeder your ways. I dooted ye were joost gane to yer accoont when I pickit ye up yonder, with the doggie howlin' and greetin' o'er ye."

"I don't see much mercy in the matter. Better far that I were stiff and cold now under the yarran bush; but I am much obliged to you all the same."

"Kindly welcome; ye're kindly welcome, young man: ye've been on the spree, as they ca' it, I can tell that weel, more by token I hae nae preevilege to school ye on that heed, seeing that I, Jock Harlaw, am just as good as ready money in the deel's purse from that self-same inseedious, all-devourin' vice."

"No, it's not that," said Jack, with a faint smile, "but I don't wonder that you thought so. I'm very tired, that's all, and there's something wrong with my head, I think."

"The Lord be thankit; I'm glad it's no that devil's glamour that's seized ye. But surely I ken the collie; how did ye come by him, may I speer?"

"So you don't remember me or the dog; you came to Gondaree with him and the other pups on your back."

"Lord save us! auld lassie wasna wrang, then; it's just fearsome," exclaimed the old man, in accents of the deepest concern and wonder. "And do you tell me," continued he, "that you're the weel-gained, prosperous, kind-spoken gentleman that helped old Jock in his sair need yon time? Fortune's given ye a downthraw; but oh, hinny, however sair the burden may be, or sharp the strokes of adversity, better a hunner times to bear a thing than to sell your manhood to the enemy of the flesh."

Jack saw there was still a suspicion in the old man's mind; it must have been hard for him to believe anything but drink could have brought a man so low, but he did not resent the mistake, and only closed his eyes wearily.

"If ye ask auld Jock Harlaw to tell you the truth," the old man continued, "he'll say that of all the men he's had ken of he never saw one that did not die in the wilderness once he had bowed the knee to the Moloch of drink. Ye may see the Promised Land, and the everlastin' hills glintin' in the gold o' the new Jerusalem; but ye maun see, like Moses on the mountain top, or on the sands o' the desert, ye'll no win oot, ance ye're like me, if the angels frae heaven cam and draggit ye by the hand."

"It's a bad look out, Jock, by your showing; but how is it, with your strong perception of the evils of the habit, and your religious turn of mind, that you have not broken yourself of it?"

"Maister Redgrave," answered the old man, solemnly, "that is one of the awful and inscrutable meesteries of the life of the puir, conceited, doited crater that ca's himsel' man. My forbears were godly, sober, self-denying Christian men and women. Till the day I left the bonny homes o' Ettrick, for this far, sad, wearifu' land, nae living man had ever seen the sign o' liquor upon me, or could hae charged me wi' the faintest token of excess. I was shepherd for the Laird o' Hopedale, and nae happier lad than Jock Harlaw ever listened to the lilting o' the lasses on the Cowden Knowes."

"And what tempted you to emigrate, and better your condition, as it is ironically termed?"

"Weel, aweel," pursued the old man, contemplatively, "my nature was aye deeply tinged wi' romance. I had heard tell o' the grand plains and forests, and the great sheep farms of Australia, with opportunities of makin' a poseetion just uncommon, and I was tempted, like anither fule, to quit the hame of my fathers, and the bonny Ettrick-shaw, and Mary Gilsland, that was bonnier than a', to mak' my fortune. And a pretty like fortune I hae made o' it."

"Well, but how did you come to grief? There must have been so many people too glad to get a man like you among their sheep."

"I had my chances, I'll no deny," said the old man. "Ilka one o' us has ae guid chance in this life, forbye a wheen sma' opportunities o' weel-doin'. But though I wrocht, and toiled, and scrapit for the day when I should write and bid Mary to join me across the sea, I had nae great luck, and mair times than one I coupit a' the siller just as I had filled the stocking. At the lang end of a', just as things had mended, my puir Mary died, and I had nae strength left to strive against the evil one that came in the form of comfort to my sair heart and broken speerit. Maybe I had learned to pass a wee thing too near to the edge when I was working—there's a deal too much of that amang men that would scorn the idea of drunkenness."

"And the end?"

"And the end was that I was delivered over bound hand and foot to a debasing habit, which has clung to me for thretty years, in spite of prayers and resolutions, and tears of blood. And so it will be, wae's me, till the day when auld Jock Harlaw dies in a ditch or under a tree like a gaberlunzie crater, or is streekit in the dead-house o' a bush public. And which gate are ye gangin' the noo?" demanded the old man with a sudden change from his dolorous subject.

"Haven't an idea; don't know, and don't care."

"That's bad," said the old shepherd, looking at him with pained and earnest looks; "but ye're looking no fit to leave this. I misdoot that I wranged ye when I thocht it was the drink. What will I do if it is the fever?"

"Let me rest here; I dare say I shall soon get over it," said Jack, with a gleam of his old hopefulness, but he was touched with the anxious manner of the kind old man, and made the best of what he was afraid would be a serious illness.

But he was happily mistaken; a few days' rest and the careful nursing of the shepherd, whose small stock of medicine had never before been broken into, sufficed to restore him, not to health, but to a state of convalescence which permitted him to stroll a little way from the hut.

Jack had had many talks with the old man, whose experience was worth something, although he had not been able to avail himself of it, and the conclusion he arrived at was that he would accompany Harlaw to Jimburah.

"I'm weel kenned there; why suld ye no get a flock o' sheep too? The doggie will do work fine for ye, and maybe we'll get a hut together, and I'll cook for ye; then when ye get strong ye can look aboot and see what ye can do."

"Anything you like, Jock," said he, wearily; "one thing is much the same as another to me now."

"Weel a weel," said the old man, gratified at his acquiescence, "there's better lives than a herd's in Australia, and there's waur. I wadna say but that after sax months or so, with the labour and the calm, peaceful life where ye see God's handiwork and nae ither thing spread out before ye, after sax months ye might find your courage and your health come back to ye, and gang on your way to seek your fortune."

"Didn't you find it dreadfully lonely at first?" inquired Jack.

"Weel, I canna in conscience deny that at first I thocht it just being sold into slavery, but as time passed I found it wasna sae devoid of rational satisfaction as might ha' been supposed. Many a peacefu' day hae I walked ahint my flock, sound in mind and body too. There's poseetions in life, I'll no deny, that's mair dignified and pridefu', but on a fine spring morning, when the grass is green, the birds a' whistling and ca'ing to ither puir things, the face o' Nature seems kindly and gracious; the vara sheep, puir dumb beasties, seem to acknowledge the influence of the scene, and there's a calm sense o' joy and peace unknown to the dwellers in towns."

The old man warmed with his subject, and spoke with such earnestness that Jack could not help smiling, far as his thoughts were from anything like mirth.

"Well, Harlaw, man is a curious animal, not to be accounted for on any reasonable plan or system. As you and I have not managed to dispossess ourselves of the complex functions chiefly exercised in the endurance of various degrees of pain which we know as life, we may as well wear them out for a time in what men call shepherding as in any other direction. They don't fence hereabout, then?"

"Not within years of it, sir; and I'm thinkin' it's just as well for puir bodies like you and me, if you'll excuse the leeberty."

"Don't make any excuse, and get out of the way of saying 'sir,' if we are to be mates. Call me Jack—Jack Smith. Mr. Redgrave is dead and buried—fathoms deep. Would to God he were, and past waking!" he added, with sudden earnestness.

"Dinna say that; oh, dinna cease to have faith in His mercy and long-suffering," said the old man, beseechingly. "I am old and fechless, and, as I hae told ye, a drunkard neither mair nor less; but I cling to the promises in this book (here he took from his pocket an old, much-worn Bible), and though the mortal pairt o' Jock Harlaw be stained wi' sin and weakness and folly, I hae na abandoned the hope and the teaching o' my youth, nor the trust that they may yet gar me triumph over the Adversary. But we must be ganging; it's twenty miles, and lang anes too, to Jimburah."

There was nothing but to buckle to the journey. Jack was weak after his illness, but he faced the road as the manifest alternative, the old man's rations having been exhausted, and further sojourn in the deserted hut being inexpedient.

He was thoroughly exhausted when the home-paddock of Jimburah was sighted. He walked up with Jock Harlaw to the overseer's cottage, the proprietor's house being unapproachable by the "likes of them."

Here he and his companion stood for half an hour, waiting the arrival of that important personage, the overseer, along with nearly a dozen other tramps, candidates for work, or merely food and shelter in the "travellers' hut," like themselves. A stout, bushy-bearded man rode up at a hand-gallop in the twilight, and spoke.

"Well, there seem plenty of you just now, a lazy lot of beggars, I'll be bound; looking for work and praying you mayn't get it, eh?"

This was held to be very fair wit, and some of the hands laughed appreciatingly at it.

"Any shepherds among you? You fellows with the dogs I suppose have stolen them somewhere to look like the real thing? Oh, it's you, old Jock, is it?" he went on, with a good-natured inflection, changing the hard tones of his voice. "You're just in time; I've lost two rascally sweeps of shepherds at the dog-trap. Can you and your mate take two flocks of wethers there? You know the place."

"Nae doot they'll be bad sheep to take," quoth old Jock, with national caution. "Just fit to rin the legs off a man with the way they've been handled; but I'm no saying, if ye're in deeficulty."

"Then you'll take them? Well, you can come as early as you like tomorrow morning. But stop; is your mate any good? *You* don't look as if you'd done much shepherding, though you've got a fine dog, by the look of him."

"He's a friend of mine," affirmed Jock, with prompt decision, "and I'll wager ye a pound o' 'bacco ye hav'na a better shepherd on the whole of Jimburah."

"Humph!" exclaimed the official, "he may be as good as most of them, and be no great things either. However, I'm hard up, and must risk it. What's your name?"

"John Smith," said Jack, steadily.

"Uncommon fine name too. Well, Smith, you can go out along with Scotch Jock tomorrow morning, and take the 1,800 flock; he has 2,200 in his. I'll send your rations out after you, and will come and count you tomorrow fortnight. Come in now and take your pannikin of flour for tonight. He knows the travellers' hut. Here, you other fellows, come in and get your grub."

He who of old boasted himself equal to either fortune enunciated a great idea. But how different, often, is the practical application to the theory fresh from the philosopher's workshop!

XXV

*"There is a tide in the affairs of man
Which, taken at the flood, leads on to fortune."*

—SHAKESPEARE

The "travellers' hut" is an institution peculiar to divers of the outlying and interior districts of Australia. It is the outcome of experience and cogitation, the final compromise between the claims of labour and capital, as to the measure of hospitality to be extended to workmen errant. Given the fact that a certain number of labourers will appear at the majority of stations, almost everyday of the year, demanding one night's food and lodging, how to entertain them? Were they suffered to eat and drink at discretion of the food supplied the permanent *employés*, abuses would arise. Said *employés* would be always requiring fresh supplies, having "just been eaten out" by the wayfarers. Also disputes as to the labour of cooking. It might happen that the more provident and unscrupulous guests would occasionally carry away with them food sufficient to place them "beyond the reach of want" on the following day, or, so wayward is ungrateful man, might levy upon the garments and personal property of the station servants after they had gone forth to their work. Such examples were not wholly wanting before the establishment of that *juste milieu*, the "travellers' hut." There, an iron pot, a kettle, a bucket, and firewood are generally provided. Each traveller receives at the station store a pint of flour and a pound of meat. These simple but sufficing materials he may prepare for himself at the travellers' hut in any fashion that commends itself to his palate. On the following day, if not employed, it is incumbent upon him to move on to the next establishment.

Jack smoked his pipe over the fire in the caravanserai aforesaid, after a meal of fried meat and cakes browned, or rather blacked, in the frying-pan which had previously prepared the meat. Old Jock performed this duty cheerfully, and not without a certain rude skill. He produced from his kit a small bag containing a modicum of tea and sugar, which just sufficed for a pint each of the universal and precious bush beverage, causing them to be looked upon with envy by their less fortunate companions. Tired out by the day's journey, Jack had scarcely energy to consume his share of the food, and but for the pannikin of tea, indifferent enough, but still a wonderful restorative in all "open air" life and labour, could not have essayed even so much exertion. At another time he would have been amused by the rude mirth and reckless jests of his associates. But this night he sat silent and gloomy, hardly able to realize his existence amid conditions so astonishingly altered.

"You're rather down on your luck, young man," observed a stout but not athletic individual, smoking an exceedingly black pipe, full of the worst possible tobacco; "you've made too long a stage, that's about it. I'm blowed if I'd knock myself up, at this time of year, for all the squatters in the blessed country."

"No fear of you doin' that, Towney," said a wiry-looking young fellow with light hair and a brickdust complexion, which defied the climate to change its colour by a single shade, "at this time of year, or any other, *I* should say. How fur have you come?"

"A good five mile," quoth the unabashed Towney, "and quite enough too. I walked a bit, and smoked a bit, you see. Blest if I didn't think I should finish my baccy before the blessed old sun went down."

"Well, I'm full up of looking for work," said the younger man. "There's no improvements goin' on in this slow place, or I could soon get in hut-buildin', or dam-makin', or diggin' post holes. I ain't like you, Towney, able to coast about without a job of work from shearin' to shearin'. If the coves knowed you as well as I do they'd let you starve a bit, and try how you like that."

An ugly look came into the eyes of the man as he said slowly, "There might be a shed burnt, accidental-like, if they tried that game. You remember Gondaree, Bill, and the flash super? I wonder how he and his boss looked that Sunday mornin'."

Bill, an elderly, clean-shaved individual, the yellowness of whose physiognomy favoured the hypothesis of prison discipline having been applied (ineffectually) for his reformation, gave a chuckle of satisfaction as he replied—

"Well, it happened most unfortunate. I 'ope it didn't ill-convenience 'em that shearin'. I hear as M'Nab (he's boss now, and they've bought the next run) has got the best travellers' hut on the river. Anybody heard who they've shopped for those hawkers at Bandra?" continued Bill, who seemed to have got into a cheerful line of anecdote, running parallel with the *Police Gazette*.

"Why, what happened them?" asked the fiery-faced young man.

"Oh, not much," affably returned Bill; "there wasn't much of 'em found, only a heap of bones, about the size of shillings. Some chaps had rubbed 'em out and burned 'em."

"What for?" inquired the sun-scorched proprietor of the prize freckles.

"Well, they was supposed to be good for a hundred or so. However, they put it away so artful that no one but the police was able to collar it; and the fellows got nothin' but a trifle of slops and a fiver."

"It's my belief," asserted the young man with the high colour, concluding the conversation, "that you and Towney are a pair of scoundrels as would cut the throat of your own father for a note. And for two pins I'd hammer the pair of ye, and kick yer out of the hut to sleep under a gum-tree. It's dogs like you, too, as give working-men a bad name, and makes the squatters harder upon the lot of us than they would be. I'm goin' to turn in."

The men thus discourteously entreated looked sullenly and viciously at the speaker, but a low sound of approval from the half-dozen other men showed that the house was with him. Besides which, the wiry, athletic bushman was evidently in good training, and had the great advantage of youth and unbroken health on his side. So when he stepped forward with his head up and a slight gesture of the left hand, as of one not wholly devoid of scientific attainment, the pair of ruffians turned off the affair with a forced laugh; after which the whole of the company sought their sleeping compartments or bunks, with but little of the delay resulting from an elaborate *toilette de nuit*.

The next day found Jack and his companion in possession of the Dog-trap out-station hut, and of two flocks of sheep, duly counted over to them by the overseer. Two brush-yards constructed on the side of a rocky hill, and half full of dry sheep manure, a guano-like accumulation of years, completed the improvements.

A month's ration for the two men (64lbs. of flour, 16lbs. sugar, and 2lbs. tea) was deposited upon the earthen floor by the ration-carrier, who arrived in a spring-cart about the same time as themselves.

"Now, my men," said the overseer, after counting the sheep and entering them in his pocket-book, "you're all right for a month. You can kill a sheep every other week, and salt down what you can't keep fresh. Smith, you'll have to stir them long legs of yours after your wethers; they're only four-tooth sheep, and devils to walk, I believe. Keep your sheep-skins and send 'em in by the cart, or I'll charge you half-a-crown apiece for 'em. You can settle among yourselves which way you'll run your flocks; though I suppose you'll quarrel, and not speak to each other, like all the rest of the shepherds, before half your time is out. If you lose any sheep, one of you come in and report. Good-morning."

With which exhortation Mr. Hazeham rode off, either by nature not "a man of much blandishment," or not caring, on principle, to waste courtesy on shepherds.

"So here we maun sojourn for sax months," remarked old Jock, as they sat at their evening meal, after having yarded their flocks, killed a sheep, swept and garnished their hut, and made such approximation to comfort as their means permitted. "I dinna ken but what we may gang along ducely and comfortably. Ye were wise to write and order the weekly paper. It will give us the haill news that's going and many an hour's guid wholesome occupation, while the sheep are in camp or at the water. We'll maybe get a book or two from the station library."

"I expect you'll have most of the reading for a while," answered 'Mr. Smith.' "What's the use of knowing that everyone is better off than one's self? One comfort is that this flock keeps me going, and I shall sleep at night in consequence."

"Ye'll no find them rin sae muckle after a week or twa's guid shepherding. There's a braw 'turn out' here—both sides frae the hut; once ye get to ken the ways o' your flock, ye'll be like the guid shepherd in the Holy Book, and they'll be mair like to follow ye, man, than to keep rin-rinning awa' after every bit of green feed."

In spite of Jack's gloomy air, and refusal to take comfort, or acknowledge interest in life, matters slowly improved. The hut was not so bad, clean-swept and daily tended by the neat handed Harlaw, who had constituted himself cook, steward, and butler to the establishment. The country was open, thus minimizing the labour of looking after the flocks, which, left a good deal to themselves, as is the fashion of experienced shepherds, mended and fattened apace. The atmosphere of the interior, cool and fresh, "a nipping and an eager air," soon commenced to work improvement in the general health of the two Arcadians.

John Redgrave had considerately written and ordered one of the excellently conducted weekly papers of the colony, which duly arrived, directed to "Mr. John Smith, Jimburah, *viâ* Walthamstowe," such being the imposing name of their post town. The weekly journals of Australia, arranged something after the pattern of *The Field*, are, we may confidently assert, in certain respects the most creditable specimens of newspaper literature known to the English-speaking world. Comprising, as they do, fairly-written leading articles, tales and sketches, essays political, pastoral and agricultural information, travel, biography, records and descriptions of all the nobler sports and athletic feats of communities hereditarily addicted to such recreations, plus the ordinary news of the day, they are hailed as a boon by all who have sufficient intellectual development to feel the want of at least occasional mental pabulum. Alike to the country gentleman and farmer, the lonely stockman, the plodding drover, or the solitary shepherd, they are at once a necessity and a benefit, occasionally a priceless luxury.

So it came to pass that after a few weeks had glided on, unmarked but by no means slowly, and the fate-guided comrades had settled down to a placid endurance bordering upon enjoyment of their damper, mutton, quart-pot tea, and negro-head, Jack began to look forward to his paper, and to digest the contents of it, from the stock advertisements to the list of new books, unattainable, alas! with a relish which surprised himself. The regular exercise, the healthful, pure atmosphere, the absence of anxiety, the sound sleep, and natural appetite had produced their ordinary effects, had thoroughly recruited his bodily and mental powers. In despite of himself, so to speak, and of the persistence with which he would declare that he was irrevocably ruined, his mental thermometer rose perceptibly. He experienced once more a sensation (and there is no more complete test of high bodily health) which he had rarely enjoyed since the blessed days of Marshmead. He felt the childlike lightness of spirit, on awakening with the dawn, which more than all things denotes an uninjured and perfect physique, a nervous system in normal and flawless condition. Wonderful is the self-attuning power of the "harp of a thousand strings," the divinely-fashioned instrument upon which, alas! angelic melodies alternate with demon wailings; and the fiend-chorus from the lowest inferno is mysteriously permitted to drown the seraphic tones which would fain uplift the aspirations of man to his celestial home.

With braced sinews, freshly-toned nerves, and veins refilled with pure and unfevered blood, John Redgrave appeared so manifestly an altered man that his humble mentor could not refrain from approving comment.

"Eh, ma certie, but ye're just improvin' and gainin' strength, like the vara sheep, the puir dumb craters, just uncommon. There's a glint o' your e'e, and a lift o' your heed, and a swing o' your walk that tell me ye're castin' awa' the black shadow—the Lord be praised for it, and for a' His mercies. I'll live to see you ance mair in your rightful place amang men, and ye'll give old Jock a corner in your kitchen, or a lodge gate to keep, when he's too auld and failed to work, and hasna strength left for as much as to drink."

"You have a right to a share of whatever I may have in time to come," said Jack, with comparative cheerfulness. "But I have lost the habit of hoping. I do feel wonderfully better; and if I *could* look forward to anything but to some fresh strange trick of destiny I should feel again like the man I once was, who had the heart to dare and the hand to back a bold adventure. But I doubt my luck, as I have had good reason to do; and I believe old Blockham was not far wrong when he said that there were some men (and he took me to be one of them) who, with whatever apparent prospects, never did any good."

"He's an auld sneck-drawer. I kenned him weel when he hadna sae muckle as a guid pair o' boots. I wadna gie a foot-rot parin' for the opinion o' a hunner like him."

"He is a stupid old fellow enough," said Jack; "but those sort of people have an awkward knack of being right, especially where the making of money is concerned. A man can't be too thick-headed to be a successful money-grubber."

"It gars one doot o' the wisdom and maircy of an over-ruling Providence whiles," assented the old man; "but I'll no deny that siccan thoughts hae passed through my ain brain when I hae seen the senseless, narrow, meeserable ceephers that were permitted to gather up a' the guid things o' this life. But that's no to say that a man wi' understanding and pairts suldna learn caution frae adversity, and pass all these creeping tortoise-bodies in the race of life, like the hare, puir beastie, if the auld story-book had given him anither heat."

"But the hare never gets a chance of a second heat, my old friend," said Jack, ruefully; "that's the worst of it; he jumps into a gravel-pit, or a stray greyhound chops him. I think I see my sheep drawing off."

So the colloquy ended for the time. But Jack doubtless revolved the question suggested by his humble friend, and asked himself whether the returning hope of which he was conscious was the herald of a gleam of fickle Fortune's favour, or whether it was an *ignis fatuus*, destined to lure him on to yet more dire misfortune.

"That can hardly be," he concluded, in soliloquy. "I can't well be lower, and he that is down need fear no fall, as the old song says."

But Jack's hope this time was no *ignis fatuus*. He had seen the lowest depths of his adversity, and though his spirit had been crushed for a while his moral nature had not suffered. And now that his health was restored he was ready to face his fate as a man should, and struggle once more to get himself a place among other men as soon as he got the chance; and the chance came soon, and in a form which he had not dared to hope.

As he sat one day under a tree watching the sheep which were feeding on a wide spread of country before him, he took a newspaper out of his pocket which had arrived at the hut just as he was starting, and on looking down the column of "local news" his eye met a paragraph which caused the blood to leap in his veins, and filled his mind with a new and sudden hope. It was this—

"We regret to hear that Mr. F. Forestall and his companion, a stockman, name unknown, have been killed by the blacks when they were on their way to take possession of some new land which Mr. Forestall had purchased. The land is again in the market."

Jack bounded from his seat in a state of feverish excitement. "By Jove! there's a chance for me yet, but I have not a minute to lose."

He was impatient to be off at once, but there were the sheep to be driven in and a horse to be got. While he stood thinking what was the best to be done he saw Mr. Hazeham riding up, and suddenly resolved to tell him of his predicament and appeal to him for help.

"Well, what do you want?" said the overseer, "and what do you mean by sitting there reading the lies in that confounded paper and letting your sheep go all over the country?"

"The sheep *have* rather a spread," said Jack, quietly, "but you'll find them all right. They are feeding towards the yard, and have a good way to go yet, but if you have a few minutes to spare I want to speak to you, if you please, and ask your help."

Mr. Hazeham looked in surprise at "John Smith," and his astonishment was considerably increased when he heard all Jack had to say. He was good-natured in the main, and not unwilling to help a man who had been a large landed proprietor, and might be again; besides, he was not a little pleased at his own sagacity, for he remembered that he had described Jack to Mr. Delmayne, the proprietor, as looking "like a swell out of luck," so he promptly replied, "Certainly I will help you, Mr.—"

"Redgrave," said Jack, reddening.

"Mr. Redgrave, I see there's no time to lose. You shall have old Scamper, he's the best horse we've got, and never mind about the sheep; a fellow applied this morning, and he's still at the huts. I shall be at my place in an hour, or less; you come up, and you shall have the horse and your wages, John Smith," he added with a laugh.

Jack laughed too, and started off as fast as he could go to find the old shepherd.

On his way his thoughts went back to Forestall whom he had never forgiven for his treachery; but death does away with offences, and he only felt pity towards the man who had supplanted him, and who had not even entered into possession of his ill-gotten lands.

"Puir fellow," said old Jock, when he heard the story, "I expect it was the same black varmints that gave Meester Waldron his death. There's naething in the way of fichting so deevilish as thae wee pisoned arrows, but I wadna hae ye too much set up. The land may be sold, ye ken."

"True, but there *is* a chance, and luck may be in my favour this time."

"Dinna talk o' luck, laddie; the Lord has seen fit to chastise your pride, for weel ye wot ye were high-minded ance, and sin' ye've taken your punishment doucely I'm fain to believe that He may see fit to reward you; and," continued the old man, solemnly lifting his hands, "wherever ye gang, and whatever happens, may the Lord bless ye, and hae ye in His holy keepin'."

"Goodbye, old fellow," said Jack, wringing his hand, while his eyes glistened with unwonted dew. "If I succeed you shall hear of me, and you must come to me, and bring the dogs with you."

Mounted on Scamper, which Jack had bought of Mr. Hazeham, he made the best of his way to the town. His first proceeding was to call at the office of the Minister for Lands: it was possible they might be able to direct him to the agents of Mr. Forestall. Jack was fortunate enough to see the minister himself, who remembered him directly, for he had felt much sympathy with Jack, and had been indignant at the way he had been treated.

"I suppose you are come about that land, Mr. Redgrave?"

"Yes, I am," said Jack, with a beating heart, and a desperate attempt to speak calmly. "I hope I am not too late. Will you tell me, sir, whether the transfer was quite completed?"

"I am happy to tell you it was not, Mr. Redgrave. The papers were drawn up, but there has been some delay in the office. Poor Forestall was eager to see his possessions, and thought he would conclude the arrangements when he came back. So I suppose we have but to transfer the names, eh?"

"Thank God," said Jack, fervently, and the sudden revulsion from fear and uncertainty to assurance sent a sudden choke into his throat which prevented his saying anymore.

The minister saw his agitation, and talked on in a kindly way, giving him time to recover.

From the minister's office Jack went to the cattle agents he had seen before, and made the same arrangements as formerly. He had not touched poor Guy's £300, and that would be enough to get stores, pay wages, and so on.

There was no delay anywhere. Everyone in the office knew how Jack had been cheated, and was ready to oblige him; so the papers were ready for him in a very short time, and once more he set out on his travels.

XXVI

"Time and Tide had thus their sway,
Yielding, like an April day,
Smiling morn for sullen morrow,
Years of joy for hours of sorrow."

—Scott

There is no need to write John Redgrave's history for the next three years. It was a time of hard and continuous struggle, large successes and exasperating failures; his stock increased largely, but there was great difficulty in transporting droves of cattle to the nearest market; plenty of water for sheep, and no danger of floods or droughts, but it was not easy at such an out-station as this to get sufficient labour in shearing-time, and the great distance the wool had to be conveyed took off much of the profits. Moreover, Jack could not make up his mind that it would be right to bring Maud into such a wilderness, with no neighbours but the blacks, who, though they had shown no hostility to Jack, were not to be trusted. He had written to Maud at first, full of hope and confident of success, and she, dear girl, had been willing to share with him the rudest log hut; but as time went on he felt how impossible it was that he should bring her to be the light of his home before he had made that home fit to receive her.

In his solitary hours, in the silence of his small dwelling-place, he bitterly regretted having left Marshmead. It was possible that he might become a very rich man if he lived to be old, but meantime his youth was going by, and happiness along with it.

But time had good things in store yet for the brave man whose courageous spirit had never suffered more than a temporary depression. On one of his visits to the town of—to buy some of the multitudinous articles required on a large station, he learnt from an old acquaintance who was there on the same errand that Donald McDonald, who had bought Marshmead, had expressed a very strong determination to sell Marshmead and go back to Scotland. His nephew, Mr. Angus McTavish, had long ago bought a very large sheep run, and was reported to be doing wonders. Jack's heart leaped at the thought of getting back Marshmead, where he had been so happy, so undisturbed by carking care. With a thoughtful brow he began to consider the ways and means. By strict economy and careful management, added to two fairly good years, he had paid off the greater part of the purchase-money, and his sheep had increased so much that, after all his losses, he calculated upon being able to buy Marshmead if only he could get a purchaser for Wondega.

He wrote, accordingly, to Bertie Tunstall, asking him to make inquiries about Marshmead, and authorizing him to buy it if Mr. McDonald was really going to sell.

Pending these negotiations, Jack was restless and excited. The thought of Maud was ever uppermost; she had expressed her willingness to wait, for years if it was necessary. At the same time, rightly judging her love by his own, he felt that she would be happier, as she frankly said, helping to make his home happy than in waiting until everything should be put in order for herself. Yet, again, how could he bring her to Wondega?

An answer came in due time: McDonald would sell, but he considered the improvements he had made on the estate, which turned out to be very slight, and the increase in the cattle would make it worth a great deal more than he had given for it.

However, he was willing to sell the place on the same conditions on which he had bought it—namely, half the money in cash, and the rest in bills at short date. Despatching another letter to Tunstall, directing him to close with the offer, Jack bade adieu to Wondega, a place endeared by no memories of love and friendship, as had been Gondaree and Marshmead, but, on the contrary, made gloomy by having been the scene of Guy Waldron's death, and his own solitary and uncheered abode during the time of great anxiety and unceasing effort.

There was no difficulty in selling the place; it was different now from the time when the two adventurers first stood on the hill and caught sight of Lake Maud; great droves of sheep pastured on the slopes, a large but rude wool-shed stood in the shelter of some trees, and a modest cottage was built in the open, loop-holed at certain heights in case of an attack from the natives. Some of the land had been fenced in, but there had been no money to spare for rail-fencing, and the rails and posts were of wood, mostly cut, shaped, and put down by Jack himself.

The land sold well, and Jack was enabled to buy back his own old place. On his way back he passed by Gondaree, and could not refrain from stopping and making some inquiries about M'Nab, who happened to be absent from the station.

The year succeeding his downfall had been unusually favourable to the pastoral interests. High prices for wool and stock, steady rainfall, new country opening, a cessation of wars and rumours of war—all these circumstances had combined to produce and sustain for squatters the most protracted term of triumphant success ever known in the Australias. Those who, without skill or energy, had by good luck purchased when stock were at their lowest, had of course been floated out on the ever-deepening tide into undreamed-of fortune and success. Those who, like Alexander M'Nab, possessed both, had gone on from one successful enterprise to another with astonishing rapidity. His name, as the managing partner in this district for the great firm of Bagemall Brothers, was constantly quoted as the exemplar of first-class management, luck in speculation, successful shrewdness, and well-deserved advancement. A magistrate, an exhibitor of prize stock, an inventor of improvements in machinery as applied to station uses, a co-proprietor of several of the largest properties in the district, a power in the state, his name was in every man's mouth. Time and prosperity had mellowed his perhaps originally aggressive propensities, and now he was popular, respected among all classes of men.

John was glad to hear of the prosperity of his old overseer, and pushed on with a light heart to Juandah. He was met with a warm welcome. Mark Stangrove looked more prosperous, a trifle stouter and merrier; the good years had told in his favour. Maud was lovelier than ever, though she was certainly thinner and paler, so John Redgrave thought at first, with a pang of compunction, but after he had been there two or three days he fancied that he must have been mistaken, for the bloom on her cheek and the sparkle in her eye were as beautiful as ever.

"Oh, Maud, my darling," said Jack, as they stood together in the veranda the evening of his arrival, "what time I have wasted! I go back to Marshmead a poorer man than when I left it, for I am burdened with a debt, and what years I have lost!"

"Don't regret the past, dear Jack," said Maud, sliding her little hand into his; "perhaps if you had never left Marshmead you would always have been a little dissatisfied with it; besides, if you had never left it we should not have met."

"I would bear it all over again if you were the prize at the end, Maud."

"Once is enough," said Maud, with an arch glance from her bright eyes.

"And I may have my prize?"

"Yes, when you are ready," replied Maud, demurely.

"I'm ready now, you saucy girl," said Jack, laughing, though he winced at the implied reproach in her words, "and I have a great mind to take you at your word, and carry you off to Marshmead at once."

"Come back when you like, my dear fellow," said Mark Stangrove, who had just joined them, "and then we'll see about it."

The week passed all too quickly, but Jack resolved that it should not be very long before he returned, and certain whispered conferences with Maud settled the time.

As John Redgrave at length reached the homestead, certain changes were strongly apparent. The once trim, orderly, and pleasant place was weed-grown and melancholy of aspect. The stables were tenantless, and bore traces of long disuse. Many of the buildings were roofless, while the materials of others had been used up for the formation of out-houses. Mr. McDonald did not "believe," as he expressed it, in improvements, nor in having one man or boy about his establishment who could possibly be done without; for this reason probably he made use of the garden as a calf paddock, and Jack's heart felt acute misery when he saw the trampled flower-beds, the broken fruit-trees, the mutilated shrubs; but McDonald was not a man whom this sort of thing troubled. To have lived in sight of such a daily desecration would have been to some men an intolerable annoyance. He did not care a jot, when duly satisfied by careful inspection that his bank balance was on the right side, that his daily steak and glass of grog were attainable, if every garden in the land had been uprooted. In other than these convictions and satisfactions he had no interest. He rarely rode over the run. He never helped to bring in the calves to brand, or the fat bullocks for market. He was by no means particular about keeping up the purity of the carefully-bred herd. He often permitted his calves to be past the proper age before they were branded, probably by the aid of his neighbour's stockmen. But with all this apparent neglect, and his whisky-drinking to boot, he kept steadily to his principle of having as little labour to pay and feed as was possible. He did not mind a few strayed or even lost cattle. If a few calves were branded by others he troubled not his head; and yet this obese, unintelligent block made more money than the cleverest man in the whole district. His secret was this, and I present it to aspiring pastoralists: he had no personal expense; he had no debts; therefore he was able to weather out the terrible financial gales when the failure of clever, hard-working men was of daily occurrence.

As Jack got off his horse at the house, Elsie came to the door.

"Eh! but it's Maister John, it's my ain bairn," she cried, "come to bless my auld e'en before I dee; oh, thank the Lord that I hae lived to see this day."

The old woman flung her arms round his neck and burst into tears.

"My dear old Elsie," said Jack, kissing her, "I am as glad to be here as you are to see me; and where's Geordie?"

"Geordie is awa looking after the cattle in the stock, but he'll be here the nicht. And oh, Maister John, is it you that's bought the place?"

"Indeed it is, Elsie, and you must tell me what has been done since I left."

"Eh, but ye must hae your dinner first, my bonny man, and I must see aboot the getting o't; but bide a wee, I'll send for Geordie; he'll tell ye a'."

Later in the evening John heard from the lips of his two faithful friends what had been done in his absence. Whatever improvements bad been made, and they were very few, were in the direction of the cattle-yards. They were larger than formerly, and that was all; but the stock had increased largely, and were in good condition. As to the lost garden, Jack thought that Maud might like to watch the gradual formation of a new one. He had got out of the habit of thinking that everything should be complete and perfect before Maud came.

After setting men to work at repairs in the stables to begin with, Jack in a few days' time rode over to pay a visit to his old friend Bertie Tunstall, who could hardly do enough to show his gladness. Jack had so much to say that the two days of his stay hardly sufficed for a recountal of all he had seen, felt, and suffered, since leaving Marshmead. In old times they used to enjoy the circulation of ideas produced and quickened by the mutual intercourse of persons who read habitually and did not permit the wondrous faculty of thought to be entirely absorbed by the cares of everyday life, by the claims of business, by plans and actions tending directly or indirectly to the acquisition and investment of money. It is given to few active professions to afford and to justify as great a degree of leisure for realizing an abstract thought as to that of the Australian squatter. He may manage his property shrewdly and successfully, and still utilize a portion, at either end of the day, for history and chronicle of old, for poetry and politics, for rhyme and reason. He can vary intellectual exercise with hard bodily labour. He may possess, at small additional cost, the latest literary products of the old and new world. He may, after the arrival of each mail-steamer, revel in masterpieces of the thought-giants, fresh from the workshop. When kindred spirits are available within meeting distance, great is the joy of the pioneers, what time the half-wild herds are gathered; the tender oxlets seared with the indelible cipher. Then arises the bustle of the body as each man lauds a favourite author or decries a pet aversion.

Life again flowed on for Jack with the peaceful security and round of accustomed duties which had filled up the days of long ago happily and so completely. Spring ripened into glowing summer with stores of fruit and flowers; with long dreamy days of sunshine tempered by breezes which wandered over marsh and mere, fresh from gentle murmurings with the wandering ocean wave. Again he saw the wild swan lead her brood of cygnets through the deep reed-bordered meres. Again he leaned from his saddle at midday and dipped his broad-leafed hat in the cool marsh waters which plashed pleasantly around his horse's feet. Once more he rose at dawn to feel the thrice-blessed sense of safety and untroubled possession of the land. Again he mingled with his fellows on terms of absolute equality; nay, more, of slight but acknowledged superiority, as of one who had bought experience, who had struggled with fate and overcome. And in the midst of the priceless sensation of contentment and repose came a fuller tide of thankfulness, a savour of keener relish, born of the unforgotten hardships of the past. Before the summer days had reached their longest John Redgrave brought home his bride.

What need to say that they were happy? The union of two such loving hearts and two such perfect tempers is sure to bring happiness. At the sight of his friend's lovely wife, and Jack's perfect delight in her, Bertie Tunstall suddenly found himself a lonely and miserable man. He said his health needed a change, and went off to town, from whence he returned in a few weeks an engaged man, and in due time made another visit to the same place, and brought back a pretty, amiable, loving little wife, who proved to be a great favourite of Maud's.

According to John Redgrave's promise, old Jock Harley was not forgotten; a place by the "ingle neuk" was offered him, but he preferred a hut of his own, and a comfortable one was built for him on the hillside, far away from the house, where he could have his eye on the cattle, though he never took the interest in them which he did in sheep, giving it as his opinion that they were "puir doited beasties, and unco hard to unnerstan'." The dog Help came with him, and was made a great pet of by all the household.

When John grew prosperous and wealthy he sent home a considerable sum to Guy Waldron's sisters, the increase of the £300 which had come to him so opportunely when he was in his direst need.

As years passed on, as the clover and rye-grass matted in thick sward over the fens and flats of Marshmead, Jack found his thoughts running much upon the education of the steadily increasing olive-branches that came, and grew, and flourished in that cool, breezy clime.

To the alarm of old Elsie and Geordie, who spoiled the rosy boys and girls to their hearts' content, Mrs. Redgrave already begins to hint at a residence in the metropolis, solely, of course, for the sake of masters and so on for dear Bertie and Maud.

For many a year John Redgrave's life and opinions have been before his countrymen and close neighbours, great and small, poor and rich. His active principles have been plain for all men to see. If he buys a thousand acres of the Marshmead Crown lands, he employs no agent, but stands up like a man and bids in person. His motto is "fair and above board." What he thinks right to do he will perform if he can, maugre land-sharks, agitators, or even his very respectable and slightly democratic farmer neighbours. Everyone in the district knows, or believes he knows, nearly every thought of the heart of that transparent kindly nature—of that hearty, jolly and benevolent Squire of Marshmead. But two of his opinions have ever excited remark or called forth curiosity. One is an intense dislike to sheep, under any and all forms of management. The other is a furious and unreasonable hostility to the extensive pastoral region which lies north of the Murray.

His tale is told. I hold it expedient in common fairness to inform my confidential friend, the reader, that the writer is acquainted with more than one Jack who abandoned the substance for the shadow; with more—many more, alas!—than one or two young, brilliant, brave, and beautiful Jacks, who, enthralled by the Circe of new worlds, served henceforth to fill her dungeon-sties, or to wander aimlessly from land to land, till kindly death released from union wasted body and ruined soul. But, alas! not with many who, like John Redgrave, fought their way back to comfort and affluence, after having gone down into the depths of misfortune,—not with many who "suffered and were strong."

THE END.

A Note About the Author

Rolf Boldrewood was the pseudonym of Australian novelist Thomas Alexander Browne (1826–1915). Born in London, he settled with his family in Sydney in 1831 after his father, a shipmaster, delivered a group of convicts to Hobart, Tasmania. Educated at W. T. Cape's school and Sydney College, Browne spent holidays with his friend John George Nathaniel Gibbes on Point Piper. At seventeen, he settled on land near Port Fairy to lead a life of squatting. This lasted until 1868, as consecutive bad seasons forced him to resettle in Sydney after twenty-five years away. Around this time, he began contributing articles on rural life to weekly Australian magazines, publishing his serialized novel *The Squatter's Dream* in 1875. Using his pseudonym, he found success with bushranger novel *Robbery Under Arms* (1888), a story of survival and adventure set in the harsh Australian wilderness. While pursuing his literary interests, Browne held several government positions, including police magistrate, gold commissioner, and justice of the peace. After nearly three decades in Gulgong, Dubbo, Armidale, and Albury, he retired to Melbourne, where he spent the last twenty years of his life.

A Note from the Publisher

Spanning many genres, from non-fiction essays to literature classics to children's books and lyric poetry, Mint Edition books showcase the master works of our time in a modern new package. The text is freshly typeset, is clean and easy to read, and features a new note about the author in each volume. Many books also include exclusive new introductory material. Every book boasts a striking new cover, which makes it as appropriate for collecting as it is for gift giving. Mint Edition books are only printed when a reader orders them, so natural resources are not wasted. We're proud that our books are never manufactured in excess and exist only in the exact quantity they need to be read and enjoyed.

Discover more of your favorite classics with Bookfinity™.

- Track your reading with custom book lists.
- Get great book recommendations for your personalized Reader Type.
- Add reviews for your favorite books.
- AND MUCH MORE!

Visit **bookfinity.com** and take the fun Reader Type quiz to get started.

Enjoy our classic and modern companion pairings!

Printed in the USA
CPSIA information can be obtained
at www.ICGtesting.com
JSHW022214140824
68134JS00018B/1049